Ghosts of Sanctuary

The Sanctuary Series, Volume Nine

Robert J. Crane

1 3 1750885 0

Ghosts of Sanctuary
The Sanctuary Series, Volume Nine
Robert J. Crane
Copyright © 2018 Ostiagard Press
All Rights Reserved.

1st Edition

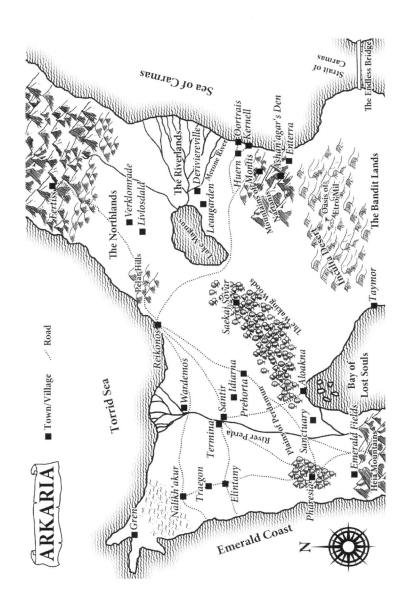

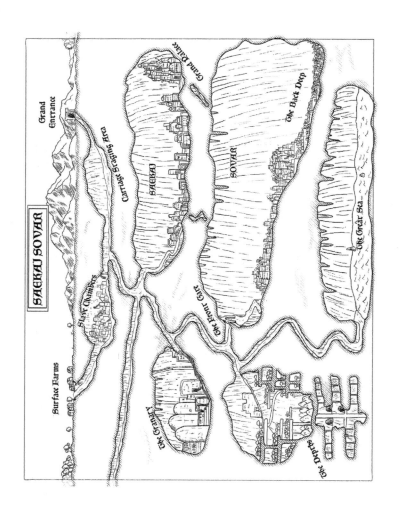

Prologue

Shirri Gadden had landed herself in trouble this time, the sort you couldn't exactly pull yourself free of without the kind of help that didn't come cheap. Shirri's problem was that she was broke, and since help didn't come cheap, it was a double pox, the sort you got right after you recovered from the last ailment.

She hurried down the street with the cloak over her, trying to ignore the pounding rain coming down. Reikonos wasn't a pretty town, not unless you were rich and lived in the parts where they had big houses and big gardens. Down here by the factories it was ugly, with black coal smoke belching out of tall brick stacks, dumping ashen residue on everything. She had a small flat near here, and it was impossible to keep it clean with all that vexation dumping down all the time. She'd heard tell from her mother of a time when the skies above Reikonos were blue, but that sounded like a falsity to her. The factories with their black clouds and smokestacks had been around for as long as she could remember.

She skirted past a pub and dodged down an alley. She'd been this way a few times before. It wasn't real safe to be wandering in this part of town after sundown, but then, there weren't a lot of parts of Reikonos where it was. Cutthroats would steal a coinpurse from a corpse more gladly than mugging a living victim; less chance they'd get caught if they left their prey dead in an alley rather than let them walk away to scream for the city guard.

Shirri heard the footsteps before she saw who was making them. It was like a constabulary bell ringing, clanging from one of the towers all around the city. She turned her head and saw them—

Oh, Davidon, she saw them.

She took to running, knowing damned well they'd catch her. They looked tall, she was short, and there wasn't a chance in a dragon's

1

mouth she'd get away from them, not in this knot of alleys. She knew them, knew them well enough to know that anyone with half a wit would have someone posted ahead, just past the empty lot on the high street.

Still, death came for those who stood still, so Shirri broke into a run. If they were honest criminals, they might write her off as a bad job, say forget about it and go drag away some drunk staggering out of Minndee's bar on the street over—

They didn't write her off.

They started after her at a run, hoots and catcalls filling the alley. She knew what a calm criminal sounded like, the sort that might have put the fear of Davidon in her and been off about their business. These weren't that type. These were the other.

The ones who enjoyed hurting people.

"Oh, no," she whispered to herself, cutting around the corner. She could see the vacant green space up ahead, across the empty street. A glance skyward proved that the clouds of smoke had covered the sky this night, and there was not even a sliver of moon to guide her. The street torches burned, making her wonder if she could somehow disappear past that lot, maybe—

One of them burst out of a side alley laughing only five feet behind her, and she knew her time was nearly up. Shirri screamed, knowing even as she did that no one would hear her, no one would help her—not in this town. Not the guards. Not the citizenry. No one.

Not in this town. Not in Reikonos. Everybody always said it: there was no hope left in Reikonos. The man behind her snatched her cloak just as she made it to the cobblestone street, the gaslights above her sending off their warm glow. She stumbled, twisting her ankle as she fell. She landed hard on the stones, her elbow cracking and a gasp of pain forcing its way out of her lips. She curled up instinctively, cradling the elbow, the ankle radiating pain of its own down her foot.

"Lookee what we got here, lads and ladies," said the burly man who'd chased her down. There were others emerging from the shadows now, their grins the first thing she saw, teeth shining in the gaslight. "Shirri ... this is why you shouldn't run when you know you owe."

"I don't have it," Shirri said through gritted teeth. The pain in her elbow was impossibly bad. She could feel the rough hints that a bone had broken there, and there wasn't anything she could do about it except lie here and hope they left her alive when they were done with whatever they intended to do. She had ideas, and every single one of them terrified her.

2

"Well, then that makes you kind of useless, don't it?" Burly asked. He was just a rough from the streets, he didn't even work for himself. It somehow made it worse that the man who was going to kill her wasn't the man who really even wanted to kill her.

"Let's take her to the wall and toss her over," a woman with a weaselly voice said, not even disguising the thrill at the thought. "Watch her spend her last moments trying to decide whether to drown or get ripped apart."

"That's always a fun one," Burly agreed. "Costs, though, paying off a guard to let you. Doing the job here, though ..." He grinned. "That's free."

"Please, no," Shirri said. The pain had faded under the panic, the certain knowledge of what was coming. She couldn't see any way out of it, no hope of rescue. They had her surrounded, they had the numbers. She had no way out, and the desperation clawed at her like a cat sealed in a sack and tossed in the moat. In her case, it manifested in the most curious way, a plea that she said, under her breath, like a ritual turned to a shield, in just the way her mother had taught her, long ago:

"*I invoke thee who hear my plea, I request thy aid, For those who are soon to die.*"

"You think that'll help you?" Burly asked, sounding vaguely amused. "I don't think you realize—"

A sound like thunder following a lightning strike rattled the nearby windows, shaking the ground beneath Shirri. She watched the toughs take a step back, uncertainly, rocked by the strange sound. There was a flash, and she looked around, trying to see where it had come from, but there was no telling, really; it almost seemed like it had come out of the building with the sharp spires and the tower that stretched up behind—

Wait. Had that been there a moment ago? Shirri's head swam with the pain, and then the sound of a door opening in the distance echoed across the street.

It sounded like hope.

"Is someone there? Help me!" Shirri shouted before Burly reached down and grabbed her, stuffing a hand in her mouth. He tasted like whiskey distilled in an old, dirty barrel.

"You hush up there," Burly said, peering into the dark. Something was moving out there, Shirri could see it. There was a sound, too, like ...

Footsteps?

"Whoever you are," Burly said, motioning for his comrades to close in, "I'd suggest just walking on this lovely evening—if you wish it to remain a lovely evening and not a bloodbath."

"I've always enjoyed a good bloodbath," came a woman's voice from the darkness, sharp and playful and proper. She stepped out of a shadow and Shirri saw her, clad in silver armor from head to toe, blond hair bound tight above her head in a flowing ponytail. She looked straight at Shirri with something akin to amusement, then shifted her fierce attention to Burly. She had the pointed ears of a pure elf, and Shirri blinked in surprise at that.

"Well, it's going to be your blood, darling elfy, so I doubt you'll enjoy this one," Burly said, chuckling under his breath. "Look at this getup, thinks she's a brave lady knight."

"She's a lady of the elven kingdom, actually," came another voice, this one from a man with platinum hair. He looked calm and composed, but wore a smile, and in his hand was a mace with a metal ball that he rolled in a circle with his wrist. He wore immaculate white robes that didn't look as though they had a speck of ash on them.

"Ain't no elven kingdom," one of the toughs said. "Who you supposed to be?"

"A bunch of minstrels out for a walk, clearly," came another voice, this one jovial and lighthearted—and completely out of place. The speaker stepped into the gaslight and Shirri gasped, as did a few of the others. He was tall, taller than any person had a right to be, and with skin as green as the ocean by the docks. He almost looked like ... but he couldn't be. "Would you like us to sing you a tune? Because that'll cost you."

"Oh, we're going to make you do the singing, greenie," Burly said, putting a dagger to the side of Shirri's face. She felt the point of the blade at her cheek. "Compliments of the house."

"I don't think this gentleman has good intentions," came the voice of another man, older, and when he stepped out, Shirri frowned. He was wearing armor, too, grey and battered. He wore a sword on his belt and kept his hand upon the hilt, and spoke from behind a helm that looked like a bucket.

"You may be dressed funny, but you're not quite as dumb as you look," Burly said. "Now ... last chance. I'm feeling generous. Go back to the carnival you all came from and we'll call this just another fanciful night in Reikonos. No harm done to any party, but—"

"Harm is about to be done." A dark shadow slipped out of the inky black night, and Shirri's eyes rolled off it. She heard the voice of a man, deep and resonant, and when she finally saw him, she realized he, too, was covered in armor from head to toe. This armor was different than the others, though—

It was entirely black, and he wore two swords at his waist.

Shirri felt her breath catch in her throat, staring at him—at HIM—him, dressed like HIM—

One of the toughs let out a laugh, but it was shrill and high and unconvincing. "Look at this fartwat! Thinks he's Cyrus bloody Davidon, he does!" He laughed again, but it died as he looked at his fellow criminals, and a dull, painful silence settled in instead.

"That's right," the man in black said, and as he stepped forward, his hands fell to his swords. Through the bottom of the helm, Shirri could see a ghostly smile. Then the swords erupted from their scabbards and were in his hands faster than Shirri could draw a breath, and suddenly—

Suddenly, she wasn't afraid anymore. "It's him," she whispered. "It's really … him."

"Not a bloody chance," Burly whispered back, awestruck. "It—no—he doesn't even—"

"My name is Cyrus Davidon," the man said, and she felt it—she *knew* he spoke true. He held the blades up, and they looked like every illustration she'd seen in every book on him she'd ever read. There was a sound of leather boots slapping against an alley floor, and then another, and another, as the criminals started to run.

"It's bloody impossible," Burly said, retreating back, dragging Shirri with him. His grasp at her neck was loosened, fading, along with his hope. "He can't be—he's—he's a bloody myth! And—and even if—if—he's been gone a thousand years—"

Shirri looked at the five of them, in the darkness, as they closed together—the woman, the green man, the elf, the knight and finally, the man in black. He stood there by gaslight, holding aloft his swords. "I was gone," he agreed. "For a while. And now …" And the smile became a grin as he seemed to shiver in the gaslight, as though a cloud of smoke from a nearby factory covered him over for just a moment, and then drifted on. Shirri felt the warmth run through her as Burly's last hope flagged, and his arm slithered off her throat, fear taking him as he ran off into the night, fleeing from the specter that stood before her, a ghost that seemed to have drifted right out of the mists of history and solidified right there, in front of her, before her very eyes.

The man in black smiled, a ghost that had come out of the night, out of the darkness—to save her. And he spoke, as she stood there, witnessing it at last—the thing the people had all talked about, hoped for, wished for, for as long as Shirri could remember …

His return. "… And now I'm back."

5

1.

"... And now I'm back."

Cyrus Davidon's words echoed through the dark alleyway, like the rattle of stones against the sides of a barrel. Their foes had fled, but he remained, Praelior in one hand and Ferocis in the other, the sense of power intoxicating, flowing through him in a way that he hadn't felt in a thousand years.

"He's struck the dramatic pose," Vaste said from beside Vara. "Is he preening? I can't tell if he's preening, it's so dark." With a flick of his wrist, his hand lit, and light sheered through the darkness as though he'd lit a candle.

"I don't know if I would go so far as to call it 'preening,'" Curatio said, his platinum hair lit in the glow of Vaste's hand. "But there is a certain element of the theatrical in his efforts this eve."

Cyrus blinked, then sighed, shoulders sagging. "You people—I can't go anywhere without a damned critique, honestly. I swear—" He sheathed Ferocis, and the world slowed down slightly. "They ran, okay? I was aiming for intimidating, and apparently I hit the mark, because, witness them, being gone—and the girl saved." He pointed at the waif of a girl standing just down the alley, blinking at them all. "Hope kindled, girl saved, now we can return to our—I don't know, etheric slumber." He frowned. "Though, to be honest—"

"I don't really want to go back in yet," Vaste said.

"Nor I," Vara said, her long blond hair flashing in the light of Vaste's spell. "That bright light, always the same shade of milk—"

"The lack of smell," Cyrus said, looking around, sniffing. "You getting this?" He made a face as a wave of something awful seeped into his nose, noxious, as though someone burned something particularly offensive. "It's like Vaste had the worst movement of his life and then set fire to the outhouse afterward."

"And there's ash over everything," Vara said, brushing at her shoulder. Specks of grey had appeared like dusty blemishes on her immaculate silver armor, conspicuous in the glow of Vaste's spell. "As though they've allowed the communal ovens to burn every hour of the day."

Cyrus looked at dark skies around them. Buildings of deep red brick stretched tall on either side, and in the distance, other towers and spires loomed, higher than the blocky structures that hemmed them into this alley. "Looks like things got ... taller in our absence. What are all these—these—I can't really tell in the dark." He waved a hand over his face, casting the Eagle Eye spell. "Are those ... I think they're belching smoke."

"Explains why we can't see the moon," Vaste said, peering toward the streets at either end of the alleyway. The glow of torch or fire in the distance hinted that they were perhaps lit the way Reikonos of old had been, though they seemed to have a different cast to them. "I thought it was just clouds."

"There is definitely a pall that hangs over this place," Vara said, looking about. "Those toughs—I know your hometown has had many a disreputable sort over the years," she looked to Cyrus, "but this seems brazen, even for Reikonos, don't you think?"

"Honestly, I'm just happy to hear your voice again—your actual voice, not that tinkling sweetness that somehow pours right into my head," Cyrus said, "and also that it didn't happen to be you accusing me of being the sort of thug we just encountered."

Vara frowned at him. "Why would I do that?"

"It used to be your modus operandi," Cyrus said, favoring her with a tight smile.

"That was a thousand years ago," she said, "and before I married your lug arse. Try to keep up, will you." She cast a look around again. "Things have changed."

"Not as much as I might hope," Alaric Garaunt said with a sigh of impatience, breaking from their ranks and striding down the alley toward the thin girl who stood, watching them all, transfixed. "The four of you stand here, catching up, as though you haven't spent the last thousand years in each others' company—"

"It's a little different hanging out in the ether versus actually being here, Alaric," Cyrus said, reaching out and touching Vara's shoulder, his gauntlet clanking against her pauldron. "There's ... sensation ..."

He pulled his gauntlet off, then ran his hand over her armor again. It felt cool to the touch, smooth. He brought his hand up and brushed her cheek, and she flushed slightly. "I'd forgotten what this felt like, actually being corporeal. It's reminding me of ... things." He stepped closer and leaned down, kissing Vara on the lips. She kissed back, wordless.

"Yes, indeed, it would appear he's reawakening in all sorts of ways," Vaste said.

"We have just saved someone," Alaric said, irritation rising as he moved over to the thin girl who was still staring, wide-eyed and silent, at the lot of them. "Perhaps someone might wish to inquire how she is doing?"

"Maybe later," Cyrus said, his lips still on Vara's. "I'm remembering—"

"That he has a groin," Vaste said.

Vara broke from Cyrus. "We all have groins, you idiot."

"Actually, we didn't, until we came out of the ether," Cyrus said.

"You didn't have brains, either," Alaric said. "And that doesn't seem to have changed." With another sigh, he offered a hand to the girl standing before him. "Are you all right?"

The girl just stood there, gaping at him for a few seconds. "You ..."

"My name is Alaric Garaunt," he said, hand still extended. "And you are?"

"Shirri," she said after a brief pause in which she seemed to be making up her mind about something. Her eyes were wide, fixed on the Ghost. "Shirri Gadden."

Curatio walked toward her, his sandals slapping upon the cobbles as he stepped away from Vaste, Cyrus and Vara. "You seemed to have drawn a fair amount of ire from those toughs, Shirri Gadden."

Her face was small and pinched. "I ... don't know you."

"You said my name," Cyrus noted. "I heard you. And you called out for us—for help. Summoned us here."

"You're not ... who you look like," Shirri said, and Cyrus could see the full retreat of belief playing out on her face. Whatever hope he'd kindled in her by his appearance, and by running off those thugs, it had faded in mere moments, and now was fully replaced by something else.

Disbelief. Hints of fear were visible as well.

"Who do I look like?" Cyrus asked.

Shirri shook her head, too quickly. "You're not him."

"Who else might I be?" Cyrus asked.

"An imposter," Shirri said.

"No imposter could manage this ego," Vaste said. "It's well-earned, the product of many battles, and insufficient time ethereally divorced from his groin. The bravado just rolls off of him, even after a thousand years."

Shirri opened her mouth, held it that way as though trying to form a question. What finally came out was, "And who are you supposed to be?"

Vaste just stared at her. "That hurts. I just saved your life, and this is how you repay me? The ingratitude."

Shirri regarded him with a careful eye. "Ahhhh ... I'm not sure you saved my life."

"Ridiculous," Vaste said, now stepping toward her as well. "They were going to kill you. I'm very familiar with the sort of hatred that turns to murder, having seen it in the eyes of more than a few of my enemies. I know, I know—you look at this face," and he brushed a hand over his massive, distorted green cheek, "and you wonder— 'How could anyone want to kill something so pretty?' But I assure you, they have tried. Envy, I assume."

"I may think with my groin, but you think with your arse," Cyrus muttered.

"And why should I not, when it's such a brilliant thing?" He turned and bent slightly, his rear jutting out beneath the robes.

"I ... should go home," Shirri said, taking a step back as Vaste thrust out his backside.

"Pay no attention to the company of fools behind me," Alaric said, extending a hand to her. "You found yourself in danger, and you sought for help. We are the answer to your call. Please." He swept the bucket-shaped helm from his head. "Let us help you."

"As fine a company of ... actors? Impersonators?" She took another step back. "Whatever you are ... as uh, convincing as you are, those toughs, as you call them ... they will be back." She shook her head. "They don't take no for an answer. And the people who give them their orders, who sent them after me ..." She shuddered. "They won't take kindly to being told fanciful tales of some long dead ..." She looked right at Cyrus, and he saw a flicker of it in her eyes again, just for a second.

Hope.

It died just as quickly, and she looked away from him. "So ... thank you for the reprieve, but ... I should be going before they—"

Thundering footsteps, like the march of an army, sounded through the alleyway. Shirri froze, her back stiff, looking like a trapped animal.

"I think they're coming back," Cyrus said, amusement and anticipation rippling through him. "And they've brought friends."

"Try not to sound too gleeful at the prospect of a fight," Curatio said, paused between Alaric and them.

"Get behind us," Alaric said, reaching out to Shirri and brushing her shoulder. She let him steer her away, pulling her back behind him as Cyrus came forward with the others. It was a moment to close ranks. "We will protect you."

"You're carrying swords," Shirri said as Vara pushed past her, the paladin placing herself in front of the thin girl, "and sticks and ... whatever that is," she gestured to the rounded ball in Curatio's hand.

"This," Curatio said, lifting it by the handle and pressing a button, "is very painful." Spikes shot out from the ball in every direction, and Shirri flinched.

Vara slid next to Cyrus and leaned into him. He kissed her again as she put a hand on his waist, sighing as they parted. "That was—" he started to say.

She slid Ferocis free from his scabbard, and he looked down at her, scandalized. She gave him an innocent smile. "I have no godly weapon of my own, and it would appear we are going into an actual fight this time. Surely you would not wish to leave your beloved and adorable wife defenseless?"

"I would not," Cyrus conceded, "but you better put it back in my scabbard after the fight." He cringed. "That ... sounded much worse than I intended it."

"Hah hah, Cyrus likes for Vara to slide a sword into his scabbard," Vaste said, brandishing his staff, Letum. "It's hilarious, because it's a reversal of the traditional roles—"

"The fight, you fools," Alaric muttered. "Do you not see this coming?"

It would have been hard to miss. Shadows were streaming into the alleyway. Where before there had been perhaps a dozen, they were returning in many times that number. More footsteps came from the exit behind them. They all wore cloaks that stretched down to their knees with high collars. The cloth was black and shone in the night, leather with a gleam to its surface like dull armor.

"We're being flanked," Cyrus said with cautious amusement. "Wife ... you might wish to watch our backsides."

"Pay special attention to mine," Vaste said. "I think a thousand years in the ether without eating anything has really toned and firmed it."

Vara rolled her eyes. "I care nothing for your backside, even if it were toned to the point of being twin hills of pure muscle."

Vaste's face fell. "Your words hurt me like sword wounds. But there is no healing spell for the damage you do me."

Cyrus let out a chuckle, then met Vara's eyes. "But ... you still like mine, right?"

"That long old thing?" Vaste let out a hiss of derision. "You practically need a woman's dress to cover it."

"It's a fine arse, husband," Vara said, patience on the wane. "But perhaps we might discuss it later. Battle first, sex later."

"I never did get things in the right order," Vaste said. "It was always battle, never sex."

"Because we never kept goats," Curatio said, voice thick with amusement.

"All of you need to be quiet," Cyrus said, "it's time to be serious and win this fight—quickly." He hesitated only a moment. "Because we defend innocents from peril. And also so that I can get with Vara afterward."

"Chavoron," Alaric said, almost pleading, "why have you left me to this fate? Were my crimes so great as to require nearly eternal penance—"

"It's been a thousand years, man," Vaste said. "And they haven't even been using innuendo until now, now that they've realized they're corporeal and fleshly again."

"It feels as though it's been eleven thousand years for me," Alaric said, brandishing Aterum and holding it high as the shadows crept in. They lingered at a distance, easing closer. This was no mad army, rushing in on them. These were men and women who had heard a tale and come to put the lie to it. "And that was just the last five minutes."

"Carnival performers," came a voice down the way, slipping through the shadows. "Look at them." A man passed out of the dark, lit by the glow of Vaste's spell. "This is what sent Broaderick running?" His voice was rich and resonant, and he let out a cawing laugh. "What a weak-teated fartwat."

"What's a 'fartwat'?" Cyrus asked, wrinkling his nose.

"I imagine it's like a near-twat, but at a greater distance," Vaste deadpanned. "For example, the man speaking to us is a fartwat because he's not close enough to be gutted—yet. But as soon as he is, he'll be a deadtwat."

"And what the hell are you supposed to be?" the man asked, peering at Vaste in the dark. "Some freak dropped out of a ship at the airship docks?" His thick brow furrowed into deep lines. A smell wafted off of him, of sweat, of worse—a failure to bathe for many years, Cyrus thought.

"Don't be coy," Vaste said, "I know what you're thinking—'This immense, brute green man is the sexiest thing I've ever laid eyes upon.' Well, I'm sorry to tell you, but you're simply not my type. You might think that's because you're a man—and it is, you know, on a surface level. But mostly it's because you're small and weak and shriveled, and obviously a coward who had to come rushing in here with thirty or fifty friends rather than walk down a dark alley by himself to see what all the fuss is about. Also, I suspect impotence." Vaste threw up a hand. "I know, I know—that should be of little consequence, given that your parts are not really my interest, but I'll tell you—impotence is just not an attractive quality for anyone but a raper."

The man just stood there, blinking. "What the hell did you just say?"

"Also, you're very stupid," Vaste said. "Sorry. I can't handle stupid. It makes me ooze sarcasm, and that wears my tasty arse out."

"That's about enough of this twaddle," the man said. He stepped into the light a little further, and his long, dark hair was matted and hung limp at his shoulders, hanging over his black coat. Now Cyrus could see an armband wrapped tightly around his bicep—white cloth with a strange, eight-point symbol in black upon it. "Shall we end this?"

"About time." Cyrus stepped forward. He cast a quick glance back; there were only ten or so behind them, and Vara was facing them, sword already in hand, Vaste just behind her, watching her back. Curatio was a step back behind Alaric, and Shirri—the thin girl—was between their impromptu lines.

Alaric stood at Cyrus's shoulder and let out a pensive sigh that cracked with ghostly energy through the alley. "After all these years … it still comes down to this."

Cyrus found himself smiling tautly, Praelior in hand. "You were expecting the world to eschew violence entirely while we were away?"

"I had hope," Alaric said, sighing once more, his own sword still in a high guard.

"There's no hope left in Reikonos," the oily lead thug said. He was smiling, entirely too amused for what he was facing. "Haven't you heard?" He reached into his vest and pulled something out in a long, smooth motion.

"That's about to change," Cyrus said, brandishing Praelior as he stared at the man.

"Yeah, well … you say that carrying a sword and wearing armor." The man finished his draw, pulling the object out of his coat. It was wooden, with metal at the top of it, forming an L shape. He gripped it at the bottom, and pointed the long end right at Cyrus. "Good luck changing anything like that." He could see a dark recess at the tip, like staring into a circular pit no bigger than his fingertip. The man pointed it right at him, and closed one eye as he stared down it lengthwise at Cyrus. "You even look like a product of the past ... so ... welcome to the future."

"What the hell is that?" Cyrus asked, staring at it as the man's finger tightened. Then there was a flash and the alleyway lit for just a moment, and a boom like thunder echoed everywhere.

2.

A thunderclap echoed down the alley. Cyrus felt the sharp impact of something strike him on the breastplate like a hard sword thrust to his right pectoral, and a clang echoed in the dying wake of the thunder. He took a staggering step, off balance for just a second before he stepped down hard again and set his feet, staring at the oily gang leader in the black coat, and then looked down, just briefly, before looking back up into the man's wide eyes.

"What the hell was that?" Cyrus asked. Something small and metal dropped from his chest plate and made a THUNK! as it hit the alley floor and rolled a few inches.

"Huh," the man with the strange object said, "that should have ... that should have killed you."

Cyrus gripped Praelior tight. "Really? I didn't feel much of anything, to be honest."

"I bet your wife says that all the time," Vaste piped up.

"Quite the opposite, in fact," Vara said.

"I hate that you always take his side now," Vaste said. "I remember when you were up for a good laugh at his expense. Remember the time you brined his underclothes when he sent them down to the laundry?"

Cyrus looked over his shoulder. "That was you?"

Vara did not meet his eyes, looking instead at the ten or so shadowy figures trying to flank them. "Thank you for that, Vaste, you utter arse."

"I smelled like pickles for a week," Cyrus said. "Every time I sweated—"

"You're supposed to be dead," the oily man said, voice dragging in disbelief. "Armor doesn't work on bullets. Everyone knows that. It's why no one wears armor anymore."

14

"But his just stopped one," one of the other shadowy thugs said. "I don't know about this, Murrice."

"You don't know much of anything," oily Murrice said. "And I bloody well saw it for myself, didn't I?" He paused for just a second and dropped his strange barreled contraption, raising his finger instead. "Get them! They can't take us all!"

Silence fell in the alley. "As far as battle cries go," Cyrus said, "I've heard better."

"Like, 'To your deaths, fools!'" Vaste said. "That's better."

"Certainly more accurate," Vara said.

"Go, you idiots," Murrice said. "Or McLarren will be most aggrieved."

"Wait, who is McLarren?" Cyrus asked, but it was too late for an answer.

The shadowy figures came charging in at them, but it was almost pathetic how slowly they moved. The closest, a woman as dirty and ragged as any street urchin, came at him with a shriek, and he spared her the blade and punched her in the stomach so hard she folded and hit the ground in a heap just past him.

"I just drew first blood," Cyrus said, and a man came leaping at him so slowly as to seem like he was sliding through tree sap. Cyrus reached out and touched his chest, then applied some strength.

The man flew through the air with a cry of surprise and landed on a fence, one of the decorative spikes burying itself through his upper arm.

"*Now* you've drawn first blood," Vaste said. "Except Vara actually beat you to it by a few seconds. She's not sparing the sword."

"One of them attacked me with a dagger," Vara said. "It didn't seem enough to just punch him in the face, so I ended him in hopes of preventing future alleyway stabbings, ones in which the victims might not possess a godly weapon and mystical armor."

"If you hadn't stolen my sword, that'd be half you," Cyrus grumped as someone tried to stab him in the chest. The knife blade bent against his chest plate, and he reached out, turned it around, and put the blade, bent though it was, in the thug's neck. He stepped aside to avoid the spurt of blood and backhanded another attacker as he did so. Both collapsed.

"Do not get complacent," Alaric said, his own blade whirling. He opened some poor fool's belly as he moved, and the victim's screams filled the alley. "We don't know what other devilry they may have at their disposal. Whatever that man fired at you, I suspect it would have had a different effect had he hit your face."

"Unless he'd hit his brain," Vaste chirped. "Then it would have had no appreciable effect whatsoever."

A tough came right at Cyrus, breathing stinking breath at him. Cyrus threw out a hand and thumped the ragged man in the nose. He already had several teeth missing, and when Cyrus made contact with his face, a few more loosened and fell out. The man flipped, landing facedown on the alley floor with a groan.

Cyrus turned his gaze back to the oily Murrice, who was fiddling with his barreled implement once more. He had a small animal skin of some sort and was pouring something down the open tubing at the front. "What do you call that?" Cyrus asked.

"It's a pistol," Murrice said, doing his work with a few quick, wary glances at Cyrus. He stopped pouring whatever it was down the tube, then threw it back in a pouch on his belt. That done, he pulled a small piece of what looked like parchment, then another of those small metal balls, and shoved it down inside with a little rod no longer than half of Cyrus's forearm.

Cyrus watched it all as the man finished his work and started to lift the weapon, drawing a bead once more …

With a roll of the eyes, Cyrus slid past him with all the speed that Praelior granted him. Murrice barely turned his head in time to see Cyrus do so, and clicked a small switch on the back of the device as he did so. He tried to bring it around to line up with Cyrus once more, arm moving so slowly …

"Do you expect me to just sit there and allow you to throw your mechanical thunder at me again unanswered?" Cyrus asked, slipping up next to the man as he brought his arm around. With his left hand Cyrus grasped the man's extended one, breaking his elbow over Cyrus's shoulder. With a cry, he dropped the weapon and Cyrus spun, catching it in one hand and then lifting it, pointing it into Murrice's face. His eyes were wide with surprise. Cyrus frowned at the device, staring at it. "How do you …?" Then he saw the small switch beneath, sandwiched under a small metal loop. "Ah." And he clicked it with his index finger.

The weapon roared, thunder echoing once more down the alley as though someone had cast a lightning spell. A cloud of smoke belched forth, and through the luminosity of the weapon's flash against the cloud it produced, Cyrus saw a spray of blood as the weapon blasted a hole in Murrice's face.

"Oh, I like this," Cyrus said, staring at the weapon as his foe sputtered, staggered back, and fell, clutching at himself. "A *pistol* …" He ran a finger over the grain of the wood along the sides of the metal tubing. "Do they come in black?"

He directed this question to Shirri, who was still sandwiched between Vaste and Curatio and looking around much like a scared cat. It took her a moment—during which Cyrus smashed the face of someone running at him from the side—to realize he was speaking to her. When she did, she blinked and said, "It's—I don't know? Maybe. They're forbidden in Reikonos, but—yes, I suppose you can have them in any color you'd like, just paint the wooden part ..."

"Hm." Cyrus slid the weapon into his belt after trying to use it once more; it failed to function. "I want one in black." He buried Praelior in some poor soul's head. They'd had a blade in hand so he felt quite justified in doing so.

"Well, I've had quite enough of this," Curatio said, his mace dripping blood. "Vara, kindly move aside so that I may—"

"I can do it myself now, you know," Vara said, smiling as she lifted a hand. "Watch this, you old heretic—"

And she cast a spell as five of the toughs charged down at her at once. It surged from her fingertips, and Cyrus knew by the mere casting that it was not just a force blast, her favorite spell, but something else laced through it—

A hiccuping burst of fire blossomed from her fingers and struck one of the charging men, setting his tunic aflame, pushing him back a few steps—

And doing absolutely nothing to the other charging thugs, all clad in similar black knee-length leather coats with the white armbands.

"What the hell?" Vara switched her target to another of the toughs and cast again, sublingually. Another small belch of flame and force sent another back barely a step, setting his arm aflame on the sleeve. With a noise of frustration, she slung Ferocis sideways and cut the others in half as they reached her.

"Oh, you can do it yourself, can you?" Curatio asked with an unmistakable smile. "Perhaps this old heretic might show a young one a thing or two yet—"

He raised his hand to the sky, and there came a thundercrack the like of which was much louder than anything Cyrus had heard the pistol make. Blue sparks rained down from the sky, finding their targets around the alley, a fork of lightning for every single one of the people there save for Shirri and the five of them—

Cyrus watched the nearest foe jump and dance from the application of the lightning to his head, and then it ceased, and the man staggered a step, then raised his head. "What the hell was that?" he asked, stumbling sideways.

"Oh, gosh, that's embarrassing," Vaste said. "It would appear Curatio's suffering some of performance anxiety that's keeping him from really unleashing himself. And after his boast to Vara, no less. I'd imagine that's quite the blow to the pride." He brought his staff around and floored one of the toughs that was running past him. "How awkward. I'm blushing for you."

"This ... has never happened to me before," Curatio said, staring at his hand.

"I hear it happens to many men," Vaste said, then, his eyes flitted back and forth. "Or so Terian told me. Long ago. In a confession of his many, many failings."

Alaric held up a hand to cast a spell, and a cone of force blasted a nearby thug into a wall, where he grunted in pain but stayed on his feet. "My spellcraft appears affected as well. I shouldn't want to have to rely on a healing spell right now, therefore I suggest we make haste in dispatching these thugs."

"Back to my strengths," Cyrus said, burying his blade in a running man up to the hilt then ripping him sideways. "And then, after the battle—another of my strengths—"

"Oh, I bet you've felt the sting of failure in that department before, Cyrus," Vaste said.

"Actually, no," Vara said. "I was quite surprised, as Archenous failed quite consistently, especially at the end of our time together."

"Turning evil probably does terrible things to your drive," Vaste muttered. "And again, she thwarts my well-aimed jape."

"She blocked your staff before it could make contact with me," Cyrus said with a grin, taking the head off some idiot who held a butcher's knife. Those that remained all seemed to be carrying weapons now, clubs and daggers and the like. He slit another in half jaggedly as they ran toward him. He only realized after that it was a woman, and shrugged. If she didn't want to be bisected, she shouldn't have carried a knife into a fight.

"Yes, I play my wifely role as protector well," Vara said, joining him and tearing some poor soul in half from behind. "The flank is now clear."

He looked down the alley and Vaste waved at him, surrounded by corpses and groaning men. "Hihi. Your wifely wife protector made a mess, Lord Davidon."

"You should clean it up, then," Cyrus said, slashing another foe down without paying much attention. These fools moved slowly. "Since it seems like you won't be much good as a healer or a spellcaster."

"Lies," Vaste said, and raised his staff. A small flame belched out from the tip, hardly more than a single stick's kindling. "Well, shit," he said as it flickered out. "This is terrible news. It would appear I've been afflicted with the same impotence as the rest of you. Damn you, Terian! Damn you for spreading this pox to me! Now I shall have to fall back upon the only other thing I'm good at—being pretty. You, there!" And he strode forward, swiftly, the Staff of Death in his hand aiding his passage like any other godly weapon. He stepped in front of one of the toughs who had come running at Alaric from out of the shadows, and the man stopped short at the seven foot troll's sudden appearance in front of him. "Cease and desist your attacks in the name of my utter gorgeousness."

Jaw dropping, the man panicked and stabbed at Vaste, who, unamused, thwacked his hand with a downward thrust of his staff. Bringing the tip up, he shattered his attacker's jaw and then brought the weapon around and obliterated his skull. "Fine," he said as the corpse fell to the ground, lacking anything above the jaw. "You people don't appreciate beauty. So I guess it's down to caving heads in, then."

Alaric buried his blade into the guts of one of his attackers, and with a spark of magic, the man was hurled bodily from the blade, and flew almost five feet before he landed, thumping roughly. "Damn," the Ghost said. "Truly, our magic is compromised."

"Did you give that spell everything you had?" Cyrus asked.

Alaric nodded. "Indeed."

Cyrus let out a low whistle, clipping a running straggler in the side of the head and knocking him either unconscious or dead; Cyrus did not concern himself with which. "You brought down the Endless Bridge with your blasts, and that barely threw a runty man a few feet."

"Something is very wrong," Curatio said quietly. "This world ... has changed."

Cyrus's hand brushed the pistol in his belt. "Tell me about it. It's not all pistols and joy, either." He frowned. "I hope something similar hasn't happened to sex."

"I expect your partner will still launch from your loins at the end with the same explosive fervor as she ever did," Vaste said dryly.

"Damned right she will," Cyrus said.

"I am right here, and I have my own opinions," Vara said, "And they are thus: you're damned right I will."

"Why don't you two just magically combine into one person already?" Vaste grumbled.

"That's kind of the point of—" Cyrus started to say, but was halted by someone hitting him from behind. He turned to find a small man standing there with a club. "Truly?" he asked, and the man cast the club down, raising his hands in obvious surrender. "Get the hell out of here," Cyrus said, pointing toward the mouth of the alley in the distance, "and if you come back, I will feed you your own entrails and nothing else for days at a time as you drown in the juices of your own colon."

"I don't know about you," Vaste stage-whispered to Vara, "but I'm definitely turned on and ready for him now."

"Indeed," Vara said, "I can hardly contain my enthusiasm for tearing off his armor piece by piece, and thrusting his—"

"Okay, you win," Vaste said, "I didn't realize I was placing my head in that dragon's mouth. I thought talk of entrails would cool your passions. Clearly, I was wrong. You're just as barbaric as him, the thought of battle making you moist."

"Don't say that word," Vara said. "Especially in relation to me or any part of me, or you'll find your guts moist from a wound."

"I would have believed you absolutely capable of that in the days when you knew I could heal myself. Now—I doubt it."

"Do you doubt it enough to stake your life upon it?"

"Maybe … *Moist.*"

Vara threw a hand around and a hiccuping force blast combined with flame caught Vaste's robes right at his belly. He took a step back from the spell force, then hastily beat at the small fire that flared on his plump, rounded stomach. "These were new robes! I got them from a tailor in Termina! Spent a fortune on them, too—"

"They have blood on them," Vara said mildly, taking the legs from beneath a running man with a slash. He hit the ground, skidded, and started to half-crawl, half-walk away, hurrying toward the mouth of the alley.

"And fire, now," Vaste said, beating out the last of the flames. "Why do you hate me?"

"Because you said the word 'moist.'"

"It's a perfectly fine word!"

"Not when used to describe me, you grotesque."

"Your sense of humor has gone as flaccid as your magic."

"And yours," Vara shot back.

"Yes, and it's as ruined as my robes," Vaste said, staring at the scorched cloth. "I bet they don't make them like this anymore, since this world has clearly gone all to hell. Did you see the runes stitched into the cloth? They're enchanted, see, to give me more magical ability to refresh my—"

"Doubt that'll do you much good now," Vara said. "What with the flaccidity and all."

Vaste's brow turned down in a scowl. "I wish much flaccidity for you in the coming minutes. A thousand years of pent-up frustration on the part of your dark-clad avenger, bottled up and unable to be spent? That'd be ironic, wouldn't you say?"

"I would if I were convinced a troll knew what the word irony even meant."

"So much hate," Vaste said, throwing down his robes again in frustration. "May you be as moist and frustrated as I am burnt and irritable right now."

"Well, we've won the battle," Curatio said. "And in good time, too."

"Indeed," Alaric said. "It seems our friends have not lost their desire for a fight, though, now putting down their weapons turning wits upon each other like blades."

"In fairness," Cyrus said, "we've turned upon ourselves for a good fight for—well, a thousand years, now, because no one else can provide the challenge of wit we need." He gave Praelior a good swing and blood flew off it, spattering the ground in a long line.

"We weren't exactly fighting all that time, though," Vaste said. "I mean, I felt mostly at peace with you people in the ether. Bored, admittedly, because some of you don't have a great deal of conversational depth outside of the strategies of great battles and proper disembowelment of your foes—"

"I'll have you know that I'm perpetually learning and curiously seeking out new things all the time," Cyrus said. "Why, look at this nifty new acquisition." He lifted the pistol.

"Right, well," Vaste said. "It would seem we've won the battle. What ne—"

A rumble filled the air overhead and something soared far over them, lights burning within it. Wood-hulled, it was massive, reminding Cyrus of the great sailing ships at the old docks in Reikonos, but flying overhead across the skies with a surprising grace, like some enormous, magical bird. It moved over them swiftly, so swiftly that Cyrus wasn't entirely sure what he saw until a moment later, when it had flown beyond the rooftops on either side. It rattled the windows around them with its passage, and almost sent Cyrus to his knees in fear of something coming down on him.

Silence fell a moment later, and they were all left staring at the black and clouded sky.

"What in the hell," Curatio asked, the city of Reikonos falling into silence as they stood in the alley, surrounded by blood and dead bodies, "was that?"

3.

"Was that ..." Cyrus just stared up at the now black sky, clouds hemming in the heavens. "Was that a ship? In the air?"

The wooden thing that had passed over them in such a roar was gone, leaving behind only dark skies, a faint glow from the streets at either end of the alley giving them some small illumination. Cyrus sniffed; the stink of this city was upon him, and he frowned as he looked up, wishing that thing—whatever it was—would come back.

"It very much looked like a ship," Vara said. "Like one I saw in a drydock in Termina once while it was being constructed. But ... flying. As though thrown by a titan."

"Very curious," Curatio said. "A flying ship."

"It's an airship," Shirri said, emerging from their midst now that the danger had passed. She regarded them warily, as though they might attack her now that all their other foes had been beaten or fled. "Only about a hundred of them a day come to Reikonos, so it's totally understandable that you wouldn't have heard of them ... I guess." Every word was laced with sarcasm.

"Well, we have been gone rather a long while," Cyrus said, throwing a little sarcasm back at her. This exhibition of ingratitude did not much impress him. "Perhaps you could understand our lack of understanding when it comes to things we might have missed."

"Sure," she said stiffly, and started to back away. "Well. I ... appreciate the help." She thumped a heel into a body and cringed, her little nose curling. "I'm sure this won't cost me ... horribly ... when the Machine finally does get ahold of me."

"What machine are you talking about?" Vaste asked. "Is it like a smith's bellows? Sending hot air up your skirt? Because I would imagine that could hurt."

"Or like one of these?" Cyrus brandished the pistol. "But bigger?"

His brows knitted together. "Do they make these bigger? Because, I mean—bigger is always better."

"Which is why I am superior to you in every way," Vaste said, then got elbowed in the belly by Vara. "Most ways." She raised the elbow again. "Some ways, then—entirely related to intelligence and suppleness of arse," he amended, eyeing her waiting elbow.

"Yeah, they make bigger pistols," Shirri said, still backing away. "Listen … ah … I should go. You all have quite the mess to clean up, after all." She eyed the bodies splayed about the alley uncomfortably.

"We can protect you," Alaric said, taking a step toward her that was matched by her taking one away from him. "If you come with us—"

Shirri let out a small, desperate laugh. "Can you get me out of Reikonos? Because that's the only way to protect me from the Machine. You may think you did me a favor dispensing with all these wastrels, but the Machine … has so many more available to them. This is a fraction of a fraction. They'll be back to eat me whole soon enough."

"Then you should remain with us," Alaric said, gesturing to Sanctuary, which now stood in the shadows. Cyrus glanced up at the building with all its spires, smaller than ever before and sandwiched uncomfortably between two other buildings. "We offer a haven for lost souls, those in need of aid."

"Look, I was just desperate when I called out—" Shirri started to say.

"And you look much less desperate now," Vaste said. "Trying to run away from five strangers who saved your life in an alleyway. Why, you're positively glowing with self-reliance. It shines through just past the feeling of disdain for us that you wear like a second cloak."

"I don't disdain you—"

"And why would you, when we're so pretty?" Vaste asked. "And helpful. And just left scads and scads of your enemies dead at your feet. Speaking of, watch out for that one, he's leaving quite the puddle." He pointed past her.

Shirri followed his warning and scooted sideways around the indicated corpse. "Thanks … uh, for everything … but …"

"She's going to make another excuse," Curatio said. "I would like to place my gold on, 'I can handle this myself.'"

"Always a favorite among the stubbornly self-reliant," Cyrus said, and then, drawing looks from the other four, said, "I know by personal experience, of course."

"Of course," Alaric said. Then, turning his attention back to Shirri, he said, "You need not fear with us."

"She won't believe you," Vara said, studying her shrewdly. "She's been running from this 'Machine' for so long she doesn't know how to do anything else."

"Mmm," Cyrus said, shaking his head. "The taste of one's own fear must get quite wretched after a while. Just running all the time, always looking over one's shoulder. I mean, I wouldn't know what that's like myself, but ... I imagine it would be horrible."

"Look, weirdos," Shirri said, still easing back. "I appreciate that you all are ... fighters, I guess? I'm not. This isn't the way things are done here—"

"All evidence to the contrary," Curatio said, eyeing the slew of bodies around them.

"Did you hear that?" Vaste asked. "They've cured all the violence in the souls of men since we were gone. Will wonders ever cease?"

"I'd say no, wonders will not," Cyrus said, still examining the pistol as he picked his way back over to Murrice's corpse and started to rummage through his belt. What was it he'd used to prepare this weapon ...?

"Yes, you're a very civilized person in a clearly civilized time," Vara said, dripping with sarcasm as Cyrus tried to contain a smile of appreciation. He enjoyed her wit when not on the receiving end of it—in much the same way he appreciated her swordsmanship. "We relics should probably just pack up our things and go, because clearly displays of violence on the streets are a product of a bygone age."

"You're all making sport of me," Shirri said, coming to a standstill and not looking amused.

"Oh, good, they still have insult-based humor," Vaste said. "Without that and magic, I'd say all the joy would be gone from the world."

"I'll let you know how sex is," Cyrus said. "Because if that was gone, too ..." He ran a finger over his own throat.

"This isn't what you think it is," Shirri said, still standing her ground.

"Truly?" Curatio asked. "Because it looks to this practiced eye as though this lot wants something from you that you are either unwilling or unable to give, and they have turned to the means they most easily understand to compel you to cooperate—violence."

"But surely it's not that, Curatio," Vaste said. "Because she says violence is gone."

"I don't know, that violence still felt pretty real—and quite good—a few minutes ago," Cyrus said.

"You sound just as randy about that as the other thing," Vaste said.

Cyrus came up with the strange ball of animal skin that he'd seen Murrice pouring in the end of the pistol, uncorked it and gave it a sniff. He made a face. "Smells like Dragon's Breath." And when he saw Vaste's frown, amended, "The alchemical substance, not like a sniff inside Ehrgraz's mouth. And I'm quite satiated as relates to violence—for the moment. But I'm sure the desire will well again soon enough. Or that I'll be called back for more, whether I'm ready or not."

Vaste blinked. "Are we still talking about violence?"

Cyrus smiled. "Maybe."

"It must have been good to be you during the heydays, before your wife conquered your long arse along with the rest of you," Vaste said.

"You have nothing to fear with us," Alaric said, extending a hand toward Shirri. "We can protect you, whatever comes."

Shirri let out a little sigh. "I don't know who you are ... but ... thanks. And ... no, you can't." She looked at each of them sadly, her gaze coming to rest on Cyrus. "If you were really him ... maybe. But maybe not even then."

"I'm really me," Cyrus said, pouring a little of the Dragon's Breath down the tubing of the pistol. He could hear it rattling somewhere in the bottom of the contraption. What was the next thing Murrice had done? He fished through the man's belt again and came up with some small, papery substance, and a little bag of heavy metal balls. Right. This. He wadded one of the papers up and stuffed it inside, then dropped the ball in after. Seizing the thin rod that was attached to another tube on the side of the barrel, he warred with it until he found a set of grooves that released it, then crammed it down the tube. "I think this is how this works ..."

"Yeah, you're packing the powder, wadding, and bullet down the barrel," Shirri said, eyeing him uncomfortably. "Then you just pull back the hammer and press the trigger."

"Hm," Cyrus said, securing the rod in back its place. He lowered the strange latch at the back—she'd called it a hammer—and laid his index finger gently across the—trigger, was it? He pointed it at one of the corpses. With a thunderous boom, smoke appeared and the corpse jerked, a new wound and trail of blood spattering the cobblestones.

"This ..." Cyrus stared at his new weapon in admiration.

"There are bigger and better than that," Shirri said. "Or worse and more terrible, I should say. That one's ... outdated. But probably the best a street thug like Murrice could hope for. They're contraband, after all. Possessing one is a crime."

Cyrus stared. "... I could have better than this?"

"It's rather like him and swords," Vaste said. "Or women. Never satisfied."

"Until he finds the best," Vara sniffed. "Then he's *quite* satisfied."

"You can't help me," Shirri said, edging away again. "Any of you. I ... I have to figure out how to leave town."

"I'd suggest the elf gate," Cyrus said, slipping the scabbard for the pistol from Murrice's belt. "Assuming it's not overrun with ... I don't know ... gnomes or something."

Shirri just frowned at him. "The gates have been closed for a thousand years. Since the time of ..." Her gaze froze on him. "Look, you play him well, but ..." she shook her head, "... I don't have time for games or imitations or ..." She looked down. "False hope. I need to scrape up the gold to leave this town, now. I'm sorry for the trouble I brought your way. You should get out of here before the survivors come back with more."

Cyrus looked at Vara. "If we're going to squeeze in a roll in the hay, we should do it before they get back. I'm thinking in practical terms, here—"

"Shush," she said, holding up a finger to him and turned back to Shirri. "What have you done to these people?"

Shirri stiffened. "I haven't done anything to them."

"What hold do they have upon you?" Vara asked.

Shirri seemed to war with herself. Caught between wanting to tell these strangers—and Cyrus was under no illusions about how she viewed them, as 'weirdos'—her troubles, but also not wanting to linger.

Haste won. "I've got to go," Shirri said, and turned away, decision made.

Alaric must have felt it, too. "We will be here should you change your mind or need our aid again. Our doors remain open to those who seek help."

Shirri looked back over her shoulder but didn't turn. She had a hunted expression on her face; Cyrus had seen it countless times before. "You'll find a lot who could use it here," she said, hurrying down the alley. "This is Reikonos, after all, and—"

"'There is no hope left in Reikonos'," Alaric said, softly, as she disappeared around the corner. "That ... is something we shall have to change." Cyrus recognized the tone, of course. He'd heard it from the Ghost before.

Cyrus stood with the others, watching the girl retreat down the alley, hurrying away. "What do you suppose has happened, to leave this place so … hopeless?" he asked, sniffing the sharp scent of the black powder still clinging to the fingers of his gauntlet. The dust blended perfectly with his metal gauntlets, but the smell helped blot out the stink of this city …

This strange, rotting city. The thought rose unbidden in Cyrus's mind.

"I don't know," Alaric said, and there was the same determination in his voice that Cyrus had heard before, "but we will find its source, and then …" he clenched his own mailed fist, "… solve the problem. Whatever it may take."

4.

"It's getting a bit fragrant out here," Vaste said, stepping over the bodies and moving back toward the gates of Sanctuary. A small wall lay at the edge of the street, only seven or eight feet high, blending in with the walls of the squarish building that rose around them. "May I suggest we adjourn back inside? Where perhaps Sanctuary will conjure us some rosewater?"

"Shall we just leave this mess here, then?" Vara asked, looking at the corpses around them. Vaste was right; already they stunk, the bowels and bladders of these attackers emptied in their moments of death. No groans of pain echoed in the alley, either. Death had come, swift and sure, at the hands of the Sanctuary defenders.

"I'm not dragging them inside," Cyrus said, easily stepping over two on his way back to the gate, "I don't care how much rosewater Sanctuary conjures, there are some smells you just can't cover up." He sniffed, looking down at a corpse, which stared back up at him with a stricken look. "Also, I'm a destroyer, not the man who rolls the corpse wagon around town. Cleaning up is someone else's department."

"This is like leaving a trail right to us," Vaste said, swinging an expansive hand over the bodies littering the alleyway. "I mean, it is outside our gates."

"If you drag a bunch of bloody carcasses inside, it's going to leave even more of a trail, fool," Vara said, scraping her boots against the cobblestones. They left dark red stains behind.

"Perhaps a short cleansing might be in order," Curatio said, and lifted a finger. A small spray of water came out of his fingertip, and washed over his boots, rinsing the ichor from them. He frowned. "I used to be able to command a pond's worth of water with this spell."

"Speaking of one of your former dowsees," Cyrus said, "I think this may be an improvement." Curatio turned the spray toward him, but it fell greatly short.

"There are curious things going on in this world," Alaric said, staring at the mouth of the alley where Shirri had disappeared. "Some strange Machine that generates fear. Dishonorable weapons that wound your foe at a distance." He glared at Cyrus.

"Because casting a flame spell on an unarmed warrior is so very honorable," Cyrus said drily. "I view this as simply an improved version of the bow and arrow or spellcraft, and if you find that dishonorable, then I don't know why Sanctuary ever had archers or wizards."

Alaric frowned. "I hear your point, and I don't like it."

Cyrus watched the Ghost carefully. "Because you can't refute it?"

Alaric was quiet for a moment. "Aye. And because … whatever that thing is, it makes me feel … old."

Curatio let out a small laugh. "You come from a world where magic was used to construct buildings the size of mountains. Where it was taken to such an extreme as to scourge an entire people from the face of Arkaria. And you find your honor itching over this small thing?" He pointed at the weapon in Cyrus's hand.

"It's not *that* small," Cyrus said, a little uncomfortably.

"Keep telling yourself that," Vaste chirped.

"It's a good size," Cyrus said.

"Old, and there are bigger, according to that odd girl. The one who doesn't think we're actually who we are."

"Clearly her judgment is impaired," Cyrus said, stuffing the pistol back in the scabbard for it, which he'd now attached to his belt. A sound in the distance caught his attention. "We should get back inside. Close the gates."

"You don't fear these men, do you?" Vaste asked, then stopped. "Oh. Right. Hay-rolling."

"Damned straight," Cyrus said. "The last thing I need is a fight while I'm having a—well, you know."

"There are serious issues in need of resolution," Vara said, familiar impatience rising.

"Yeah, and I'm one of them," Cyrus said, picking his way over the last of the bodies and into the open gates. He glanced around; he hadn't seen much before. His Eagle Eye spell was now working—at least one spell still did—and now he could see the yard that surrounded Sanctuary.

It was pitiful compared to how it had been before. Where there had once been acres of space, enough to contain a barn, workshops, and

29

archery ranges, there was now only fifteen feet or so of grass before the start of the building itself. An old tree remained in the yard, growing up and over the wall. Its branches hung over into the alleyway.

The walls, too, were much reduced. Where once they'd boasted a curtain wall that could be held against almost any attacker, now it was but a small partition from the street, one that Cyrus could have climbed with only a little effort.

"Need a bigger wall," Cyrus muttered, and before his very eyes it elongated, going at least three feet higher. "Better," he said, and looked down the way. To grow it any higher would risk making it out of alignment with the walls of the buildings on either side.

"Sanctuary itself will cloak us once we're inside the gates," Alaric said, stepping next to Cyrus.

"You're in favor of a retreat, too?" Vaste asked, coming up behind them. "Or are you just hoping Cyrus's personality will become less thorny once he's found relief?"

"I'm not thorny, you uncouth pile of elephant turds," Cyrus said, rolling his eyes. "I'm the same as ever—and if you don't stop trying to throw cold water on my modest plans for this next half hour, I'm going to have Sanctuary conjure a goat in your quarters the next time you sleep. I bet you'll wake up excited to see that."

"Disturbing," Vaste said.

"Agreed," Vara said, giving the troll a shove from behind. He stumbled past Cyrus and into the yard. "Now let's get off the street."

"Does no one want to continue this fight?" Vaste asked.

"Now who's thorny?" Cyrus asked.

"We face an unknown host in an unfamiliar land," Curatio said, stepping within the walls as Alaric and Cyrus moved to shut the gates. "Only a fool would invite that sort of trouble when there is no clear goal. And presumably, at some point, the city guards would become involved in such a conflict. Being new in this city, I should think we would like to avoid running afoul of the authorities—at least until we have reason to do so."

"I hate your logic," Vaste said, watching the gates close soundlessly. Cyrus dropped the heavy steel bar across it, securing them closed. "Because it feels like us going back inside this place again, not to come out for a thousand years more."

"It will not be that long," Alaric said with a faint smile, stepping up the small rise—only three steps now—to the great doors of Sanctuary.

Cyrus's eyes ran over the facade. It looked much the same, but smaller. Where before Sanctuary had boasted towers at each corner, now it consisted only of the central building, and perhaps a tower at its center, as ever, though he could not see it from where he stood. Passing beneath the great lintel he realized that the stained glass window above the entry was smaller now as well, barely large enough for a man to pass through.

"If we go by Cyrus's endurance, I'm sure it won't be," Vaste said.

"For that comment, I shall prolong our encounter," Vara said. "Beyond your puny ability to imagine."

"Trust me, I will be doing my level best not only not to imagine," Vaste said, "but to plug my ears so as not to hear. And perhaps to beg Sanctuary to conjure more layers of stone between us to defray any noise."

Cyrus listened to them snipe at each other with only the slightest attention. His gaze instead roamed the foyer. The second-level balcony and the massive hearth to his right seemed much reduced. As did the lounge to his left, comprising only a half dozen seats, and ahead, the Great Hall ...

Was little more than a small dining room, with a central table set for a half dozen. Food waited upon the table, and silence reigned over the guildhall.

It was in flawless condition, not a gash upon the walls, no sign of burns nor attack, but ...

Nothing was the same anymore.

"It's so different," Cyrus said under his breath, eyes coming to rest on the central staircase just to the right of the Great Hall. It was a fraction of the size it had been before, barely wide enough for one person to walk up at a time.

"Sanctuary changes to accommodate the space needed—and given," Alaric said, also sweeping the room with his gaze. "Moving our old guildhall into the heart of the city would be rather more attention gathering that we might wish—assuming we could find a place where it would even fit."

"I didn't really have a chance to look before, seeing as we appeared here and immediately had to run outside to give help to a person who apparently would have preferred death, but ..." Vaste gave a small sigh, "it really is different."

"Everything is," Curatio said, steady as a stone. "A thing you will learn, watching the world change around you ... nothing ever stays the same except perhaps the nature of people. Things will change, the world will change. But people, with their petty vanities, their cravings for power, even their basic interactions ..." And here he favored

31

Cyrus and Vara with a very knowing look that made Cyrus blush, "... those remain the constant as everything else moves."

"Forgive me," Alaric said, and Cyrus turned to see him fading, etheric and cloudy, "but I wish to get a better sense of the world around us ... and what shape that change has taken ..." And then he was gone, faded into mist and evaporated into the air.

"I believe I'll take stock of what has changed within these walls," Curatio said, looking around. "With spellcraft diminished, seeing that the Halls of Healing remain and are well-stocked seems prudent." And then he moved toward the stairs, walking up the spiral with a purpose.

"Shit," Vaste said, eyeing Cyrus and Vara with undisguised discomfort.

Cyrus looked at his wife. "So ..."

She stared back. "... Yes?"

He smacked his lips together, finding them suddenly dry. "... Perchance ...?"

She did not move. Did not smile. Just looked back at him, evenly. "Yes?"

"Would you like to see ... uhm ... if our quarters are in the same place?" Cyrus asked.

She just stared back at him. "No."

He felt a hint of deflation. "No?"

"No," she said, clear.

"Thank the gods," Vaste said, letting out a sigh.

"No," Vara said, still staring at Cyrus, eyes starting to take on a deep burn. "I wish to tear every piece of armor from your body, one by one, then shred my way through your underclothes, covering you with bites and kisses such that my fervor will leave its mark upon your very skin—"

"Damn," Vaste said.

"—and when we are finally unclothed, I will press myself naked against you, continuing to assail your senses with my nearness," she stepped closer to him, fierce determination in her fiery gaze, "my fingers playing against your flesh until you can stand it no more—and then I shall commence—"

"You really are an evil bitch," Vaste said.

"—and the ride will be longer than the year and more you took away from me going to Luukessia—"

"I hate this so much. My life. All of it. Whose 'last hope' were you, again? A randy warrior's, right? Not the last hope of the elves, surely."

"—for it shall be slow, almost agonizingly so—"

"More like Cyrus's last hope for physical intimacy, ever."

"—and in the best of ways—"

"Why did I come here? I could have stayed in my mansion in Termina. Sure, they looked at me funny there, but they didn't subject me to this sort of torment—"

"—and by the end you shall be begging me to end it, to let you finish your race—and I shall—but only once I have had my fill." Vara extended a hand, waiting. "And it shall take me quite some time before I have had my fill."

Cyrus swallowed. "Oh. Goodness."

"There is no *goodness* here," Vaste said, head bowed, shaking it. "None. I have made a terrible mistake. First a thousand years in the ether, and now this. There is not nearly enough separation between us all. Not enough stone in this city to muffle the noises I shall surely hear, even were I to go down to the dungeons and bury my head under fifty soft pillows."

"Shall we?" Vara asked, hand still extended.

"Absolutely," Cyrus said, taking her hand in his. They reached the stairs in seconds, and Cyrus found he had to keep up. When they were at a suitable distance not to be overhead, Cyrus spoke again, in a low whisper. "How much of that was simply to torture him?"

"Some," she said, after a short pause. He watched a slow, satisfied smile creep across her face. "The words, perhaps."

"But not the thought?"

She shook her head, still almost dragging him, at a run, up the stairs. "Not at all. I might have let it remain unspoken, but ... this was always going to be your fate."

His eyebrows rose. "Truly?"

She smiled as the staircase wound to its close only a few short stories up. "It has been a thousand years, and we've just had a battle." She paused, and he stopped himself as she fell into his arms. The kiss was long and amorous, and when they broke, she was grinning. "And ... you are not the only one who feels it ..." She dragged him onward, and he happily let her.

5.

Vaste

It wasn't the fact of Cyrus and Vara having marital relations that felt like a burr under his considerable skin. Vaste had known them both since before they'd shared a bed. These things were expected, healthy, even, he told himself, even as the faint noises began to come from somewhere up the stairs.

No, he thought as the first grunt wafted its way down a few flights to him as he stood in the foyer, alone, it wasn't that they were going about each other like two furious wolves somewhere above his head. It wasn't that at all ...

It was that they were doing it ... and he had absolutely no hope of such a thing for himself.

"Gah," he said under his breath, to the empty foyer. It rang in the quiet, a not-soft moan coming down the stairs, echoing through the cylindrical tower where the staircase reached up.

Vaste studied his surroundings with immense dissatisfaction. Like Cyrus, he too did not care for the change he saw around him. Everything was smaller, he observed with distaste. He even stood awkwardly, as though he might now brush the lower ceilings with his head. They were plenty tall enough to guarantee he would not, but still ... it was a change.

And he did not like this change.

A sharp gasp drifted down the stairs, and he grunted, rolling his eyes. "I want more stone between us, Sanctuary."

Silence.

"You hear me?" he called. "More stone. Heavier doors." He paused. "Good gods, they left their door open, didn't they? They would. Just to spite me, because their intimacies make me ... uncomfortable."

There was no reply. Vaste listened. "You can't talk, then?" He shuffled his feet, staring at them. They were encased in boots now; heavy and leather, with blood stains at the toes. "I almost imagined I could hear you with the rest of them, over the last thousand years. Talking softly in the background, unable to get a word in edgewise with this crowd forever yammering." He looked at the dark corners of the room at the high ceilings. "No?"

He stared at his feet a little longer. "I wish you could talk. Hell, I wish anyone could talk right now. Shout, preferably. For hours. Nonsense, if necessary, anything to fill the air …" He stared at the staircase, wondering how far up Curatio had gone. Closer to the source of the noise, another moan making its way down now. No, he wasn't going that way to seek conversation. If anything, he'd be better off getting further away.

Vaste turned, looking at the door. It was shut but not bolted. Outside waited the empty yard … and the gate beyond.

"Alaric!" Vaste called, shifting back and forth between his feet, looking around. The smell of the fire in the hearth, the warmth of it seeped in, but it didn't feel like it had before. There was no real warmth here, in this cold quiet. The strangely artificial silence was broken by the occasional gasping cries of the couple somewhere above him, rutting about like angry chipmunks—probably going for each other's nethers the same way, too. "Curatio!" He waited a beat. "Anyone …?"

"Ohhhh!" A gasp echoed down the stairs, and Vaste cringed.

"Okay," he said, "that's quite enough of that." A few steps carried him to the door and he opened it. The darkness outside was near complete save for the fleeting glow of lamps somewhere over the wall, beyond the entries of the alleyway.

He paused, hesitating. There was a new world out there, one that had questions—and maybe answers. They'd been dropped here in this place, only the faintest direction given, that almost silent voice he would have sworn he heard throughout their thousand year journey through time—

Save her.

And then they were here, out the door, in the dark, rushing once more to help those who seemed beyond help. He had little opinion of this Shirri save that she seemed desperate, and yet desperately uncooperative with them when they offered to protect her. Vaste shrugged; humans were peculiar creatures—a moan from inside affirmed his opinion and caused him to roll his eyes—and he had long since become accustomed to most of their peculiarities.

But pride? That seemed to be Shirri's chief affliction. And it was hardly an exclusively human quality. He'd seen much of it among his own people, after all, before he'd even left Gren.

Or maybe it was suspicion? There was a fair amount of that among the trolls as well. She'd stared at Cyrus most peculiarly, as though she'd known him—or doubted him. And that led him to a most interesting conclusion:

That the man in black armor, at least, was known in these strange days.

His mind raced with the possibilities. All these new revelations—there were ships that sailed the air like the ones that in his days had cut through the rivers and bays around Arkaria! There were weapons that could shoot a ball of metal through the air!—all these thoughts and more crowded in on him, and Vaste felt himself drawn, as Alaric had been, to look for the answers.

"Yes! Yes!" A deep voice echoed from inside the halls. Vaste closed his eyes and shut the door behind him, hearing the soft click as it shut.

"Someday, perhaps ... I'll find someone to make those sorts of noises with," he muttered under his breath. "But it'll be more tasteful. More artful. Less ... stylistically abhorrent? I don't know."

Something gnawed at him, though, some combination of things he'd heard this night ...

But he shook them off; there was nothing for them yet. No point in worrying about that which he could not even be sure was a thing worth worrying over.

Vaste took tentative steps forward, toward the gate and its heavy bar. He started to reach for it, then stopped himself, listening.

No sounds in the alleyway. But in the distance, he heard something ... voices. Shouts in the night.

They were seeking this place. Perhaps in their haste, the survivors had forgotten where it happened.

Either way, they seemed some distance off. But unbarring the gate ... no, he couldn't afford to do that. But how could he pass if not—

"Oh." He felt a flush in his cheeks. Foolish, really. Raising his voice a little, he said, "Sanctuary, make me an exit, and then close it behind me after I pass."

He stood in the silence for a moment, and suddenly a section of the wall had simply ... disappeared. He made a face of grudging admiration. "Good show," he muttered and passed through. When he looked back, the gap was simply gone, solid stone replacing it.

The voices were still echoing in the distance, and Vaste had no desire to linger. It was time to move on, to see this world and the wonders it contained. He kept Letum at hand, secure in the knowledge that any who came at him with a knife would get a split skull for their troubles. Cutpurses and prowlers be damned, he needed to see this city, this world, and—

A grunt somehow echoed its way through the streets—familiar, loud, and passionate. He frowned, recognizing the voice of Cyrus Davidon. "The window, too? Really?" He looked up, unable to see the tower above the shadowy eaves of the building. "You people really need to learn to shut doors and whatnot. For privacy's sake— and everyone's sake, really."

Gathering his cloak about him and lifting his cowl over his head, Vaste stooped to make himself just slightly less conspicuous—fat chance of that at his height and girth, but he did his best anyway— and off he shuffled down the alley, trying to get the hell away before he could hear another sound from Cyrus and Vara … and so he could get a taste of this new world he found himself in.

6.

Shirri

The streets were quiet once she'd left those freaks behind. It wasn't that Shirri hadn't appreciated their help, odd as they were, violent as they were—she knew worse had been coming at the hands of those Machine thugs—it was more that she'd resented it.

Resented that she'd needed help at all.

"I don't need help," she muttered under her breath, the streets of Reikonos passing in slow movement as she strode through. Her cloak was gathered about her, her eyes flitting through the shadows. Were other servants of the Machine out there, watching her, even now?

Surely. But maybe, if she was very fortunate, they'd be inside, peering out their windows at her. The gaslamps around her burned quietly, the faint crackle nothing like a real wood fire. It had been some time since she'd seen a real wood fire, though. They were not common in these days. Not since gas had come into its own. That and oil—both far more plentiful than wood here.

Her steps on the cobbles echoed like signals sent out to waiting servants of the Machine: *She's here!* It was enough, quite enough, to make her pick up her pace, but also to try and soften her footfalls. These were the hours when most of Reikonos slept. There were, of course, still carriages about, still factory workers coming off the odd shift and walking home. Her eyes crawled toward the horizon. There, in the north, looking down upon the city, it sat, ever watchful.

The Citadel.

And beyond it, somewhere in the dark, were the cliffs and the shore and the airship docks and the port. From there one could hear the crashing of the waves, a sound she missed. A sound she hadn't heard since ...

Shirri shook her head, detouring around a clump of horse manure still sitting in the street. They spoke of steam engines small enough to drive carriages, elsewhere in the world, but only a few had made their way to Reikonos as yet – she'd heard. She had yet to see one. Little came first to this backwater. Coricuanthi, yes. In the domains of Imperial Amatgarosa, surely. Perhaps even in the closer kingdoms of Firoba.

But not in Reikonos. Not in Arkaria.

Not here, at the edge of the world.

Shirri clasped her cloak tighter. It wasn't cold, but the evening's damp was slowly soaking in, chilling her. The spectacle of watching so many servants of the Machine killed? That was chilling as well.

She'd only said the words. Surely that couldn't have brought back …?

No. It was foolishness. She hadn't even meant the words, really. She'd needed help, and she'd blurted some insipid, silly fairy tale that her mother had told her. That was all. Speaking mere words wouldn't bring back Cyrus Davidon. He'd been dead for a thousand years.

And yet …

No. Foolishness. Shirri's eyes darted, watching a man in a top hat who passed on the other side of the street, his dark cravat standing out against his white shirt. He was dressed finely, too finely to be out at this hour, she thought.

Yet he passed with barely a glance, that was all, not even slowing to indicate he gave a damn about her. She thought she saw the sparkle of a monocle in the light of the gaslamps. It could be; they'd become quite popular since arriving on these shores from Firoba.

Shirri ducked down an alley anyway, after checking it was clear. The brick was dirty, ash dusting it from side to side. The light of the gaslamps faded behind her as she slipped into the dark. Did they know to look for her here?

Surely not. If they had, the servants of the Machine wouldn't have needed to follow her before. They would have just waited for her here.

Down the alley, picking her way through the piles of ash and the heavings of chamberpots, she found the old staircase. Tucked away, leading beneath the street, she slipped down it after checking to be sure that no one had followed her. The scuff of her boots was muted against the layer of ash that had fallen on the steps, and she left fresh footprints as she descended to the basement apartments. The building soared another six, seven stories in the air, looming over the alley. Here was where the city started to get tall, stretching into the core, toward the Citadel. Away from the industrial sectors, the factories and smokestacks, but downwind.

These were the slums, the tight-knit warren of alleys where clotheslines lay strung between the buildings, and the once-white cloth of even the freshest washing was dusted grey after an hour on the line.

Down she went, stopping at the door, pausing with her hand on the knob. It turned without even the key, and Shirri let it swing open, silence and darkness waiting for her within.

She opened her mouth to speak, to call out—and then stopped. The door had been locked when she'd left—

"Mother?" she called, letting her voice permeate softly into the rooms within. She stepped inside, reaching for the lamp that sat always in the sconce to her left. She found it, the oil sloshing within, and lit it swiftly.

Its glow cast the suite of apartments in a pale orange light, revealing a most disturbing scene.

The apartments had been turned over. Not a stick of furniture remained whole; the couch was splintered, the wood backing broken cleanly in two, stuffing spread over the rug, which had been pulled from its place in the center of the room and jumbled up on one side of the room. Every item was on the floor, in a pile, every possession they had broken or bent in some vain effort to find ...

It.

"Mother," Shirri whispered, frozen in place. She dared not raise her voice, not now. What if one of them—or more—were waiting in the bedroom?

Yet she couldn't just ... stand here. She needed to know. Needed to know if mother was ...

Gathering her courage, Shirri took a breath. Then another. Then counted to five ...

With slow steps, she picked her way through the debris toward the open bedroom door. The silence in the apartment was oppressive, almost purposeful, as though someone was quelling every normal rattle, every usual snore that permeated through the walls and the ceilings to rain down upon her in these low hours of the morning.

Her breath seemed louder, too, and the thudding of her heart within her chest struck its own rhythm, reminding her of the drums when the bands played at the local taverns. It beat, louder, faster, the closer she got to the door.

It felt like miles, but also inches, and when she reached it, she paused, a slow breath sneaking out as though to herald her arrival at the most convenient place for an ambush. She expected a hand to shoot out and grasp her around the neck as she stood there, gasping, a dark and lecherous servant of the Machine breathing stinking breath through rotted teeth at her as he made his furious demands.

But no demands came, nor any hand either. Shirri gathered her courage and rounded the door and found ...

Nothing. There was nothing in the bedroom, and no one. The furniture was all smashed, the armoire, the cabinet, the bed, and nothing remained whole and in one piece ...

But there was no body, either.

"Mother?" she called again.

Only silence answered her.

With stumbling steps, Shirri turned from the bedroom. They'd gotten her, then. They'd gotten Mother. Taken her ...

Where?

To one of their illicit hideouts, surely. Kidnapping was nothing new for the Machine, even if their motive in this instance was different from what it usually was.

Shirri's legs buckled again, and she stumbled, catching herself on the remains of the couch. It creaked, the broken wood buckling, and she barely avoided a tumble into one of the piles of her sundered possessions. They were few, but those few had been precious, mementos ...

And now they were gone. Like Mother.

Despair rolled down upon her like black thunderclouds, and Shirri stayed there, uneven, bent almost double. Her hand lay on that broken couch, though it offered no support. It was like her life here—empty, save for Mother. And now ...

Now here she was, the Machine after her ... and Mother was gone.

"What am I going to do?" she asked herself, though a tingling on the back of her scalp told her she already knew the answer.

She let out another long sigh. Those fools, then. The ones from the alleyway, the ones idiotic enough to interpose themselves between her and the Machine. No one who knew better would have dared.

But they're not what they seem. This was firm, like conviction, in her mind. *That man in black is not ...*

He can't be.

"But maybe they could ... help," she whispered to the empty apartments.

It was as thin a hope as any she'd ever hung on, but somehow that faint wisp—like smoke from a fire long put out—got her to remove her unsteady hand from the wreckage of the couch, and place one foot in front of the other, up the stairs and back out into Reikonos, carrying her on unsteady legs back from whence she'd just come, seeking that faintest of hopes.

For it was all she had left.

7.

Cyrus

Cyrus's breaths came in gasps, his wind having left him in the last exertions. His legs were splayed across the bed, his skin covered in perspiration, his long hair draped over the pillow which rested a few inches above his head. When they had finished, he had not quite managed to crawl back up to lay his crown upon it, instead collapsing where he was, his bride tucked against his side, her own head resting upon his chest as it rose and fell.

"That was … as good as any of our times in the old world," Cyrus said, breaths still shallow. "Better, even, for being so long in the coming."

"Yes," Vara said, "it's almost as though you've had none of this sort of companionship since your wife died." She spoke with ringing irony, her eyes facing up, the beams hanging above them in the tower room. She reached a hand down and tweaked him, making him jump slightly. "Why, if one didn't know better, I might say you've been entirely celibate for a thousand years and more, dear sir."

"Oh, don't pretend as though I were doing anything after your 'death' but pining for you and orchestrating revenge," Cyrus said, brow puckering.

"So you told me in our ethereal interlude," she said, strangely quiet. "But you also told me that Administrator Tiernan was possessed of a desire to—"

"She might have been possessed of it," Cyrus said, trying to close this door before it opened too far and a titan came strutting out for a fight, "but I was not."

"Hm," Vara said. She didn't seem impressed by his denial. "You are a strange man, then, not to find yourself possessed of fleshly desire in

42

the absence of—well—in absence."

"I don't think I was possessed of much but a mourning spirit at that point," Cyrus said, pulling her closer, his fingers brushing against the smooth flesh of her ribs as he dragged her up for a kiss. She did not protest, meeting his lips with equal pressure. "Surely you would have felt the same, had our roles been reversed," he said once they'd parted.

"Hmm … perhaps," she said, low and steady. "I would have mourned for an appropriate amount of time, given that we'd been together for two years before said event. I think at least a few days of grieving would have been in order before moving along."

"A few days—" He started to rise, and caught a glimpse of the puckish smile ghosting her lips. "Oh, you devil—"

She laughed, leaning down to kiss him once more as she rose. He watched her in her nakedness as she froze, sitting on the side of the bed. "… Did you leave the door wide open?"

"Hm?" Cyrus sat up; down in the pit beneath the stairs that led out of the tower room, the door hung wide on its hinges. "Oops."

"And the balconies thrown wide, no less," she said, frowning as a breeze whipped through, stirring the curtains. There was little but a view of glowing lights to the horizon, city towers with lanterns in them in the distance to be seen, but nonetheless … "Anyone could have heard our … carrying on."

"Well, I hope they enjoyed it as much as I did," Cyrus said, settling back and dragging himself up to his pillow. It was soft, yet firm enough to allow his neck some rest. His body felt slack, the tension all bled out by battle and … this. He drew another deep breath and it flowed out, leaving him resting in comfort.

"I doubt it," Vara said, frowning as she pulled the sheet around her and passed through the balcony curtains, into the darkness beyond. The sheet trailed behind her like a dress's train.

"Where are you going?" Cyrus asked, watching her thin figure through the shears.

"I want to see this new world with my own eyes," she called back. "To look upon it from above, not below, in that dark alley. I want to see what it's become."

Cyrus got up, the feather bed giving as he pushed against it. He poked his head through the curtains after her, and once he was satisfied that no one had an immediate view of them, he trailed after her, placing himself at her back, leaning against her thin figure as she leaned into the stone railing. "And what do you see?" he asked, kissing her neck.

"Smoke," she said, pinching her nose with one hand and keeping the sheet snug about her with the other.

Cyrus sniffed. A sulphuric smell like rotten eggs filled the air, different than the simple stink of the open sewers and cast-off chamberpots of Reikonos of old. Chimneys belched black clouds, blotting out the sky, and another of those flying ships passed overhead a few miles to his left, churning through the air toward some distant point by the waterfront.

"Truly?" Cyrus asked, letting his nose remain unclasped. He would adjust to the stink, he was sure; he certainly had with the pungent aroma of Old Reikonos. Surely the new was not that different. Time and exposure would do the trick, but he had to gut it out in the meantime.

"Yes, I truly see smoke," Vara said dryly, not bothering to turn around. She did, however, unclasp her nose. "I expect that unless your Eagle Eye spell has worn off, you would see it, too."

"I do see the smoke," he said, staring into the haze of the distance. "But I also see ... familiar sights." He pointed around her to the Citadel, standing tall in the center of the city. "And new ... wonders," he shifted his finger to the airship chugging along in the distance. He let his gaze fall to where it should be—ah, there it was. "And the places of old."

She followed his pointed finger. "Reikonos Square. It's still there."

"Indeed," Cyrus said. "But so much else has changed ..." He let his finger drift over the horizon, the buildings so different in their jumbled arrangements than how they had looked in his day. "You know, I think we're not far from the old markets."

"Indeed," Vara whispered. She shivered, and he could feel her back move subtly against his chest.

"You're thinking of Isabelle, aren't you?" Cyrus asked.

"She could—and should—still be alive," Vara said with a sigh. "Though it's doubtful she is here in Reikonos if what you said about her when last you saw her was true."

"I think she'd left Endeavor for good," Cyrus said. "She was living in your parents' house in Termina when last I met her. It was a brief encounter, and I was ... out of sorts, but I doubt she came back here."

"You probably have the right of it," Vara said. "She was always more connected to the family than I was. To lose our parents, and then me ... I doubt it was easy for her after that."

"I expect not," Cyrus said, pressing closer to her. "Perhaps we can go see her." He hesitated. "Is it just her you're curious about out there?"

"No," Vara said quietly. "When we were in that alleyway, one of those idiots said that there wasn't an elven kingdom anymore. It makes me curious … about the state of things west of the Perda. Of how my people are doing."

"But there wasn't a kingdom before we left," Cyrus said. "We saw to that, remember?"

"It would be difficult to forget," she said, turning her gaze away. "But nonetheless, I wish to know—was the curse of our kind broken with the death of Bellarum? Do my people have a viable state … or …" and here she looked at him again, and there was a dark hesitation behind her eyes, "… did losing me actually cost them their last hope?"

"I'm sure they're fine. The elves are a resilient people. But we'll have to go, of course. See for ourselves." His eyes drifted across the horizon to where the airship moved in the shadows, the torches on its deck making it easy for him to follow, its outline shadowed against the clouds of black smoke that hung hazy over the city. "On one of those. You know, once we've gotten the lay of the land here."

"Or we could teleport," Vara said. "Provided it still works. Personally, I wouldn't care to trust that I could become ethereal on command just yet, should one of those come crashing to the earth with us upon it."

"Or that we could be resurrected from such a fate," Cyrus said, frowning. "How do you think it is that magic is so … hobbled in these days?"

"I don't know." She leaned back against him, the bare flesh of her shoulders pressing against his chest and causing him to stand just a little straighter in response. "The world seems closed in like the city with these clouds around it. So much is mystery to us. So much remains to be learned about what has changed. So much to be seen." She rounded on him. "And we shan't be experiencing it here, in the confines of our bedchamber."

He paused, eyes flitting about as he searched out a response to that. "No … but … uhm …" Words failed him.

"Come, let us go and see this new world with our own eyes," she said, brushing past him with a lazy trace of the hands through his chest hair. It tickled, causing him to tense.

"Right now?" he asked as she walked back inside leaving him exposed to the world. He followed after, a few steps behind, his bare arse tensing further as the wind blew through.

"There is no time like the present," she said, removing the sheet and tossing it back upon the bed as she traced a path back to her armor. She paused there, naked, stiffening as though she could detect some other scent in the air. "Unless you have ... some other notion in mind?"

"I'd like to see this new world," he agree, doing a little stiffening of his own as he watched her—she was just standing there, and yet ... "But ..."

She inclined her head slightly, and turned, and he could see the hint of a smile she tried to conceal. A tease, then; she knew what he was thinking. She padded across the floor gracefully, stopping to touch his face with one hand, to give him a long, lovely kiss as she drew his cheek down with it while the other ...

Cyrus smiled, then twitched as she found home with it.

When she broke from the kiss, it was to a wide grin. "We shall go and see this new world, then."

"Sure," Cyrus said, a little hoarsely, his mind firmly fixed within these walls now.

"In twenty minutes, perhaps," Vara said, bringing his lips to hers while her other hand ... wandered ... She broke once more, and now she was grinning. "Maybe thirty," she said, as he lifted her and she giggled, so very unlike her, at least with anyone else, and they fell back into the bed and left the new world and all its mystery and majesty safely outside, for later.

8.

Vaste

"This new world is simply terrible," Vaste muttered as he wandered down a street, looking at the buildings. He kept his cowl over his head, shadowing his face and hiding under the eaves. Lamps burned on every corner and he wondered what oil powered them; they didn't smell like the ones of Old Reikonos, that was certain. These had a stranger scent, more full and slightly less acrid.

Not that there wasn't stench enough as it was, even by the standards of someone born in the swamps as Vaste had been. Chamberpot leavings still remained in the streets, though now they were more likely to cover cobblestones, like in the elvish cities he'd been to, rather than the dirt that had lined most of the streets in Reikonos and the Human Confederation in his day. There was even an effort to differentiate the road, with its cobbles, from walkways along either side, where pedestrians could move.

No carriages rolled along, not at this hour, and Vaste wondered at that. Old Reikonos ran twenty four hours a day. This new Reikonos though, at least the part he was in, seemed quite asleep now. Perhaps there were markets somewhere still active, but for now he encountered only a few people, all of whom seemed quite content to stay far away from him and his mammoth frame, even hidden as it was under a cloak.

And the way the few people he'd seen had dressed ... Gone were the tunics of old. Now most people seemed to wear cloth shirts of the sort worn only by the trendiest types in the days before. He even saw one in some strange suit of black with only a shirt beneath for a white highlight. It made him shudder, some strange association with Cyrus and his armored garb brought to mind. Who else could stomach that much ebony in their wardrobe?

No one. No one save for Cyrus.

The new lamps cast more light. But that wasn't necessarily to his benefit, Vaste thought as he passed one, feeling exposed under its glow. The shadows were his ally, especially given what he'd heard from that alleyway tough.

"And what the hell are you supposed to be?" he'd asked.

As though he didn't know what a troll was. Absurd! Who could possibly not know a troll when they saw one …

A nagging feeling in his stomach persisted nonetheless. Reikonos was changed, and change, mysterious as it was, was a form of uncertainty. Uncertainty bred doubt, and doubt had settled in Vaste's belly like curdled milk. He needed to know the shape of things in order to eliminate it. Perhaps things had just changed too much in the time they'd been gone. He'd known the shape of the world when they'd gone away. Arkaria had been well-defined, clear from corner to corner. All threats were vanquished, all troubles put at end.

But now … now it felt like darkness had crept in like this smoke that lingered overhead and deposited its ash everywhere. There were gangsters in this very city, some mysterious "Machine" that Shirri, the strange human who'd apparently summoned them here, was terrified of. That hadn't been the state of Reikonos when they'd left. It had its crimes, certainly, but … tyrants run rampant? Hardly.

Now, though …

Vaste slowed as a square loomed ahead. Statues rose over the buildings that seemed to grow taller the closer he got to it. He could see the road detour in a wide circle around it. It was not Reikonos Square, but some smaller plaza, perhaps what had once been a green for feeding animals. Now the space was taken up by the two statues, stories tall, taller than the buildings around them, which was no mean feat.

He shuffled closer to the sidewalk, peering into the darkness. The right-hand statue held a torch in hand, and wore flowing robes. It was a kingly figure, crowned, and standing almost equal in size to the lefthand figure, which …

Was much more familiar.

The statue was of an armored man, and as Vaste stared up at it, he counted the height—seven, eight stories high. Taller than any of the buildings in old Reikonos, but here it was only slightly taller than those in this area. Others rose in the distance, much higher than this. But here the statues dominated the area. And the armored one …

It lacked only for a helmet, its long hair, open stance, and sword extended skyward capturing the likeness perfectly.

"Son of a whore," Vaste breathed, staring at it. Damned if he knew who the cloaked and crowned one on the right was, but this—the armored one? There was no mystery for him there. The face even looked like him—mostly.

It was Cyrus Davidon, in all his glory, staring out over the city of Reikonos—or at least this section of it.

Vaste just stood there, trying to catch his breath, until it soured in his nose, like everything else, and he finally knew how he felt about it.

"To hell with this new world," he said, not caring if anyone heard him. "I want to go back to the old one, where they worshipped megalomaniacs I could kill without feeling guilty about it." And with a long sigh, he stared up at the likeness of his friend, wondering what the hell else was wrong with this place that he couldn't presently see.

9.

Cyrus

"Where did everybody go?" Cyrus asked as he tromped down the narrower staircase, the smaller foyer waiting before him as he rounded the last spiral.

"Perhaps they decided not to wait for us," Vara said, a step ahead of him. The sweet smell of smoke now permeated the foyer once more; the hearth to their left was burning as they emerged, the pop and crack of the flames casting just enough heat to make Cyrus feel warm in the slightly chill air.

"Or perhaps they simply couldn't deal with the caterwauling coming from upstairs," Curatio's clear voice, tinged with amusement, echoed from the lounge.

Cyrus made his way over to find the healer sitting languidly in a chair. "Apparently you didn't have a problem with it," he said.

Curatio merely raised a platinum eyebrow. "I have heard worse. But also better." The corner of his mouth quirked up in silent judgment. "Vaste, I believe, has gone on."

"And Alaric hasn't returned?" Vara asked, settling into her own chair.

Curatio shook his head. "Nor do I believe we should wait for him. He will find us in his own time, and his exploration could take … many hours. Days, perhaps even."

Cyrus frowned. "I thought Alaric was back. I guess I forgot how often he tended to disappear."

"As you should know by now, being in the ether is no simple matter," Curatio said. "There is certainly more to it than ever I realized."

"Indeed not," Vara said. "I would have a hard time commanding myself to disappear for more than a fragment of a second, as yet."

"It is much the same for me," the healer said, "though of course I only preceded you into Sanctuary's embrace by a year. It took Alaric some ten thousand years to become the Ghost; we had but a tenth of that time before this moment came."

"I can do this," Cyrus said, and his hand turned ephemeral, for just a second, then solidified again. "But that's about the limit of it."

"It might be handy should you find yourself unable to dodge a sword or thrown object," Curatio said with a thin smile, "but I think you'll find it insufficient to the task of, say, dodging an entire army and their swords."

"What do you think we should do first when we get out there?" Cyrus asked, the desire to charge out the front doors and see … *everything* chafing at him. He felt as dazzled as a child in a toymaker's shop, unsure where to look first.

"Perhaps a simple tour of the town would be in order," Curatio said. "A chance to acquaint ourselves with the changes to Reikonos— and maybe reacquaint ourselves with the few things that have not changed."

"I should like to inquire about the state of things beyond Reikonos, personally," Vara said, sounding a little preoccupied. "After all, quite a bit more of my life was spent outside the city gates than within them."

"Indeed," Curatio said. "Perhaps the day will come soon where we will be able to return this hall to its place in the Plains of Perdamun."

Cyrus blinked. "I … hadn't even though about that. I wonder how those lands are doing?"

Vara started to answer, but cocked her head. "Do you hear that?"

"N—" Cyrus started to say.

"Yes," Curatio said, his own attention on something beyond. "It's at the gate."

"What is it?" Cyrus asked.

"A knocking," Vara said, already in motion. She hurried to the doors and then opened the rightmost, silently upon its hinges. She stuck her head into the night, paused, then turned back. "It's the girl. The one who summoned us."

"Let us be wary," Curatio said, caution falling over his features. "She might be captive to the enemies pursuing her. It is possible they are looking for vengeance for their lost army."

Cyrus snorted; it tickled his throat in a way he hadn't felt in a thousand years, and he enjoyed it so he immediately did it again, prompting Curatio and Vara to stare at him. "Sorry. But I've fought armies, and these people—they're street thugs, back alley muggers that turn immediately soft when confronted with a real soldier."

"They did not immediately retreat when faced with us," Curatio said.

"They did once they realized their numbers counted for nothing," Cyrus said. "Bullies and cowards. They attack with overwhelming force or not at all."

"Come," Vara said, disappearing through the doors. Cyrus followed, slipping out into the night behind her. Once out of the warmth of the foyer and its crackling hearth, he felt the chill of night slip through the cracks of his armor like he'd been dipped in a mountain spring. He suppressed a shiver as he stared up, the sulphuric aroma of smoke once more worming its way into his nose, so thick he could taste it on the back of his tongue.

"Shall we open our gates?" Vara asked with a whisper, crossing the short distance to the heavy gate. A weak thumping was coming from the other side, like someone striking the metal with a palm.

"Just a moment," Cyrus said, and drew the pistol from his belt. He'd placed the curious scabbard for it upon his left hip, where Ferocis had rested until Vara had appropriated it—and now the scabbard—for herself. He clicked the small lever back, finger hovering over the trigger as he pointed it at the crack where the gates met. "Now I'm ready."

Vara sighed, reaching for the bar holding it all closed. "How do you suppose Vaste made it through here without unbarring the gate?"

"He is of Sanctuary," Curatio said. "It would not be difficult."

"He could climb over the damned wall," Cyrus said, not looking away from the gates.

"Witness the egalitarianism of my husband," Vara said, taking the bar in both hands and lifting it. "I submit to your ministrations, and you leave me to do the heavy lifting. It is as though we're in bed all over again."

"You do the work while I protect you," Cyrus said with a smile. "Does that not seem reasonable?"

"Perhaps I should take that little toy while you lift the bar," she said, setting it to the side. She returned presently, and paused at the gate as another knock sounded.

"You don't know how to use it," Cyrus said.

"You point in the direction you wish to fire and click that little thing your pointer finger rests upon," Vara said.

"And after that?"

"I haven't the faintest idea. Click that lever and then point and shoot again, I suppose."

"It has to be reloaded first," Cyrus said with a slightly patronizing air. "Which takes time and knowledge."

Vara sighed. "Very well. Show me later, and I'll take up the burden."

"It's a terribly dishonorable weapon for a paladin," Cyrus said, bringing the pistol in closer to him. "You should just leave this to me."

She narrowed her eyes at him. "You are only saying that so I do not take away your new toy."

"Well, you already took one of my toys away today," Cyrus said, nodding at Ferocis, which she now drew, hand poised on the gate door. "Forgive me for not wishing to share absolutely everything of mine with you."

She smiled faintly. "Have you not heard the truth of marriage, husband? What is mine is mine, and what is yours is also mine."

Cyrus's brow wrinkled. "I don't like that truth of marriage. It sounds one-sided."

"Much like every argument you'll ever have with your wife, my dear Cyrus," Curatio said with a smirk. Cyrus looked over to find him with his mace at the ready, spikes deployed. "I, too, am ready, in case you forgot I was here."

"You are awfully quiet sometimes," Cyrus said.

"I think it's more that you two are so loud that anyone with a less forceful personality fades into the background," Curatio said.

"Yes, I'm certain you've always been such a wallflower in life," Vara said, letting the door creak open slightly. "That must be how you became the gladiatorial champion of the Protanians."

Curatio grimaced. "I do so miss the days when you lot were ignorant of my failings."

"Yeah, because it left us unable to bust your ass when you'd point out our failings," Cyrus said with a careful smirk.

"So very true," Curatio said as the gate swung open and Shirri Gadden stumbled in, hand raised as though to pound the metal door once more. "It does not appear to be a trap," he pronounced as she regained her footing.

Vara started to close the door behind her but stopped, mid-swing. "Mother of Life, look at that."

"What?" Cyrus peered through the gates. "Oh. Well. That's … unexpected."

Curatio shifted position to look out, and his eyebrow rose as he caught a glimpse. "Hm. Indeed."

The alleyway was clear, the cobblestones clean of all the blood that had been left in the wake of their battle. Not a corpse was in sight, either, every last one vanished as though no fight had ever taken place there.

"No one could have washed away what we'd done here," Vara said, leaning forward and looking to either side. "Blood does come up that easily nor quickly."

"Maybe some sort of new invention …?" Cyrus asked, staring out into the alley. "Some way to easily remove blood from every surface?"

"Don't be ludicrous," Vara said, "surely there is no such thing." But she looked at Shirri, nonetheless.

"Uhm … not that I know of," Shirri said, looking as though she'd been caught quite by surprise by the question.

"It's not ludicrous to think they might have come up with a way to remove blood from cobblestones or clothes or—whatever," Cyrus said. "It is a problem. I can't tell you how many perfectly good tunics I've ruined by cutting someone to slivers while wearing something I'd rather not have gotten bloody. Because once you get it on your sleeves, it's over. That tunic is forever relegated to the battle pile, you know? And it's not as though it's all that farfetched—they have ships that fly here. Something that removes bloodstains doesn't seem like all that much to ask."

"I would think the bloodstain removal would have somewhat limited practical applications for any but you," Curatio said with some humor.

"Not so," Cyrus said, holding up a finger. "Think of what your natural healers could do with it. Why, Arydni told me of—"

"We have a guest," Vara said, impatience in her voice. "Could we perhaps save the wonderful talk about the innovations of tomorrow for another time, perhaps when we don't have company?"

"I still want to know where those bodies and bloodstains wen— oh," Cyrus said. "Sanctuary."

"Indeed," Vara said. "For when you want something to disappear without a trace, you should consult the thing that made us disappear for a thousand years."

Cyrus frowned. "Does this mean that the key to bloodstain removal was here in my grasp all this time? Because if so, I have to wonder why Sanctuary never revealed it could clean my tunics before—"

"I apologize for our failure to greet you in the manner which you deserve," Curatio said, stepping forward to Shirri. "We are ill prepared for a guest, and have been so long out of polite company that our manners have faded in the interim." He bowed, low, before Shirri. "I am Curatio Soulmender." He raised back up, and smiled. "At your service."

"Yes, uhm, well, okay," she said, regarding him with a curious—and wary—expression. She took in his robes—which, Cyrus noted with some amusement, were spotted with blood—and then turned to favor Vara and Cyrus with a short examination.

"What brings you back our way, Shirri Gadden?" Vara asked, holding her head high, in that slightly imperious way she had. "More trouble?"

Shirri hesitated. "Yes," she said, seeming to decide forward was the only way. "I—my mother has been taken by the Machine."

"Scoundrels," Cyrus pronounced. "Where is she? We'll get her back."

"General," Curatio said, a note of warning ringing out, "recall you have no army at your immediate disposal."

"We are an army," Cyrus said, "we five."

"A somewhat diminished one," Curatio said. "Perhaps we might get our inquiries answered while we wait for the other two of our number … and offer our guest some refreshment?"

Cyrus prepared to argue, but a small rumble from his stomach brought to mind that while he'd indulged one appetite recently, he had not eaten in a thousand years. And now he thought on it … he certainly felt it. "Maybe we should, uh …"

"I believe there is a feast upon the table in the Great Hall," Curatio said, stepping over to the stairs and opening the door to the foyer. "Perhaps we might retire there and sup and converse until Vaste and Alaric have returned."

"An excellent idea," Cyrus said, stepping up to the entry, putting out a hand to invite Shirri onward. "Shall we?"

"Uhm … sure," Shirri said, delicately making her way forward with some uncertainty, as though she were being led into the lion's den.

"And I'll just bar this gate myself, then shall I?" Vara asked, sarcasm strong enough to wilt the grass around her.

"You're a strong, capable woman, dear," Cyrus said, favoring her with a smile as he returned his pistol to its place on his belt. "Did you say a feast, Curatio? Because I'm sure our guest is hungry."

"I'm … not hungry, but … all right," Shirri said, trailing in Curatio's wake as they made their way across the foyer to the Great Hall—less great now that it was smaller. She looked around curiously. "Where … are your other two friends?" The door closed behind them, and Vara, still wearing a deep frown and muttering under her breath, began to make her way toward them.

Cyrus stopped on the Great Seal, following Curatio's lead. "They'll be back shortly," he said, beating the healer to the punch. "They're just ... taking a look around, I expect." He forced a smile, eyes darting toward the food waiting upon the table visible through the doors in the hall. "I'm sure they'll be along any time ... once they've gotten a little better idea of what to expect here in this new world ..."

10.

Vaste

"I take it you weren't expecting this?"

The Ghost's voice punctuated the silence of the night, and Vaste turned, tearing his eyes from the pedestal base of the immense Cyrus Davidon statue, copper, smelly—of course and nearing eight stories in height. Vaste's stomach rumbled; he could not decide whether he was ill or hungry, and wondered if he should find it in himself to eat were a meal presented to him right now.

"Even Cyrus, with his ego as large as this statue, would not expect … *this*," Vaste said, pronouncing the last word with great distaste. "Did you know about this? Before we arrived, I mean?"

"No," Alaric said. He had come out of the ether now, the last traces of mist and smoke wafting off his cloak, his battered armor hidden beneath it and his helm missing. He looked like an old traveler covered against the weather, though his bulk suggested strength, or perhaps armor. Vaste knew it contained both. "I was as trapped within the ark as you were, unable to look out until the moment we were summoned. Everything you see here is almost as surprising to me as it is to you."

Vaste raised an eyebrow at him. "'Almost'? You had some inkling that Cyrus was to become a deity?"

Alaric flashed a quicksilver smile. "I was there during the ascent of the Gods of Arkaria. I saw them rise before I entered the ark the first time, and so, when I emerged in your era … finding them to have elevated themselves up as they had … *that* was a surprise. Going under as we did, giving the legend of Cyrus Davidon some thousand years to propagate, to seep into the minds of the people of this land? No, I don't find it curious that they would build an immense statue to him, or take his name in a gasp the way you would have Bellarum or Mortus …" The smile faded, and the Ghost stared at the pedestal base, where Cyrus's name was carved along with a litany of other titles. "No, for me it does not come as much of a surprise."

"This is, perhaps, the most unfavorable view I've ever held of humanity," Vaste said. "And I've hated your people on many occasions before. Thought of you in the trollish way—as little less than skittering bugs upon Arkaria, there to serve my race. Sure, I mostly gave up those beliefs when I left Gren, but now—now, in this moment, finding that your species have decided to deify my friend the lunkhead—I think I may be heading back around to an even dimmer view of your kind."

"Cyrus did amazing things," Alaric said.

"I know," Vaste snapped. "I was there for them. But he also did many, many harebrained things, things which I assume have been forgotten to the ravages of time, or that perhaps were carefully culled from the historical record by someone who realized that if they disclosed that he was once seduced by a dark elven spy who stabbed him in the back and left him for dead mid-freaking-battle, people might not quite have the same respect for him. For the sake of— Alaric, he doesn't even remember to close the door before—"

"Yes, I heard before I left," Alaric said, turning away. "But in fairness to him, that's at least as much on Vara as Cyrus."

"I suppose," Vaste said, shuffling uncomfortably, drawing his cloak closer to him to hide him. It was chilly, though. "Are there monuments to her as well?"

"Smaller ones, and usually with him, but … yes," Alaric said.

"What is it she says? 'Bloody hell.'" Vaste let out a low breath. "I mean, really, Alaric. The delusion, putting *him* on the pedestal—it's almost like Gren of old. Next there'll be a goat parade."

Alaric let out a little chuckle, then quieted. Soberly, he asked, "What really bothers you about this? Is it truly that there is a gargantuan statue to your old friend here—"

"It is gaudy. I mean, stylistically, it resembles his arse—too tall, too hideous—"

"—or is it that you fear that while he is remembered," Alaric said, studying Vaste in a way that made the troll most uncomfortable, "you might perhaps be forgotten?"

Vaste just stood there for a moment. "I'd forgotten how annoying it is when you pierce my heart with your keen insights. And to think I had missed you while you were imprisoned."

"I missed being ambulatory," Alaric said, flinching ever so slightly, "and not in immense pain."

"Very well," Vaste said. "Yes … I find it irritating that he might be so well remembered and I might be utterly forgotten." He threw a hand back the way he'd come. "Did you hear them in that alley? They didn't even know *what* I am, let alone who I am. They picked out Cyrus Davidon right away—and no wonder, with this statue of him blotting out the very sky—but Vaste the troll, wise, true, brilliant, firm and supple of arse—no, we not only don't remember him …" His voice dropped to a hush. "Alaric … they didn't seem to know what a troll was at all."

"This worries you, then?"

"We're not a quiet people," Vaste said. "And there are ships flying through the air, to and fro, and I imagine not just from the other side of the city based on the speed at which they're traveling. They're coming from far-flung lands. Can you imagine how closely that would help knit the world together? With teleport spells, we could travel from Termina to Reikonos in seconds. Commerce and trade and travel was near instantaneous for those who could afford to hire a wizard to carry them and a small amount of goods. But this—" He gestured to an airship in the distance, moving across the sky as though it had sails that were catching a strong breeze. "Cargo. Masses of people. No reliance on wizardry—people could be coming from all over. Massive transport, not just teleport. The implications are staggering—"

"And you think—"

"I think that those idiots—admittedly probably not very worldly—in the alleyway … didn't know what a troll was." Vaste swallowed, the churning feeling in his stomach making him want to sit down. Or perhaps bend double and heave. "It leaves me with a very, very bad feeling, Alaric. My people were not wise. They were not well regarded. The fact that they are now unknown in the largest city in Arkaria …"

"It *was* the largest city in Arkaria," Alaric said, holding up a hand as though that mere act would assuage the worry charging through Vaste's mind. "We do not know that it remains so, nor what shape this world has beyond the walls of the city, nor, indeed, within them, entirely, yet."

"I don't see how with those things in the sky that this world grows anything but closer together," Vaste said. "Trade between the humans and the elves opened up everything, and ushered in peace, prosperity and communication between your people and those long-eared, insufferable arses like nothing before. Those ships," and he pointed again at another airship, coming from a different direction, "herald a web of communication and knowledge and goods exchanged that we could scarcely have imagined even if we thought the shackles of magical control by the Leagues would be utterly thrown off. The idea that my people are out there, somewhere, and unknown—"

"To idiot street thugs about to assault strangers in a back alley of Reikonos?" Alaric wore a faint smile, and Vaste felt the light sting of his sarcasm. "Of course. These people are, after all, surely the most knowing and worldly and elite among us. It is absolutely inconceivable that they might possess a gap in their knowledge of creatures in this world."

"You are dismissing my fears," Vaste said with a sigh.

"I would caution you not to embrace a fear that has yet to prove itself true," Alaric said. "There is plenty to worry about in any given day without resorting to worrying about the things that are entirely unfounded—and this remains one of them. We don't know what has happened to your people, nor even if these fools in the alley knew of what they spoke. Wait. Learn. Ask questions of those who would know such things … and then, if your investigation yields worrying results, by all means, worry."

"I just can't bring myself to think that way, Alaric," Vaste said. "Why, if I didn't worry about the impossible things that have never happened, I'd be firmly stuck without anything to worry about at all."

Alaric let out a soft chuckle. "I think we both know—given all that seems to happen around Sanctuary—that is untrue."

"But …" Vaste said, staring up again, "… they built a statue of him, Alaric."

"Many of them, in point of fact," Alaric said, looking evenly at Vaste with his lone eye. "All throughout the city."

Vaste stood there, sullen. "Is there at least *one* of me?"

"My search has been hardly exhaustive, but as near as I can tell … no." The Ghost folded his arms before him. "But neither are there any of me, or of Curatio. Most of our comrades have been similarly neglected."

"And who's this ineffable bastard?" Vaste threw a thumb over his shoulder at the other statue, the one next to Cyrus, robed and standing tall.

"I believe that is the Lord Protector of Reikonos," Alaric said, turning his eye toward the Citadel. "As near as I can garner, he is the leader or ruler of this place now."

"Not someone we know, then," Vaste said, looking up at the very human ears on the statue of the Lord Protector.

"He certainly doesn't look like anyone I know," Alaric said, giving the statue a glance. "Though I have found no name given in my examinations; he is merely called the Lord Protector, 'Our Lord' or 'Our Protector.'"

"Well, I'm going to guess based on my governing criteria of statues that he's either an idiot or a tyrant," Vaste said, and when Alaric looked at him questioningly: "Well, look who else they built a statue to. And the only type of person who builds a statue proclaiming their own amazing-ness would have to be a tyrant of the highest order."

"Perhaps," Alaric said, "but forgive me if I reserve judgment until I know more. This city, while certainly not without flaws—some you have seen and some you have not—is also a place of wonder, and whoever rules it has some small knowledge of making it so."

"Maybe," Vaste said, stingily conceding this. "But still ... look who they worship!" And he threw his hand out to point at the Cyrus statue again. "Mark my words, Alaric. Goat parades will follow this—this—idiocy."

"I rule out nothing," Alaric said, a trace of humor playing across his face. "But perhaps you might look more charitably on your sworn brother once you have a chance to better digest these ... changes."

"I doubt it. Statues of Cyrus. Goat parades." He let out a sigh. "I hate this town already. Again."

"Then let us finish our business here with expediency, that we might move on," Alaric said, placing a hand on his shoulder. "Come—let us return to Sanctuary. For I suspect that our friends are waiting for us even now ..."

11.

Cyrus

"I'm glad we didn't wait on the others to eat," Cyrus said, mouth full of a turkey leg as he gnawed it madly, trying to take every succulent scrap from the bones. The skin was perfectly roasted, the meat within tender and juicy. Delicious, really.

The hearth in the Great Hall roared along one side of the room, and torches flickered in sconces lining the walls. There might only be one table within the room now, Cyrus reflected, but it was a grand one, laden with innumerable delicacies.

"I had quite forgotten the simple joy of eating," Curatio said, attacking a salad of greens with fresh tomatoes and sliced cucumbers with a fervor. It had been dressed with some sauce he'd poured from a bottle, and Cyrus eyed the entire bowl with great skepticism. He had his eye on a roast of beef rib that lay just to Vara's left, and motioned to her for it. With a roll of her eyes, she paused in her own eating and handed it to him. He sliced a piece the size of a boot and tore a strip loose with his teeth.

"Manners, husband," Vara said, her own fork poised before her mouth, similarly laden with greens. *Elves,* Cyrus thought, carefully suppressing an eyeroll. "Our esteemed guest seems to have lost her appetite by the mere act of watching you attack your food like a feral hog its dinner."

"What?" Shirri looked up from her empty plate. "No, I'm not—"

"She's not even looking at me," Cyrus said, barely waiting for a bite of beef to slide down his throat before rebutting that clear falsehood.

"For good reason," Vara said. "If you could see yourself—"

"My appearance didn't seem to bother you earlier."

"You didn't have half a cow in your mouth then."

"No, but I had a lovely taste of elf in it when I—"

"I see the newlyweds are still arguing." Alaric's voice rang out in the hall as he appeared in a dense patch of mist that formed in the corner, another shape coalescing along with him, larger—

"Vaste," Curatio said as the troll took a staggering step forward out of Alaric's fog. "How was your ethereal transit back to us?"

The troll looked slightly greener than usual to Cyrus's eyes. "Nauseating," Vaste said, stumbling a step sideways. "And not just because of the statuary along the way."

Cyrus met Vara's curious gaze. "Statuary?" she mouthed to him. He shrugged; often he had no idea what Vaste was talking about, and he had learned it was better if he didn't ask.

"How did you just …?" Shirri was on her feet, backing away from the table. Alaric and Vaste had appeared almost directly in front of her, and her eyes were narrowed, blinking furiously as though she could somehow clear them from her sight like the afterimage from looking into the sun. "You were not there a moment ago."

"I can see why you'd be confused," Vaste said, "being as there is no magic in your time, apparently." The troll sauntered up next to Cyrus, sniffing. "Is that roast beef?"

"The rib, no less," Cyrus said, lifting the plate toward him. "How's your stomach?"

"Getting better by the moment," Vaste said, snatching it from him and pulling out the chair next to him. "You wouldn't believe what I've seen. Truly, we've come to a dark time in humanity's history, perhaps even worse than when we left. They've given up their dangerous worship of gods who want to kill them and turned to even falser deities."

"Vaste," Alaric said with a great sigh.

"Oh shit," Cyrus said, eyes wide with concern. "Who are they worshipping now? Malpravus?"

"I wouldn't rule it out," Vaste said, tearing a strip off the beef. "This is amazing," he said, distracted as he chewed. "I mean, really, I wouldn't have thought Sanctuary could outdo your mother's cooking, but—truly, this is a masterpiece—"

"Who is worshipped here?" Vara asked, leaning forward. "What danger are we in for? Is there some cult to worry about, like the Hand of Fear?"

"Entirely possibly," Vaste said serious, chewing a lump of fat. "When you see, you won't believe it. The depths these people could stoop to, why I wouldn't be surprised if there are human sacrifices in every square on the morn; children gutted while still alive, caterwauling for mercy from their false gods—"

"Vaste," Alaric said, a little more warningly.

"Oh, fine, they worship *you*," Vaste said, settling his look on Cyrus. "Everyone here loves you. Are you happy now?"

"Happy?" On the contrary: Cyrus felt like he'd been poleaxed squarely in the forehead. "They worship ... me?"

"Much like your little elven wifey in her home country back in the good old days, yes," Vaste said, ripping another bite directly off the bone. "You are beloved here. And I? I am forgotten. Lucky I have this beef to ease the pain and—let's just get it out there—fear for my very life in the midst of a society plainly gone utterly mad."

"The elves did not worship me," Vara said, sounding deeply annoyed.

"They practically fell over themselves kowtowing to you," Curatio said. "What else would you call it?"

"Wisdom," Vara said with a glimmer of amusement. "The elven people have a great appreciation for quality."

"So does Cyrus, apparently," Vaste said, still burying his face in a slab of beef. "And other parts, as well, I would guess."

"Truly, they worship me?" Cyrus looked around the table, finally settling his gaze on Shirri, who still stood, staring at the spot where she'd seen Alaric and Vaste appear.

The question seemed to jar her out of her stupor. "Well, I mean ... they worship Cyrus Davidon here." She stared at him, and a hint of disbelief emerged on her pinched face. "So ..." And she shrugged.

"What is that shrug supposed to mean?" Cyrus asked.

"Clearly she doubts your godhood, my lord," Vaste said, still gnawing the bone. "Shall I call forth your priests to deal with this heretic?"

"You of all people should know that before I was apparently elevated to god," Cyrus pointed out, "I was an actual heretic, pursued and hated by—well, everyone. Or almost everyone. I didn't think it included you—"

"I liked you before everyone else liked you, even your bride," Vaste said, eyes on his meal and not on Cyrus. "Just remember that when your true believers come for me for belittling your long arse. Or maybe be-longing it, since you can't little that thing."

"I am still stuck upon the idea that he is worshipped," Vara said. "Are you certain of this?"

"There are statues," Vaste said. "Many statues."

Vara made a face. "Appalling."

He shot her a sour look. "There are some of you as well."

Her expression lightened a shade. "... I suppose it can't be all bad."

"I think we might have missed a most important point," Alaric said, sliding up to the table and delicately taking hold of a turkey leg for himself. "First of all ... our guest does not appear to have eaten."

"I'm ... fine," Shirri said. "Really. It's the middle of the night." She looked over the table with a wary eye. "You've made a feast in the middle of the night. Seems a bit much."

"As you wish," Alaric said. "But ... you have also returned to us at a most curious moment, after so recently spurning our help." He grew serious, the turkey lingering in his hands uneaten. "I can only assume something has changed your mind about taking our aid."

Shirri stood there, looking like she might stumble over the word. "My ... mother ... she's been taken by the Machine."

"Really?" Vaste asked. Then he nodded at Cyrus and Vara in turn. "Our mothers are dead." He looked at Alaric. "Yours too, I assume." He was met with a nod, then looked to Curatio. "And you? Yours didn't end up with eternal life?" Curatio shook his head. "So," Vaste turned back to Shirri, "you have us at a disadvantage, what with our mothers being dead and yours only being kidnapped. Count your blessings."

Shirri's mouth fell open. "I—what?"

"He's just being Vaste," Cyrus said, a pained look creeping over his face. "How do you know your mother was taken by this ... Machine?" His look deepened into a frown. "Also, what the hell is this Machine?"

"Yes, I admit I, too, am curious about the defining attributes of this group you've mentioned," Alaric said, stroking his chin. He'd taken his helm off and placed it on the table like a council meeting of old, and Cyrus was not too distracted to note it. "Tell us about them."

Shirri drew a breath and held it, her small face puffing out at the cheeks like a fish Cyrus had once seen in a glass tank at a show of wonders. "Well, the first thing, I suppose, is ... the Machine is everywhere."

"Are they here right now?" Vaste asked. "In my pants? Is that what I feel tickling my leg?" He looked down. "Oh, no, that's just my hand. And perhaps a bit of au jus I've spilled." He reached for a napkin and dabbed at himself.

"They're a group of ... *businessmen*—" Shirri started.

"Why does she say that word like she means 'criminals'?" Vara asked.

"—who engage in ... every facet of life in Reikonos," Shirri said. "They sell captive labor to factories for a fraction of the cost of a day's wage for a normal worker. They essentially own them—"

Cyrus slammed a fist on the table. "Dammit, I freed all the slaves, and some ass comes along and puts people back into it. On that basis alone, they are my enemy."

"Something I'm sure they'll come to regret very soon," Vaste said, still focused on his lap. He looked to Curatio. "Have you anything for removing gravy stains?"

"Talk to Sanctuary about that," Curatio said, a little snippily, "I'm hardly your launderer."

"Twenty odd thousand years old and you can't tell me how to remove a stain?" Vaste asked. "What the hell have you been doing with your life?"

"Please, go on," Cyrus said.

"This is my only pair of robes that fit right," Vaste said. "This is an emergency!" He paused. "Oh, you meant *she* should go on. I'll just keep my wardrobe woes to myself, then, shall I?"

"Please do," Vara said, looking at Shirri. "So … this Machine is into slavery for profit, are they?"

"They also run all the prostitution in the city," Shirri said. "Every single lady or man of the night—they answer to the Machine."

"Whoring, slaving—why, they're in all of Terian's favorite businesses," Vaste said. "Say—I wonder how he's doing—"

"He's dead, naturally," Cyrus said, prompting Vaste to pause his attention toward his lap. "Dark elves only live a thousand years. He's right at the end of that."

"I would not be so certain," Alaric said. Without elaborating, he turned back to Shirri. "Please—do continue. What else does the Machine have its tendrils into?"

"Local elections," Shirri said, "paid protection for businesses. They collect a premium each week to ensure that your business, shop, stand—whatever—doesn't suffer from criminal attack."

"And if you don't pay, then your business will suddenly suffer a criminal attack—from them, yes?" Curatio asked, slight smile creasing the elder elf's face. "A scheme almost as old as I am."

"There's more of course," Shirri said. She looked pinched, and Cyrus had to wonder if this was her natural state or one brought on by anxiety. She was certainly small of face, regardless. "Usury, blackmail—you name it, the Machine is involved in some form. All the powerful unelected positions in the city? Fixed by the Machine."

"So … who runs the Machine?" Cyrus asked, feeling his pulse steadily rising. The mere existence of such a thing as this Machine made him agitate to bring his own particular form of justice down upon it. "Because a visit from us … might just throw a wrench into their gears."

"No one knows," Shirri said.

"Oh, someone knows," Vara said.

"No one down here on the streets knows," Shirri said. "Maybe up in the Citadel, someone does, or in the Cliffside district—"

"What do you bet the 'Cliffside district' is where the big mansions are still?" Cyrus asked.

Shirri nodded. "It is. Everyone knows that."

"We didn't know it," Cyrus said. "At least not for sure. Just because that's where they were in my day—"

"Yes, very well," Shirri said, cutting him off. "Can we …" She bowed her head, studying her lap. "… I hesitate to ask, but …" Here she drew another breath, heavier and tighter. "… Is there anything you can do to help me? To help my mother?"

She looked to Alaric, and he smiled. "Of course." Then he turned his head, slowly, to look at Cyrus. "Guildmaster?"

Cyrus blinked, feeling once again like someone had smacked him in the head with a weapon of some stripe. "Me? This one's on me?"

"You are the duly elected Guildmaster," Alaric said with a slight smile.

"I don't think anyone at this table voted for me other than Vaste," Cyrus said.

"And I regret it immensely," Vaste said, a spoon filled with mashed potatoes stopped inches from his lips. "Why, if I'd known it would lead to your eventual deification I would have voted for Vara. Or that leaf-eating idiot."

"I voted for you," Curatio said.

"You'd have voted for a shrubbery at that point if it'd meant you could cast away the Guild leader medallion and be left in peace to run your Halls of Healing," Cyrus said.

"I doubt I'd have found many shrubberies as capable as you," Curatio said, "at least not since the days before the trees entered their slumber."

"Alaric," Cyrus said, tone approaching beseeching, "… don't ask me to be in charge. Let me be the general again." He reached into his collar and swept the chain from around his neck, taking care not to rip his hair out by catching it in the links. "My days as Guildmaster were … fraught. Let me go back to doing what I was best at—"

"Killing people and destroying shit," Vaste said.

"—and you go back to leading us," Cyrus said, "in all but combat." He held out the medallion, dangling at the end of its chain.

Alaric eyed the medallion. "I don't think—"

"Oh, come on," Vaste said, "he's already a god in this city. Don't pretend the four of us with any sanity remaining will look to him for leadership before you. We're mad, but we're not what I will now call 'Reikonos mad.'"

Cyrus smiled faintly. "He has a point."

Vara put a hand on Cyrus's arm. "I would follow you, you know."

Cyrus looked deep into the sparkling blue of her eyes. "You have. It led to your death."

Vara looked slightly stung. "That was hardly your fault."

Cyrus's smile faded. "It was entirely my fault. I provoked the fights that led us to that moment."

"And changed the face of Arkaria forever," Curatio said, leaning forward, elbows upon the table, fingers upon his face. "Do not diminish yourself or your accomplishments, Cyrus."

"I'm not trying to," Cyrus said, and looked right at Alaric, who stared at him with that one good eye. "I'm not trying to—look, when I make a decision, I will be looking to you for approval when I do it. We all will. You would have remained the Master of Sanctuary if you hadn't gone under that bridge, hadn't sacrificed yourself to Bellarum and the others. I'm Guildmaster because you made the brave choice, and accepted the brunt of consequences I called down on you—"

"You were hardly the only one who struck a blow in that fight," Alaric said. "And you had the courage to fight it, unlike me. I was prepared to sacrifice one of our brethren to keep a horrific peace. For that, you think I should be leader? Because I failed to dare the status quo, when the status was oppression by those who would think themselves our betters?" He shook his head. "No, Cyrus—you led this guild bravely when I was too afraid to confront the evil that sat upon the throne of this land—"

"Bullshit," Cyrus said, medallion trembling as his hand shook. "You didn't just confront the evil, you threw yourself bodily into their torture chamber and took endured years of pain to spare the rest of us until we could fight them on even footing—"

"You spat in the eye of evil and I appeased it—" Alaric said.

"You wisely steered us from a fight we couldn't win, and I shoved myself and all my friends into its waiting maw—" Cyrus said.

"I will lead us," Vaste said, rising, hands spread out in either direction. "I am wise and just, and all I ask is that you bow to me, call me a god, and bring me some pie." He looked down the table. "Oh, the pie is already covered. Never mind that last one. Bowing and calling me a god shall be sufficient." And he leaned to grab the pie.

"Perhaps we could settle this issue of leadership later," Vara said, clearing her throat uncomfortably. "It seems likely, after all, that if we were to go and fight this Machine on behalf of recovering Shirri's mother, we would probably defer to Cyrus's strategic and tactical guidance, at least in the short term."

Alaric was quick to reply. "It is true; I have never been a general, and never led anything more than the smallest of armies. My knowledge in these areas is considerably less than yours, brother. I bow to you in this."

"Just don't think passing the medallion on who leads the fight absolves you of this discussion later," Cyrus said, reluctantly pulling the chain back. With a hesitant glance at the circular pattern of runes upon its surface, he placed it back over his head and slid it beneath his breastplate.

"I am certain it will be a stimulating discussion," Alaric said with a smile.

Shirri seemed to stir to life again, her face resting up her hand, elbow on the table. "Sorry, I, uh … fell asleep there during all that … macho posturing or whatever you were doing."

"They were deferring to each other endlessly," Vaste said, mouth full of pie. Shirri watched him eat, a look of disgust creeping over her face. "It was quite sad to watch, like two old men arguing over who enters a door first. Just go, you old jackasses, before one of you keels over dead from age."

"Says the thousand year-old troll," Vara muttered.

"I do have one question," Cyrus said, looking at Shirri. He felt a certain swell of confidence, knowing that the rest of them had marked him to be their leader, at least in the fight. *This one thing I can do,* he thought. "What … does this Machine want from you so badly that they would kidnap your mother?"

Shirri froze, hesitating. "I … can't say," she finally coughed out, her words almost inaudible.

A moment of silence hung over the table before Vaste piped up. "Oh, a secret," he said, hand filled once more with a gluttonous helping of pie, poised to cram it into his mouth. "You'll fit right in around here," he said, smiling, as he shoved it in.

12.

"Our first objective should be to find and assault the nearest stronghold of this Machine," Cyrus said as they strode down the steps of Sanctuary and into the waning night. Light was showing somewhere beyond the high walls, hints of the sun on the rise in the distance. He looked in the direction where the sky was brightest and decided that must be east.

"How will we find it?" Vara asked as Alaric raised the bar on the gate and then opened it for them. Cyrus passed through first, into the empty alley, all trace of last night's massacre now faded away.

Cyrus stared in either direction. Lamps glowed at either end of the alley but the light was fading in the dying of night. "I don't know. We could ask—"

"Someone who knows," Curatio said, looking pointedly at Shirri, who stood right in their midst. Cyrus turned to look at her, and the others followed until all five were focused on her.

Shirri looked uncomfortable at all the attention upon her. "Well ... yes, I know where their nearest office is. It's not exactly a secret."

"Interesting," Alaric said. "I should think it would be, given that this organization dabbles in so many hideous fields of endeavor. I would think that being open about their locations would invite retribution."

Shirri just blinked at him. "Nobody would dare."

Cyrus cracked a smile. "Doing what no one else would dare do is something of a specialty of ours."

Shirri's breath seemed to catch in her throat, and she muttered, "I've cast my lot with dead people. Dead, and they don't even know it yet."

"Oh, I think we know we're dead," Vaste said, "haven't you seen this idiot's monuments?" He chucked a thumb at Cyrus. "They don't build those to the living, sweetheart." He paused. "Unless this Lord

Protector fellow is still alive."

Shirri frowned. "Of course he's still alive. The nearest, er, office for the Machine is this way." She pointed to their left. "Six blocks away."

"You lead," Cyrus said, nodding to her, and with a hint of reluctance, Shirri started in that direction.

"I know the two of you are really trying to push leadership onto anyone else," Vaste said, "but you could have turned to one of us who has been around a while rather than delegating to the lady who summoned us out of the peaceful ether into a horrific hellscape filled with statues of the man in black armor and groupies who probably worship him and wish they could bury their heads in his lap like some elven icon with terrible hair and worse judgment."

Vara's brow puckered. "My judgment is excellent. And my hair is just fine."

"If it was that great, you wouldn't wear it in a ponytail all the time," Vaste said.

"I need it out of my eyes when I fight, you fool."

"I can vouch for the fact that it's quite lovely when down," Cyrus said. "Very full of body, lustrous, really—"

"I'm sure it looks wonderful all piled beneath her on the bed as you labor atop her," Vaste said.

"It looks just as wonderful when it hangs loose as she labors atop me," Cyrus said with a wicked smile.

"This is the most bizarre thing I have ever done," Shirri muttered ahead of them, "and the strangest people I have ever met. Why have I cast my lot with them again?"

"Desperation, my dear," Curatio called to her. "It leads you curious places."

"No shit," Shirri muttered, almost under her breath.

"I, for one, am curious why the ruler of this city would tolerate such activity," Alaric said, as they came out upon the main street at the alley's end. Cyrus's gaze swept in either direction. The city certainly looked … different.

Gone was the hodge podge of wooden shanties and stone houses with thatched roofs. Replacing them were houses of clay and brick with tiled rooftops. There was a more uniform look to the city now; not cleaner, but more orderly in a way that Cyrus could only think of as "modern." As though the nicest, best-built buildings of the Reikonos of old had become the decrepit places of this city, and a new breed of superior structure had sprung up in their place.

"The Lord Protector?" Shirri asked, leading them to the right down a cobblestone street lit by lamps that glowed orange. "He never comes down out of his tower anymore. They say …" She hesitated, looking around, as though someone might overhear them. "… Never mind."

"I'm very interested in what this ephemeral 'they' have to say," Vaste said. Cyrus looked at him to see that he had his cowl over his head and was walking hunched over. When he caught Cyrus looking, he shrugged. "Don't want to be too much of a spectacle."

"You're not any smaller when you hunch over," Cyrus said. "You look like two people huddling under one cloak. Maybe even four; two piled upon the tops of two others' shoulders."

"As though you're all small of frame," Vaste shot back. He straightened himself, looking uncomfortable. "I was stooping further before, but after that pie I'm afraid I might leave a mess on these pretty streets should I bend too far. If it was old Reikonos, I wouldn't hesitate, because all I'd soil would be mud. But here, I'm afraid I'd ruin their cobblestones and then strong guards would appear and present with a bill for damages, which I'd feel compelled to hand to Curatio to pay." When everyone just stared at him, he said, "Because he's lived so long, doubtless he has money."

"You have a mansion in Termina, fool," Vara said, "and an income stipend for life."

"Yes, but the man who gave that to me is dead thanks to some utter arse chopping his head off and burning his body," Vaste pointed out. "Also, my natural life-span was supposed to cease some nine hundred years ago, so I'm not counting on them having kept it for me."

"You may be pleasantly surprised, then," Vara said. "Elven law specifies that such decrees are to last an elven life span—though I suppose whoever is now in charge of the kingdom—or whatever it is—might have changed it in our absence."

"There is no elven kingdom," Shirri said, frowning over her shoulder.

"Tell me of the elves," Vara said, picking up her pace to come alongside Shirri, who looked as if she were readying herself to take a sudden leap away from the elven paladin in her shining armor. "Where are they?"

Shirri blinked a few times. "Pharesia, of course, and Amti. And some are here, some in Termina, and Emerald Fields—"

"Hey, Emerald Fields and Amti are still around," Cyrus said. "Good for them."

Shirri looked at him strangely, then turned her attention back to Vara. "But mostly Pharesia and Amti."

"Of course," Vara said, smiling slightly.

Shirri looked a little discomfited. "You're one of the whole elves, then?" She eyed Vara's ears.

"My name is Vara Davidon," Vara said, giving her an intense gaze. "Do you know of me?"

Shirri looked taken aback, then met her look with a touch of defiance. "I know of Vara Davidon. Everyone knows of Vara Davidon. But you are n—"

"I *am* Vara Davidon," Vara said, stopping her with an outstretched hand. "My people live for some six thousand years and I have been gone but a thousand. I left this land when I was thirty-four. Do you know this truth of my peoples' lifespan?"

"Yes," Shirri said. "Of course."

"Then you doubt I am who I say I am," Vara said, eyes narrowing further, hand still placed to obstruct Shirri's forward motion. "You doubt my husband, too, then—and my friends."

Shirri looked around at them each, slowly. "I … don't know your friends."

"But you have no one else to turn to," Vara said, "so although you don't trust we are who we say we are, you are still stuck asking us for aid."

Shirri looked down. "I … have no one else. And …" She looked up, and that glint of desperation was in her eye. "And there is no one else who would spit in the eye of the Machine the way you have."

"I think you mean 'gouge out the eye of the Machine the way we have,'" Vaste said, stepping up. "We killed some thirty of their people. I assume based on your other statements that no one else in this city would so much as touch one of them, yet we killed thirty, and could have killed more."

"You did," Shirri said, with great reluctance. She stared at her feet once more.

"We have done something that no one else is capable of or would dare to," Vara's voice was strong and confident. "Why do you doubt we are who we say we are?"

Shirri's gaze flicked up to her. "Because you're clearly crazy, taking on the Machine."

"You're taking on the Machine as well," Vara said, her own eyes narrowing at Shirri. "You could have sought them out, made peace with them—given them whatever mysterious thing it is they want from you. But instead you've run, then watched strangers fight them on your behalf, and now are leading us into their den. A more suspicious person might suspect a trap."

"I'm not trapping you," Shirri said, taking a step back. "I'm …" Her voice trailed off. "Using you, I guess."

"Someone's finally found a use for Vaste," Cyrus said, breaking into a smile.

"I have many uses," Vaste said. "For example, Vara has me stand next to you so that you may bask in the reflection of mine and my arse's glory."

"You also make an excellent pie disposal," Curatio pointed out.

Shirri looked at each of them. "I just told you all I'm using you."

Alaric cleared his throat and smiled benignly. "Yes."

Shirri blinked. "And ... you don't have ... anything to say about that?"

"You desire our help," Alaric said, "and we have offered to render it." His smile remained. "Thus, we have consented to work for your purposes, for we find the rescue of your mother from the clutches of these—these—"

"Fiends," Vara said.

"Gangsters," Cyrus said.

"Syphilitic turdwagons," Curatio said, drawing everyone's attention to him. "It was better than whatever Vaste was going to say."

"Damn you, healer," Vaste said. "It *was* better than what I was cooking up."

"We find no fault in you for wishing assistance," Alaric said, stepping up next to Vara and looking at her—ever so gently—until she turned her hard gaze away from Shirri. "All find themselves overmatched, overwhelmed at some point in life. And with the foes you are up against, it seems that aid is needed from a source more willing to clash with such ..."

"Worm-infested anuses!" Vaste shouted, and when Curatio looked at him, "Beat that, you old elf!"

"I don't think I care to try," Curatio said.

"You require force, and we are here," Alaric said, "willing to help. So—we put ourselves at your disposal."

"But you ... could get hurt," Shirri said. "These people ... the ones who work for the Machine ... they're not all street thugs like the ones you encountered in that alley. Thousands work for them, across all walks of life in this city. They have their fingers in everything—"

"Have they had their fingers in my pie?" Vaste asked. "Because I cannot abide that."

"They have had their worm-infested anuses in your pie," Vara said.

"Those bastards," Vaste said. "Vengeance will be ours for this atrocity."

"As strange as we may sound," Alaric said, "and as strange as some us may *be*—"

"He's talking about you, you know," Vaste said, elbowing Vara. She shot him a scathing look. "What? You sleep with a seven-foot tall human in black armor with a pathetically underwhelming arse. Some elven icon you are."

"She sleeps with someone a whole city worships," Cyrus said smugly. "Beat that—troll."

"You don't know what you're getting into," Shirri said, raising her voice at last. "If you do this—it won't end with just getting my mother back."

Alaric still smiled. "I expected not." He wheeled his attention to Cyrus. "General?"

Cyrus took a quick breath. He was ready for this. "If this Machine is what you say it is, we'll need to roll across their operations in this part of the city quickly to prevent any sort of response. It's a little like conquering a whole map in one night—I assume they're entirely headquartered here in Reikonos, nothing outside the gates?"

Shirri made a very strange face. "No. There's nothing outside the gates."

"We need to at least overwhelm their entire presence in this area," Cyrus said, "but if we could, I'd recommend we hit everything they have in the city. Every office, every building—we treat it like a war to be won, and we take it to them without mercy. No survivors to let them know what's coming, just a straight up attack on their forces and outposts until we find our objective."

"I might have some qualms about the 'no survivors' bit," Alaric said stiffly, "making allowances for any secretaries or other non-combatants we find in these places—"

"If this criminal enterprise is what she says it is, Alaric," Cyrus said, trying to hold back a little, "they're aiding and abetting slavery, forced prostitution, general thuggery, and who knows what else. Anyone who dabbles in that is hardly innocent."

"Perhaps not," Alaric said, "but neither does it make them subject to summary execution at the edge of our blades. You may kill all those who raise a weapon against you, but to strike down the unarmed and surrendering—"

"Aye," Cyrus said, burying his further objections. They welled within him, along with perfectly good arguments—*There is no justice in this city, they have committed great offenses against the weakest*—but he held them in his heart and they did not pass his lips. "But we need to be prepared, then, for a reprisal—and much sooner than we might have otherwise see."

"Any reprisal they sit fit to levy, we shall both endure—and cram back down their throats as though they were our own blades." Alaric paused. "Which is likely to happen, us burying our blades in them." Vaste cleared his throat, and then waved the head of his staff. "Or whatever you carry," Alaric conceded.

"I can't believe I'm doing this," Shirri muttered.

"Do you have objections?" Alaric asked.

Shirri just stared at him. "Yes. I have objections. I have worries, concerns, fears—I have all of those." She bit her lower lip. "But I also have a mother who's been taken by these criminals, and so I have no hope left ... save for you." Cyrus detected an insult she bit back at the last. "So ..." She gestured with an extended arm down the street. "Shall we?"

"Let us," Alaric said, and they began to walk once more.

"I have a question," Vaste said, coming up alongside Shirri now, "oh, expert of our day. What ever happened to the trolls?"

Shirri looked at him, most peculiarly. "A ... what?" She stared, then seemed to get it. "Oh. Is that what you are?"

"What do you think I am?" Vaste asked. "Never mind. You have no idea, do you?"

"I haven't been outside Reikonos," Shirri said, and here Cyrus detected a hint of self-consciousness. "But I've never heard of anything that looks like you."

"What about the goblins?" Vara asked. Shirri stared at her blankly. "The gnomes? The dwarves?"

"I ... there are some from other lands," Shirri said. "Dwarves, I mean. And gnomes, I guess? Small people, about yea tall?" She held a hand to her knee, then raised it to her waist. "And dwarves?" When Vara nodded, she said, "I've seen some of them, coming in on ships from Coricuanthi and Imperial Amatgarosa and Firoba, but ..." She shrugged. "If there were any on Arkaria, I don't know of them."

"This is clearly Vara's fault," Vaste said gravely.

"My fault?" Vara asked, giving him a vicious look. "Explain."

"After you died, the elves were so grieved that they decided to wipe out your most hated foe—the gnomes," Vaste said. "And after they had accomplished that *small* task—"

"Har har," Curatio said.

"—their bloodlust could not simply be sated by going home and chewing on vegetables, as your kind does for reasons I cannot begin to fathom. No, then they must have widened their war, and the dwarves, goblins, and even the trolls surely felt their ancient and pointy-eared wrath."

There was a second's pause, and Shirri said, "That's not—"

"A most illuminating speculation," Vara said, "and just as delusional as any descriptions of your arse that don't include the words 'fat,' 'oblong,' and 'a waste of space.'"

"See?" Vaste said, pointing at her. "Elves are unrelentingly vicious."

"What about Saekaj Sovar?" Alaric asked, a tightness in his voice.

"Yes, Alaric is worried about his progeny, the Lepos clan," Vaste said.

"It's … still there," Shirri said, frowning. "Tough to believe, I know, but at least a quarter of the ships that come through Reikonos come from there."

Something about what she'd said prickled Cyrus's ears. "Why did you say that it's tough to believe Saekaj is still there?" he asked, drawing in a deep breath. Despite their recent feast, the smell of fresh bread from a nearby bakery was making him hungry again.

Shirri just stared back at him, skepticism drenching her features. "Come on. Don't pretend you don't know."

"Of course we know," Vaste said grandly, "it's why we're asking you stupidly basic questions about the shape of the world; we desire to make ourselves look like fools in front of a near total stranger who is already using us to rescue her mommy. It's the only way to spend your days, striking down gangsters in back alleys and then asking elementary questions of the people you save, trying to convince them that you're long dead adventurers from better days, back when people weren't so starved for meaning in their lives that they'd be driven to worship empty heads of cabbage mounted on a set of black armor."

"I wouldn't ask if I knew," Cyrus said, ignoring Vaste's fusillade. "You've said a few things that have left me wondering—you mentioned the gates haven't been opened in a thousand years; that this Machine has nothing outside Reikonos's walls." He let his eyes wander. "Everything else is so built up in here … I find it hard to believe they wouldn't have expanded the city outside the walls by now, given how crowded it seems to have become. And then you talk about … these other races that are simply … gone from these lands." Cyrus stared at her, watched the suspicion cloud her small face. "What has happened here? This obvious thing you think we know?"

She watched him for a moment, still as a statue, then gave a light snort. "You are a fine thespian."

"My swordplay is no act," Cyrus said, "and neither is my demeanor now. Answer me—and tell the truth. What lies beyond the gates of Reikonos? What happened in the land beyond that would make Saekaj's survival … unbelievable?"

She stared at him, her eyes slightly wider. "Truly, you don't know?" They narrowed just a little. "You don't just take me for a fool?"

"I take you for a person who seeks aid," Cyrus said, trying to keep hold of his thinning patience. "This is my price. Now answer me."

"Fine, then," she said, shifting her gaze to her toes. "You ask what is beyond the gates? A moat—hundreds of feet wide, and deep, too." Shirri looked up. "And no way across it, save to swim."

A grinding, worrying feel crawled into Cyrus's guts, a thin trickle of worry like a thread being spun stronger. "And ... beyond that?" *Reikonos never had a moat before ... to dig such a thing would be ... an undertaking of gargantuan proportions ... why would they ...?*

She did not speak for a long moment, studying him as though pressing to see if some facade would break, and he would laugh, confessing to trying to trick her. He did not, and after long seconds, she answered. "What waits beyond is ... death, of course. For any who are thrown over and choose to swim rather than drown. Death waits beyond, in all the lands between the River Perda and the Sea to the east. Death that came—supposedly in the days after *you* left." Disbelief was audible in her voice. "Came across the lands like a sweeping plague, devouring all life swept before it. A horde, a grey-skinned horror that came from out of the mountains northeast—"

"No," Cyrus whispered, his mouth suddenly quiet dry.

"Damn," Alaric said, bowing his head.

"It can't be," Curatio said, looking quite stricken.

"Torrential, uncontrollable shits," Vaste said, his deep green paling by several degrees into a near grey.

"No, I don't jest ..." Shirri shook her head. "They are out there, still, waiting—in case an airship crashes, and they occasionally do, losing all hands, should those things reach them before a rescue ship can ... They wait beyond the moat, afraid to cross, as they have for the last thousand years ... this eternal enemy ... this ..."

She started to say the name, but Cyrus raised his voice, and they spoke as one:

"Scourge."

13.

Cyrus's world spun around him, vertigo creeping into his head like a titan had bound him to a giant maypole and flung him in the air. His nose filled with the scent of fear, like blood, and it pounded through his veins and in his head, throbbing beneath the temple. He could almost taste the vile stink of putrid death coming from the east, over the horizon, as he would have thought of it, but it was not just east, and it was not over the horizon—

It was close. It was just beyond the gates.

Cyrus's legs felt suddenly weak, as though bordering on collapse. A stone seemed to have formed in the center of his chest where his heart had been. Oh, it still pulsed in there, but now it was weighted, threatening to drop into his belly, into the bile that churned there. He put his face in his hand and, distantly, he could hear Vara say his name, feel her touch him on the shoulder.

"Dammit," he said, the world faded in sound around him. The distant buzz of some herd creature had stilled and he was left with a question that boiled out. "How did they get from Luukessia to here?"

"The same way the Protanians originally reached Luukessia to kidnap me," Alaric said, next to him now, and speaking in a slow, soothing voice. "There is a land bridge that connects north of Fertiss to the very northern portions of Syloreas. Indeed, I myself encountered the Protanians for the first time around the place where I believe you first met the Scourge."

"Pinrade," Curatio said, looking quite pale. "That was the name of the place."

"In my day it was Pinradeonage," Alaric said, "but yes ... I expect that was the place. Beyond it lay a few further villages, after which it became entirely too cold for a human to survive long, even in the summer. But a Scourge ..."

"They must have showed up after we left," Cyrus said. "Worked their way through the cold lands ... and ... fallen upon Arkaria ..." His voice sounded otherworldly, from some other plane of existence beyond this, it was so faded and hoarse. He looked to Shirri. "And they got ... all the lands? From the sea of Carmas to—"

"To the river Perda," Shirri said, surprisingly calm. Didn't she realize what this meant? How *they* had destroyed—

"They must have destroyed the bridges on the Perda," Curatio said.

"And Reikonos?" Vara asked. She, too, seemed paler, but composed. "How does it still stand?"

"The Lord Protector enlisted every man and able woman and child into service once the Scourge arrived and began to sweep across the lands like a blight," Shirri said, still looking at them all as though they were simpletons for not knowing this. "They began outside the main gate, anything that could be used as a shovel was to be used. And they dug a trench moat, spreading in either direction from that point, deep as a river, until finally they hit the ocean—"

"He had them build a moat," Cyrus said in quiet awe. "Around the entirety of the city. That must have taken ... astounding resources."

"Every person available," Shirri said with a shrug. Plainly this was just dead history to her. "Using discarded boards and old axes and their hands if they had nothing else. A trench in a ring around the city. They called it the Miracle of Reikonos." When everyone stared at her, she seemed to take it as a prompt to go on. "Because while every other city west of the Perda fell, Reikonos stood."

"But Saekaj Sovar—" Alaric said.

"Like I said, it's there. I guess they barricaded themselves in for a while, and somehow now they have a tower from which to launch airships." Shirri shrugged. "I don't know how that happened or how it works, but ... they have one. And it keeps out the Scourge, I guess."

"Brother ..." Alaric said, putting a hand on Cyrus's other left shoulder, while Vara had one on his right. "We all share blame for this."

"Indeed," Curatio said, voice scratchy and hollow. "We are all culpable in our own ways."

"Our actions are directly responsible for—" Cyrus cut short his thought. "It was bad enough when it was Luukessia, but now our ... our sins have come home to Arkaria and ..." His stomach tightened and for a moment he thought he might vomit.

"There is no act without some consequence," Alaric said. "Every move we make carries the seed of some further tree of action in the future. And when you deal with undertakings such as ours, to cleanse the land of gods, the consequences can be … unforeseeable."

"My failures," Cyrus said, "are innumerable, and the consequences so vast and blighted as to beggar belief."

"Yes," Vaste said, "they truly are. How did you get promoted to god again? Talk about failing your way to the top."

"These were not your actions alone," Alaric said.

"I struck at him, Alaric," Cyrus said. "I—"

"You did not strike at him at all, in fact," Alaric said.

"You shoved me out of the way and stood in my place to be struck down," Vara said calmly. "If anyone bears fault in this, it is Mortus for trying to murder me, not you for trying to sacrifice yourself in my stead."

"While I would blame myself for not shoving you out of the way first," Curatio said. "Or taking your place."

"And I bear the blame because I should have seen Mortus coming and hurried our evacuation," Alaric said. "Bellarum later admitted to manipulating him into leaving their meeting in his realm early, simply to spite us and drive him into our path. A bit more alacrity on our parts—or even perhaps a little more begging and humility on mine—and we might have walked free from that place."

"I, on the other hand, was a perfect saint," Vaste said, "at least, compared to all you blame-shifting fools who decided to war with a god. I came to the aid of my friends in their hour of need and helped strike down an evil son of a bitch who imprisoned countless souls after death to the point that once he shuffled into death they all came screaming in rage at anyone who moved." He examined his clawed fingernails. "Why, I'm a damned hero, helping to free Arkaria from the yolk of false gods who tried to grind the land under their boot for ten thousand years. Too bad no one remembers me that way."

"Vaste has a point," Alaric said.

"Damned right he does," Vaste said, then lowered his voice to whisper, "*Hero,*" while pointing at himself.

"If Mortus hadn't built his power on imprisoning the souls of the dead, none of this would have happened," Alaric said. "While we had our own role in his death, it was hardly for us to predict what would happen afterward."

Something about that sat badly with Cyrus, but when he saw Vara and Curatio nod, he decided not to argue—for now. "Perhaps," he allowed. "It just …" He closed his eyes, still stinging under the weight of emotion that welled up every time he thought of those grey-skinned, rotting things. "It's hard not to believe that we had a hand in making this mess."

"We did," Alaric said softly, "and we will do all we can to make right our mistakes—if indeed we made one. I cannot justify the consequences of what we have done ... but neither could I justify letting the land of Arkaria sit under the yolk of the gods. Bellarum moved us all into these positions and cared little for the consequences. Now he is gone, and the consequences are ours—and we shall deal with them. But first—" And he turned to Shirri. "There is a more immediate need for our help right now."

Shirri blinked a couple times. "Oh ... are you all done with your ... history lesson? Debate? I don't really know what you're doing here, honestly."

"We're girding ourselves for a tea party with your mother, obviously," Vaste said. "And if she's as cheerfully lovely as you, girding is going to be necessary."

Shirri blinked, taking a slight step backward. "I'm not—I mean, I'm ... nice."

"I'm sure you're a perfectly wonderful person under normal circumstances—" Alaric started.

"You're self-involved enough to make our living god over here look humble in contrast," Vaste said, pointing at Cyrus. "No mean feat, that."

Cyrus felt a low growl begin in the back of his throat. "Will you leave me out of your insults for once? Perhaps you're so flighty and empty of skull that the consequences of our actions past carry no weight, but I, for one—"

Vaste sighed loudly enough to interrupt Cyrus. "Oh, it's to be this way, is it? Fine. Fine. I believe there's a hero—and a villain—in all of us."

Silence fell at his words. The wind kicked up through the Reikonos streets just then, and they all stood there. "That's ... a lovely metaphor, Vaste," Curatio said. "Very insightful. We do, indeed, possess great capacity for wrong—and right—given the changing of circumstances—"

"Oh, no, I mean it quite literally," Vaste said, tongue playing over his teeth as he made a face that looked as though he was trying to get a taste out of his mouth with his tongue. "I just realized—Sanctuary made those bodies disappear from the alleyway? And some of our friends, of course, died in the defense against Bellarum—"

"Yes, some of us did," Vara said acidly. "Apparently so brutally that they were unable to be reconstituted."

"Right," Vaste said, "and then the corpses just vanish—poof. And a meal appears on our table." He arched his eyebrows. "Do you get what I'm saying here? I don't think those bodies in the alley just disappeared. I think Sanctuary takes them, turns them into a tasty beef rib through magical reconstitution—"

"Oh, for the sake of the gods—" Curatio said. "This? This is where your mind goes now?"

"I think they're in my teeth," Vaste said, tongue running over his front teeth. "Our own heroes and these villains, stuck there, in my teeth, possibly for all eternity, now that I live forever—"

"Sanctuary does not reconstitute the dead and feed them to us," Alaric said with great patience.

Vaste paused, tongue upon his front teeth. "It doesn't?"

"Hardly," Alaric said, then paused. "It's more probably the stone block that once made up the miles of our walls that you ate." And he smiled, beckoning Shirri to lead them on. She did so, and they began to move once more.

"I actually feel worse about eating old stone," Vaste said, "no matter how expertly it's prepared. Does Sanctuary not think me worthy of the good, villainous meat?"

Vara made a noise of impatience as she moved to follow Alaric and Shirri. "Count your blessings you're not eating human, as you were complaining of just a moment ago."

"It seems to have worked out fine for you," Vaste snipped back. "And it doesn't bother me—I subsisted on a diet of human meat as a child. It makes you stronger. Though it does taste a little gamey."

"Lovely," Cyrus said, the only one left behind as Curatio moved to follow the others.

"Oh, don't pretend you wouldn't have eaten troll if they'd put it in front of you as a child," Vaste said, still picking his teeth. "Still, reconstituted stone. That's worse than elf food, you know. Branches and leaves and such." He gave Cyrus a subtle glance. "Hardly fitting fare for a living god."

Cyrus let out a sigh and turned to follow the others. "Let it go, will you?"

"How can I?" Vaste asked, hurrying to follow him. "Look at you! They gave you everything! You ended up with everything. Statues. Your wife lives and breathes and—lustily does things to you that would make most of us blush—"

"You do seem a deeper shade of green."

"It's probably just nausea from hearing you two go at it," Vaste said. "But the point is, Cyrus—" And he sagged. "My life ended up counting for zero. I was an outcast and hated in Gren, I was always on the fringes in Sanctuary—"

"Dumbass, you were a member of the Council," Cyrus said. "In the thick of things."

"Because I knew you," Vaste said. "Reflected glory, that was all."

Cyrus let out his own hiss of impatience. "Well, you are walking in my shadow just now."

Vaste looked down. "Oh. In a literal sense, yes. How ironic." He stepped sideways and moved to walk next to Cyrus. "Do you not see how well things turned out for you in all this?"

"Most of my friends are dead," Cyrus said. "I was raised in a society that hated me, and when I found out my mother was actually alive, she was dead within a year." He turned his head to favor Vaste with a fiery look. "Now I find myself in a strange world where my actions in the past have led to the complete destruction of most of my homeland and the possible annihilation of several different races."

Vaste twitched slightly. "There are some among your people who'd consider that a good thing."

"I'm not one of them," Cyrus growled. "Do you really think— beyond the obvious things I'm grateful for, such as my life and that of my wife—that I am in any way 'living the dream' at this moment? Do I really have it so much better than you? In consequence and bounty, am I so much better off than you, Vaste?"

"You have Vara," Vaste said quietly. "Do you need anything else?"

His words pricked into Cyrus's skin and ran cool through his veins, soothing him as though a draught of some tonic. "Perhaps not," he said, glancing ahead and noticing Vara with an ear cocked in his direction, even dozens of paces ahead now. She wore the trace of smile. "But ... I do feel an enormous responsibility to correct these ... mistakes."

"Of course you do," Vaste said. "You wouldn't be Cyrus if you weren't burying your feelings of guilt over something you were only tangentially involved in while acting as a brave and sane person would." He paused for a thought. "Perhaps that's why they worship you. Sanity and bravery. Such a rare combination among your people. It should be celebrated whenever encountered. I'd argue they took it a bit far with the godhood—"

"Meanwhile, in Gren, they're still waiting for it to appear even once."

"Well, I did leave," Vaste said, "so it's not as though they really saw it, did they?" His voice grew muted, and Cyrus regretted even mentioning Gren. "What do you suppose happened to them? The Scourge?"

Cyrus shook his head, trying to be cautious in his reply. "The headwaters of the Perda are too deep for scourge to cross. I ... suppose I don't know. Perhaps your guess about the elves and their wroth is ... accurate."

"I heard that," Vara said. "Insult my people again by assuming our part in genocide and you will find yourself on the receiving end of elven wroth." The look in her eye was dangerous.

"I think she means it," Vaste said, and then he gave Cyrus a shove at the shoulder. "Go on. Make her mad."

"I'm a fool, but I'm not that much a fool," Cyrus said. "I don't know what happened to your people. But almost anything is possible, I suppose." He lowered his voice to a whisper. "Including elven wroth. They do get mad sometimes, you know."

"I know. I think I'm about to see it now," Vaste whispered loudly.

"Hmph," Vara said, turning away from them both and saying nothing more.

"Are you really so worried about counting for nothing?" Cyrus asked, after another minute or two of walking. The scenery around them was changing; the buildings were growing taller, the stone block giving way to reddish brick, so different from the white stone of the buildings of his day. "About your life mattering for naught? Because you did great things, Vaste. Aided us in—"

"Aided *you*," Vaste said. "I'm a mere second fiddle to a god. What does that make me? A lackey?" He made a rude noise. "I am clearly the brains if it's you and I on an adventure together. Remember the Temple of—"

"Yes. It would be hard to forget."

"I was plainly the brain in that scenario," Vaste said. "You were the brawn."

"Is that why I had to decapitate the troll bandits to claim our reward?"

"Absolutely. The brains do not need to sully their soft, beautiful hands with stinky troll blood."

"So you admit trolls stink?"

"*They* stunk! Do you know how long it had probably been since Byb Hirrin and his lot had bathed in anything other than swampwater? I mean, really. I, on the other hand, enjoy the Sanctuary showers very regularly—"

"You could stand to enjoy one right now ... lackey."

"Oh, that's cause for a dinging," Vaste said, and with speed garnered from the staff of Mortus, brought the tip of his weapon down on Cyrus's helm, causing it to ring and Cyrus's head to ache.

"Ow," Cyrus said, grabbing his helm. "That genuinely hurts now."

"Good," Vaste said. "Gone are the days when you could simply smart off to me and have no consequence thanks to your own blazing speed. This is my equalizer," he brandished Letum, "and remember well, Mr. Fancy God, that you while you may be the only one remembered, some of the rest of us ascended with you."

"Duly noted," Cyrus said, the resonant sound from his helmet finally dying down. "And ... I haven't forgotten you, Vaste."

"Of course you haven't," Vaste said, "I just rang your helmet like a little bell. Anytime you're in danger of forgetting me, I'll do it again, too."

"A potent reminder," Cyrus replied.

"Yes, it's like you in that regard," Vaste said. "Now ... do you have your mind upon the task at hand?"

Cyrus looked ahead, to where Shirri was leading the way with Alaric at her side, Curatio and Vara trailing them by a few paces. They were almost fifty paces ahead of Cyrus and Vaste now. "I do. As much as I can, anyhow. I suppose we should catch up."

Vaste shrugged. "They're not going anywhere fast. Perhaps we should let Alaric do what he does best." He gestured with the tip of his staff. "You know, with our skeptical new recruit up there."

Cyrus frowned. "Her? You think he's trying to ... recruit her? To what?"

Vaste wore the hint of a smile. "To what Alaric always recruits people to." A little trace of regret twisted his lips, exposing fangs. "To join us and become part of a happy band of people striving to help others."

14.

Shirri

She traced her path along the street in silence, the armored man with eyepatch and the greying beard walking alongside her. Shirri kept one eye on the street ahead, and one on the man at her side, and wondered which she needed to watch more sharply for danger.

"I won't strike you down, if that's what you're wondering," the man named Alaric said. He sounded amused—at her expense, no doubt.

Shirri reddened and turned away from him. "I wish I knew that was a certainty."

"If I meant to strike you down, would it not have been more effective to simply let those enemies of yours do it in that alleyway earlier?" Alaric asked calmly.

"There are powerful reasons for them not to," Shirri said, looking away and into the basement window of an apartment unintentionally. A child no older than six was sitting in it, looking up at her. He tossed a casual wave at her, and she waved back without thinking about it. "They want me alive...for..." She looked at him, a little hesitantly, "...reasons."

"Your secrets do not concern me," Alaric assured her. "Keep them, if they make you feel safer."

Shirri shivered. "Nothing makes me feel safe anymore." She stared into the distance, where the sun was casting its rays from below the horizon, lighting the eastern sky. "Probably because there is nowhere safe for me any longer."

"Your world does seem to be constricting around you," Alaric said with a light nod. "I won't pry into your secrets, but … I admit curiosity to what has compelled this group to pursue you as they have."

"They just destroy people," Shirri said, and she could tell by the flicker of a smile from him that she'd said it too quickly. "It's what they do." At least that wasn't false.

"Some make that their purpose in life," Alaric said after a brief pause. "And from what I have seen of this ... 'Machine' ... and the people in their employ, I do not have a hard time imagining that is true. But there is always another side to a coin, and here I wonder at their motives—pure venality? Greed? Simple lust for power? Or is there something more, beneath the surface of this organization?"

"There's less to them than meets the eye, if anything," Shirri said, drawing her cloak around her. It wasn't cold, but she still felt a chill, thinking about the trouble she was in, of her mother being taken. No good was coming, not now. Not from any of this. Certainly not from these ... *strangers* was the most charitable word she could summon up to describe them—whom she'd turned to for help. "They care about maintaining their power, their dominance here. Nothing else. And they will employ anyone who can aid them in that. Corrupt or decent. Whatever gets them closer to their goal."

"Interesting," Alaric said, seeming to ponder that. "Then this world is not so different from the one I left."

"Yes," Shirri's voice was dry, "it's almost as though you woke up this morning and it's exactly the same as the one you're from."

Alaric smiled once more. "You don't believe that we are who we say we are."

"I don't even know who you are," Shirri said, shaking her head. "Or the elf with the platinum hair. Or the ..." She looked back at the green one, so tall and unbelievably large. "... Whatever he is. A 'droll,' did you call him?"

"'Troll,'" Alaric said with a smile. "Though droll does perhaps fit him better."

"You're just strange travelers to me," Shirri said, shrugging. "Maybe you got off an airship from Firoba yesterday or the day before, given how strangely you talk. Maybe you're circus performers from another land, dressing two of your own up in the garb of our ... legends." And here she looked back at the blond-haired elf, and, further back, the man in the black armor. "I don't know what your game is, and so long as the punch line's not at my expense, I suppose I don't care."

"It must be difficult to go through life so isolated as to not care about those around you," Alaric said. "To intentionally blind yourself to misery so long as it falls on others and not yourself."

"It's Reikonos," Shirri said with a condescending smile. "No one cares about anyone else here. No one worries about their neighbor or—whatever it was like in the days of Cyrus Davidon, or the days after that, or even the more recent days, like my mother talks about. This city has changed. Wolves are at the door, hiding themselves like sheep. That'd be the Machine. You let them in, you think they're just some poor, suffering person with their head down in need, like you? Then you find out they're not." She cocked her head at him. "You know why they call it 'the Machine'? Because it's made of interchangeable pieces, just like they make in the factories. Pull a few out, they'll replace them with others. The Machine keeps running, always moving toward what it wants and never breaking down."

"Fascinating," Alaric said, almost a whisper. "They sound truly lost."

Shirri let out a mirthless chuckle. "*That's* what you think of when I describe to you a cartel bent on making misery into profit?" She raised her eyebrows in amusement. "You are truly naïve for someone so old."

His eyes twinkled. "You have no idea."

"I don't have a care, either," she said. "If you can help me, I suppose I'll be grateful. Maybe take my mother and the little money I have, and try to get passage to Emerald Fields or Termina or even Binngart, across the sea in Firoba. That'd be safest." She stared straight ahead once more, her footsteps carrying her in even paces toward her destination, a little lance of fear spiking along her back. "You should get out of here before things get any worse. Better to get away from the Machine than shelter in ... whatever your home is, here."

"I doubt that very much," Alaric said, "but if it is your choice, I will respect it, as I respect your desire to keep your secrets. I hope, before we part ways, that you will see that there is hope yet in this place."

"There's not," Shirri said.

"Then why are you walking with us?" Alaric asked, that small smile now seeming insufferable to Shirri. "Why have you not started your flight to this Firoba already?"

Shirri started to lie but something stopped her. "Because I can't just leave her behind."

"Then you hope for a resolution that sees your mother returned to you," Alaric said.

Shirri bowed her head. "Like a fool ... I suppose I do." Her smile was bitter. "Now who among us is naïve? Trusting in a Cyrus Davidon impersonator and his team of thespians." She stopped and raised her hand to point at a building across the street and down a block. It was a multi-story apartment building of red stone, with glass display windows and a storefront on the first floor. "They're in there. Or at least it's their nearest post."

The blond-haired elven woman caught up, eyes anchored upon the building. "A candle shop?"

"They use it as a front," Shirri said. "Candleworks in this city are wholly owned by them. They've run every other maker out."

"That's quite indecent," Vara said.

Shirri wanted to laugh. "It is what they do."

"This it?" the one dressed as Cyrus Davidon asked, reaching them at last with the green one at his side.

"Indeed, so she says," Alaric said. "Two men stand out front. Sentries?"

"Poor ones, if so," the platinum-haired one said. Curatio, was it? "Their eyes are on each other, not the street."

"What do they have to fear?" Shirri asked. "The city is theirs."

"Me," the black-armored one said, his voice a husky, determined growl. She looked at him in mild alarm; it was a threatening noise that he made, but his attention was entirely on the Machine's storefront. He started toward them, crossing the street, on a direct line for the two out front. "They will fear me."

"Well, he hasn't lost that finely-tuned sense of the dramatic in the last thousand years." Vaste sighed and then hurried off after him. "Wait for me! If you're going to crack skulls, I want a piece of them."

"You just ate," the blond haired elf said. Shirri could not think of her as ... well, as Vara. She didn't fit the image Shirri had ever had of the Shelas'akur and wife of ... him.

"I'm not going to eat *them*," Vaste said, shooting her a look of mild reproach as she stepped off the curb to follow him and her ... husband. "Besides, anyone who gets assigned guard duty on a sidewalk outside a store in the early morning is bound to be empty of head."

"Shall we?" Curatio asked, stepping up next to Alaric. "I don't wish to leave our friends to this destruction on their own. They might get up to no good."

"Indeed," Alaric said with that maddening smile, "and I'm sure your unquenchable desire to inflict unholy elven wroth upon humans has little to do with your calculus in this."

"I got over that long ago," Curatio said, smiling back, "when I finally met a human whose head was so thick that my efforts to bash his skull in came to naught."

Alaric drew his sword, and Shirri almost gasped. The faux Cyrus ... he was so ... bizarre a spectacle. But this man ... this Alaric ...

There was something about him …

"Wait here," Alaric said, smiling with encouragement. "We shall be back shortly."

"I doubt it," Shirri said as the two of them hurried off across the street. The Cyrus impersonator was already almost to the watchmen, who were regarding the approach of a black-armored figure with some discomfort even before he shed his cloak and entered a full charge, no weapon drawn. "But I'll be waiting … at least until I see you get slaughtered," she said, considerably lower, stepping back into the shadows of a nearby alley to see what happened next.

15.

Cyrus

The first of the watchmen on the sidewalk flew through the window, no need for Praelior. The shattering of the glass resonated richly through the canyons of the street, and the scream of the second watchman as Cyrus lifted him over his head and threw him through the next window provided a similar satisfaction, the urge to destroy anything and everything he encountered something of a throwback to times when Cyrus could recall venting his righteous rage upon the unrighteous.

"Feels like Enterra all over again," Vaste said as Cyrus leapt in the front window, drawing his sword as he did so. "Except above ground … in the Reikonos of the future … with taller opponents … no Emperor or Empress … and there's only five of us. Exactly like Enterra, except for that."

"Yes, it's stunningly similar," Vara said, leaping next through the shattered window into the darkened shop, Ferocis in hand. Display hutches with glass tops ringed the storefront. A thump in a back hallway resulted, a moment later, in five toughs in ragged black coats pouring out of a back counter and leaping out at them—

"Trouble, as always, arrives right on time," Vaste said from somewhere behind them as Cyrus leapt into the fray, Vara at his side.

Praelior moved with swiftness, taking hands, taking arms, taking lives. Blood flew freely, as did limbs and screams. The work of a skilled swordsman was hardly called for here, in a place where his foes drew daggers and dirks rather than blades that would give them any sort of reach. His greatest challenge was keeping from striking Vara's armor when he threw an overly enthusiastic stroke.

"Now it's a butcher shop," Vaste said, once they were done. He sounded mildly disappointed, having been boxed out from attacking them himself, Vara and Cyrus standing between him and the fight. "Though usually they keep the slaughter in the back."

"Come with me, fool," Vara said, dragging the troll by his black robes toward the door through which the toughs had appeared. "You go upstairs?" she asked Cyrus.

He let his gaze sweep the room; there was indeed a staircase just inside the entry door, no partition to separate it from the storefront. "I can do that," he said, storming toward it.

Cyrus swept up the stairs and found a series of open doors leading off a hallway. He stopped here, noticing another staircase just down the hall, winding its way up to the third floor. He moved toward the nearest door, which was partially open, and elbowed it wider as he stepped inside. A man was caught, frozen, sitting at a table, a plate of chicken bones in front of him.

When he saw Cyrus he shoved back from the table, rising as he drew a pistol from his belt. Cyrus drew his own in reply, and thumbed the hammer back, raising it to aim before the man got his partway up. Pulling the trigger, the hammer of Cyrus's pistol fell, and a soft click sounded.

The man completed his aim, pointing the long tube end right at Cyrus's face. He came around the table wearing a smirk, but kept his distance to at least ten feet or so, out of sword's reach. "Misload it?" the man asked, seemingly amused by Cyrus's misfortune.

"I don't know," Cyrus said, shaking it slightly. "I poured in the powder first, then put in that little bit of parchment—"

"Wadding," the man corrected, voice dripping with amusement.

"—then the metal ball—"

"Bullet," he said.

"Right, that," Cyrus said, looking at the pistol. He thumbed the hammer back once more. "But ..." He shrugged.

"Well, you know," the man said, adopting the air of a conciliatory teacher who'd taken a particularly dull-witted pupil under his wing, "sometimes they just fail." He motioned at his own belt, where two more pistols hung. "Smart to carry a spare or two, in case."

Cyrus looked at his own, examining it, but keeping it pointed in the man's direction. "How do they fail?"

"You must be quite the fool to use a weapon you don't know anything about," the man said, still smirking. "Perhaps you should have stuck to that meat cleaver in your other hand." He laughed, scoffing. "But all right, since it'll do you no good, you—you have quite the inadequate impersonation going on there, friend. Cyrus

Davidon? Pff, as though that's not been done over and over. Sometimes, when the hammer falls, it fails to produce the spark necessary to ignite the powder." His grin grew wider. "No spark, the powder doesn't blow, the bullet doesn't get propelled out of the barrel, and because of that, you die. Basic knowledge." He raised his weapon high and his arm grew tense. "All for want of a little fire."

Cyrus stared at the back of the pistol, where the hammer landed. Now that it was thumbed up again, he could see a tiny, pin-sized hole, and ran his index finger over it. "So ... I just need a little fire ... here?"

"A little late for that now," the man said, "but y—"

Cyrus's pistol rang out, and the man staggered, an angry red hole having appeared in the center of his forehead. A drizzle of blood ran down the side of his face. His mouth moved as if to speak, but no words came out.

"A little fire, I can still do," Cyrus said, taking a couple steps forward and gently wrenching the pistol from the dying man's grasp. He keeled over, and Cyrus bent, unbuckling his belt. "Good advice about carrying extras, though. I think I shall take it." And he buckled the man's belt above his own, adjusting it so that the pistols rode at the small of his back, at his front, and on the hip beside his own holster. "Might need some adjustment later, but ... many thanks." He looked at the man, who was now twitching in death. "A little late for you, though, I suppose."

"Are you now so used to conversing with us folks deemed long dead," Curatio said, entering the room behind him, "that you feel the need to talk with those who truly are?"

"Just offering thanks where thanks are due," Cyrus said, turning to look at the healer, whose mace dripped with red. Cyrus ran a hand over his purloined belt and new pistols. "How do I look?"

"A question best asked of your wife," Curatio said, "but for my part, I would say, 'Garish.'"

"You wear white robes everywhere, what the hell do you know about what's fashionable?" Cyrus asked, brushing past him as Alaric emerged from a room at the end of the hall, his own weapon now covered in red. "What do you think, Alaric?" he asked, gesturing to the belt.

"It doesn't go particularly well with your boots," Alaric said after but a glance, immediately sprinting up the stairs to the next floor. "Or your honor!" he called back.

"He's on that honor thing again," Cyrus said.

"Yes," Curatio said dryly, following behind him, "it's almost as though he lives for it."

Cyrus hurried up the stairs to find the Ghost clashing with a young man with a dagger. "Put it down!" Alaric said in his harshest voice. The youth, quaking, slashed at him.

The blade passed ineffectually through Alaric's torso as he turned to mist, and the youth's jaw dropped further. The boy looked at the weapon in his hand, then back up at Alaric.

"Put it down, leave this place, and never take up arms as part of this Machine again," Alaric said, putting his sword, Aterum, to the youth's neck.

"Okay," the young man said, letting the dagger clatter to the wood floor with a heavy rattle. "I just ... needed the money."

"Find an honest trade instead," Alaric said.

"But not candlemaking," Cyrus said, brushing past them, "as apparently you'd end up working for the same people.".

"Where is the woman?" Alaric asked, keeping his weapon at the boy's throat as Cyrus checked the rooms off the hallways behind him.

"What ... woman?" the youth asked. Cyrus cast a look back and saw the boy's hands shaking in the air.

"The Machine took a woman," Alaric said. "Where is she?"

The boy was trembling from head to foot now. "You're ... going to have be more specific. They take a lot of women. From all sorts of places."

Alaric's face tightened, and he raised his hand so the blade was more cleanly positioned. Cyrus paused to watch, keeping one eye on the stairs up, presuming more enemies awaited up there, and the other on Alaric's interrogation.

"I—I—when was she taken?" the boy asked, dissolving into stuttering wildly.

"This very night," Alaric said.

"None of our guys went out last night," the boy said. "Could it have been, uhm ... the coal yards guys? Over on Market Street?"

Alaric surveyed him with that lone eye, his anger like a blinding flash to Cyrus, who almost wanted to look away from the seething wrath, even though it was not directed it him. Like the sun, though, it made him uncomfortable to stare at it. "Do you have prisoners here?"

"Uhh ... next floor up ... second door," he said, still shaking.

Alaric looked to Cyrus.

"On it," Cyrus said and sprinted up the steps.

Coming out the top of the stairs, Cyrus found a veritable gauntlet of trouble waiting for him. He looked back as he emerged, the hallway running parallel to the stairs filled with five thugs wielding pistols.

Grimacing, he dipped his head, pointing the top of his helm toward them, so as to expose his neck as little as possible, and poured on Praelior's speed—

They began firing before he'd even fully emerged. The spang of the metal bullets rattled against his armor with each impact, thunder echoing in the hall.

Cyrus crested the stairs and drew his own pistol, aiming at the foe farthest from him, a man who wore brightly colored clothing beneath his black leather coat. Red shirt, green sash around his waist, and his pants were a wild shade of purple. "You offend mine eyes," Cyrus pronounced, and fired, making the man's shirt even redder.

He dropped the pistol and drew another, taking aim at the next farthest fellow, this one in ragged clothing. With the speed of Praelior at his fingertips, it was no difficult feat to aim carefully, down the carved notches at the end of the barrel, and then send a bullet right into that fool's face.

Now he was upon the nearest of them, the man still holding his pistol, his stunned jaw dropped almost to his ankles. Cyrus cleaved his head from his body with a quick swipe, then shoved the still moving carcass aside and plunged into the next, and the next. When he was done, his five foes were dead, not one of them with a chance to reload their weapon.

Putting the blade of Praelior under his arm but careful to let his hand rest upon the pommel, he paused and retrieved his two dropped pistols, then reloaded them, the whole process taking less than thirty seconds with Praelior's aid and careful movements. The weapons securely replaced upon his belt, Cyrus took up Praelior in hand once more, and now had godly strength, speed and dexterity—plus he had four pistols at his easy disposal.

"I could have killed you eight times while you fidgeted with those damned things." Alaric's voice almost causing Cyrus to jump in surprise. He hadn't even heard the Ghost approach.

"Admittedly, it's no force blast spell," Cyrus said as Alaric surged past him, kicking open all the doors all on the floor except the second, "but it seems useful to have a means of answering a ranged attack."

"They are weapons without honor," Alaric said, sweeping his gaze around the last of the rooms he'd opened. Cyrus peered past him; it was sleeping quarters, just as the other three had been. Badly tended, with unmade bedrolls that looked like they'd been unmade forever.

"Yes, because plunging metal into your foes is dishonorable," Cyrus said with irony of his own. "Why, no one should die that way.

Speaking of—what happened to the boy dunder downstairs?"

"He lives to see the error of his ways," Alaric said, situating himself in front of the last door. "Perhaps a chance at redemption will allow him to find the courage to change."

"Or he could just warn his comrades at the coal yard that we're coming, guaranteeing we'll run into a lot of those bullets you find so dishonorable," Cyrus said.

"Then they will reveal themselves for who they are, and we will kill them nonetheless," Alaric said.

"Easy for you to say when you haven't been shot by one of them yet," Cyrus said. "I assure you, they are not gentle in their arrival, and unguarded flesh will be torn asunder as easily as if a dagger were to pierce it."

"Then it is fortunate that we are guarded," Alaric said, and smashed the last door with a heavy kick, ripping it from its hinges. He was through it less than a second later, rushing into the room with sword at ready.

"But not everyone is," Cyrus said, following after him, already sober to the spectacle within.

There were six women in the room, all huddled as far from the door as possible. There were no windows, no light, and the women were filthy, the smell of an overripe chamberpot causing Cyrus to draw a quick breath and hold it before he proceeded deeper inside.

Alaric whispered something, and a faint glow appeared at his fingertips. Nessalima's Light, Cyrus realized—though sadly muted. It was barely more than a candle's worth of illumination.

"It is all right," Alaric said. "We are here to save you. You will be free to go."

The women huddled, shrinking from him as Alaric took a step forward. Cyrus followed a step behind. "I don't think they're quite hearing you, Alaric—"

"It's him," one of them whispered, and the muffled moans of fear stopped instantly.

"It's who—oh," Cyrus said.

"My lord," one of the women said, scurrying forward, dragging her ragged clothes behind her and throwing herself on Cyrus's leg. It took all he had not to recoil, not just from her utterly filthy appearance, but from the idea that a strange woman would anchor to his leg like a child. "Is it you, my lord? We have prayed for you, for your deliverance from this evil—"

"It would appear we've found some of your worshippers," Alaric said. If he had any feelings on the subject other than amusement,

Cyrus could not detect them in his tone.

The other women came at him then, flinging themselves upon him, grabbing at his armor and clinging, crying, begging for salvation. "Ahh ... yes ..." Cyrus said, "I am here to save you."

"What is all this?" Vara's voice came from somewhere out in the hall, and she appeared a moment later, greeted with the spectacle of her husband being clutched around the legs and waist by six strange, extremely dirty women.

"It's a rescue," Cyrus said, trying to hold back the sense of rising claustrophobia that came from being stuck in a dark, confined room with people clutching at him.

"You're doing it wrong," Vara said. "You're supposed to get them out, you know. Not just stand around with them grabbing you."

"Just be glad I don't wear Terian's old armor or they would have impaled themselves trying to thank me or greet me or—whatever," Cyrus said.

"Worship you," Alaric said. Now there was amusement.

"Come along," Cyrus said, trying to gather them all up. "It's time to get out of here, ladies." And he began to usher them toward the door, and then the stairs. They were crying, gratitude rushing out in tears, confessions of some sort, blubbered and almost incoherent, and all of them seemed to be talking to him at once. "Yes," he said, trying to manage that panic he felt within at all these people vying for his attention, gripping at his arms and his legs and his entire self, "I know, it must have been terrible, but you're all safe now. I'll see to it."

"Listen to your god," Vaste said from the landing below as Cyrus limped his way down, half-carrying at least three of them and trying to keep one of them from inadvertently impaling herself on Praelior in her desperate enthusiasm to be near to him. "For truly he has come to lead you from out of the darkness and into the light."

One of the women let out a shriek at the sight of Vaste, and two others screamed immediately after her. "Thank you for that, you ass," Cyrus said, cringing at the sound as he escorted the women—some now actively fighting him to keep away from the troll—past Vaste. "This is why you're forgotten, in case you wondered. Because you don't make anyone's life easier."

"Seems a fair trade," Vaste said with a shrug, going on past him and up the stairs. "I get to enjoy my life while making you miserable, and you get to be worshipped in your afterlife."

"I'm not dead yet!" Cyrus called after him, struggling to get the women downstairs.

"Give it time," Vaste called after him. "Another day or two of being worshipped like this and you'll be begging for death."

Cyrus did not argue with him, as he was still trying to fight to get one of the women, screaming now, in notes of wild hysteria, carefully gathered back to him to get her out of this miserable place. In any event, part of him wondered if the troll might be right.

16.

Shirri

Shirri had been watching the street for some time, a small crowd gathering in front of the shattered store windows, peering in, unable or unwilling to step inside for a closer look or to aid the wounded guardsmen—or whoever else was inside. She'd heard screaming from within, sounds resonating out from the shop shortly after her bizarre companions had entered, and ... well, she hadn't much cared to look closer after that. Someone was injured, perhaps dead—Shirri had seen quite enough of that for today—for an entire lifetime, really—and it was scarcely daybreak.

"What do you suppose is happening?" a man in finery asked, his black coat possessed of tails that reached almost to his knees.

"I hear screaming and shouting," a woman in a very tight corset with a massive hoop skirt answered, unable to keep the delight from her voice. Shirri was wandering closer, possessed of perhaps a little curiosity, and confident that as the crowd kept gathering, she could shelter herself within it. "This is the most exciting thing that's happened on this block since the last riot!"

Shirri had crossed the street and was only fifty or so feet from the building now. There were probably twenty or even thirty people gathered out front now, shoving a little, the back ranks pushing the front into the building so that someone could report back on what was happening, the front ranks shoving back, unwilling to get too close. Back and forth, the crowd surged, and Shirri kept well clear of it.

A hubbub came from within the building now, a hue and cry above that of the assembling crowd, and Shirri stopped where she stood as the front ranks shoved the back ones into the street, pushing to remove themselves clear of the door as something emerged—

It was the Cyrus Davidon impersonator, some six dirty, wretched women clinging to him and sobbing and crying and screaming to the heavens—or to him, possibly—as he dragged them out, a determined scowl on his broad, handsome face. Shirri had long imagined him— the real him, not this imposter—though she did not perhaps assign quite as much mythological importance to him as most in the city. When she pictured him, she pictured someone more … august, perhaps. More serious. Less … flippant than this imposter.

Oh, certainly, this fellow was muscled. And tall. And wore the armor well. And was handsome, in his way, which was not as ruggedly and obviously handsome as she might have imagined. There was a stunning clarity to the sort of handsome she had envisaged for Cyrus Davidon, and this man lacked that. He was a more subtle kind of handsome, the sort you had to stare at for a while to appreciate. It did not blind in a blast of summer lightning, but perhaps crept up on you and made you think, "Yes, I suppose he is not terrible to look at …"

Not what she'd imagined at all. Which was why, among many other reasons, she was sure that he was not, in fact, Cyrus Davidon.

"Come on, then, ladies," the Cyrus Davidon impersonator said, dragging himself clear of the front door with his train of women attached all about his person. Three had him by the legs, two clung to his waist and another seem to be climbing his shoulders as though trying to ride him like some sort of upright horse. Even with the woman's arm locked around his forehead, Shirri could see the scowl of impatience and displeasure at being so thoroughly manhandled— or perhaps womanhandled, in this case. "Off you go." And he began to shuck them loose, taking care that no injury came to them. "Go back to your homes, your families—wherever." And he lifted the highest off his shoulders and set her, squirming, upon the cobbled sidewalk.

"I have nowhere to go, my lord! Protect me!" she screamed and hurled herself back at him, wrapping her arms around his neck as he tried to pry loose another. This set loose another round of wretched wailing and clinging as the women tried even harder to hold onto him.

"You, there!" the Cyrus impersonator shouted, voice like a bolt out of the sky, aimed at the man with the long tailcoat. "Help this woman." And he pulled loose one of the ones at his leg and bodily moved her toward the fellow, who took hold of her arm in surprise.

"Help her … what?" he asked, seemingly stunned. He was blinking furiously, but he maintained his hold on the wailing woman as she fell to her knees trying to get back to the Cyrus impersonator.

"Help her find a place to stay that's safe," Cyrus said, pulling loose another from his waist and shoving her toward the stunned woman in the hoop skirt. "And you, too. See that this one is well cared for."

"I—what?" the woman in the hoop skirt asked as the woman clung to her, fighting for only a second to get back to the Cyrus impersonator before burying her head in the hoop skirt.

"All of you," the Cyrus impersonator said, "I charge you to help these women." And he handed off another to a stunned looking factory worker covered in soot who seemed utterly surprised at having a ragged female prisoner pushed at him by a tall man in black armor that was dressed like ... well, *Him*.

Peeling off the last few, the Cyrus impersonator relieved himself of his captive worshippers and pushed them off on waiting members of the crowd who simply stared at him.

"Are you ... really him?" asked a teenage girl, stepping out of the stunned crowd.

The Cyrus impersonator paused, and Shirri could see him in profile. The breezy attitude he'd displayed before the battle in the alley was gone. His face was like a thunderhead, and she did not dare get closer, watching as he simmered for a moment, then spun on them.

"*I am Cyrus Davidon!*" he boomed over the street. People who'd been watching the spectacle from nearby took a step back, a block away they stopped in their tracks. Glancing down the street, she could see that even three blocks away some had paused to look around, such was the volume and fervency of this tall pillar in armor. "This," and he threw up his thumb at the building behind him, "has been a place of great evil. The Machine, as you call it, takes from people, it takes people, and it chews them up, grinds out everything good, and all in the name of its own power."

This caused a furious blinking in the crowd, mouths to fall open. "My ... my lord ...?" the man in the long coattails asked, half bent into a bow already. "What would you have us do?"

"Let the word ring forth from here," the Cyrus impersonator called—very theatrically, Shirri thought, lending credence to her idea that he was some sort of actor, "that I have returned, and that I am at war with the Machine and anyone who stands with them. If you wish to die, get between me and them. If you wish to live ... help me, or help those caught in this Machine's terrible grasp."

And with that, he was apparently done and disappeared back inside. Shirri took the opportunity to sidle a little closer to the edge of the crowd, to listen to the reaction that followed.

"I ... I think that was actually him," the man in coattails said, jaw moving up and down slowly even after he'd finished speaking. "He spoke to me. To me!"

"He was so tall," the woman in the hoop skirt said. "Did you see? It was just as I always heard. Taller than any man I've ever seen."

"He spoke with such fire," said another, a woman dressed in the simple garments of a textile mill worker. She ran her hands down her heavy sleeves. "I could feel the chills run through me at the sound of his voice." She shivered. "It was so ... resonant."

"He's back!" the man in the coattails said again, still holding to the woman the Davidon impersonator had thrown at him. He looked at her now, blinking, as though realizing he'd been given a task. "I—I will see that you are taken great care of, my lady. The best, only, for you."

She did not hear him, unfortunately, for she was still wailing with hysteria and now burst into sobs on the coattailed man shoulder. He patted her back gingerly.

Shirri, for her part, was left staring as the others entered a sort of conversational circle that reinforced what they'd seen. She thought about stepping in, about being the breath of reason, of criticism, but ...

"It was him," one woman said, one of the captives, wailing with ... joy? "It was truly him ... he saved us! *He saved us!*" And her cries might have reached the heavens, they were so full of elation.

Whatever words of protest she might have offered faded, melted in Shirri's mouth before they could be born from her lips. And instead she listened with a hard, coarsened heart, as the others sang the praises of a man she knew couldn't be anything but a fake.

17.

Vaste

"I think I hear a Cyrus Davidon speech," Vaste said, the staircase moaning beneath his weight as he ascended. He'd gone up so many flights already, and yet this climb seemed interminable, like rising to the top of the tower in Sanctuary of old. At least that was over with. The new Sanctuary had much less climbing, and Vaste was all the happier for it. Provided Cyrus and Vara could learn to shut their damned door.

Vara had paused on the stairwell, just a little ahead of him, her head cocked to one side, listening. "Indeed."

Vaste watched her as she resumed her upward climb. "Well?"

That prompted a puckering in the lines of her forehead. "Well what?"

"How is it?" Vaste asked. "The speech. You know, graded for its excellence."

She shrugged lightly as she came around the bannister and into the short hallway at the top of the stairs. Here there was no upper staircase, but instead a ladder that led to a trapdoor. The roof, Vaste suspected. "It's not bad," Vara conceded, pausing as she looked at the doors around them. Two were open, two were not. "I give it a three out of five, perhaps. He's done better."

"You took all the fire out of him earlier," Vaste said, catching a glimpse of Curatio moving around, a flash of white robes in one of the doorways.

"Fire is not the problem with this one," Vara said, thinking it over. "He's plenty angry. It's his audience. He does better with fighters, and he's talking to civilians, and worshippers, no less. They're positively agape, and he doesn't know how to handle that."

"Yes, he's always done much better with people who hate him," Vaste agreed. "I think he's overly attached to putting a sword through people, but that's less my problem than yours."

"It saddens me that I've reached the point with you that I don't know whether you're making a lascivious comment or not," Vara said, peering in at Curatio and then stepping forward to join him.

"Oh, that wasn't lascivious at all," Vaste said. "Lascivious would be—"

"I think I've had quite enough of this for one day," Alaric said as Vara and Vaste entered the room where he'd spied Curatio. The Ghost was standing before a table, back to them but looking over his shoulder. "Between our newlyweds' refusal to shut a door and your constant banter, I wouldn't mind letting this rest, at least a little while, as we focus upon other matters."

"Well, I'm not done, so—*holy Cyrus Davidon!*" Vaste said, suddenly seeing what waited on the table in front of Alaric.

There was gold, although not an immense quantity. But what the scene lacked in gold pieces, it made up for in jewelry and strange stacks of paper all placed throughout the table. Things were piled on every surface in the room, art and other items that Vaste knew instinctively were the ill-gotten gains of the rabble that ran this place.

"Finally we have your mind on something besides the gutter," Curatio said with a smile.

"My mind can operate on multiple levels at the same time," Vaste said. "The gutter is merely the beginning for me. The real challenge is that it's not as though my audience is going to realize that I can thread my lowbrow humor in with the works of great elven philosophers, so I'm always dragged down to the lowest common denominator. I—oh, who am I kidding? Elven philosophers are boring and self-important."

"Whereas you are merely self-important," Vara retorted, "which is why you're taking it so hard that your good friend has been elevated to godhood while you remain an unknown artist of the smutty joke format."

"Your words sting me," Vaste said, frowning. "But I take solace in knowing that your blade does not."

"For now," she said, lifting one of the stacks of paper that sat on the table, bound together. It was no more than a few inches long, and a couple wide. She pulled one free. "These look … strangely familiar, though I know I have not seen one like this before." She held it up, and upon it was the same face that Vaste had seen on the statue next to Cyrus's.

"That's the Lord Protector of Reikonos," Vaste said, taking it from her hand and looking at it. "Lots of watermarking and funny writing on this." He flipped it over to find a stamped picture of the Citadel upon the back. "What the hell is this?"

"It looks a lot like those notes of currency that one of my bankers in Termina used to try and foist off on me," Cyrus said, entering the room, his brow down in a scowl that only lightened minutely when he saw Vara. It was a subtle thing, probably one the warrior didn't even realize happened, Vaste observed. At one point it had made him coo with amusement to see the fiercest warrior in all the land go all smitten and doe-eyed—or as close as he got—over the fiercest paladin in the history of all history ...

But now it just left him cold, and he turned away.

"I thought it was something of a joke, the idea of paper money replacing real gold you could hold in your hand," Cyrus said, taking up the paper from Vaste. Vaste gave him an annoyed look; it had been snatched so quickly, and without so much as a by-your-leave before he took it. "I never figured it would catch on, but judging by this place ..." The warrior tossed down the paper, not even bothering to hand it back to Vaste. How rude. And typical.

"It would appear it was an idea ahead of its time," Alaric said, also frowning. "But there is still gold."

"Indeed," Curatio said. "Nothing could ever replace the feeling of a solid coinpurse clanking against your side as you walk."

"Clanking against what on you, exactly?" Vaste asked with a frown of his own. "You're a healer, you don't wear armor."

Curatio lifted his robes to reveal a fine layer of mail at his ankles. "Now that it's no longer heresy ... you really should get some of your own. And perhaps a nice mace, too."

"I have a staff that splits open heads faster than Cyrus can devour a beef cutlet," Vaste said. "Keep your damned mace."

"I assure you, if I had no regard for table manners, I could eat beef faster," Cyrus said.

"Darling, you already have little regard for table manners," Vara said, sotto voce.

"Yes, but I said 'no regard,'" Cyrus said. "It's a fine distinction, but—"

"Shirri's mother is not here," Alaric said, head bowed as he stared at the purloined goods around the room and the pile of monies upon the table before him.

"No," Vara said. "We have checked every room and the basement. This house is one half barracks for these thugs, and one half prison house for … whomever this Machine desires. But her mother is not among the captives, unless she was hiding among the dirty women flinging themselves upon Cyrus."

"A common occurrence through the years, as I recall," Vaste said, drawing an ireful look from Alaric. "What? I make no promises; if a choice witticism passes that involves vulgarity, you cannot expect me to pass on it as though it were a salad."

"Especially when it rings so heartily true," Vara said, drawing a wounded look from Cyrus. "Sorry," she whispered to him, "but it really was simply too good to pass up."

"All this silliness aside, we are no closer to our goal than when we arrived at this place," Alaric said. "Many lie dead in these halls, but we have come no closer to—"

"That youth that you tried to set on the right path," Cyrus said, clearing his throat. "He suggested something about a coal yard on Market Street being the next nearest or most logical place to keep a kidnapping victim?"

Alaric paused, pensive. "Yes, you are right. A thin thread, but a thread nonetheless. I suppose we must move onward."

"If I may," Vara said, holding position as the others started to move. "Before we leave, I suggest two courses of action."

"And they are?" Alaric asked, with a stiffness of his own. It was plain to Vaste that something was brewing beneath the surface of the Ghost's mind.

"First, we throw all this out the window to the crowd below," Vara said, nodding at the nearby windows. "Enrich them at cost to this Machine."

"An excellent suggestion," Curatio said, "and one that will surely please Cyrus's assembled legion of worshippers below." The warrior let his eyes roll irritably at the healer's comment, but did not reply.

"And second, we set fire to this building and let it burn," Vara said, almost standing at attention.

That drew a moment of silence. "Yay," Vaste said, "we're going to set fire to this tinderbox of a city. I am highly in favor of this plan, because anyone who worships Cyrus Davidon as their gods needs to be purged from the very surface of the earth with scourging fire. Good thinking." He clapped Vara on the shoulder.

She sent him an acid look. "The air is wet; rain is on the horizon. The fire will likely not have much chance to get out of control, but it will deny this place as a safe haven to this Machine. We should treat all such properties of theirs thusly, and send them a message that their secret leaders will receive loudly and with great clarity."

"'Your money will be stolen and all your other shit will be burned,'" Vaste said, "'Signed, Sincerely, Other Criminals Who Wish to Steal From You And Burn Your Shit.'"

Alaric let out a soft guffaw, most unexpectedly, before composing himself. "I think Vara is right. I think that will send a necessary message about what is happening in this town now that we have arrived."

"'Hark, peoples!'" Vaste cried. "'Cyrus Davidon has returned, and in his vengeance he will be stealing lots and lots of shit, and burning much more of it! Woe betide you should you live or have your business next to one of these terrible Machine hideouts, for your shit will perhaps also be burned—you know, 'by accident'!'"

"Your duncery is growing entirely too pronounced," Vara said.

"I am merely pointing out that our control of fire, and Curatio's of water, is not nearly what it once was," Vaste said. "Cities have burned with less spark applied. We should exercise great caution here."

"I thought you wanted to scourge my worshippers from the very earth," Cyrus said dryly.

"Oh, you of all people should recognize I was being dramatic," Vaste said. "I have no more desire to leave Reikonos a scorched ruin than I do to go live in the ragged boneyard of Gren, a lonely hermit with none but the dead for company."

Alaric nodded. "We shall throw this all to the crowds, and burn the rest." That said, he nodded, and Cyrus stepped forth, shattering the window with his gauntlet while Vara and Curatio began to gather up the bills and coins.

The Ghost, meanwhile, stepped closer to Vaste and leaned in as the shattering sound of Cyrus clearing the glass from the corners of the window nearly covered his whisper. "And what do the dead here have to say, Vaste?"

Vaste paused, listening carefully. "Very little," he said. "But unlike the muted effects of magic, I find them entirely absent." He listened, but there was only silence. "Strange things are happening in this place, Alaric." He had heard little else to suggest that there were any dead lurking—a curious thing for a city of Reikonos's immensity.

"Indeed," Alaric said as Cyrus scooped up a handful of gold in front of them and turned to the window, shouting something at the crown below and then loosing it all. "Many strange things are happening in this place. The silence of the dead is merely another disquieting one. The dampening of magic, the rise of this Machine ... these infernal 'pistols'—"

"Don't be such an angry old man, Alaric," Cyrus said, scooping another armful of gold and money.

Alaric merely grunted. "Concern yourself with your honor and not my age … whippersnapper." The Ghost smiled. He glanced at Vaste, "We should, perhaps, help them," he said, and moved to do so, seizing vast bundles of the notes. Taking his turn at the window, he began hurling them out.

Vaste could hear the shouts and squeals of the crowd below. "Reminds me of the sound pigs make at a trough," he mused, not bothering to assist. The others had a formed a chain of sorts, and the money, gold and jewels were making their way out. He could do little to assist; they had a system worked out, and his bulk would only get in the way.

And so he watched, instead, as they threw their pilfered treasures down unto the crowd, showering them with largesse. Something about the whole spectacle unnerved him, leaving him unsettled and longing for the days when the whispered voices of the dead came to him in moments like this, providing a strange comfort by their very presence.

18.

Cyrus

"Do you truly believe this coal yard is the place that this Machine has chosen to hide Shirri's mother?" Vara asked as they threaded their way down the stairs. The noise of the crowd from outside was surging wildly, shouts and cries echoing into the building through some of the windows they'd broken in their ascent.

"Hell if I know," Cyrus said. "Everything about this Machine is muddled thus far. We don't know who they are, other than some criminal brotherhood. We don't know where they make their headquarters, only that they seem to have a heavy presence in the streets of Reikonos." He shook his head. "There's so much we don't know." The scent of blood and stink of death washed the hallway they passed through, and Cyrus saw the bodies of the five men he'd slain on his climb, sprawled across the floorboards as they moved toward the downstairs. "This whole world is a great mystery."

"Time has merely had its way with the world you knew," Alaric said from behind him, causing Cyrus to pause at the top of the stairs. The Ghost approached. "The players and places may be unfamiliar to you, perhaps the world has grown wider since we left, given Shirri's talk about lands beyond the seas, and the distance these airships can sail … but it is still the world we knew, with other elements simply layered atop it. We will find our way, in time." He drew himself up to a commanding height. "And we will start by knowing Reikonos as you once did."

"Glad you didn't say as I once did," Vaste said. "Because my experience with this town was very poor. Did I ever tell you about the time I went drinking at a dark elven establishment down by the docks with Terian? I thought the patrons were going to try and make me their mistress." He slapped his backside. "You know, because of this."

"I assumed it was because of your pretty face," Cyrus said.

"I'm sure that was a factor."

"We'll need to ask Shirri about this coal yard," Cyrus said. "We can start getting to know Reikonos again by ripping this Machine up by the roots."

"'Roots' doesn't really work for a 'Machine,'" Vaste said, pensive, and almost quiet with the crowd noise seeping into the building. "Perhaps ... 'destroy it down to the gears' might be more apropos."

"Where's Curatio?" Cyrus asked realizing the healer was not present. He heard thumping footsteps above, and then sniffed; smoke was in the air. "Oh, that's right."

"Yes, he's carrying out our dictate of scorching the Machine's resources," Alaric said. "I imagine it's going to take a more sustained effort than usual because of the magical constraints."

"It is taking quite a bit more effort than usual," Curatio's voice shouted from somewhere above. "In fact, if any of you would care to start a fire or two on that floor and the ones below, it would aid me greatly." There was a pause, and something shattered above. "I suggest aiming for a ripe pile of bedding to allow your spell to catch—and it will catch quickly."

Vara stopped, looking into one of the rooms. Cyrus glanced in as well. It was a bare-bones sort of dormitory, with a few bedrolls spread on the ground. Vara took one, he took another, and they both conjured fire that lit them.

"This is disappointing," Cyrus said with a frown at the small fire he'd started. "I'd just gotten good at magic, too."

"Well, you'd gotten adequate, at least," Vaste said. "For a warrior." And he sent a spiraling little ball half the size of Cyrus's fist into another bedroll, lighting it up. "It would appear that in addition to the denizens of this world deciding to go insane and back Cyrus, the natural order has gone mad as well in a bid to equalize our spellcasting abilities."

Cyrus summoned a ball of fire roughly the same size as the one Vaste had commanded and sent it into yet another bedroll. The heavy scent of smoke was beginning to fill the air thickly here; black clouds were seeping up to the ceiling. "Yet I remain a stronger swordsman."

"And I can smack you with this staff as many times as I—" Vaste started to say.

Cyrus drew his blade and rapped Vaste neatly across the knuckles on one hand, then the other, causing him to drop Letum in surprise.

The Staff of Death tumbled from his grasp and Cyrus snatched it out of the air with ease, then rapped Vaste lightly once upon the forehead.

"Oww!" the troll said, hands racing to the place where Cyrus had struck him. He looked down at the warrior with one eye squinted closed in pain. "Well, I don't care for that at all."

"It's not much better through a helm," Cyrus said, tossing the staff back at him. Vaste caught it.

"Brothers, I suggest you expedite your fire setting," Alaric called up the stairs. "Things appear to be ... heating up down here."

"First I'm struck on the head by this dunce," Vaste said, still squinting in pain, "and now Alaric deals a horrifically pedestrian pun. My disappointments continue to abound."

"I would think that would pale next to the knowledge that Cyrus is a god and your people may be extinct," Vara said.

"I was just speaking of the disappointments of the last two minutes," Vaste said. "I just assumed you'd had enough of the earlier ones by now."

"I should like to hear no more complaining about extinct species and friends worshipped as gods," Curatio said, descending the stairs to join them in the hallway, "as I have gone through that before and you didn't hear me bitch about it."

"I think people simply had greater emotional fortitude in our day," Alaric said.

"Yes, this younger generation is forever complaining about something," Curatio said.

"On the plus side," Vaste said, "no one can accuse us of holding back critical information, like, say, 'The gods are not really gods,' 'They really want to kill you, Cyrus,' or maybe, 'Anyone can learn magic.'"

"Or, 'Your mother is still alive,'" Cyrus added.

"I'd perhaps add, 'I have lived nearly forever,'" Vara said, "or, 'Our guildhall is a sentient life force with the ability to magically allow me and others to turn ethereal.'"

Alaric and Curatio were silent, and Cyrus noted much looking around from them, some study of their own shoes.

"Well," Alaric said at last, gesturing to the stairwell, "shall we?" And he hurried to take the lead, Curatio following just as swiftly thereafter.

"Oh, we busted their asses," Vaste said with mild glee. Then, with a quiet pause, he added, "Do you think they've told us everything now?"

Cyrus looked at Vara; she looked back. There was a small flicker of reserve. "I hope so," Cyrus said, unwilling to commit to anything further. "But either way ..." He shrugged. "It all comes out, you know—in the fullness of—"

"Yeah, yeah," Vaste said, following their elders down the stairs. "I wish it would come out sooner. You know, when it might be helpful to know in advance?"

"If wishes were horses, we wouldn't have to walk to the coal yard," Cyrus said, heading down after him, letting Vara lead. "Which brings up a gripe I have—the reduced size of Sanctuary's grounds leaves no room for a stable."

"I'm sure you could put in a plea with Sanctuary to let you have Windrider again," Vara said, "were you so inclined."

Cyrus frowned. "I would like to see Windrider again—though I know Windrider is not naturally a horse." He smiled, just a little. "How curious that we spent a thousand years with Sanctuary in the ether and I don't feel I know that much more about it or its aims than when we first went in. A thousand years to end up with—well, this." And he made his hand fade, just slightly, and only for a second.

"I can do little more," Vara said, and her entire body became hazy for slightly longer than Cyrus's hand had, but she slipped right back into solidity, the haze evaporating like an early morning fog. "What about you, Vaste?"

"I can do at least as much as you," the troll said, half a staircase down, "but I don't wish to make this natural beauty vanish." He waved a hand to encompass his whole body. "There's just not enough of it in the world, especially now. It'd be a crime to remove more."

Cyrus let out a dry chuckle as they descended the last staircase into the shop. It was still a chaotic mess, but quiet inside. Outside, though—

That was another story.

It looked to Cyrus's eyes like a near riot was breaking out in the street. People were stooping and shoving, trying to lay hands on every piece of gold and scrap of money that they could. Alaric and Curatio had paused just inside, surveying the scene.

The Ghost spoke first. "We must do something about this."

Vaste slapped the head of Letum into his open palm. "Like crack some skulls?"

"No," Alaric said tightly, "I was thinking a bit more along the lines of peacefully solving the problem, not making it worse through violence."

"Are you sure?" Vaste asked. "Now that my healing spells are encumbered, I'm finding violence is really the only thing I'm good at." He peered at Cyrus curiously. "Is this how you feel all the time?"

"You're good at quite a number of other things, my darling," Vara said, patting Cyrus on the shoulder. "As he should know by our open door policy."

"Oh, thanks for reminding me of yet another affliction I've dealt with in the last few hours." The troll sighed. "It's injustices all the way down here, I tell you. It's as though the universe or the God of Good, or whoever's left smiling—no, frowning—down on us, studied my entire life and said, 'Oh, you dislike your own people and their stupidity and their violent aggression? Wouldn't it be hilarious if you came out of your thousand-year slumber to find that the intelligent troll girl you'd always hoped to find has been wiped off the world with the rest of your kind, guaranteeing that your beautiful light and wonderful arse will never be passed on to glorious, fat troll babies. Oh, and you'll also lose that magic that makes you so special and be forced to beat people with sticks like a common troll." He sighed loudly. "Next thing you know, I'll be afflicted with stupidity, and perhaps scarred."

"You are scarred," Vara said, pointing the marks on his forehead and face.

"Yes, but these scars add a rugged, manly quality to my face," Vaste said. "They're character builders that only add to my handsomeness. I'm talking about the kind of scars where someone just rips your face nearly off—you know, like your husband did to Orion."

"His face was my canvas and my fist was like a brush," Cyrus agreed.

"'Twas beautiful work," Vaste agreed. "Or hideous, rather." He looked over the crowd. "So … no busting heads? This is a real shame. I have so much disappointment and anger to work through. Also, some sexual frustration that—"

"Perhaps Alaric and Curatio might have been right about our generation's emotional incontinence," Vara said.

"Agreed," Cyrus said. "There are some things that would be best kept to ourselves."

"That is how I feel about almost all of our conversations that involve a free exchange of emotion," Alaric said. "Perhaps we should adopt a 'stiff upper lip' policy, at least in public? We can always trade confidences back at the guildhall."

"This idea sucks," Vaste said, "because I know that really, you're all just looking to exclude me from your confidence-sharing circles. Alaric and Curatio have each other to confide their secrets in, Cyrus and Vara share not only secrets and a bed, but a free exchange of revolting innuendo—"

"We share a lot more than that, big fellow," Cyrus said.

"But I—I am the fifth wheel in all this," Vaste said. "I have no one to confide in, unless Vara is feeling merciful—and I think we all know that this is a state unlikely to come but once every thousand years, so—"

"This riot is getting worse," Curatio said. "And we have business to attend to elsewhere."

"Shut out of emotional support everywhere," Vaste said. "So much hate."

"We'll talk later," Cyrus said, and stepped up to look over the crowd, moving past Alaric. "This could be a challenge, but if I can get their attention—"

An earsplitting whistle shrilled from behind Cyrus's ear and he cringed. Glancing back, he saw Vara with two fingers in her mouth. A hush had fallen on the street, and everyone had stopped right where they stood, awestruck at both the sudden noise and the sight they'd now seen beyond it.

Cyrus surveyed the stunned crowd, and then nodded his thanks to Vara before raising his voice to address them. "You know who I am," he said, and whispers ran through the lot of them, every eye fixed on him.

"The world's biggest bag of human feces, wrapped up in black armor?" Vaste whispered.

"I have liberated this money," Cyrus said, trying to set his mind to the task of oratory, knowing there would be more from Vaste that he would have to ignore, "for you, the people. From the Machine. And yet ... here you stand, fighting amongst yourselves for scraps of paper." He stooped and grasped a fistful of gold, lifting it up as he stepped down onto the sidewalk in front of the building. He offered it to a woman in haggard clothing; she stared at it for a moment before taking it gently, no sign of the vicious squabbling that he'd seen only a moment earlier, before Vara had commanded their attention.

Cyrus looked over the crowd easily; not one of them stood anywhere close to his height. "Is this what you've become in my absence? Chickens pecking at each other over mere seeds? For what is this paper, these notes?" He gestured to a man who'd filled his hands and his pockets with them; they were stuffed and overflowing. "They're seeds. Seeds you hope to plant, to exchange for what you perceive to be a better life. And if you are starving, then perhaps they will find use in that way." He looked over the crowd. "Are you starving?"

There was an uncomfortable murmur. Looking up and down the street he decided this was not a district of utter poverty and despair, though it was certainly grimy from the ash. "I thought not." He took a few of the notes out of the man's pockets, and handed them to another woman, one who looked thinner and more careworn. "Is this good reason to plunder and destroy each other, then? For paper?" He waved one of them. "For chunks of metal?" He pulled a small coin out of his own purse; it was from before he'd left with Sanctuary. "What does this mean to you? What are you willing to do to get it? Kill your fellow humans? Harm them? Strike their eye from their head?" He made a motion as though to throw his elbow, miming a hit he'd delivered a thousand times. "Is that who you are here? Someone gets in your way ... you strike at them?" He listened to the silence. "Is that who you think I am? Some coarse plunderer who would kill or harm anyone for a piece of gold?"

A woman in front of him shook her head, then lowered her eyes from him. "No, Lord Davidon."

He handed the coin to her, and she took it, looking up at him. "You are right. That is not who I am."

He turned and began to stride back through the crowd. "I threw this out so you might have it. I did not throw it out so you could simply display your strength over each other—allow your might to make obvious which of you is strongest. That is the way of the Society of Arms—the place where I was raised, and whose ethos I rejected. Strength does not make you mighty, and it does not make you right." He took a step back up in front of Alaric and the others; a fire was blazing bright in the building behind them now, smoke pouring out of the upper windows. "For any one of you who wishes to test their strength because you think it makes you right, I invite you to step forward now, and challenge me. Let us see who is strongest."

"Let us see indeed," came a voice from the back rank of the crowd, and a man in a knee-length black leather coat with a white armband— the Machine's symbology on it—came striding forth with five others trailing him. He shoved his way through, and then the crowd started to clear for him, screams and cries as people saw him, saw what he carried—

A pistol.

Cyrus saw the glint of dark menace as the man started to raise it, as did each of his fellows. Six pistols, all traveling upward, the crowd screaming and surging out of the way to give them clear aim—

Right at Cyrus—

And the others.

Cyrus reached for Praelior, shoved his hand toward the hilt even as he moved swiftly, trying to thrust himself in front of one figure in particular—

Vara.

But a volley of thunderous shots rang out before his hand could reach the hilt and before he could throw himself in front of her. The pistols flashed like lightning, like spells crashing through the canyons of the Reikonos streets, and Cyrus watched the smoke puff from the barrels and knew that he could not stop the bullets from finding their intended targets.

19.

The sound of metal bullets on his armor, their impact clashing plate against chainmail underpinnings, rang through Cyrus down to his very bones. They turned his armor into almost a bell, clanging constantly against him as he moved sideways to try and shield Vara with his body. The sound of the thunderous shots rang in his ears as he moved.

His fingers brushed the pommel of Praelior and suddenly the frenzy of movement—the tightening of his every muscle as he surged forward, of the screams he could now hear from the crowd, slowed impossibly, the drip of sweat down his back—all of these things ran through him along with the bile of fear as he turned and bowed his head forward, slipping in front of Vara.

But the shots were already loosed, and there was nothing to be done.

Cyrus had lost count of how many he'd felt. Three? Four, perhaps? Now that he had Praelior in hand, his wits seemed to come back to him. Vara was safely behind him, and—

She shoved him, pushing him aside so she could step forward, Ferocis in her own hand. "Are you mad?" she asked, eyes blazing as she stared at him, speaking so rapidly that it probably sounded like gibberish to anyone not handling a godly weapon. "I have armor of my own, you fool!" She was flushed and burning at the cheeks, pale white skin lit up with a fiery red glow.

"I was trying to protect you from this new threat," Cyrus shot back, "it came so fast—"

"Yes, well," Vara said, "none of it came my way, and these idiots are simply standing there, almost unmoving, now that we have weapons in hand."

"I suggest we dispense with this enemy," Alaric said, his own sword drawn, speaking just as rapidly as them. "Before they can conjure some other honorless devilry with which to attack us."

Cyrus leapt, aware of Vara and Alaric following. They covered the distance off the steps and down into the street before the men— clearly toughs in the same mold as the others Cyrus had encountered in his dealings thus far with the Machine—could recoil from the vision of foes descending upon them in a blur.

With his first strike, Cyrus tore apart the one who'd led them. He was not merciful in his strike, cleaving the man uncleanly a little above the waist. Without healing spells, there would be no surviving the attack, and that gave Cyrus a measure of thin triumph as he cut him through. The next fell easily, and the next, and then—

Cyrus turned back to find that Alaric and Vara had done their parts, and the six men were dead or dying in the street.

"My—my lord!" a woman said, raising a hand to Cyrus, emerging from the crowd, which had stepped back to let the battle unfold when they'd seen the guns. "You ... you're unharmed!"

"Did you expect any less?" Cyrus asked.

"You moved ... so fast," another man said, mouth slightly agape. His jowls were hanging, and his eyes were unfocused. "I could scarcely see you. Truly ... you are him."

"I am him," Cyrus said, his voice low and menacing. "And woe be unto anyone who challenges me."

"I challenge you all the time," Vara said, so swiftly she knew none would understand her. "It works out rather well for me."

"You're special," Cyrus replied under his breath.

"I'm special, too, I'll have you know," Vaste said, only a step or two behind them, scraping the tip of his staff on the gutter, blood and other refuse of battle sliding down it. Cyrus looked; a few steps from Vaste lay a man with his skull split asunder. *I guess the troll managed to get one as well ...*

"Few would argue it," Alaric said, his own blade covered in gore. "Perhaps now we should—"

"... Tend to your wounded?" A soft voice from behind them prompted Cyrus to turn. His eyes fell upon the steps to the building, where stood a figure with crimson spreading across his white robes—

"Curatio," Alaric breathed, and he was at the healer's side in but a moment, his sword sheathed. "Brother. How—"

"I do not possess a godly weapon for speed nor a complete set of armor, unfortunately," Curatio said, holding up his hand, which bled from a wound in the middle of it. He grimaced, and it pumped a small volume of red down to soak his sleeve. The robes were soaked almost to his elbow, and he tried to flex his hand but it ended with a grimace. "I was struck in the volley, unfortunately." Another little drizzle of blood came pulsing out. "I believe ... this may be a problem."

"You know what else is a problem?" Vaste pushed up to them, looking down at Curatio's wound. "Vegetables. Vegetables are always a problem. They don't taste very good, and you're supposed to eat them."

"You don't," Vara said acidly.

"And apparently that's a problem," Vaste said. "Look how short-lived my people are."

Curatio let out a small gasp of pain, and stared daggers at Vaste. "How did they hit me and miss you?"

"Not because I ate vegetables, that's for sure," Vaste said, patting his ample belly.

"I can still see the bullet in there," Cyrus said, peering down at the wound. A small black piece of dark steel glinted within, hidden under the pulsing beats of the flowing blood. With each pulse, it would emerge for a second like a ship at the shore on low tide, and a moment later be swallowed up again.

"I have tried a healing spell," Curatio said, grimacing, "but it only buried it further. I shall need to remove this ... metal ball ... before I can properly close even such a small wound with magic."

"Do you truly think your magic is up to this task?" Alaric asked. "With the limits as they are?"

"If this were buried in my belly? Perhaps not," Curatio said, forcing a smile. "But I think, in the hand ... yes. We shall have to hurry, though. I need to return to Sanctuary."

"Damn," Alaric said and looked at the bodies in the street. There was a wild murmur running through the crowd; all the money had been scooped up, but still the crowd remained, watching Cyrus, waiting for him to speak. Cyrus looked back at them, a little warily. He wasn't sure how to leave this, but he felt a pressing need to move on.

"We need to get to the coal yard," Cyrus said, then nodded at the fallen bodies of the pistoleers who had attacked them. "Staying here will draw more interest from the Machine, and for no purpose. If we mean to rescue Shirri's mother, we need to be on about it."

"I need to remove this ball," Curatio said. "Much the same as I once had to remove the water from your lungs before you could heal."

"I'm not saying you don't," Cyrus said, "I'm just saying—we could do it here, if need be. A little whiskey, a dagger—"

"On the balance," Curatio said, "I would rather do this in the Halls of Healing, where I have disinfectant at the ready to stave off infection and clean cloth to buttress the wound while it heals." He arched his eyebrow and nodded up at the candle shop behind them, where black smoke churned out of the broken windows on every floor. "Also, this building is on fire, and I make no guarantees as to how long it will be before it collapses."

"This is a poor place from which to perform a surgery," Vaste said, and he reached down, steadying the elf with an arm around his shoulders. "New plan—I take Curatio back to Sanctuary to heal, and the three of you—" he looked sideways, and Cyrus followed his gaze to where Shirri emerged, watching them suspiciously, from the crowd, "—you four, I suppose—move on to the next target."

"I don't think we should divide our forces," Alaric said. "Not in the face of their superior numbers."

"If we don't get to the coal yard now," Cyrus said, "we're going to lose our advantage of surprise, and their superior numbers are going to count for a lot more. Forewarned is forearmed."

"I see no need to hold up your continued progress," Curatio said, grimacing. "I can deal with this. Doubly so with Vaste's help. It is a minor matter, but I need Sanctuary's aid to keep it from becoming a much greater one. This is little different from removing an arrow, save for I have nothing with which to grasp the damned thing. Let us be on our way, and you on yours, and we shall rendezvous soon enough."

"All right," Alaric relented. Cyrus watched the Ghost, and it looked to be a near thing. "But as soon as we are done at the coal yard, I will return to Sanctuary to find you there, and bring you along with us via—"

"Via turning into smoke and dragging us nauseatingly through the ether, yes," Vaste said. "My stomach will look forward to it not at all." He hefted Curatio and started down the sidewalk, past Shirri, back the way they had come. "Hold on, old man, I'll get us to Sanctuary in what'll probably feel like the blink of an eye to you—so … say, a year?"

"Hilarious," Curatio said as the two healers began to recede through the crowd, people moving out of the way to let them pass unchecked.

"I've often been told I am," Vaste said.

"Probably by dead people who simply want to humor you so that you will talk to them," Curatio said.

"Or by alive people who wish to get bullets removed from their hands," Vaste said.

Curatio paused for a moment. "You know, you really are endlessly entertaining, a fellow of near-infinite jest."

"Better."

Cyrus watched them go, their banter receding beyond his ability to hear it. He looked out to the crowd for a moment, wondering how best to disperse them. Alaric stirred behind him, and then whispered in his ear. "It would be best if this mob went on about their day and did not follow us to where we intend to go next."

"Aye," Vara said, joining Alaric at his other shoulder, "it will be much more difficult to hide our approach should we appear at the head of an excited crowd that takes up half the street."

"I'll work on it," Cyrus said, and stepped up. The smoke was already drifting into the sky behind him, fire starting to appear at the windows of the Machine's outpost. "Good people ... return to your homes. Go on about your business."

"But—but my lord!" one of the women shouted, and he recognized her as the one with the massive hoop skirt. It was sullied and tarnished now, looking as though it had been stepped on many times in the scramble for the money. "You have returned! Should we not remain with you?"

Cyrus paused, then shook his head. "I have much work to do. This city ... needs me to go and do ... stuff."

"Very smooth," Vara said.

"I'm trying to keep our plans secret," Cyrus muttered, then raised his voice again. "You will hear of my doings, and you will know that I am the one doing them—"

"Who taught you language?" Alaric asked. "Was it Erkhardt? Because he was supposed to aid you, not set you back to infancy."

Cyrus cleared his throat. "You will know it is I by my deeds. I will cleanse this city of many troubles. Tell everyone you meet that I have returned. Tell them that I am working here, in the streets and in the shadows, to ferret out wrongdoing. Tell them—"

"Tell them little else, for we have somewhere to be," Vara muttered.

"Tell them I'm back," Cyrus said, "and watch for my sign. Help one another—and await the day when I call upon you to join me." With that, he raised his sword. "For it will come—and soon."

20.

Vaste

"I know I complain about how terrible this place is—and it is terrible," Vaste said, walking with Curatio, his arm threaded under the elf's, helping to keep him on his feet. "But … it is somewhat nicer than in our day. At least this part of it." He scanned the streets with their high buildings of brick that rose into the sky on either side of them. "And tall. So tall. It's impressive, really."

"It's like walking in a box canyon," Curatio said, wincing, blood still pumping from his injured hand. He was faltering, Vaste knew, the steps becoming more difficult the longer they walked. "You never know who is watching you from above, or what bandits might come from a hidden cave to try and snatch your purse."

"Walked in a lot of box canyons, have you?" Vaste asked.

"Indeed," Curatio grunted, laboring as he walked. "Not intentionally, but when you travel the lands as much as I have, you do tend to find yourself in a few over twenty thousand years or so. The last one I went into—and this was slightly before Sanctuary—I found myself in a nest of bandits and was forced to use lightning and fire to kill them all."

"A proud day, I'm sure," Vaste said, hearing a peculiar sort of drag to Curatio's words.

"Well, it was nice to stretch the old spells without fear of getting dubbed a heretic," Curatio said, still struggling. "So I suppose that was one advantage."

"Pretty unlikely that you'd be so fortunate as to go unwatched in this sort of man-made box canyon," Vaste said. "Why, there are people everywhere now."

And there were. Reikonos was bustling to life, the sun up, the people in motion. Small crowds made their way down the sidewalks while horse-drawn carriages filled the streets. Vendors were hawking food on the corners, shouting their wares to the heavens. Vendors of fresh and less-than-fresh fruits and vegetables were setting up on the sidewalks. As Vaste passed a cart of turnips, he looked away, making a face. "Revolting."

"Apparently I need to stave off vegetables to become more like you," Curatio slurred. "I cannot believe that they failed to find you with a single shot and yet managed to hit me."

"I had my staff in hand, Curatio," Vaste said, laboring only a little under the elf's weight. It was of greater difficulty to stoop to thread his arm around the elf than it was to carry him whole. But probably less eye-catching, if only marginally. "It was no great difficulty for me to watch where they were aiming those barrels and simply move out of the way before they fired."

"Ah, devilry," Curatio said. "Not having a godly weapon has once again cost me greatly."

"'Again'?" Vaste asked. "When did it cost you before?"

Curatio let out a long sigh. "When Vidara chose Alaric for her favors over me, of course."

"Wait ... did he actually do anything with her?" Vaste asked. "I thought he rather turned her down."

"I have no idea," Curatio said and let out a soft moan of pain. Vaste couldn't be sure if it was related to his injury or the thought of the former Goddess of Life with Alaric.

"Well, either way," Vaste said, "she turned on us in the last battle with Bellarum in a desperate gamble to try and save her own hide, so I'd say you did well in avoiding the traitorous wench."

"Somehow I don't think my life was all the richer for lacking ten thousand years of companionship with a goddess," the healer said, sounding quite irritable about it.

"Well, when you put it like that," Vaste said, "by gods, you should have doubled your efforts."

"I don't think that much would have helped either," Curatio said, voice weakening a smidge.

"Stay with me, Curatio," Vaste said. "I don't know if you realize this, but if you pass out, I'm going to have to try and remove that bullet myself, and I'm deathly put off by the mere sight of blood."

"You're a healer," Curatio reminded him.

"Yes, which allows me to magically heal wounds before the sight of them makes me ill," Vaste said.

Curatio let out a small moan. "Well ... I certainly wish I could oblige you in this."

"Me too," Vaste said, scanning the street. "Me too."

There seemed to be no shortage of humans in this place. Where the Reikonos of his day had been composed of trolls and dark elves and gnomes, the occasional dwarf and who knew what else, the number of humans in this one was overwhelming. The only difference seemed to be more variance in the shades of their skin. "That's new," he muttered to himself, seeing a human with near ebony skin walking down the street, dressed much more smartly than most in this district, and in a very different style. He had a serious bearing, and went right past without giving Vaste's stooped-over frame nor Curatio much of a look. "Did you see ...?" Vaste started to say.

"I see pain," Curatio said, voice growing more weary. "And more pain. That is all, at the moment."

"Your loss then," Vaste said. "Humanity has taken some turns in the aesthetics department since we left."

"Yes, the garb here is most peculiar."

"Not what I meant, but—" Vaste stopped midsentence, his eyes caught on something in the crowd ahead. He'd been looking for more people of that ebony skin tone when his eyes had caught a flash of green.

Of green ... skin.

He saw it again in the distance, and blinked. There was someone in a cloak, with a cowl pulled up, standing tall above most of the humans in the street. He peered, and saw a bob of dark hair, then a face—

"Oh my dead gods," Vaste said, and his mouth fell open and he nearly stood up straight.

"Aigghhhh," Curatio grunted, resisting Vaste's attempt to stand taller. "What the hells are you doing?" the healer asked, trying to pull back as Vaste accidentally nudged his wounded hand.

Vaste stared, straight ahead, blinked again, and—

Yes. It was a troll woman with lustrous black hair and perfect green skin, wearing a cowl. She was probably a block and a half away, just— *right there*—and he lurched forward.

"What are you doing?" Curatio struggled against him, pulling at his arm, still wrapped around the healer. "Sanctuary is this way." And he pointed to a cross street.

Vaste looked up again, transfixed. Where was she? She'd been there, just a moment ago, standing tall over the heads of everyone else on the street and now—

She was gone.

"I saw a beautiful troll woman," Vaste said, barely a whisper.

ROBERT J. CRANE

"I don't believe you," Curatio said. "There are no beautiful troll women."

"Well, this one was," Vaste said, his voice taking on a dreamlike quality.

"Which is why I think you have seen a mirage," Curatio said, still pulling back against Vaste's attempts to go forward. He had to find her, catch up to her and—"Or a delusion."

"I'm not the one wounded here!" Vaste said, trying to lift his head up, up, trying to get tall so he could see her again. She had to be there—she'd been right there.

"Then it was prompted by the sight of my blood, clearly." Curatio fought against the attempt to stand taller. "You are going to expose yourself, fool."

"There was a troll woman walking down the street here," Vaste said, tugging at him as he stood. "I saw her."

"It doesn't matter now," Curatio said, brandishing his wounded hand. "We need to get back to Sanctuary so I can tend to this. I am in pain!"

"So am I!" Vaste shot back. "Do you know what it's like to live in the shadow of Cyrus and Vara's bedroom antics, knowing you might go to your grave having never experienced such pleasures?"

Curatio fell silent, and Vaste paused, eyes still fixed down the street, a cold realization trickling down his back as what he'd said filtered through his consciousness.

"... Never?" Curatio asked.

"You're in a lot of pain," Vaste said, trying to brush it under the rug like a shattered vase. "I didn't say 'never' as in never ever, I—oh, hell. Yes, it's been never ever. I came of age in Gren, fitting in about as well as you'd expect, and after that ... well, I think you lesser races are a little too flimsy and intimidated for me." He raised his head again. Where had she gone? "But this woman ... she was a troll. Tall. Mighty. But—dressed smartly, like a normal human!"

"There is no such thing as a normal human," Curatio growled. "But ... your point still stands. Do you see her?"

"No," Vaste said, blinking. Perhaps she truly had just been a figment of his imagination.

That was a disheartening thought. Part of him wanted to rush ahead, check in every door near where she'd vanished, look within every shop within miles, ask every person standing on the sidewalks if they'd seen her.

But that would be a sure way to generate much attention for himself, and no good could come of that. Not while Curatio's wound needed tending. "We should get back to Sanctuary," Vaste said, trying to fix in his mind this location. He tried to burn the memory of the buildings here into his mind so he could return later, to recall this place even days or weeks from now, should the need arise.

Putting his arm more firmly around the weakened Curatio, he turned down the cross street and began to walk back toward the alley where Sanctuary waited. But his thoughts stayed behind with the troll woman he'd seen on the street.

21.

Cyrus

"You have taken a woman," Cyrus said, his blade against the neck of a young tough who stared back at him wide-eyed with horror, "from her very home, and hold her captive. Tell me where she is and I will make this swift." Alaric coughed behind him, and Cyrus rolled his eyes. "Tell me where she is," Cyrus amended, "and I will maybe perhaps consider letting you continue to draw breath."

"Hell of a deal," Vara said, doing a little eye rolling of her own. "Just break his limbs until he talks."

Cyrus shot her a look, as did Alaric, but the Ghost spoke first. "You've made a stunning transformation into a dark knight." The smell of coal dust was heavy in this place, almost oppressive, and it hung in the air worse than the ash in the city.

"As it turns out, paladin is just an artificial title created by the Leagues to keep spellcasters weak, yes?" Vara kept her gaze intent on him. "So ..." She shrugged.

"That's not—entirely accurate," Alaric said with a sigh. "And I would hope you would have your own personal moral compass regardless of what the so-called gods saw as a worthy path."

"Can I—can I just get a word in here?" the tough asked, Cyrus's blade still at his throat.

"Do you think it's wise?" Cyrus asked, pushing Praelior—ever so gently—against his throat.

"Gurk," the man said, then, more hoarsely, "Maybe not."

The coal yard had not been quite what Cyrus expected. There had only been a small shack on the premises dedicated to the Machine, the entirety of the rest of the place being consumed with running the actual coal yard. Even at this hour groups of men in the yard were doing the hard work of shoveling coal into wheelbarrows that were then carted out onto the street and off to their destinations.

"I have my honor," Vara said, "but I am not above asking difficult questions of human refuse at this point."

"But does your honor not ache at the idea of physically harming someone just to get them to talk?" Alaric asked.

"Have I done so yet?" Vara asked, arching an eyebrow at him. Cyrus got it.

So did the man with the sword at his throat. "Ohh, you're not going to actually hurt me," he said, and let out a breath of clear relief. "That is—just so fortunate, because—I was about to tell you everything, honestly."

Cyrus reached out and struck him in the chest, causing him to grunt in pain. A couple ribs broke under his hit. "They're paladins; I'm not."

"Thank you for making that clear," the man said in a weak, pained voice. Now Cyrus was having to fight to keep him upright against the pull of gravity. "Okay, I'm ready to talk again."

Cyrus looked back to see Vara with a gleam of triumph in her eye and Alaric looking wearied and possibly annoyed, though it was difficult to tell under his helm. "Tell us what you know about this woman you've taken."

"I didn't take any woman—uh, tonight," the guy said, wheezing and clutching at his side, "neither did anyone from here." Cyrus lifted the blade higher, pushing it a half-centimeter or so deeper into his neck. "Whoa, whoa! You want a woman? I can get you a woman. I can get you five women. A hundred. We take them all the time, I'm just saying we didn't take any this morning or last night—"

"Confession may be good for the soul, but I doubt trying to mollify us in this way is going to increase your chances of survival," Cyrus said.

"I—I—what do you want from me?" the man asked, still clutching at himself.

"Decency," Alaric said, staring at him hard, his eye focused on the man. "Which is plainly not forthcoming."

"Tell us about the Machine," Vara said. "Who runs this place? Who do you report to?"

"Are you crazy?" the man asked, eyes growing wide. "They'll kill me."

"That'll happen pretty definitely if your head comes off," Cyrus said, pushing the sword in just a little deeper. "But if you survive us, you might just be able to run from the Machine. Die now for certain, die later maybe—tough choice, but it's all you've got. Choose."

"You're not going to kill me," the man said, and nodded at Alaric, "not in front of your old man. It'd offend his honor."

Cyrus looked at Alaric. "Maybe you should leave."

Alaric stood there, stiff and still for a long moment. "Perhaps I should," he said at last, and he vanished in a cloud of mist which fell to the floor and then receded out the door.

Cyrus turned back to the man with a gleam in his eye, and pushed Praelior just a little deeper, enough to break skin. "Now that we're alone ... I've grown weary of you, and I doubt you have anything interesting to say. Prove me wrong in two seconds or say farewell."

"I don't believe you," the man said, jutting his chin out defiantly. "You wouldn't—"

Cyrus pushed the sword in, and the artery in his neck began to leak, a little at first, and then more. The man's eyes lit up in surprise as the blade began to cut into his throat. "Wait, wait—" he said, and Cyrus pushed just a little deeper—

The man's hands flew to his neck, trying to restrain the geyser of blood shooting out. "Gurkkk," he said, and Cyrus mumbled a healing spell under his breath. It wasn't much, but then, neither was the wound—

The man brought his hands back from his neck to reveal a slight gouge that remained beneath the blood that covered his throat. He drew a couple of rasping, experimental breaths, and looked Cyrus right in the eye. "What ... did you just do to me?"

"I healed you," Cyrus said, "but I won't do it again, so ... talk."

The man seemed to stagger on his feet, eyes racing left to right, playing for time. "About ... what?"

"All right, I'm killing him," Vara said, unsheathing her sword.

"No, no, no!" the man said, throwing up a hand at her. "You—you, I believe. Okay, I will tell you—uhm, I report to a man named Touhmes, and he works out of a mill about ten blocks from here at the corner of Crescent and Mill Street. His boss is a guy named Tirner Gaull," the man said, still rubbing at his neck, "And Gaull—well, I don't know where he works. But he shows up every now and again when I'm at the flour mill."

"How many other hideouts does the Machine have in this area?" Cyrus asked.

"Hideouts? None," the man said.

Cyrus's eyes narrowed, but Vara beat him to the question. "What else does the Machine have in this area?"

"They own half the buildings in town," the man said, still rubbing his neck and looking quite stricken. "They don't use them themselves, but—I mean, they have rent collectors and they charge—oh, they make you pay through the nose."

Cyrus frowned. "Why would they demand payment through a nose? Would not it be simpler to just take it from their hand?"

"What?" the man asked, putting up his hands. "No, that's not—it means—"

"Oh, I think it's figurative, the nose thing," Vara said.

"Ohhh," Cyrus said. "It was very confusing. I tried to imagine people stuffing those paper notes up their noses for safe keeping. Seems like it would hurt."

"Indeed," Vara said, and then took Ferocis and put the tip right up the man's nose. "What is your name?"

He stared at the blade sticking out of his nostril. "Guy."

"How original," Vara said. "Now, Guy ... what is the Machine's response going to be to someone attacking their operations in the city?"

Guy's eyes were wide and focused on the sword blade in his nostril, crossed as he stared at the tip of his nose. "I don't know. It's never happened before. No one's been crazy enough to cross the Machine like this until you two came along."

"Hear that?" Cyrus asked, "Guy says we're special."

"The thousand years of life, the songs sung to your deeds, and all the statues had not already convinced you of this?" Vara asked.

"Well, it's nice to have a reminder every now and again."

"Are we about done here?" Guy asked. "Because I need to catch an airship somewhere. I hear Vanreis is nice this time of year. Maybe Muceain or Suijnara. Binngart, even, though those fricking Rannin are a stiff bunch of—"

"I'm nearly done with this kidnapping, possibly murdering piece of swine," Cyrus said. "You, my lovely bride?"

"Yes, I am quite nearly done with him," Vara said, and pushed the sword just a millimeter further up his nasal passage. "A little force blast through the tip of my sword and I expect his brains will empty all over the wall ..."

"Ahhhh ... normally I wouldn't believe you're a mage of any kind," Guy said, "but your hubby there already showed me the whole 'healing light' bit, so, uhm—please don't?"

"I have a feeling there's something you're not sharing with me, Guy," Vara said, leaning toward him, "and this bothers me. You might even say it makes me ... irate." Her voice was steady. "You see, we came here looking for a certain woman, and while you've been very forthcoming in the name of saving your own skin—I still don't have what I want. And as my husband here can tell you—when I am disappointed, I tend to handle it … poorly."

Guy stared at the end of his nose. "I'm … so sorry to hear that. Probably comes from the upbringing. You should blame your parents. Were you overindulged as a child or—ah—ah—AHHHHHH!"

Vara pushed the tip and forced Guy to standing on his tip toes to keep Ferocis from impaling his skull or simply ripping his nose off. "My childhood is not a topic of discussion here. We're talking about the last secret you hold; the one you're keeping back from us in hopes of fleeing this place with your miserable life intact so that you may take it and go slithering back to your masters, able to say, 'But at least I did not tell them this!'" Her voice went nasal and mocking, a solid imitation of Guy's. She leaned in. "But you will tell us. And then you will go catch an airship to somewhere far from here. Either your life in Reikonos is over, or your life, in total, is over. Make your choice swiftly."

Only a half-second of calculation passed through Guy's eyes before he started to speak again. "Okay, so maybe there is this one thing that came to mind when you mentioned a woman being taken—"

"I had a feeling your memory required some jogging," Vara said, then slapped him gently on his belly where it overhung his belt a little. "Like the rest of you."

"If this person was taken locally, but they're not in any of the local grab houses—that means, uhm," Guy went on, "they're not women being put to, uh, immediate use." He swallowed heavily.

Cyrus gripped his sword hilt tighter, and Vara, sensing it, held up a hand behind her to stay his blade.

"Anyway, if this lady was taken for reasons other than, uh—well, other than, uhm—the—"

"Other than selling her as a slave or a woman of the night," Vara said tightly.

"Yeah, that," Guy said hoarsely. "She'd probably be held in a central location." His eyes darted to Cyrus. "I don't know where that is. Somewhere past the statue. The big one. In Davidon Park. Can't miss it. But beyond that, I dunno. That's as far as I've ever gone with any of the bigwigs that have come through, so you're going to have to talk to someone else higher up the chain if you want the exact location."

"They named a park after me?" Cyrus asked, pressing his lips together. "Finally I get to see if the likeness is good."

"It's not," Guy said. "You don't look anything like Cyrus Davidon."

He seemed to realize he'd erred, and his eyes went back to wide. "I mean, uh—it's a terrible likeness. The sculptor should be fired. Then, uh, exposed to fire. Many, many pistols fired at him—at his hands. Maybe his eyes, since they've failed so completely—"

"You've been gone a thousand years," Vara said in a conciliatory tone, "how would a sculptor have accurately chiseled out your good looks after this amount of time?"

"Clearly needed to hire an elf who'd met me," Cyrus grumbled, then shifted his attention back to Guy. "What do we do about him? Seems to me if he knows where this supposed central location is for the Machine, he might be holding it out on us."

"I don't think so," Vara said, withdrawing Ferocis from Guy's nostril and wiping it on his shirt. "He seems like the sort of low-level flunky who'd be intentionally excluded from such things, even via gossip."

"It's true," Guy said, nodding. "I am very low-level. I am a flunky. I don't even get to clean the boots of the big guys."

"Very well," Vara said, regarding him with indifference. "I'd suggest you hurry to catch your airship. It would be a true shame if your employers were to catch you. Though I have a feeling they're about to be busy for a while chasing their own tails—and possibly us."

"Good luck with that," Guy said, bolting for the door and disappearing through it, the shack rattling as he bounced off the frame.

"What do you think the likelihood is that he runs straight to his masters?" Cyrus asked, walking to the door and looking out to make sure some Machine ambush hadn't encircled them while they'd been talking to Guy. The coal yard seemed to be functioning as normal; orders coming in, orders going out.

Well, they'd fix that in a minute.

"Low," Vara said, stepping past him and out into the open air. The sun was rising, and her cloak trailed behind her, a layer of grey ash already covering it from merely walking around this city. Her armor did not shine as it usually did, and it reminded him of the time in Termina when Santir's ash had covered it over during the battle upon the bridge. "Did you see the look in his eyes? He'll be running from them for the rest of his life, at least in his mind."

"That doesn't pain me," Cyrus said, making his way toward a group of workers a couple hundred feet away who had stopped and were watching them as they made their approach. "We should probably warn this lot before we blow up the coal yard, right?"

"'Blow up' is accurate," Vara said. "With all this coal dust in the air, the explosion will be audible for miles. Windows will shatter all over the city."

"Perhaps we should leave this one standing, then?" Cyrus asked, pausing in his approach toward the workers.

"I think not," Vara said. "It will send a very loud signal to the Machine, one which I believe we want them to get. The workers can be cleared, and there are no apartment buildings around here. I expect the explosion, while loud, will do little more than minor damage to the buildings on either side." She pointed behind them. "Some sort of metalworks," then to their left, "a mill," and finally to their right, "and that place looks to be an empty yard, the building long demolished. If ever there was a locale ripe for making an explosive statement, I believe this is it."

"All right," Cyrus said, then turned back toward the workers, "there's a fire in the building over there," he pointed toward the shack. "Fire!"

That did the trick; the workers scattered without any further question, running as fast as they could toward the exit, taking up his call and screaming it to the heavens. Others came running from back of the coal yard, legs pumping as they blew past Cyrus and Vara, calling it for themselves. "FIRE! FIRE!"

"Seems everyone knows what a dangerous place they work in," Cyrus said, tacking toward the gates of the coal yard wall. He could see movement out on the street, and peered ahead before sighing.

"It would appear some of your admirers have followed you," Vara said with a barely concealed smile. "And look—they've multiplied."

They had indeed. There were far, far more of them here than there had been at the candle shop. It was the milling mob they'd hoped to avoid, though larger and more sedate than the original unruly bunch. Cyrus caught sight of a few familiar faces—among them, the man in the long coattails, the woman with the hoop skirt, still minding their charges from the candle shop.

"I thought I told those two to take care of the women we rescued," Cyrus muttered under his breath as they approached the open gate. "Yet here they are, following in my wake like a disobedient dog, with their rescuees in tow."

"But such loving pets they are," Vara teased. "You must promise me that even after they declare themselves completely and totally for you that won't leave me for one of them. Especially the fellow in the long-tailed coat." She snorted. "I couldn't abide losing my man to someone dressed in such a ridiculous manner."

"It's all right," Cyrus said, "I'm more drawn to blue women in leather pants."

Vara's eyes narrowed tightly. "Do you recall those relations that you had hoped to have with me later?"

Cyrus blinked. "Well, I'd been thinking about it, yes—"

"Consider them cancelled. I have a sudden headache at the mere thought of that harlot."

"And here I thought you'd forgiven her after all the help she gave us," Cyrus said.

"I have," Vara said stiffly. "Mostly. It's you who needs to watch your step."

Cyrus muted any reply he might have made, instead shifting his attention to how he might deal with this crowd. "I suppose we'd better disperse them; the men yelling 'FIRE!' outside a coal yard don't seem to have done the trick, after all."

"They're blinded by their love for you," Vara said.

"Who isn't?" he asked with a smirk, but her rolled eyes told him that he might be pushing too far after having already crossed the bounds once. "Other than you, you most clear-headed of souls."

"Idle flattery will not win back what you have already lost for this evening, Lord Davidon."

"Such a shame," Cyrus said. "I had a feeling Alaric was going to keep us running all day anyhow." He raised his voice. "Did I not tell you—"

Vara clamped a hand down upon his wrist, silencing him. "Don't be angry at them."

"Why, because you have the current monopoly on anger and don't want any competition?" He smirked, and once more she rolled her eyes, though a small smile played on her lips her and annoyance had clearly broken. Cyrus raised his voice to address the crowd once more. "How nice to see you all again," he said, unable to keep the irony out of his words, "especially so soon after I thought you would all go home to await my word."

"We await your word, Lord Davidon!" someone shouted from the back of the crowd.

"Very well," Cyrus said, stepping out of the gates. "The word is this: Run." He aimed a thumb behind him. "This coal yard will explode in mere minutes, and I want all of you out of here before it does. Grievous wounding could follow for any too close to the explosion, and so ..." He gestured, pushing his hands toward them. "Run." When no one moved, he sighed, then stared down the cross street that met the gates of the coal yard in a T. "At least go over there," he said, pointing to a corner a block away, in front of a butcher shop. "If you're standing here when this place blows up, you're likely to catch a mouthful of brick, and that'll ruin anyone's day."

"Nothing can ruin this day for me," came a voice laced with fury to his left. Cyrus leaned out from behind the gate and caught a glimpse of an elf dressed in the old style; a tunic covered in runes, ears pointed at the heavens. His face was youthful; if human, he'd have been in his thirties, with perfect teeth bared in a furious grimace. When he saw Cyrus, he drew a sword from beneath his brown cloak. Chain mail glittered at his neck and at the edge of his sleeves. The blade he carried was a broad sword of the old style, the kind of craftsmanship that made any human blade look like cheap garbage, fit only for practice swordplay. The elf stepped forward, keeping his blade low. "For this day, I have found another impersonator of the great Lord Davidon." He brought the sword around, pointing it right at Cyrus's face. "And for this insult ... it will my very great pleasure ... to remove your head from your shoulders."

22.

Shirri

A crowd had gathered once more, and Shirri was watching it with a wary and jaded eye. Her pulse ran at a rate far above normal, the coal dust crowding her sinuses and making her want to sneeze or cough.

She'd been waiting outside the coal yard for what felt like an hour but was probably just a few minutes. Every moment seemed like an eternity when she perched outside a Machine business or safe house, as though she were dangling herself in front of a feral beast that wanted to eat her.

No, Shirri didn't much care for that, and kept her cowl up. It was the flimsiest of disguises, but many people wore cowls in this city to keep the ash from the smokestacks from falling on them. At least it allowed her to blend in.

"You seem uneasy," a soft voice came from beside her, and Shirri nearly jumped from her skin. A moment ago she'd been alone, and now—

Now, Alaric stood next to her, his grey beard having lost the thin layer of ash that had accumulated during the walk. It was as though the coal dust and ash she'd seen upon him when they'd parted at the gates a few minutes ago had been washed clean.

Except ... that wasn't how it worked. He didn't look wet, as though he'd splashed his face. It was simply ... gone, the normal grey of his beard returned.

Shirri shook her head at him. He'd also come out of nowhere. "I don't know how you do that," she said, and she wasn't sure to which mystery she referred.

"They call me the Ghost," Alaric said with a smile, "for obvious reasons."

"Mm," Shirri said, a non-committal grunt. "My mother?"

"Not here." Alaric grew slightly stiffer. "I left Cyrus and Vara to ask more pointed questions of one of the Machine's servants than I felt comfortable doing."

Shirri frowned. "But ... if they follow your command and you're the leader—"

"I am not."

"Well, they seem to want to make you the leader," Shirri said.

"So they do," Alaric said, still stiff. "It is a misapprehension on their part; my leadership would call for greater scruples than they currently wish to employ. If they don't desire to follow that ..."

"Well, you kind of left them to do whatever they felt called to do, so ..." Shirri looked at him out of the corner of her eye, trying hard not to insult him given that he was one of a very, very few people actually available and willing to help her. "Doesn't that mean you sort of ... condone what they're doing?"

Alaric let out a deep sigh. "Perhaps I am. Perhaps I have." A weary look washed over him. "Perhaps I simply see the world moving in a direction that suggests honor is a thing of the past ... as am I."

"That's pretty deep," Shirri said, rubbing her eyes, "for so early in the morning."

"The day grows strong," Alaric said with that same faint smile that hinted at just the barest touch of mocking. "You cannot run forever without wearying."

"I'm not doing much running right now," Shirri said. "The walking is killing my feet enough as it is."

Alaric grew quiet for just a beat. "Are you safe on these streets?"

Shirri broke into a frown. "What do you mean?"

"This Machine ..." Alaric said. "They seem to take a great number of women."

Shirri lowered her head. "Yes, they do. It's one of their chief trades, I guess. Shipping them out from here to ... wherever. Lots of trade for them. But not just women." She looked up and shrugged. "Pretty men, too, I hear, though fewer of them."

"How do they go about this?" Alaric asked, and his countenance had grown stony.

"You name it," she said. "Grab them off the streets, if a Machine agent sees one they like the look of. Follow them back to their house, make a sport of it, rob the place, threaten or kill their family. I hear they like to find one young woman and then check her sisters and mother, see if they can make a package sale out of it." Shirri shuddered. "Sorry. These are the things you try not to think about."

"I don't know that I've ever been more revolted in my life," Alaric said. "Where do they send them?"

"All over the world," Shirri said. "Firoba, Imperial Amatgarosa, Coricuanthi. There's demand for us light-skinned backward savage sorts everywhere."

Alaric frowned. "Beg pardon?"

She stared at him. "Savages. Arkarians."

"I don't understand," Alaric said.

"We're the least developed place on the globe, Alaric," Shirri said. "Arkaria is a mess. Any one of the nations of Firoba could probably conquer the livable part of Arkaria if they weren't so busy fighting among themselves. And Imperial Amatgarosa and Coricuanthi— they've set up colonies before west of the Perda and abandoned them. We're not worth the trouble of maintaining a supply line, I hear."

"This doesn't make sense," Alaric said, looking at Reikonos around them, smokestacks in the distance chugging out a steady stream of ash. "This city ... it seems ever so much more prosperous than when I left."

Shirri laughed, but the sound was dull and ashen, like her cloak. "Oh, no. It's overcrowded. It takes fifty ships a day of food at minimum just to keep the populace from starving and rioting. People are the only resource we have in this city. The mills, the factories ... they're all driven by supplies coming from Emerald Fields, from Firoba—cut those off, this city withers and dies. We'd starve within the fortnight. No one lays siege to us because—who would want us? It's disgusting and dirty here, and the labor is already dirt cheap. No jewels, no minerals—even across the Perda, where they do have land and some resources, it's not worth the conquest. Everyone would rather fight for the golden cities of Amatgarosa or the green veldt of Coricuanthi or even the bickering principalities of Firoba—though they tend to unite pretty quickly if anyone outside of their continent turns an eye toward them. We're not worth the trouble," she said, still smiling ruefully. "So everyone leaves us alone to rot, and just takes our best export—people."

Alaric stood very still for a very long time. "I find this ... disturbing."

Shirri shrugged. "Anyway, you asked if I was safe on the street? Outside my little difficulty with the Machine, I'm perfectly safe from anyone but a cutpurse or a pickpocket. And they'll mostly just take your things, not your life. I'm too short, too thin, too unappealing for the Machine's skin traders. They want tall and lustrous, with good teeth and ample bosoms." She shrugged. "I'm perfectly safe on the street. Safer than you or your lot."

"Why would you say th—" Alaric turned his head as Shirri raised a finger to point at the gates of the coal yard across the way. He followed her finger to where Cyrus was being faced down by an elf dressed in the old style, a sword pointed at the warrior in black. "Oh," the Ghost said, and faded into mist before disappearing.

Shirri just stared at where he'd been a moment earlier, her eyes frozen, now staring at a shop halfway down the block. "How … the hell … does he do that …?" she muttered under her breath. And yet, of all the mysteries she'd encountered, somehow this one didn't cause the pressing sense of anxiety that the others provoked. After all, she reflected, turning back to watch the Cyrus Davidon impersonator's confrontation with the elf with the sword, it wasn't as though she hadn't seen any sort of magic before these strangers had shown up …

23.

Cyrus

"Wait," Cyrus said, peering at the elf as he closed, raising his ornate blade in a high guard. Cyrus let his hand fall to Praelior's pommel, felt the power run through him. The elf slowed; he was quick but lacked the enhancement bestowed by a godly weapon. Particles of dust seemed to freeze in the air before Cyrus's eyes, and the thick smell of ash and ruin that lingered in this place paused within his nose, settling as though it would never leave.

Cyrus stared into the elf's face, peering at him. It truly was youthful, which could mean anything for an elf. He could have been 5900 years old or less than forty; it would be impossible for him to tell, though Vara could likely make an accurate estimate of it.

"I will not wait to strike you down, dishonorer of the memory of the great one!" the elf said, swinging his sword high and preparing to bring it down on Cyrus.

Cyrus merely sidestepped out of the way and let him swing through to find nothing in his path. The elf staggered, the resistance he'd expected in the form of Cyrus's body merely gone.

The elf swung his head around, evincing surprise at Cyrus's sudden movement. He brought his blade back up, face contorting with anger. "Trickery, is it? You show your lack of honor—" And he came at him again.

"I know you," Cyrus said, sidestepping once more. "You used to pal around with that idiot dwarf—the one that stayed in the Southwest tower. I had to go up and visit him once because of a complaint about the smell in his quarters—"

The elf froze, then rage split his countenance. "You—lie!"

"No, I assure you the smell was quite real," Cyrus said, "like old leather boots soaked in brine—"

"You—are—not him!" The elf swung wildly once more, blade dancing just a foot from Cyrus's nose as he watched it slide slowly by. "Cyrus Davidon is dead!" The elf drew back his blade. "Humans do not live a thousand years!" And he swung his sword again.

The elf's blade clashed with another, ringing out. Cyrus watched it impact and took a step back; it had met Ferocis in midair and was easily turned aside.

"What about me?" Vara asked, holding the Warblade before her, her eyes locked on the elf's. "Do you find me similarly afflicted in lifespan ... Hiressam, wasn't it?" The elf's mouth fell agape. "I recall you from the year of the siege. We manned the bulwarks together one cold night when the dark elves pressed in. You told me you were from ... Traegon, wasn't it?"

"But ... you died?" The elf—Hiressam—sounded as though his voice had turned to ash.

"Yet I stand before you," Vara said, as his blade withdrew and she kept hers at guard before her. "As does my husband."

The elf stood there, utterly still, for but a moment. His eyes flicked, wide, from Vara to Cyrus, and then back again. He moved, swiftly—

And fell to his knees, grabbing his weapon by the blade and thrusting the hilt between the two of them.

"My Lord Davidon ... my Lady Shelas'akur," he croaked, head bowed. "I beseech you—forgive me. So many imposters have besmirched your names these last thousand years. I have but tried to do my part to keep the stain of these usurpers from your honor."

Alaric appeared out of mist, his own blade drawn. "This ... is a curious spectacle."

Hiressam looked up, and his mouth fell even wider. "Lord Garaunt?"

Alaric cocked his head. "I recall you ... you came to us after the fall of the Dragonlord."

Hiressam nodded and bowed his head once more. "I served loyally for many years." He looked at Cyrus. "I was with you in the Trials of Purgatory ... in Enterra ... at Termina ... and at Livlosdald and Leaugarden. I fought in your Gradsden Savanna campaign and ..." Here he looked down once more. "I failed you ... after that."

Cyrus felt a small tingle. "You left when I was declared heretic, didn't you?"

Hiressam seemed to bow his head so low Cyrus did not know how he managed to keep from snapping his own spine. "It is my greatest regret." He raised his head, tears in his eyes. "I abandoned you at your hour of greatest need. And when you went to fight—to save us from the gods gone mad—I was not there." He swallowed; Cyrus could almost imagine the lump in the elf's throat. "It is my bitterest regret. I was a fool who made a terrible error—one I have a spent a thousand years trying to atone for."

"Indeed," Cyrus said. "That's quite the long penance, Hiressam— especially for a transgression I didn't even recall, nor one I would have held you to account for." He stepped forward and offered a hand to the elf. "Many people left when I was declared heretic. Practically the entire guild, in fact. You could hardly be blamed for not wanting to fight back the entirety of Arkaria."

"But you fought back the entirety of Arkaria." Hiressam looked up at him with dull eyes. "You ended the tyranny of the elven kingdom that year. You fought back and toppled the unjust and corrupt Human Confederation. With fewer people than ever, you stormed the very realms of the gods with your loyal chosen and changed the world." His eyes were aglow. "And I—in my disloyalty—failed you." And here he bowed his head once more, thrusting his hilt toward Cyrus.

Cyrus exchanged a look with Vara, who shrugged. "Uhm, well ... I'm not going to execute you for something you did a thousand years ago that wasn't even a crime then, so ... I'm not sure what you want to do here, Hiressam."

"And we have other places to be," Vara said. "In fact—" And she threw her hands up and then waved them at the crowd, who had stepped back to let this clash play out, awestruck and quiet. "Get the hell out of here, the coal yard is about to explode!"

She was not quiet nor nice about it, and the crowd began to flee, going from a ripple of uncertainty about it to a full break-and-run panic in a mere second. When they were safely on their way, Cyrus thrust his hand at Hiressam again. "Come on," he said, "let's get out of the way so we can blow up this coal yard and be on about our business."

"What business is that?" Hiressam asked, regarding Cyrus's hand with a sort of careful awe, then taking it and allowing himself to be pulled to his feet.

"Breaking apart the Machine," Cyrus said, "rescuing a young woman's kidnapped mother from them. You know, the usual—doing good."

Hiressam blinked twice. "Breaking ... the Machine?" He blinked once more, utterly neutral of expression. "You don't play small, do you?"

Cyrus smiled. "Well, after you've wrecked the gods of Arkaria, helping an old lady cross the street seems a bit of a comedown. Even destroying a well-established network of criminals is a slight step down from where we were, but … with magic being what it is …" And he stuck out his finger, casting the fire spell, and trying to focus it as large and as angled as he could.

A burst of sparking flame shot from his fingertip in a parabolic arc toward the interior of the coal yard. It was tiny, no more than the size of one of the bullets he loaded into the pistols, but it streaked into the yard. About a hundred feet in, it seemed to spark, and there came a flash—

The boom that followed a second later sent Cyrus flying, hurling his legs above his head and tilting him into the street. He landed like he'd been flung by a god, armor rattling as he rolled to a stop some fifty feet from where he'd started. His head rang as if Vaste had clapped him on the helm with Letum over and over for a fortnight, and a little blood oozed out of his nose.

"Perhaps next time," Vara's voice asserted itself loudly into his consciousness, which seemed dark around the edges, "you might warn us so we can step farther away before you blow something up."

"I'll … keep that in mind," Cyrus said, warring against the gonging in his head that seemed to be trying to disrupt his ability to hold a thought. A hand appeared before him. He took it and was pulled to his feet. He found himself looking into Alaric's eye, which twinkled with amusement. "That just passed right through you, didn't it?"

"I am a ghost," Alaric said with a smile, then bent to offer Hiressam a hand as well. The elf was bleeding from a cut in his forehead, but had maintained his grip on his sword through the flight. That was the sign of a true warrior to Cyrus.

"Yeah, I wanted to be one as well," Cyrus said, tapping on the side of his helm. He could hear it, which he took as a sign, along with Alaric and Vara's statements, that he had not gone utterly deaf from the explosion. "But it would appear I'm just a junior ghost, unable to manage the feats of excellence that a full ghost can."

"You'll get there," Alaric said, now standing before the mighty flames that were towering out of the coal yard. "Provided you keep your distance the next time you light something extremely combustible. Perhaps, in fact, it might be better left to me while you indulge a good run to your next target—General."

"I'll keep that in mind," Cyrus said, opening and closing his jaw, trying in vain to equalize the pressure in his head. It was as though he'd gotten water in his ear that he couldn't get out no matter how hard he tried. "Sometimes I have a hard time delegating the dangerous tasks."

"It's not dangerous for me," Alaric said. "I could have stood in the middle of the yard and lit it afire. Keep that in mind next time."

"Let us hope it is a while before there is a next time of that sort," Vara said. There was blood on her face as well, though from where he couldn't tell. It stopped shortly beneath her helm, and he realized after a brief moment of trying to get his thoughts together that she had probably healed it. "Lest the city be blown over by the mere effort on our part to knock over this Machine."

"You have chosen a worthy target," Hiressam said as the light of a very small healing spell danced upon his forehead, and Cyrus saw Vara's hand twinkle. Hiressam reached up to feel the spot where his wound had been and a small smile spread across his lips. "I had forgotten the touch of magic in these days. It has been so long since I have even seen it."

"Do you know what happened to it?" Cyrus asked. "Magic, I mean?"

Hiressam shook his head. "When you killed the gods, the Leagues were overthrown—here, and back home. I thought it would result in more spellcasters—and it did, for a time. But without the Leagues, it wasn't taught as it once was. Five hundred years ago, spellcasters started to diminish. We were already sundered, with over half the land lost to the Scourge. Other principalities were closing in. It just … sort of disappeared, almost overnight, I would say. Now, as divided as this land is, there is no unifying force. You will still find magic in Pharesia—or you did, when last I was there. But elsewhere …" He shook his head. "It is as near to gone as you could imagine."

"That's disappointing," Cyrus said, and looked at the billowing flames of the coal yard. "I have questions—so many questions. Ones you might be able to answer better than our other guide." He looked around and saw Shirri lurking a short distance from Alaric, watching them carefully, and opening and closing her mouth like she, too, was trying to regain her hearing.

Hiressam stared at him for a moment, then hit his knees once more, thrusting his sword's hilt at Cyrus. "I failed you before," he said, speaking over the crackle of the flames. "I abandoned you in your darkest hour." He looked up, and his eyes burned like a reflection of the fires raging in the coal yard. "I will not fail you again. And I will never, ever, abandon you—" His gaze flicked to Vara as she came to stand next to Cyrus, "—either of you—again." He bowed his head. "My sword is yours, as is my loyalty—if you command it."

Cyrus looked at Vara, and she looked back at him. "Magic is near useless here," he said. "And we've decided to bite off quite the large chunk in taking on this Machine. Right out of our long slumber, too."

"I have doubts about this Shirri," Vara said, low. "Probably as many as she purports to have about us. Hiressam was a true member of Sanctuary in the days when he stood with us. I find no more fault in him leaving when he did than I think you do." Cyrus nodded along with her, and she went on. "Trust will be a difficult thing in this new world, and we seem to be accumulating new hangers-on already." She pointed to the crowd, which was already meandering back, some more quickly than others. "It would be nice to have one who believed in us before we died and disappeared. Someone who understands that by our absence, we have missed much."

"Aye," Alaric said, causing them both to jerk as he entered their conversational huddle in a ghostly glide. He smiled at their surprise. "In a world new and unproven, it is nice to have some tried and true brethren to rely upon."

"Hiressam," Cyrus said, turning back to the elf, "Rise." When he did, Cyrus waved a hand at him. "Welcome back to Sanctuary." And then, inspired, he smiled, and said words that had once rung like a small, welcoming bell, in his own heart: "Welcome home."

The elf's trembled as he stood, and he drew a breath. "You don't know ... how I've longed to hear those words this last millennia. It has been ..." He stopped and looked away, into the fire, then, after a moment to compose himself, he looked back to Cyrus, Vara, and Alaric, each in turn. "I will not fail you again," he said, resolve hardening his voice, "and if I may serve you with my life—or my death—you need but ask."

"Let's hope it doesn't come to that last thing," Cyrus said, clapping him on the shoulder. "Now come on—we've got a mill to go knock over and a Machine to break to pieces." And he was off once more, Vara at his side, Alaric and Shirri but a few steps behind him.

And now, too, Hiressam, Cyrus realized as he cast a glance back, the elf walking with pride and determination as he trailed in their wake, the crowd slowly getting themselves together to follow once more. "Looks like we're beginning again after all, Vaste," Cyrus said under his breath. And to this, he saw Vara smile.

24.

Vaste

"That is not how you do it!" Curatio's shout echoed through the Halls of Healing, and indeed, probably through the whole of Sanctuary. It was done largely through gritted teeth, and Vaste caught a scent of his stale breath, hints of the feast they'd had before leaving to assault the candle shop, as he tried to hold the Healer's hand still to extract the metal bullet.

"I'm sorry I haven't practiced my surgical skills the way you have in the last twenty thousand years," Vaste said, jerking Curatio's hand back to center again, a pair of blood-covered tweezers far too small for him to wield clenched in his fingers. "And furthermore, I'm sorry you've had your instrumentation built for people with tiny fingers and not, you know, normal-sized ones—"

"There is little normal about you, *my friend*," Curatio said, looking away as he seethed. The last words came bitterly, cursing Vaste, though the troll little cared. Pain brought out even minor grievances and inflamed them far beyond proportion. "And I begin to suspect your mind is not on the task at hand."

That much was probably true. Vaste sniffed, the scent of blood aggravating his nostrils. This was hardly where he wanted to be, after all. He made to move the tweezers again, attempting to make another go of extracting the bullet, but brushed a flap of hanging skin and then the bone, which caused Curatio to groan and yank his hand away.

"Are you paying attention at all to what you are doing?" Curatio cradled his wounded hand.

"Well," Vaste said, brandishing the tweezers, "I haven't accidentally jammed these in your eye yet, so … yes. At least somewhat."

"Give them to me," Curatio said, snatching them. He turned and opened a drawer in the desk that sat along one wall of the Halls of Healing, then sat stiffly upon the small bed where they'd been working, closing his eyes for a long moment.

"Are you going to meditate now?" Vaste asked, watching him, then eyeing the door.

"I'm going to lower my heart rate before attempting the delicate removal of this foreign object lodged in my body," Curatio said, not opening his eyes. "Enhancing my calm is instrumental in insuring that I do not accidentally stab myself in every exposed nerve while trying to clumsily strike at this as though it were a foe to be crushed."

Vaste eased back from the bed. "I'll just give you the space to do that, why don't I?"

One of Curatio's eyes opened, slitted, and found him. "Stay right where you are. If I pass out, you'll need to do this while I am unconscious and unable to resist."

"You make it sound so romantic," Vaste said, prompting Curatio to snort, a reluctant smile playing at the corner of his lips as he closed his eyes once more. "How long is this going to take?"

"Not long, I hope, since I have mere minutes to cast the healing spell before the time runs out," Curatio said, then opened his eyes. Turning slightly pensive, he looked down at the wound. "Let us hope the constrictions upon magic in this new world have not diminished the window for the efficacy of healing spells."

"That would be unfortunate for your hand," Vaste said. "And you, I suppose."

"Indeed," Curatio said, positioning his hand upon his lap. "I can envisage a host of unfortunate consequences as a result." He gritted his teeth and looked up, taking the tweezers delicately in hand. "Now—if you'll pardon me for a moment—"

He brought the tweezers down with greatest delicacy into the open wound, peering intently at the work he was doing. He moved subtly, slowly, and Vaste licked his lips as he watched. A bulb of sweat ran down the elf's forehead, and his brow furrowed, dropping it past his eyes. "Damn," Curatio breathed, reaching up to mop it with the hand holding the tweezers.

An inspiration struck Vaste. "Hold on," he said, and snatched up Letum where he'd left it resting on the wall. He grabbed it at the top and swung it low and slow until it was touching Curatio's wounded hand.

Curatio sucked in a deep breath, and with amazing sureness, slipped the tweezers back into the wound. It was over in a moment, the metal ball dropping from beneath their pronged grasp and clinking onto the stone floor. A muttered incantation and it was done, the wound closed tightly, only pink skin beneath a thin layer of drying blood to mark its passage.

"Clever," Curatio said, pushing Letum away now that the job was finished. "It diminished the pain and sped up my reaction. It was as though I could do the thing in slowest movement, but with elevated acuity."

"Don't thank me, thank the God of Death for making it possible," Vaste said, clinking Letum's bottom tip against the floor with a thud. "After all, I'm guessing he doesn't get much thanks, given that he essentially destroyed all of Arkaria."

"I hope Arkaria sees it that way," Curatio said ruefully, rising to his feet. "For I doubt many who inhabit these halls do."

"Yes, there is an epidemic of blame that goes around every time the scourge pop up in conversation," Vaste said. "As though any of us intended to unleash that bloody horde. All we wanted to do was save you and Vara and our own beautiful arses—in some of our cases, anyway—not destroy everything."

"And yet … the consequences remain," Curatio said. "I may aim that weapon at you," and he pointed at Letum, "intending to merely rap you upon the head as you have so often done to Cyrus of late, but if you move even slightly toward it, I might strike out your eye by accident. And while the intention was not there to harm you, you would nonetheless—"

"Look like a beautiful, green, immense version of Alaric, but with more majesty and less mystique," Vaste said. "Curse the loss of magic that would force me into an eyepatch for life."

"You haven't lost it yet, fool," Curatio said with a thin smile. "And hopefully you never will. Magic remains potent enough that I believe we could heal such a small thing as an eye loss."

"That's good," Vaste said, drawing a hand to his cheekbone, "because I've finally seen something with them worth looking for again, and I'd hate to lose that now that I've found—"

"Oh, gods, you're on about this troll woman again, aren't you?" Curatio said, flexing his hand experimentally.

"I saw her, Curatio. Beautiful and tall and green and—"

"Yes, yes," Curatio waved him off.

A burst of mist ran across the floor then, growing into a pillar the size of a man and coalescing into the form of Alaric Garaunt, and all in mere in seconds. Vaste frowned, staring at him. With Letum in hand, he did appear much more slowly than without. Vaste reached out and brought down his staff, right onto Alaric's head as he appeared—

"Ouch," Alaric said, the staff rapping him squarely on the bucket-shaped helm and staggering him back a step as he appeared. He flinched and then opened his good eye, locking in on Vaste. "What the hell was that for?"

"I was testing something," Vaste said. "Are you always vulnerable when you appear like that?"

Alaric sighed, reaching up to adjust his helm, which had gone slightly sideways from the blow. "Perhaps. I can't recall anyone ever striking me coming out of the ether like that."

"You should be wary, then," Vaste said. "If you appear before someone who has a godly weapon, you come so slowly that it makes you easily strikeable."

"Thank you for that insight," Alaric said, sounding more annoyed than grateful.

"I live to help," Vaste said.

"And also to find a troll woman, apparently," Curatio said. He wore a smile, and was looking at Alaric.

"What is this?" Alaric asked, finally leaving his helm alone.

"I don't think—" Vaste started to say.

"He found a troll girl," Curatio said. "On the street. Or so he says. I did not see her myself."

"You make it sound like I imagined—" Vaste started.

"A troll woman?" Alaric was smiling now, too. "Truly?"

"Yes, truly," Vaste said. "She was right there, plain as the eyepatch on your face, taller than the crowd, green as sweet swamp moss—"

Alaric and Curatio exchanged smiles, and Vaste found his blood boiling. "You're making fun of me," the troll said.

"Not at all," Alaric said, then touched the spot on his helm where Vaste had struck him. "Perhaps a little bit. But I have seen so many of my guildmates fall under love's intoxicating spell. I suppose I never thought I would see it from you, Vaste."

"I'm not in love," Vaste said crossly. "I've merely seen a beautiful troll woman in a town and world where I'm told there are no more trolls, let alone ones that might catch my fancy. Forgive me for being slightly … uh … intrigued."

Alaric's smile was infuriating. "It is nice to see you go this way at last, brother."

"Stop 'brothering' me," Vaste said, grumbling. "I don't even know where this woman is. Perhaps Curatio is right. Perhaps she's just a figment of my sexy, overactive imagination. Maybe she doesn't exist at all except in my longing, in my dreams, in those watches of night when I awake and am—"

"I don't think I need to hear anymore about this," Alaric said, looking to Curatio. "Cyrus and the others have moved on to a mill, and are on their way there now, after encountering a former member of Sanctuary."

"Truly?" Curatio asked. "Who was it?"

"His name is Hiressam," Alaric said.

"Sounds like an elven name," Vaste said with distaste.

"I recall him well," Curatio said. "He is indeed an elf—from Traegon, as I recall." He frowned at Vaste. "And what is wrong with elves?"

"They're arrogant and annoying," Vaste said. "Don't we have enough arrogant elves among our little band already?"

"You can never have too many elves," Curatio said, smiling once more.

"Yes, you can," Vaste said. "I think the limit is two, and no more. After that, all you get is arguments about who is oldest and wisest and fairest—and you know, whatever else you people argue about when you get together. The best vegetables, perhaps." He shuddered.

"We will take our allies where we can," Alaric said, "and thus far, he does not exude arrogance. A heavy dose of regret and longing for the old days of Sanctuary, it appears—but not arrogance."

"Who wouldn't consider hanging around with us and killing gods the highlight of their life?" Vaste asked. "I mean, really, how do you even find something exciting to do after that?"

"You should ask Cyrus and Vara," Curatio said. "Though I think the answer would involve a door being left open—"

"Crass," Vaste said, looking at the door to the Halls of Healing and wishing he could walk through it. He felt a strange tear; duty lay at the mill, with Cyrus and the others, but—

Had he really seen that troll woman?

"I can tell the calling of your heart, my brother," Alaric said. "You should go and look for her."

Vaste cocked an eyebrow at him. "Truly?"

"I will go with Alaric," Curatio said. "I don't imagine one more godly weapon will contribute greatly to our fight, and there's little one healer can do in these conditions."

"Go and look for her," Alaric said, shifting to stand next to Curatio. "I will come and aid you once I've returned Curatio to the others."

"Well, that'd be two godly weapons out of the task at hand," Vaste said, shaking his head. "No, you go, Alaric. Help them. I probably won't get into much trouble on my own—"

Alaric's and Curatio's snickers drowned him out, and he paused, annoyed.

"Sorry," Alaric said, "but I find every time someone says something of that sort to me, they immediately land themselves in immense trouble."

"You're not wrong," Vaste said. "Perhaps you should look in on me after a while."

"I will," Alaric said, putting an arm around Curatio, as the two of them started to fade. "Take great care in following this dictate of your heart, my friend. It is a new world after all, and while we are quite accustomed to you and how you conduct yourself ... this city might not be quite ready for two of your kind wandering about." And with that, he was gone.

"It never was," Vaste said, turning upon his heel and going for the door, a spring to his step. "Not even when there were many more of us here." And off he went to seek out the one who might remain.

25.

Cyrus

"I'm sorry, who are you? What is this?" An insipid, sniffing little man in a black suit with a white shirt hidden beneath it made his way over to Cyrus as they entered the mill. Cyrus could understand the sniffing; the place had an oily, musty smell that irritated his nostrils.

"This …" Cyrus said, looking around, "… is an inspection." There was a whole lot of grinding going on, a mechanical monstrosity making deafening noise as it churned, spinning slowly as it worked the grains. He couldn't entirely see the process, but it was interesting to hear the hisses of hot air being belched out of machinery, the whistle of it out of others. Cyrus would have estimated a hundred, two hundred workers were in this room. Steel catwalks interlaced above them, providing an easy look-down for anyone spying from above. A few souls were doing just that, occasionally shouting down upon the browbeaten workers, every one of whom had the same hangdog look.

"That's preposterous," the little sniffing man said. "Why, we're paid up with the appropriate authorities. You have no cause to inspect us."

Cyrus turned to look at Hiressam. "That's how it works here? You just pay them and they don't inspect you?"

The elf shrugged. "It's corrupt, yes."

"Truly," Cyrus said, bringing his head back around. Vara stood at his shoulder, her own cloak pulled tight. "No, I don't like that. I don't like that at all."

"I don't give a fig for what you like," the sniffing man said. "If you have a problem with it, take it up with your superiors at the inspection board."

Cyrus raised an eyebrow at that, then stepped closer to the little man, whose eyes grew larger. Cyrus recognized the look; he'd just realized for the first time that the big, scary men who normally stood behind him in any dealing with the government weren't actually, physically standing behind him right now. "I don't have any superiors," Cyrus said, "at the inspection board or anywhere else. I am a law unto myself. And my law is about to be applied to the men who run this place." He leaned in closer, to the point where he could smell the sniffling man's breath. "Where are the men who work for the Machine?"

The sniffing man pursed his lips and all the color went out of them. "I—I—"

"Think very carefully as you answer," Cyrus said, drawing Praelior. "Ask yourself: 'Is delaying this large and threatening man—this muscular specimen of decency and goodness'—"

Vara coughed loudly. "Mmm. Sorry."

Cyrus rolled his eyes at her. "'Is delaying this handsome, large and threatening man worth my very life?'" And Cyrus shot her a sweet look, which she returned by smiling and barely keeping in a laugh. *Ah, well. At least she thought it amusing.* If he was being honest with himself, half of what he did anymore was to impress or amuse his wife. Turning his attention back to the man, he added, "And trust me—it would only be a short delay. This isn't a large place, and after turning you into a slippery stain on my boot, I will find them. Quickly."

"They are in the offices," the man said, pointing at a nearby metal staircase that wound its way up to the catwalks above. There in the corner of the room was a large, jutting section of brick that exposed only a few glass windows to hint at its purpose. It looked down over the factory floor, and Cyrus scowled. The workers needed to be watched, he supposed, but they didn't seem particularly ... voluntary. He studied the one closest to him and saw chains. Chains that bound the man into line along with others.

"What the hell is this all about?" Cyrus asked, leaning to point at one of the chained men. "Do you pay your workers?"

The sniffling man's mouth opened. "I—I am not in the payroll department—"

"Slave labor, then," Vara said. Her eyes grew narrow and her voice cold.

"It's—they're—" the man started to say.

Cyrus decked him with one punch, leveling him and knocking him into a piece of mill equipment. It hadn't been something he'd intended, but neither did he feel particularly guilty about it. The man slumped, and Cyrus reached down, searching his pockets for keys. He came up with a whole ring of them, black steel and jangling, and tossed them to Hiressam. "See if you can figure out which of those unlocks the chains on these workers. Let's free the slaves again, shall we?"

"Aye, m'lord," Hiressam said, sweeping into action. He leapt down to the nearest machine, with its group of workers huddled around it. They were all staring up now, almost oblivious to the shouts of overseers now thundering down from above. They'd all seen Cyrus's punch lay out the sniffling man—here and nearly to the end of the mill, Cyrus realized, seeing so many faces looking at him at once.

"Well," Cyrus said, shedding his cloak, "no point in bothering with the element of surprise anymore."

"Indeed not," Vara said, carefully draping her own cloak over a nearby railing. Cyrus had merely let his fall to the floor. "When my husband insists on knocking out diminutive idiots who present little to no physical threat. And where the entire mill can see it, no less."

"He was basically a slaver and admitted to it," Cyrus growled, drawing Praelior as the clang of boots on the overhead walks echoed down to him. "Forgive me for not simply letting him walk away after that admission."

"I don't fault you for it," she said quietly as she drew Ferocis. "Hell, I was considering belting him myself. But," and here her eyes glimmered with amusement, "you cannot possibly expect me not to give you shit for it, you intemperate man."

"'*Handsome*, intemperate man,'" Cyrus added. Her smile grew bigger as a couple of thugs drew closer, leaping over the railings to the nearest staircase and running for them both.

Cyrus blurred into action, ramming Praelior's hilt into the face of the nearest one. They were wielding daggers again, as though no one in this city save for Hiressam had the sense to carry a blade with some reach to it. At least they could have carried pistols, Cyrus thought, putting the other one down with a viciously hard punch. The man went airborne for a few feet and slammed into a piece of machinery, making it rattle and then grind to a halt.

"Gee, I hope I didn't just break something important in this slave shop," Cyrus said as the deafening noise faded. The sound was quickly replaced by the men who'd been working around the machine. They held up their chains and started to rattle them, shouting a garbled mix of excitement and supplication.

"I don't think you've broken nearly enough in here," Vara said, greeting an incoming overseer with a kick that sent the man flying. He hit the catwalks above and the entire upper level shook. Then he came crashing back down on a grinder, and a moment later— Cyrus cringed. It wasn't a pretty thing, what the machine did to a human body. He could clearly hear the sound of crunching bones half a hundred feet away, and the spray of blood was blessedly short, if astoundingly geyser-like. "I don't know that I would have broken that—or at least not in quite that way," he said, still cringing. "That's no way to go, even for a slaver."

"My conscience remains clear," Vara said, raising her gauntlet as another overseer ran up and slashed at her with a whip. She caught the end of the lash on her gauntlet and wrapped it around swiftly, then yanked him forward with the speed granted her by Ferocis. Taken completely by surprise, he flew toward her, and she met him with a punch that smashed his face into a nearly unrecognizable mass.

Below, Cyrus could see Hiressam hurriedly unchaining the captives. They were running out as soon as they were freed, bolting for the doors in ones and twos. Each manacle had to be unlocked independently, which made Cyrus wonder how exactly they let these people out in the evenings. *Probably just keep them chained up everywhere they go*, he thought. *If they let them leave at all.*

The plight of the slaves was momentarily forgotten as Cyrus heard thundering footsteps above. The door to the office in the corner was now thrown wide, five or six men running above them across the catwalks. The clanking was prodigious, heavy boots on strong metal, but the sway of it at the joints where it was bolted together made it sound as though the whole thing might come crashing down on them at any moment.

"We're about to have company," Cyrus said as Vara threw a punch that sent an overseer into a piece of machinery, hard. He met the metal with his spine, and Cyrus heard something break. The man's eyes fluttered, and down he went, keeling over as limply as if he'd had his head lopped off.

Vara showed little interest and even less remorse. "Good. I feel compelled to right many wrongs today, and to make many a man wake up either changed of mind or not wake up at all."

"Well, you're succeeding on that score," Cyrus said, casting another look to the most recently fallen of the overseers. He didn't feel much pity for them either; such wantonly cruel inflictions of harm on chained people? And not even prisoners who'd done some terrible wrong like murder. These were slaves, taken against their will and bound for cheap labor. It all turned Cyrus's stomach, and although he did not wish to do violence to them quite as strongly as his wife did, the desire was still present, burning like an ulcer in the pit of his

156

stomach.

"HALT!" A voice crackled down from above, and Cyrus looked up. Several of the pairs of boots running across the catwalk had already reached the stairs and were descending. One pair, though …

One pair was taking its sweet time.

Cyrus looked over the others. Grubby toughs, exactly what he'd come to expect of the Machine thus far. Interchangeable pieces of corruption, with a foul air and foul aura about them. Their hair was greasy, their skin dirty and ash-streaked in a way that coupled naturally with the cruel expressions that had settled on their faces from long wear. Their black leather coats were the cleanest thing about them, those armbands with the symbology of the Machine clearly issued with the coats in some sort of mass production, to let the people of Reikonos know that they were dealing with the gears of the Machine. The look on their faces, though—Cyrus could always tell a cruel man by looking at him; they had a certain expression almost burned in, like a stain upon them.

The toughs hung close by the stairwells, watching Cyrus and Vara from across the room as the last of them—the master who'd shouted a halt, descended more slowly, taking his time. Cyrus cast a look at Hiressam; the elf had freed fewer than half the slaves, by Cyrus's reckoning. There were so many slaves, and so many keys. Cyrus wondered if they all used the same key or if they simply had a different key for every set of manacles. That seemed a ridiculous idea, yet it was taking Hiressam seemingly forever to loose them.

"What have we here?" Vara asked, coming over to stand by Cyrus as they awaited the ringleader of the Machine's garrison in the mill. Blood dripped from her left gauntlet, running into the lobstered crevices. "Another of these ignorant fools?"

Cyrus scanned over the toughs that awaited their master. Once more, he saw some pistols drawn, a few daggers, but not a single one of them possessed a sword with any reach. He reached down to pull one of his own pistols, figuring on firing them all in rapid succession if need be, dropping any of the shooters with his own-placed shots before they could manage to fire. "I'm glad you wore your helm today," Cyrus said, trying to step carefully in front of Vara.

She caught his motion and shoved him aside, frowning. "My armor can catch their rounds almost as well as yours."

He gave her an even look. "Your mystical steel cannot catch the bullets as well as quartal, my dear. While you may have many superior qualities, the metal of your armor does not become more resistant simply by virtue of you wearing it."

She seethed, and then nodded slightly, allowing him to step in front of her. But the moment he did, she took the pistol he had at the small of his back. A click indicated she had drawn back the hammer. He did not bother to look at her, not now, not when he knew she'd be wearing a smile of satisfaction. She placed her wrist on his arm, steadying herself. "I take it by watching your motions that the explosion as these things go off causes them to jump quite a bit?"

"Aye," Cyrus said, seeing the legs of the arch villain of this place emerge around the last set of stairs from the catwalk. "Keep your hand on Ferocis when you fire and it shouldn't be much of a problem. More startling than anything, but I expect if you didn't handle it properly, it might throw off your aim."

"We wouldn't want that now, would we?" Vara asked, breathing slowly and steadily behind him.

"Indeed not," came the voice of their enemy, descending now the last set of steps. If there had been any doubt in Cyrus's mind that this fellow was of a different mold than the toughs that surrounded him, watching him descend the stairs put an end to that notion.

He wore fine leather boots that had plenty of mud and dirt on them. They rose to mid-calf, and were met there by bloused pants. Not the sort a simple dandy would wear, either; coupled with the dirty boots, Cyrus already formed the image of a man who was equally comfortable fitting into society or getting his hands dirty in the manner he chose. The man wore a long waistcoat, black like any Machine member, and it covered a red tunic of the old style, the sort Cyrus hadn't seen yet in this city. It was all very well made, and a sword peeked out from beneath the coat at his waist. The man had his hand on the pommel, and the look on his face when he came down the last set of steps?

Pure cruelty, mingled with a resonant confidence. His hair was shoulder length and dark, and his face was ruddy enough that Cyrus's image of a man who was no dandy was confirmed. His knuckles looked worn, like they'd thrown their share of punches, but his face lacked scars, which told Cyrus he was good enough to avoid being hit.

"I suppose you call yourself Cyrus Davidon," the man said, looking amused. He shifted his gaze to Vara. "And that means you don't have to tell me what your name is, darling."

"Oh, I'm looking forward to putting one of these bullets between this one's eyes," Vara said.

"The pistols make it hard for me to take you seriously as the real Cyrus Davidon," the man went on, still smirking. His voice was different, his accent out of place in this Reikonos, Cyrus realized. It was a strange thing; people here tended to speak faster, clip their words in odd ways, but this man …

He spoke a lot closer to what Cyrus was used to. And his hand just rested on the pommel of that sword, which—

Cyrus's blood ran cold, and he elbowed Vara, vambrace clinking against the armor at her belly.

"What?" she whispered.

"His sword," Cyrus said, mouth suddenly very dry.

"You like this?" The man drew his blade, and seeing it come free—and fast, too, far faster than had it been a normal sword—sent icy chills running down Cyrus's skin. "I've had it for a long while. Longer than you might believe." The man leered at him.

It was curved at the front edge, had a thick wooden hilt, curved at the guard—and looked horribly familiar. The man took it and pointed it right at Cyrus. "Now that we know your name, let me tell you mine—I am Tirner Gaull, and I am—"

"A thief and a murderer," Cyrus said, rage pumping through his veins as he stared at the blade. "Where did you get that sword?"

Tirner Gaull blinked at him, still amused, and then looked at the sword as though seeing it for the first time. "Why, it's mine, of course. Has been for … so very long."

"Before it was yours—it was mine," Cyrus said, "and my mother's before that, and my father's before that." He stared at the edge, fury coupling with hunger and a keen, sudden desire to see that sword ripped from Tirner Gaull's grasp. "Its name is Rodanthar, and it is called the Saber of the Righteous …"

Cyrus stared him down, cool resolution blazing through his heart, replacing that sense of worried alarm that had overtaken him when first he'd laid eyes on the blade. This would, perhaps, be a difficult fight.

But it would be worth it to take back what was his.

"And I'm going to rip it back from your dead fingers."

26.

Vaste

Finding the place where he'd seen the beautiful troll girl was not particularly difficult. Vaste's memory, even for the complex and convoluted streets of Reikonos, was more than equal to the task. He followed the sequence of turns he'd made when dragging Curatio back to Sanctuary, ignoring the stink of the city, ignoring the rising clatter of wagons, the whinny of horses and the streams of well-dressed and ill-dressed people, all in peculiar clothing, and even one rattling, thumping, strange machine upon wheels that he couldn't explain.

None of that mattered at the moment. Oh, certainly, it'd all be worth looking at more closely soon—save for perhaps the fashions. Those he didn't give a fig about. After all, it was unlikely they made those fancy waistcoats with the long tails in his size. Only one thing mattered now.

Finding her.

He made his way to the exact spot where he'd seen her. There, in the midst of swarming people upon the sidewalks, he paused, the crowd streaming around him. Some of them wore the most appalling colognes, the sort of thing that wouldn't have been out of place in a swamp. He attracted more than a few looks, he could tell, but kept his cowl up and remained bent nearly double, which still carved out quite a sizable space upon the sidewalk.

The scent of burning coal and ash was thick in the air, and looking at where his cloak covered his arm he saw a heavy dusting of grey. He peered up at a smokestack in the distance. Whatever it was they were creating here, it certainly seemed to leave quite the mess. He choked a little on the air thinking about it. Reikonos had never exactly smelled like posies, but it seemed much worse now, as did everything else.

But it would be worth the change if he could just find—

She'd been right here. The crowd ebbed around him, leaving him room, probably wondering what such a large man was doing stopped in the middle of a sidewalk. He caught a few grunts of displeasure as people detoured around him. They all seemed to be in an incredible hurry. Where did they need to go? And so quickly?

He shook that thought off, focusing on what was important. She'd been standing here, and then, when he looked again, she'd been gone. If she'd moved to her right, she'd have been in the road. He took a couple long steps over, drawing sounds of exasperation from passersby who practically had to dive out of the way to avoid his bulk as he moved. Vaste gave no care for their inconvenience; his was clearly much larger, now being trapped in a city of Cyrus Davidon worshippers and hemmed in by the damnable scourge, which brought out Mopey Cyrus, which was perhaps even more annoying than Insatiably Lusty Cyrus.

Reaching the curb, he looked down. It was a mere six inches or so, and the road, while slightly uneven because of the cobbles, was hardly low to the point where the troll woman would have simply disappeared to below head height had she stepped down into the street. No, she didn't go this way.

Looking forward, then back, he returned to his position in the middle of the sidewalk, drawing more noises of consternation and a, "Well, I never!" from some tutting woman. He gave little consideration to these morons who revered a man in black armor who was not a god and never would be to Vaste, no matter how mopey or insatiable he became. Or perhaps because of those things. Vaste could see the faults in Cyrus Davidon as clearly as he could the subtle lines on the back of his own hand. They might not be visible to others, especially at the distance most people kept from him, but they were there.

Just like the cracks in the Lord Davidon persona. Vaste had known Cyrus for too long to see him as anything other than a man. A brilliant tactician and strategist? Certainly. But blind in his own ways, and frail and fallible. How long had it taken his pigheaded arse to finally get together with Vara? Pride had gotten in the way of that, even though the two of them had been practically magnetized for each other from the start. A blind idiot could have seen that they should be together, and probably a few had, it was so obvious.

"I won't make the same mistake," Vaste said, thinking back to the troll girl. He'd seen her right about here ... and then she'd disappeared ... she hadn't gone forward or back, or toward the street ...

Which meant she must have gone into the building.

It was a rather obvious conclusion now that he thought about it. But perhaps he'd been too busy dragging a healer with a wounded hand back to Sanctuary to come to it. Yes, she must have gone into the building. He stared at the door, the glass-paned windows that revealed a storefront that specialized in …

Jewelry? What a peculiar thing to dedicate a shop to.

Of course, Vaste had seen a similar shop or two in Reikonos of old, but he'd thought it similarly absurd then. Ostentatious, actually. Having grown up in a place where the biggest priority was finding your next meal—especially in the famine days after the war—the idea of ornamenting yourself with finely crafted gold and jewels seemed as pointless to him as bathing would probably have seemed to his old friends back in Gren.

He regarded the door cautiously. Out here on the street he could avoid any serious scrutiny, it being a public place. Stepping in there, though … that might provoke uncomfortable questions such as, "What the hell are you?" And, perhaps, some screaming.

But there was nothing for it. Vaste was no Cyrus Davidon, content to let his own personal Vara slip away. He stepped over to the door, crushing some idiot's foot along the way ("Ow! Watch yourself, oaf!") and elbowing past two others, eliciting a series of grunts, and then threw the door open and walked inside, still bent nearly double, and not just to avoid knocking his forehead on the doorframe.

A bell jangled as he entered the shop, clutching his cloak tightly closed from within, so no one could see his green hands. He kept his face down, hoping the cowl would shadow him enough. It was fairly dark in here, in spite of the windows. Poor sunlight angle, he supposed, or maybe just the clouds of smoke that hung over this city occluded the sun. He hadn't dared look up to see, at least not since he'd left the alley outside Sanctuary.

Someone moved ahead of him, and a polite and very human, possibly quite old, voice asked him, "Can I help you?"

"I'm looking for someone who came in here earlier," Vaste said, trying to keep his delivery as smooth as possible. Best not to alarm this woman.

He could hear the catch in the woman's voice; this was clearly not a request she was used to receiving, and it took her back a step. "I'm sorry," she said, "You're looking for—"

"A woman, yes," he said, still keeping his head down. "Very tall. Stately. Also green. Pointy teeth. You'd probably know her if you saw her."

"Ahhh ..." There was doubt in her voice, and Vaste almost sighed. He couldn't tell just by listening whether she was stonewalling or truly hadn't seen the troll woman.

"Did you see her or not?" Vaste asked, deciding to just drop the charade. He stood to his full height, jangling a chandelier he hadn't even known was there as he slipped his cowl back and let his cloak open on the side, exposing Letum.

The woman's eyes widened as she looked up—and up—and up yet more to stare into his face. Her mouth fell open, worked up and down a couple of times, and then she pointed wordlessly to a staircase in the corner of the room. "I'd never seen her kind before. Thought maybe she came from Firoba. She ... rented out the room on the second floor just today." The older woman swallowed, now quite pale. "I don't want any trouble."

"Good. I'm not here to give you any," Vaste said, moving past her toward the stairs. He paused, looking into a glass display case at a ruby ring that was particularly impressive. "You know, I don't go in much for jewelry, but that is quite fetching. I think it's a little wrong for my skin tone, but still—quite fetching."

"Thank you," she said as he strode on toward the stairs, sounding uncertain whether she was grateful or confused. It didn't much matter to him either way, as he was quite intent on reaching the second floor as quickly as possible, the stairs shaking as he ascended. Once he got there, there was but one door. The stairs resumed heading upward just down the hall.

Vaste took a deep breath and sauntered to the door. He tried to compose himself mentally. His first words to her needed to be right: witty, charming—brilliant, even. They needed to set the stage for everything that could come after. To open her mind to the immense possibilities inherent in his mere presence here. He was, after all, witty, suave, possessed of immense intelligence, once skilled at magic—though that was obviously a problem these days—and carried the staff of a dead god.

Why, who wouldn't be interested in him?

He raised up his hand, trying to decide on that opening line, the one that would set the tone for all that would follow, and just as he'd almost decided between the two obvious entries—

The door swung open and there she was, as beautiful as he remembered.

Her hair was long and lustrous, black as perfect coal. Her skin was a shade of darker green than his own, like a grape from the temperate lands around Sanctuary in the days of old. Her eyes were suspicious, but a perfect chestnut the like of which he had not seen outside of rich woodwork.

Vaste stood there, hand still raised, mouth slightly agape, the mental pendulum swinging back and forth between the two brilliant opening phrases for their sure-to-be endless conversation—

But all he could think of to say, as he stared at her beauty and their infinite possible future together was ...

"Hihi."

27.

Vara's pistol roared in Cyrus's ear. If she felt half as furious as he did at the sight of Rodanthar—his father's sword, his mother's sword—in the hands of this black-hearted, thieving villain, the blast of the weapon in his ear made her sentiments clear.

Tirner Gaull did not drop his smirk as she shot at him; Rodanthar came up as he turned sideways. Vara's shot was well-placed, but was deflected off the edge of the blade as Gaull held it up as a kind of shield along his flank. It was surprisingly effective given that the bullet moved entirely too fast for him to do much more than give his best guess where it could go, even with the enhanced speed the weapon surely afforded him.

Cyrus drew one of the remaining pistols and fired it at him, aiming lower. Gaull flexed, stepping back as Cyrus took aim, Praelior in one hand to allow him to match Gaull's reflexes, the other holding the gun steady as he lined up the sights on Gaull's thigh.

The billowing of smoke that followed his shot clouded Cyrus's vision for an elongated second or two, but when it cleared he saw Gaull a few steps from where he'd been when the shot rang out, still smirking. The bullet must have passed cleanly beyond him, Cyrus concluded, and he dropped the pistol to grab another.

Vara fired another shot now, having pulled another pistol from his belt without his notice, and it went off like an explosion in his ear. Her aim was true, but once again Rodanthar caught the metal projectile along the surface of the blade, intercepting it before it could turn Gaull's face into a bloody mess.

"Damn!" she said in his ear, the word almost lost among the ringing sound. She sounded furious.

Cyrus had one pistol left, and he put a hand on it—

Just as the toughs clustered behind Gaull loosed their own volley.

Cyrus could see the bullets dancing through the air, moving like little metal arrows in quick flight. He could not reach out and tap them from the air, though for a second he thought he might. Vara brought Ferocis up to her face, holding it before her cheek as one of the bullets clanged against its surface and another caused her to make a grunting sound and drove her back a step. When he glanced at her, he saw a small, dark, indentation in her otherwise spotless breastplate, and the deformed metal ball, flat on one side, came rolling off as she grimaced in pain.

One of the shots took Cyrus in the side of the neck as he ducked, stinging like a wasp had crept between the links of chainmail under his gorget. He reached up quickly to be sure it hadn't somehow gotten him through the armor, but he felt no blood, only a stinging welt. Another took him cleanly in the chest and bounced off without even the dent that Vara's armor showed. Another caught him under the exposed armpit when he'd reached up. It felt as though someone had poked him there, but between chainmail and plate, he barely felt it and certainly not as keenly as the hit to the neck.

"It seems we near the end of our volleying," Gaull said, still grinning that broad, infuriating smile. He oozed patience in a way that few Cyrus had met did. He brought down Rodanthar, his form that of a very skilled swordsman. "Shall we settle this with crossed swords like the men of old?"

"I am a man of old," Cyrus said, letting the hand fall from his last pistol and striding forth, Vara a couple steps behind him, "so that suits me just fine." He did not move with the full alacrity Praelior granted him; if Gaull had not guessed at his advantage, Cyrus felt no need to betray it to him. Let him think Cyrus a pale imitator; he'd be disabused of the notion when his neck lay open by Praelior's edge, his life's blood oozing out and Rodanthar safely back in Cyrus's hand.

"Excellent," Gaull said, waiting for them, eyes gleaming. Any of the toughs they'd encountered thus far would have rushed them. Not Tirner Gaull, though. He waited, sword at ready, watching both Cyrus and Vara. "I get so tired of these dagger-wielding fops who think that jerking a pistol out will somehow bring me into line with their whims." He looked Cyrus over. "You, though ... you have the look of a man who imitates with precision. I bet you even know how to use that sword."

Cyrus cut the distance between them to a mean yard before he raised his weapon to a high guard, then brought it down with all

Praelior's speed. "I do indeed."

Rodanthar flashed out with equal speed, and Gaull turned aside his attack with ease. "Good," Gaull said, seemingly unsurprised, save for a flicker of movement in his eyes, at the revelation of Cyrus's ability. "I have so longed for a good fight with someone who not only knows what they're doing, but presents a challenge." The smile did not fade one whit. "Perhaps I was hasty in judging you an imitator. Is that Praelior in your hand, then?"

"It is," Cyrus said, coming at him again. Gaull stepped back, still smiling, apparently content to lose ground and keep his head and limbs intact. Cyrus's blade whizzed neatly past his extended hand and missed cutting into his waistcoat by little margin indeed. Without undue haste, Gaull carefully brought back his weapon, pulling it to a forward guard, not too high. It was the mark of a good swordsman.

"I always wondered what became of it," Gaull said, eyeing the blade almost enviously. "Is that, then, Ferocis that your elven wife holds?"

Cyrus did not look back; he could hear Vara clashing with the toughs. It did not sound as though it were going particularly well for them. "Indeed," he said.

"Very good," Gaull said, narrowing his eyes as Cyrus came at him again. He fell back once more, allowing Cyrus to continue coming at him with hard, broad strokes designed to blast apart Gaull's defenses. The clashes were surely rattling the man, striking pain to run down his hands and arms to the joints. Gaull, while lithe, was not particularly large. He seemed to favor his agility over trading the heavy hits that Cyrus had learned to dish out at the Society of Arms. No man—especially one with no armor—could stand long against these sorts of hits. His grip would fail, eventually, and then he'd be left at normal speed against Cyrus, who had a fine idea or twelve about hanging Tirner Gaull from the catwalks by his guts.

"And how did you come by that sword?" Cyrus asked through gritted teeth. He readied another attack, but did not want to be obvious about it. Closing with Gaull was his best strategy, though knocking the sword loose of his hand would produce a similarly enjoyable outcome.

"Less than a hundred and fifty years after you left Arkaria," Gaull said, with a zeal Cyrus found distasteful. "I led an expedition into the swamps north of what used to be elven territory. You probably know the place—where dwelled those green-skinned monsters—or at least what few of them remained." His grin grew wider, uglier. "They'd warred among themselves for so long, you see. They could scarcely put up a defense."

167

Gaull blocked another of Cyrus's strokes, turning it aside with alarming ease. Cyrus began to feel a creeping sense of concern as Gaull's eyes glittered with growing triumph. "There was one, though. A champion among their kind. Strong. Fearless. Capable. He fought us, tooth and claw, and he killed so many of my fellows. But in the end ... he fell." And Gaull dashed in, striking at Cyrus driving him back a step now. "A dagger thrust or twelve in the back when he was fending off the attacks of others ... that sorted him out."

Timer Gaull struck a glancing blow against Praelior, turning the weapon aside as Cyrus was about to redirect it to shatter the man. He stepped nearer, and Cyrus prepared to raise a knee to his unarmored gut. Before he could gather his balance to do so, though, Gaull reached out and shoved him.

Force ran through Cyrus's body, the same sort he used to punch men across entire rooms. It did not hurl him, the weight of his armor saving him from free flight. But it did make him stumble and lose his footing. Cyrus hit the edge of one of the raised walkways and tumbled into a pit where slaves had labored. The landing stunned Cyrus even as the slaves broke his fall, their cries beneath him as he came crashing down like the pleas of the damned.

"Was he a friend of yours?" Gaull called, dropping to his knees and thrusting. The tip of Rodanthar found Cyrus's armpit, open wide as he splayed out over the fallen slaves, and a soft hit turned into blossoming pain. Cyrus jerked, and felt hot blood rush out as he rolled away from Gaull. "The troll?"

Cyrus came back to his feet, trying ignore the groans of the slaves he'd just rolled over, and the pain that was starting to scream from under his right arm. He transferred Praelior neatly to his left and clenched his right fist. He was on a lower footing than Gaull, who stood, again patiently waiting for Cyrus to make a move against him. The confidence he displayed, coupled with having drawn first blood, made Cyrus uneasy.

"Indeed he was," Cyrus said, tasting a little blood in his mouth. He found a place where he'd bitten the inside of his jaw upon the landing from his fall. "His name was Zarnn, and a finer warrior you could not meet."

"I imagine not," Gaull said, remaining utterly still, his sword swinging leisurely around his legs, no worry displayed for any impending attack from Cyrus. "But even the strongest of bull creatures can be bled down, can't they?" And here he smiled more broadly. "I mean ... look at you. A legend. And yet I've drawn your blood."

"Don't count on it doing you much good," Cyrus said, and he mouthed the words to a healing spell. The pain mitigated, but a little trickle of blood remained.

"So magic does still exist in these lands," Gaull said, watching his fingers light up with envy. "I have long wondered."

"Wonder no more," Cyrus said. "Ponder instead how long you'll live with my sword in your guts."

Gaull let out a bark of a laugh. "I have other matters of more consequence to set myself to, should I need for entertainments." He smirked. "To wit—"

And he thrust his blade down into the fallen slaves, burying it up to the hilt in one man's back as a strong gasp made its way through. Without pause he thrust it into another, Rodanthar red with the blood of an innocent—

Cyrus saw a red of his own as Rodanthar's edge came up fouled by Gaull's heinous deed. He leapt across the gap between them toward Gaull's smiling visage, fury pounding through Cyrus's veins.

Tirner Gaull met him with a sure stroke, one that struck at the gaps of plate between Cyrus's cuisse and codpiece. It let out a mighty clang as Rodanthar met the chainmail cleanly, and another sharp poke was Cyrus's reward even as Gaull seemed to fade before his hard slash, the tip of Cyrus's sword slicing cleanly toward Gaull's neck but failing only centimeters away as the Machine henchman bent his back in an almost dancelike move.

Cyrus stumbled on his landing, the pain in his leg hobbling him a step. He kept from crashing down, but Gaull was upon him, striking at his back most expertly. He found the spot where Cyrus's backplate ended and delivered a poking blow. Under the assault of a normal sword, it would have a pinprick at best.

But with Rodanthar in Gaull's hand, it was much more. It opened a wound at least an inch in length as Gaull dragged his blade across, pulling the chainmail links with it. It bit into the tissue and fat, stinging Cyrus as he staggered away.

Gaull did not let up, however, lifting his blade and thrusting it into Cyrus's side, once more finding the place where his plate armor wasn't, and driving the tip of Rodanthar between the seemingly impregnable mail in order to drag small wounds across Cyrus's skin. He struck there, then at the back of Cyrus's knee where the greaves gave way for a small space—

Cyrus fell to his knees, the pain of these small wounds enough to stagger him but not fell him completely. He threw himself into a roll in hopes of coming up in a more solidly defensible position. He was unsure whether it would work, but tried it anyway. Gaull was so quick, though, he seemed to be everywhere at once—

And he was after Cyrus, striking him mid-roll, catching him under the gorget as Cyrus began to rise again. Gaull sliced him with a long scratch into the flesh of his neck, missing the artery by a hair's margin. As Cyrus tried to move sideways to counter, he fell—

Once more, Gaull was upon him.

"Truly ... I expected more," Gaull said, greeting him with a solid punch to the face that rang Cyrus's head even through the blow. "From a legend, after all, from Cyrus Davidon? I guess there's even less to you than I always thought—" Gaull raised up Rodanthar, poised to deliver a death strike upon him—

28.

There it was, his father's sword, the sword his mother had used in her conquest of the trolls, the sword he'd given to Zarnn to fight the gods—

And it was about to driven into Cyrus's own face.

Tirner Gaull let gleam only a momentary flash of triumph before he brought it down. Gaull was a boastful one, Cyrus could tell, but he wasn't foolish enough to let his boasting distract him. The motion of the blade as it descended was dizzying, the end point coming straight for his face where he had no defense for it—

It clanged as another blade turned it aside.

Ferocis struck it cleanly away and then swiped up, forcing Gaull to dodge back, lightning fast as a silvery figure dashed before him, interposing herself between Gaull and Cyrus.

"He is so much more," she said. "For example, he's also a husband to a very, very vengeful and occasionally protective wife."

Gaull let out a laugh. "That's less about him and more about you, I would think."

"Ah, but he managed to win me," she said, coming at Gaull with as much fury and perhaps a touch more speed than Cyrus had mustered in his assaults. "And that is no small accomplishment—though I doubt a fool like you would understand what it means to win the heart of a woman."

"I find little interest in a woman's heart," Gaull said, eyes gleaming as he turned aside her attacks as well. "In favor of other, less troublesome and more satisfying parts."

"Such as the mind, I do hope—though I doubt you have the class or wit to enjoy that, either," Vara said, slashing at him. Gaull took the blows with grace, and to Cyrus's surprise held onto his sword all the while. "Even if you somehow managed to unlock that."

"What need have I to joust with some lady's wit?" Gaull asked. "None I have met could match you in this regard, and still—you will fall before me." He countered one of Vara's blows particularly hard, and nearly scored a blow against her chainmail. "Too slow," he said, and danced back again. "Armor makes a sluggard out of you."

Too late, Cyrus realized that Gaull was brilliant at striking at the weakest points of their armor. He'd been fighting and living and fighting more for a thousand years while they'd dwelled in peace in the ether.

And unfortunately, that edge in skill showed.

Cyrus was pushing to his feet, fighting the pain. He'd murmured the incantation for the healing spell, but it was doing little in proportion to the damage Gaull had done. In addition, he felt a prickling through his body, and his fingertips glowed red.

He grunted; Cyrus had reached the end of his magical energy, and unlike before, when he might have been able to drag some more out of Praelior, now things felt curiously empty. As though he were trying to pull water from the air.

"Your defense is good, as far as these things go," Gaull said to Vara, dodging one of her attacks. She was faster than Cyrus, but Gaull seemed a step above. His footwork was perhaps the finest Cyrus had ever seen, always certain, never in doubt. "You have a natural skill." Gaull gave a leering grin. "But I've been doing this for nearly a thousand years, my dear; what have you been doing in that time?"

Vara swiped at him and he turned her aside sharply, exposing her flank. He struck then, and Cyrus heard the breaking of the links of her chainmail, and his breath left him as a sharp splash of crimson splattered the dull machinery beside her.

Vara sank to a knee, her face in a tight grimace, as Gaull raised up his sword. There was nothing between him and the back of Vara's neck save air, and as Gaull shot Cyrus look of satisfaction, he began to bring down the sword.

29.

Shirri

The sounds coming from the mill were not encouraging. Shirri could hear them—a dash of screaming, a hint of cries, more trouble than she might have estimated given the ease with which her newfound allies—good heavens, she shuddered to consider these weirdos that way—had gone through the Machine's previous outposts.

A swirling blast of grey mist materialized next to her, and from it emerged Alaric and Curatio, causing Shirri to draw her breath sharply. Alaric wore a smile, subtle but present because of her obvious discomfiture, and she glanced away from him with impatience and annoyance at his obvious glee from startling her.

"I take it the liberation of this place from the Machine goes well?" Alaric asked.

"Slaves keep running out," Shirri said, folding her arms before her. "People keep screaming inside. I suppose that augers well for your people."

"And, let us hope, your mother as well," Alaric said.

"Let us hope," Shirri whispered, though she did not dare to hope any longer. For all she knew, her mother had been summarily executed by the Machine sometime in the night.

"Do not despair," Curatio advised, "for despair ages us all long before our time."

"Is that your secret?" Alaric asked with great humor. "Failure to give in to despair?"

"That and a life energy that seems to fail to deplete," Curatio said with a twinkle in his eye.

"Get my mother back and perhaps I'll stop despairing," Shirri said as another bunch of slaves came running out of the mill, beating a hasty retreat into the city streets. Probably heading to the homes they had before the Machine had snatched them.

"If that's what it takes," Alaric said. "But I am curious—why does everything here seem so hopeless?"

Shirri let out a sharp laugh. "You're joking, right?" He stared back at her evenly. "You don't see it?"

"I see a city more prosperous than the one I left," Alaric said, "I see houses more impressive than the ones that stood here before. I see—"

"I see grey, grim lines everywhere I go," Shirri said, looking at the ash that gathered in the joints between cobbles along the road and sidewalk. "I see a city choking, barely able to breathe from the black smoke piping out of every chimney. I see food that's brought in and sold at prices that make the richest in the city balk. I see no easy ways out, unless you want to ride an airship over the deadly grey hellscape between here and anywhere else—and plenty do, they're so starved for hope. I see a Machine that watches over this city with a constant eye, waiting for someone to show some talent, some ambition. And the moment they do, the Machine swoops in, finds out what's special about you, discerns how they can bleed you dry—and then they do." She bowed her head, all passion expelled; now she was tired and limp as a wet rag. "So tell me, Alaric—what is there to have hope about?"

"That things will get better," Alaric said. "That now that we're here, something will change."

"I'll believe it when I see it," Shirri said, giving him a tight, cynical smile. "Because so far … all you've done is break a couple of the Machine's fingers. And I'm guessing they're going to punch back—soon. You've scarcely seen what they have to offer yet."

"Then I suppose we have something to look forward to," Alaric said, with a thin smile of his own. Unlike her he actually did seem to feel, and perhaps even be pleased about more trouble rolling their way.

"Yeah, well—" She started to reply, but a sharp scream, different from the general shouting, from the mill cut her off, and Alaric was only there for another second before he vanished into mist, leaving her standing there with Curatio.

30.

Cyrus

The sword was descending on the back of Vara's neck, and Cyrus was too far away to do anything about it. He gasped for breath in the dusty air, choking on terror.

Vara was on all fours, Ferocis still in her hand but unable to push herself back up. Blood drained from the hole in her chainmail beneath the armpit.

Cyrus's eyes met Vara's as the blade came down. His mind ran desperately through his options, but could come to only one conclusion:

Gaull was going to take her head off. And given the enfeebled state of healing magic now ... Cyrus wondered if they would even be able to reattach it once the deed was done.

A sharp, electric bolt of fear ran through Cyrus's guts. He stared into those stunning blue eyes as the sword traversed its last inches to the back of her neck, and he felt like he could read her thoughts—

Pain.

Fear.

And a glint of ... cleverness?

Her eyes went dull and unfocused as he stared at them, turning a kind of hazy, almost grey—

And the sword passed cleanly through the back of Vara's neck—

Then slammed into the floor with great force, striking loose chips of stone that flew in all directions.

"What the hell ...?" Gaull asked, blade all the way down at the floor—

Vara's head was still firmly atop her shoulders.

She rolled and kicked him, and Cyrus saw at last—

She'd gone ethereal, just for a moment, as the sword came down upon her.

Vara rolled to her feet and rose, huddled over, her blade in hand and pointed at Gaull defensively. She was still wounded, still badly injured, but her guard was up again and Gaull was staring at her, one arm over his stomach and the other keeping his blade aloft defensively. He had a look of fierce determination on his face, Cyrus could see it even though Gaull was turned sideways in profile to him. The next attack was coming, and soon—

Cyrus drew his last pistol, clicked the hammer and pointed it right at Gaull's head. He jerked a little too hard on the trigger as Gaull lunged forward—

Gaull's scream was high pitched with fury. He staggered back, blood running down his face where the bullet had creased his cheek. It was split wide, and part of his ear lobe was missing. Gaull threw a furious look in Cyrus's direction, then Vara's, but neither seemed capable of rising to fight him.

"You—you—" Gaull lunged toward Vara. He was still lightning fast and sure-footed, and her weak defensive guard was not going to be enough to turn his blade away.

"NO!" Hiressam leapt into the fray and turned aside Gaull's blade with skill, though not speed. Gaull saw him coming and twisted, elbowing the elf, who turned to mitigate the blow. Gaull came around and tried to cleave Hiressam's head from his body with fury and his enhanced speed, but again, the elf was one step ahead, going defensive and moving back, carefully, though slowly, and allowing Vara to become the third point of a triangle comprised of him, her, and Gaull.

Vara reached out to strike at Gaull, and the Machine henchman was forced to counter her while Hiressam made a probing strike. Gaull tried to lash back but Hiressam was already guarded, taking no chances against his faster opponent.

Cyrus lurched to his feet and tried to come into the fray, but Gaull slashed at him, driving him back after seeing him out of the corner of his eye. "This is not my end but yours," Gaull said, batting Praelior aside when Cyrus made a weak thrust of it. His hand was numb and he felt as though he had little left to give, his attack so frail an infant might have been able to guard against it.

"Is that so?" Vara asked, and a force blast pulsed from her fingers, distorting the air around Gaull as it threw him back a few steps. Cyrus moved into position next to Hiressam and Vara, forming a tight defensive line opposite Gaull.

Tirner Gaull stared back at them, Rodanthar held high. "I nearly beat all three of you."

"You came nowhere close to beating me," Hiressam pointed out, coolly but proudly.

"Legends," Gaull said with a derisive snort. "Legends indeed."

"Don't knock my legend," Cyrus said. "I did just give you a new scar, after all. You won't be quite so pretty when next we meet, Gaull."

Gaull touched his cheek, and his eyes flashed like furious lightning had gone off behind them. "When next we meet ... I'll take your sword, kill your wife—or worse. Perhaps some combination thereof." And he grinned. With a faux salute, Gaull leapt over a piece of machinery and was gone.

"Excellent timing, Hiressam," Cyrus said, slumping against a nearby support beam made of thick metal and folded to be all right angles and strangeness. "Though I admit—I am a little concerned that you decided to go toe to toe with a godly weapon with nothing but regular steel in your own hand."

"Do you remember this sword?" Hiressam asked, holding it up. It was ornate, with a curved edge and a very fine hilt with a couple jewels in it.

"I can't say that I do, though it looks very well made," Cyrus said, cringing. The pain was seeping in now.

"It was handed to me by the Gatekeeper of Purgatory," Hiressam said, "on our first time through. On subsequent visits, I gained these rings," and he flashed his fingers, "and my armor," running blade up and down his body. "None of them is nearly as impressive as a godly weapon, to be sure—but they do speed me up." The elf smiled. "Make me stronger. So while this Gaull had an advantage, it was not as unfair as he probably thought."

"It was unfair enough that he downed two people with godly weapons and took only a scarring blow to the vanity in exchange," Vara said, leaning against another support beam. "If I hadn't possessed the ability to go ethereal ..."

"You'd be headless," Cyrus said, drawing a ragged breath as the adrenaline of the battle fled and he was left with a weak, hollow feeling. "And I'd be a widower. Again."

"I'm sure the ladies of Reikonos would love that," Vara said, lifting her fingers and letting the glow of white light fill the air. She cringed as it died out. "That did ... so very little."

"It staunched the bleeding," Cyrus said, looking at her wound beneath her arm. "Keep in mind the effect of phantom pain; it probably did more than you feel."

"What has happened here?" Alaric's voice cut through the quiet hum of the mill as he appeared in a gust of black smoke. Gone were the screams of the slaves in their pits, replaced instead with little but the faint clank of some machine working without its masters.

"It's a long story," Cyrus said.

"Some arse killed Zarnn after we left Arkaria," Vara said. "He is now a well-practiced swordsman in the employ of the Machine, and he nearly killed us both," she indicated herself and Cyrus, "and would surely have done so if not for every trick in our respective bags and the perfectly timed intervention of Hiressam."

"Okay, it's not that long a story," Cyrus conceded. "But it's filled with drama. That son of a bitch Gaull admitted to killing Zarnn and slaughtering the last of the trolls—"

"Perhaps not quite the last," Alaric said quietly. "But nonetheless, this Gaull sounds like quite the villain, to admit such wrongs freely."

"Why would someone with that amount of skill and power come to work for the Machine?" Vara asked, pushing off the beam and grimacing as she did so. A fresh drip of blood ran down her side. "Why not carve out his own fiefdom? I mean, he nearly bested the two of us and ended up with scarcely any damage to show for it."

"I came at him too hard, too furiously," Cyrus said, unwilling to try standing on his own just yet. "He was too canny for me by half. I played right into his hand."

"Hothead," Vara said.

"You should talk."

"Neither of you should be talking at the moment," Alaric said, raising his own hand as the glow of healing light came over it. Cyrus felt some of the pain subside, and noticed that Vara, too, looked relieved. "Where did this man go?"

"He fled out the front of the mill," Cyrus said. "Or the back, perhaps; I didn't catch his direction after he leapt behind that machinery."

Alaric's lips puckered with concern. "We should leave, then— provided our business here is concluded?"

"Wait," Vara said. "We haven't searched the offices for Shirri's mother."

Alaric shook his head. "I swept the rooms upstairs before I appeared to you. They are thoroughly empty."

Cyrus looked to Hiressam. "You got all the slaves out?"

Hiressam's eyes flicked down. "All but the ones he killed."

Alaric's expression turned stony. "This Gaull ... he killed slaves?"

"Out of pure spite," Cyrus said. "Or to taunt me, perhaps."

"Heinous," Alaric pronounced and motioned at them to go. "Let us go. We should see if we can track this Gaull down." His face hardened further. "I cannot countenance leaving a rabid dog to prowl the streets, after all. For any else who are harmed in his path ..." The Ghost shook his head, and there was a kind of fury mingled with sadness and resolve in his eyes. "I would see his end come before any more are harmed."

31.

"Why are you here with me?" Shirri asked Curatio as they stood upon the street corner outside the mill gates. She'd felt drawn to move closer once the scream had come and Alaric had left in his cloud of mist. She had thought that he'd run inside, but to her surprise, he'd remained by her side, keeping a careful watch on the gate, mace hanging by his side, spikes not deployed. "Shouldn't you have gone in with him?"

"He is plenty enough assistance for any who need it, all on his own," Curatio said with a tight smile. She looked behind him to the factory across the street, workers still coming and going on some sort of a break as though nothing at all were happening over here. She caught a few curious looks from them, faces smudged with black and clothing even dirtier, but no one came over. They lingered close to the gates of their own factory, as if an invisible tether kept them there. "I believed keeping watch on you in case of trouble might be more useful."

"You need not worry on my account," Shirri said, looking once more toward the gate. "I can take care of myself."

"On the contrary," Curatio said, polite but unsmiling. "You have already needed our help twice this day." He looked up. "If you count last night as part of this day, and I do."

"I didn't *need* your help," she said simply. "But ... it was ..." She searched for the word.

"Helpful?"

She rolled her eyes a little. "Indeed. It was helpful. It was true, there was little I could do against all of those who came after me ... especially the second, bigger group..." She shook her head. "But I

180

could have made good my escape from them, provided they didn't kill me. It only felt hopeless. Looking back, there were avenues of escape available to me. I panicked."

"Ah, so now you find hope," Curatio said, and this time, he did smile. "A curious thing your hope appears to be, so very ephemeral. It comes and goes like Alaric."

Shirri let out a breath of impatience. "I don't have hope, all right? I have plans. There is a difference."

"Indeed," Curatio said. "Plans can be waylaid. Hope, though? It never leaves you unless you surrender it."

"That's very ... trite," Shirri said. "In fact, it's almost—"

"What the hell is this?" A guttural voice came from behind them, causing Shirri to wheel.

Machine thugs were always dressed the same and came in crews, matched like eggs in a basket. Six of them were striding up the street now, in their black coats with the white armbands, a patrol that was probably usually laughing and gawking as they moved to strip citizens of their valuables, to practice the thuggery that made them hardly distinguishable from a street gang. That was a hallmark of the Machine's thugs versus the regular sort; Machine thugs happily operated, without fear, in daylight. All other criminals feared the Machine enough to keep their activities out of sight.

Their attention was on the mill, but it shifted almost as soon as Shirri turned. Smoke was billowing out the windows now, and Shirri hadn't even noticed it happening. She turned back to look at the thugs, who'd focused on her—her and Curatio, and were heading toward them with intent.

"We should—" she started to say.

"Stand right here and greet what's coming without fear," Curatio said, stepping in front of her, his long white robes swishing as he moved. His mace was behind his back, one hand clamping the wrist of the other to steady it. Without the weapon, he might have looked like a monk in a meditative pose. Perhaps that was even what the thugs would think, a man in white robes stepping up to greet them fearlessly. Some elven priest naively walking into their waiting arms.

"What's going on here?" the accent of the leader was distinct, not even from the street—he had come from the gutter, Shirri guessed. He had that rough sound to him, and his face was bent in such a way that she knew he'd been in many fights. "We got an elven priest and some little slip of a thing outside a burning mill that's under our protection."

"And I'm sure you are fierce protectors, indeed," Curatio said.

"Why, surely small women and tiny children are intimidated by you every day."

That one sent a ripple through the thugs—and Shirri's stomach. They were egotistical bullies at the best of times, and provoking them didn't seem like a wise path.

"Who are you supposed to be?" the leader asked, stopping a few feet from Curatio. She could practically see him drawing courage from the pistol in his belt and the friends he had watching his back.

"Why, I am a revenant returned to life, my dear man," Curatio said. "Come back to this place to haunt your very nightmares."

That one took a minute to land. The leader's face screwed up, eyes narrowing, lips puckering as he tried to take make sense of the words but failed. "Whatchoo say—?"

He didn't get a chance to finish, because Curatio brought the mace around and winged him on the side of the head before Shirri even got a chance to think through what might happen next. The leader's eyes fluttered as it struck, and though it didn't utterly cave in his skull, the mighty crack made her cringe.

Curatio did not take that as a stopping point, however; he was not moving nearly as fast as the Cyrus or Vara impersonators, or even Alaric, but he certainly had alacrity on his side. He moved smoothly to the next nearest of the thugs, punching his mace forward and landing the ball in the man's nose.

Blood exploded out like someone had smashed a rotten piece of fruit. The thug keeled over, out, and the man in white moved on as the others began to scramble into action.

Curatio's mace swung high, then low. It battered another thug unconscious, catching him in the temple and leaving a bloody spot behind when he ducked and moved past a dagger to slam it home in another's belly. The "OOF!" was loud enough that she suspected it could be heard blocks away, and the recipient of the blow fell to his knees, clutching his midsection and wheezing to try and get a breath in his body.

"This is the problem with consigning your will to a gang," Curatio said, taking the legs from beneath another with a sweep of his feet. The man thudded to his back loudly. "You make subservient your own thoughts, your initiative, and when someone goes and knocks over the brains of your operation with the first strike, you're left without thoughts of your own. A dangerous thing, letting others do your thinking for you—" He threw the mace back at one of the last two toughs, both of whom were only steps from Shirri but a few more from Curatio, who had worked to his left as he'd made his way through them. The mace sailed into the face of one of the last two, crushing his nose and probably many other things, though Shirri missed the rest because the man crashed to the ground as the mace went sideways, coming to rest out of anyone's reach. "Though not as dangerous as me," Curatio said with a smile.

"You won't get away with this," the last thug said, ripping his pistol from his belt and bringing it up. Curatio was already sprinting forward, trying to cut the distance between them, but the last thug was surprisingly clear-eyed; he had a bead on the elf and was thumbing back his hammer, finger coiled on the trigger. Shirri watched it unfolding, and her mind calculated how it would go.

He'd fire before Curatio could reach him. The bullet would hit the elf, and he'd go down. There would be no dodging it, no avoiding it. The thug was squinting, one eye closed, preparing his aim as he clicked the hammer back—

Shirri drew a sharp breath and exhaled words that she hadn't said in ... years.

A bellowing sound of thunder cracked over the street and lightning lanced from her hands, a bolt pure and furious and true. The last thug jerked as it hit him, his thumb contracting and straightening before he could finish cocking the hammer of the pistol. He stood there, frozen in time for just a moment before Curatio paused, inches from him as the forks of lightning finished dispersing themselves—

The thug fell over dead, his face a rictus of horror, his eyes bulging out.

Curatio gave her a look, very slight smile showing itself as someone pounded around the corner of gates; it was Alaric, with the others— the new elf, Hiressam, with the Cyrus and Vara imitators only steps behind him. The last two, in particular, looked quite bloody; though she saw no sign of obvious nor gaping wounds upon them, they did move a little slower than they had previously.

"What happened here?" Alaric asked, taking in the fallen Machine thugs with a glance.

"Something very interesting indeed," Curatio said, stooping to pick up his mace. "It seems there is more to our new friend Shirri than meets the eye." And he smiled, sending little chills down Shirri's arms, her back—everywhere, really. "Much, much more."

32.

Vaste

"You're probably wondering why I've knocked upon your door," Vaste said, trying to recover after his insipidly stupid opening. (Hihi? Who even said that, other than him?)

The beautiful troll woman regarded him with mingled curiosity, her lower fangs protruding over her lips as she stared at him intently. There seemed to be intelligence there, didn't there? Was he imagining it? Would his fantasy be ruined as soon as she opened her mouth and muttered, "Ungh? Grunnnt"?

But she didn't say that. Instead, with perfect fluidity and grace to her speech, she said: "I did wonder."

"Oh!" Vaste tried to contain himself, but failed. "You … you used a two syllable word."

She stared at him, then her eyes narrowed further. "I frequently do, when the situation calls for it."

"'Fre-quent-ly,' that's three syllables," Vaste put his hand on his chest. "Be still my heart. 'Si-tu-a-tion' is four—"

"Who are you, and why are you at my door, critiquing my word choices?" she asked.

"Gods, 'critiquing.' That's—"

"Who are you?" she asked, voice rising.

"I'm sorry!" he said, throwing up his hands. "My name is Vaste—"

"Who?"

"Damn you, Cyrus Davidon, for hogging all the glory," Vaste said. "As you might notice, I am a troll."

"I'm hardly stupid, thank you," she said, frowning all the deeper. "It would be hard to miss."

"Hah! Yes, indeed, it would be difficult to miss." Vaste drew himself up to his full height, aware of the blood pounding through his veins. He was flushed, he was sure of it, but he was equally sure he didn't care. There was a beautiful troll woman in front of him! "Ahm … I have just returned from a, uh … long trip away … and … I was wondering … are you the only one of your kind here …? Because … I'm not seeing many of my own sort around Reikonos … at all." He finished, trying to keep from verbally hemorrhaging his enthusiasm all over her.

She stared at him, and then seemed to loosen up just a little. "I'm the only one of my …" She looked him up and down. "… our … sort here, yes."

"And what a wonderful specimen of our sort you are," Vaste said, nodding furiously as he looked her up and down. "Do you mind if I ask what your name is? Where you came from? What sort of—"

"Hold your horses," she said, the cloud of suspicion returning. "One thing at a time, will you?"

"Right, right," Vaste said, still feeling like he was speaking so rapidly that his words might have been an out-of-control carriage, the horses gone wild and dragging it any which way they cared to. "One thing at a time. Indeed. I am Vaste. And you are …?"

A pause. "Birissa," she finally allowed. "My name is Birissa."

"And where do you come from, Birissa?" He couldn't control the question; it simply shot out.

Now her eyes narrowed more deeply. "Hang on," she said. "From whence do you come?"

"That's a … fair question," Vaste said, thinking very, very quickly about how to answer it. None of the ones that came blazing through in such rapid succession seemed to be sensible. "I come … from very far away," he finally settled on. "Very, incredibly far away."

She settled back on her heels and crossed her arms in front of her. "If you can't do better than that, I'm not sure I care to tell you where I come from."

"That's perfectly fine," he said, still gushing, in spite of his best efforts to plug it. "I can't think of anything less important right now than knowing where you're from. What's important is where you're going and how I can be of assistance, and indeed, of great help … in, uh … changing the course of your, uhm …"

And here he came to a loss for words. Nothing he was thinking was sensible, he was not so far gone as to be blind to that. How did one say, 'I want to marry you and have your babies!' to a total stranger, after all, following thirty seconds of conversation? And not have it come out utterly desperate and ridiculous?

She was looking at him as though he were an idiot, and he couldn't blame her. "I'm sorry," he said. "It's just ... been a very long time since I've seen a fellow troll. I suppose ... I gave up hope, especially when I arrived here. I thought ... all our kind had been wiped out." He put his head down. "Perhaps you know what I mean ... what a truly wretched feeling it is ... to feel like you're alone in the world."

Her stare was piercing, but after a moment it lost some of its intensity, replaced by a flicker of warmth and perhaps ... longing? "I do know something of that," she said, letting her arms fall to her side. They brushed the long cloak she wore, not dissimilar to his, stirring it back to reveal something that made him blink. Twice.

"Uhm ... you carry quite the blade," he said, looking at the flash of a scabbard that her motion had revealed.

She stepped back self-consciously, trying to disguise it, but it was far too late for that. She was only a little shorter than he, and the blade she wore on her belt went almost to her ankle. It was longer than Praelior, longer than Aterum, longer than Ferocis—maybe almost the length of any two of them combined, and at least one and a half times the width of any of them.

"I—" she started to say, and here he saw a flush of embarrassment.

"You don't have to explain," Vaste said quickly. "If I had a sword and I were answering the door in a strange city, I would surely be wearing it. Hell, I might even greet whoever knocked with it already drawn. People are a suspicious lot, after all, not exactly the most accepting of those who are somewhat different ... taller ... greener ... prettier ..."

"You think I'm pretty, do you?" She sounded almost amused by it. That impressed him further; it took real wit to be amused, to approach the compliment with humor. Any idiot could take it onboard sincerely; it took brains to twist it around and throw irony into it.

"I do," Vaste said, trying to gallop on past that, "but I'm more impressed with your mind right now."

"That was clear from the syllable counting," she said.

"Where I come from ... I was an outcast from my people," Vaste said. "And an anomaly, because I liked to ... think." He let his eyes dart, because the way that had come out was far too superior for his taste and comfort.

"I find thinking a wonderful alternative to not," Birissa said, eyes flicking over him with amusement. "It's your very great misfortune if you were raised in a place where that was frowned upon."

"I know, right?" he said, letting it out like a great gasping breath air surging back into his lungs, like he was finally able to exhale after a decade of keeping something in. "It was a nightmare! And—" He started to say more but was interrupted by a sudden burst of mist appearing in the hall. "Uh oh. Something weird is about to happen, just—don't let it scare you."

"What are you t—oh." Birissa stared as Alaric formed out of a column of misty grey. "Who is this and what is he doing in my hallway?"

"We've encountered a problem," Alaric came straight to the point.

Vaste swallowed hard. "I'm sure you have. There's always a problem to be had with Cyrus around."

"Indeed," Alaric said, and a dark glimmer of amusement passed over him. "We have to return to Sanctuary immediately."

"Alaric," Vaste said sharply, nodding his head to Birissa, who watched them both with something between amazement and curiosity, with perhaps a speckling of horror. "I'm rather busy at the moment."

"Who's your friend … who can appear and disappear out of a cloud of fog?" Birissa asked, looking over Alaric.

"Birissa, this is Alaric," Vaste said hurriedly. "Alaric, Birissa. Now, go evaporate, will you?"

"We require your presence immediately," Alaric said. "Things have taken two rather dramatic turns."

Vaste sighed, a noise of exasperation and annoyance. "Again, with Cyrus, I don't see how they couldn't, but—I really need some time here, Alaric."

"For what?" Birissa asked, one eye watching him more intently than the other.

"Bring her as well," Alaric said, eyeing Birissa. "She carries a large sword; perhaps she might like to use it."

"Don't assume she's violent just because she's a troll—" Vaste started.

"I do like to do a bit of hacking and slashing when warranted," Birissa said.

"Well, shit," Vaste said, sagging. Then, to her, he said, "You really are perfection, aren't you?"

"Thank you, I think," Birissa said.

"Meet us back at Sanctuary," Alaric said. "We'll be in the Great Hall. There are things to discuss." And with that, he was gone in a puff of smoke, the mist reeling itself back out of a nearby window through the permeable crack around the sill.

"How the hell did he even find me?" Vaste asked, throwing up his hands.

"We're two trolls in the middle of city that lacks our class and wit and sophistication," Birissa said, shrugging. She drew the door closed and produced a key with which she locked it. "Your friend seems interesting. I'd like to go hear him out."

Vaste let his own eyes narrow at her. "Because you find yourself intrigued by me, as a person ... or because you're drawn to the violence he's apparently promising?"

She paused, thinking for a second. "It's more the latter than the former, honestly. I don't know you that well yet, and you seem strange. But I'm new in town and my skills run toward violence." She shrugged. "Sorry."

Vaste just blinked at her a few times. "You know what? I'll take it. Let's go," he said, and off they went, her trailing in his wake, and a little smile on his face as she followed him down the stairs.

33.

Cyrus

The sting of the wounds Tirner Gaull had inflicted had not faded by the time Cyrus had returned to Sanctuary and settled in one of the seats in the Great Hall. The physical wounds certainly hurt, there was no denying the truth of them, no matter how many times Curatio attempted to knit them closed.

But worse than the physical wounds was the sting to pride, and the knowledge that Gaull—that bastard—had killed Zarnn and taken Rodanthar.

Cyrus stared at a dish heaped with buttery mashed potatoes, pieces of the red skins still within, and found himself wishing to shove them away in spite of a pressing hunger. Vara, next to him, seemed similarly preoccupied. She smelled of sweat and of blood and wore the same grimace as Cyrus, more pain that wouldn't depart.

Curatio sat across from them, eyes flitting down the table to Shirri, who sat in the seat closest to the door, at the far end of the table. A more conspicuous and isolated spot she could not have chosen. Hiressam was the only soul near her, and he was a couple seats closer to Cyrus. Shirri's was face partially occluded by the shadows that came from the flickering of the flames and the incomplete light that shone down through stained glass windows behind Alaric.

Alaric sat at the head of the table. There had been no argument this time, just the Ghost taking his rightful position, in Cyrus's eyes, though he did evince a measure of distaste at the configuration of the table. Cyrus guessed it was the rectangular nature; Alaric had always preferred a circular arrangement.

"We can change the table, you know," Cyrus said, stirring the Ghost out of a long, silent stare that he'd directed at an unresponsive Shirri.

"Later," Alaric said, dismissing him with a wave of the hand. "There are more important matters."

"Yes," Vara said, stirring, another grimace pulled from her lips at the mere motion. "There are. Such as what is hobbling my magic so thoroughly that I can barely cast two near-ineffectual healing spells before I run out of magical energy." She held up her hand and it glowed faintly red for a moment before fading away.

"I used to be able to push the limits of my magic when I had Praelior in hand," Cyrus said, slapping a hand onto his scabbard. "Now I can hardly cast anything, as Vara said." He let his hand slip from the scabbard further around; he'd lost all but one of his pistols in the fight at the mill. With his magic hamstrung, he felt the loss acutely, and cursed Tirner Gaull under his breath once more.

"One of our number didn't seem to have much difficulty casting a rather strong spell," Curatio said, turning his gaze to Shirri.

"What did I miss?" came a singsongy voice from the entry as the doors thumped closed. Cyrus turned to find Vaste striding across the room.

"Tension," Hiressam answered under his breath as Vaste came into the Great Hall, someone trailing a few paces behind him. "Mostly tension."

"Oh, good, I love tension," Vaste said, and now Cyrus could see the figure trailing behind him. It was a troll woman, probably as tall as Cyrus if not slightly taller, a cloak of the old style draped over her shoulders and neatly closed at the front with a simple clasp of brass. Vaste threw himself into the oversized chair next to Curatio and the troll woman followed with a little more reticence, slipping quietly— amazingly quietly, given her size—into the seat next to Shirri's end of the table. She studied Shirri with a flicker of brief interest, then turned her attention to the food in front of her.

"Hello," Cyrus said to her with a tight smile.

She looked right at him. Like Vaste, her lower fangs protruded from behind her lips, giving her a jutted-jaw look. "Hello," she said, simply and with more careful elocution than Cyrus had heard from any troll other than Vaste.

"I'm Cyrus," he said.

"Birissa," she said, and then her eyes fell to the rack of rib in front of her. Without so much as a by-your-leave, she picked up the whole of it and put it on the plate before her with a grunt, then daintily picked up her silverware and cut a massive piece, shoving it into her mouth while the others watched in a stunned silence.

Vaste was the first to speak. "Gods, you are impressive, woman.

That is the sexiest thing I have ever seen in my life."

"Yours is the life of a grotesque," Vara muttered under her breath, so low that Cyrus hoped he was the only one that could hear it.

"Now that we're all here—old and new," Alaric said, removing his helm and placing it upon the table, "it seems we can begin."

Cyrus sat there, déjà vu running through him. "This feels like the wrong room for such a conversation. Shouldn't we adjourn to the Council Chambers?"

"I don't believe they're there any longer," Vara said. "Did you notice when we went up the stairs earlier?"

Cyrus stared at her. "No, I hadn't. My mind must have been elsewhere."

She blew air between her lips impatiently. "What about after?"

Cyrus shrugged. "I was hungry."

"Classic Cyrus," Vaste said with great good humor. "You are quite the character, my friend. Why, your appetites are probably the reason why these people worship you, for who could fail to appreciate such drive?"

"Where do you suppose the archives are, then?" Cyrus asked.

"They will have moved somewhere appropriate, I am sure," Alaric said, "but this is hardly the time to discuss—"

"I should like to do some journaling later," Vara said. "I would hate to think that my diary was lost in the ether."

"Yes, who knows who could be reading it, then?" Vaste asked. "All sorts of ethereal beings could be having many great laughs reading the comedic courtship of Cyrus and Vara." He made his voice into a high imitation of hers. "'Today I met a lunkheaded warrior who offended all my sensibility but still inflamed my loins in such a way as I have never felt since emerging from the ice baths of paladin-hood. Why, I think I might have even felt a stirring in that one tiny, special spot I discovered when I was alone in the dormitories after hours'—"

"I have killed many today," Vara said darkly, "killing one more won't make a difference to me."

"I like you people already," Birissa pronounced, her mouth full of a whole hen. It all stayed in her mouth as she spoke, though, not a speck flying out. Which was a mark in her favor as far as Cyrus was concerned.

"I feel like our courtship was more romantic than that," Cyrus said. "It was as though were drawn together unstoppably—"

"Like your sword to an enemy's entrails, I'm sure," Vaste said with unfettered amusement. "Still, as fun as this may be, I feel like we've hashed it out enough in the last thousand years." He settled his hands upon the table in front of him, watching Birissa eat out of the corner of his eye. "So, what did I miss?"

"Shirri cast an impressive lightning spell," Curatio said. "Out of nowhere."

"Zarnn was killed by a man who now works for the Machine," Cyrus said, "and he wields Rodanthar."

"His skill is impressive," Vara said. "He nearly bested both Cyrus and me at the same time, with our godly weapons in hand. If not for Hiressam, he might have triumphed."

Vaste nodded, face screwed up in concentration. "Indeed, indeed. What's a Hiressam?"

"I ... am Hiressam," the elf said, stirring in his place nearly across from Vaste.

"Good gods, I didn't even see you there," Vaste said. "Oh! You!" He pointed at the elf. "I remember you now. You were friends with that smelly dwarf."

Hiressam flushed. "He was ... not smelly."

"The hell he wasn't," Vaste said. "I went up to his quarters one time to deliver a complaint—I think it was the fourth or fifth he'd received, because we kept having to move people off his floor." The troll threw his arms wide. "This is a mystical place with special magics and indoor plumbing, things the like of which most of Arkaria has never seen. Even it couldn't keep the smell off your friend, I don't know if he was taking mud baths in pig shit or what, but he had a stink problem."

"It was truly terrible," Cyrus said. "Like socks brewed in brine and worn on a long march."

Vaste nodded. "And then used to wipe your arse after a heinous movement. And left to stew for six months."

Vara made a slight gagging noise. "That's enough of that, and I'm not even eating."

"You need a stronger stomach," Birissa said, now extracting the chicken bones. She simply pulled them out of her mouth and it was as though all the meat had been boiled from them.

Vara stared back at her, just for a moment. "I'm sorry—where did you come from? Because we were given to understand from the man who nearly killed us that the trolls of Gren were wiped out some eight hundred plus years ago."

"Wouldn't know anything about that," Birissa said, picking up a lump of aged, yellow cheese from a plate of them and sniffing it. She made a face but then shoved it into her mouth anyway.

Vaste mopped his brow, eyes fixed on her. "This is so ... amazing."

"Where are you from, then?" Cyrus asked as Birissa chewed the cheese. She seemed to be trying to decide whether she liked it or not.

"Not here," she said, finally just swallowing it down. She stared down at the plate she extracted it from, eyes narrowed, pronouncing judgment. "Not bad," she decided, and grabbed another wedge, white this time.

"Do any of our new guests have any information about the Machine they'd like to share with us?" Alaric asked. His face, too, was slightly shadowed, but he seemed less patient and more straightforward than usual, especially in council. New people, Cyrus decided. Their presence was probably throwing him off.

"Don't know anything about a Machine," Birissa said, finishing the second lump of cheese and making a face. "Just got to town last night."

"It's just as well," Vaste said, practically gushing. He was practically falling all over this Birissa in a way that Cyrus could not recall seeing from the troll before. "They're just a bunch of gangsters trying to choke the life out of the citizens of Reikonos. Not the sort you'd want to associate with."

She paused as she started to pick up the sautéed breast of a duck. "I think I might have run into a couple of those when I came in at the airship docks. Tried to shake me down for money. 'Give us some gold, or your visit is going to end in the local apothecary,' something of that sort." She stared straight ahead in concentration.

Cyrus's gaze flicked to Hiressam, who nodded. "That ... is the sort of thing that low-level Machine operatives would do. Shakedowns for gold, platinum, silver, valuables."

"My goodness," Vaste breathed. "I'm so glad you weren't hurt."

"Mmm," Birissa said, the duck breast having evaporated from her fork. "Too bad they can't say the same." She spoke with the same near-indifference she exhibited toward Vaste.

"What happened to them?" Vara asked.

"They stumbled headfirst into a running airship engine," she said, swallowing without missing a beat or evincing any more emotion than she had at any point during the entire meal. "It exploded after the first went in, but I made sure the second followed anyway, crammed him right in there tight as a drum. Thought they should be together in death." She surveyed the table in front of her and pointed at a bowl of squash. "What's that?"

"It's squash," Vara said. "It's a vegetable."

Birissa made a noise of distaste and screwed up her face by sticking out her tongue. "No need for that, then." And she stood up and reached for a suckling pig instead, drawing the entire thing over to her, the apple falling out of its mouth onto the table.

"This is just getting better and better," Vaste said, a deeper shade of green than any grass Cyrus had ever seen.

Birissa shot him a tight smile and went to work on the pig as Cyrus averted his eyes. She had better manners than any troll he'd encountered save for Vaste, but that was not saying much and he had no desire to watch it any further. "So …" Cyrus said, redirecting his attention to the end of the table, "Shirri knows magic?"

Shirri did not stir, staring at the table before her, hand draped upon it, her plate still empty.

"So it would seem," Curatio said. "The lightning spell she produced was quite impressive, given the constraints we've encountered on magic in this place. It was more than I would have been able to muster in similar circumstance. And furthermore, there was no trace of red glow upon her hand when she concluded it. It would surely have run any of the rest of you—save perhaps Vaste—dry of magical energy immediately."

"Shirri," Alaric said quietly, "magic has faded from this land. From where did you learn your spellcraft?"

"From my mother," Shirri said, breaking her silence at last, though she did not stir from her statue-like position.

"This grows more interesting," Cyrus said. "The same mother that the Machine has somehow taken?"

"She is not as strong as she once was," Shirri said, eyes flicking up. "And they took her in her sleep, I believe. Probably gagged her, or perhaps knocked her unconscious."

"The Machine doesn't much like dealing with squirming captives," Hiressam said, his smooth voice like a balm to Cyrus's jangling nerves. "In their kidnapping activities, it is very common for them to club their victims insensate. More than a few have died in the process, but it keeps things quiet."

"Have you had many dealings with the Machine?" Vara asked him.

"Here and there," Hiressam said, shifting in his seat. "I have opposed them often, though never as grandly or obviously as you have this day. I have fought them in quiet places, struck them where there was no chance to be seen." He looked down, plainly uncomfortable. "They are without honor, and I considered fighting them to be no less than a charge given me by …" He cleared his throat. "Well, it was a duty for me, and one I undertook as often as I could, but … that was not terribly often. They move in numbers, they do so boldly, in daylight. The city watch is theirs, for all intents and purposes, and turns a blind eye—"

"An Alaric eye, I like to call it," Vaste said.

"—to their activities," Hiressam said, undeterred by the troll's interruption, though he did evince a confused expression for just a beat. "That makes it difficult to oppose them without exposing yourself. To do so means that they will come for you. And there is not a corner of Reikonos where their influence does not extend. Cross them, and if they should find out about it, they will find you. And they will make an example of you." He swallowed and looked down again.

"Who runs this organization?" Alaric asked. "Whose hand guides—"

"Whose arse sits upon the throne of the Machine?" Vaste asked.

"What an incredibly inelegant way to ask the same damned question as Alaric," Vara said.

"Elegance is for little girls in dance classes," Vaste said. "I like my way better."

"It was delightfully crass and to the point," Birissa said, nodding in agreement, the suckling pig now little but bones.

"I could not say," Hiressam said. "Whoever they are, they have guessed at the truth of their vulnerability. If I had such a name? I would go straight for them. Bury my blade in their neck in silence if need be, and let the Machine fall to pieces without them." He shook his head. "No. Who runs them is a carefully guarded secret, of necessity. There are many who would oppose the Machine, both from places of honor, such as I do, and also baser motives. There are countless criminals in this city who feel their fortunes would rise if the Machine would but move aside and permit their competition."

"And they hold the levers of government, too?" Cyrus asked, thumping a palm upon the table, feeling the grain of the wood upon his bare hand. "How high does that go?"

"Not too high, I would say." Hiressam reached out, pulling a dish of spinach mixed with a heavy cream close to him. He spooned some out on his plate experimentally, then tried it. Apparently satisfied, he took another scoop while answering. "For example, the Lord Protector remains above their influence. He probably does not even realize what is going on down here."

Cyrus frowned. "How can you be sure?" He leaned toward Hiressam. "If this powerful fellow has a corrupt watch and countless—I don't know, whatever instrument of elected government they have across Reikonos—how do you know he's not in on the scheme and just collecting the profits from his tower?"

Hiressam stared at Cyrus blankly. "I ... can not believe you would say that of the Lord Protector."

Cyrus stared at him. "Why would I not? I don't know this man—"

"But you do," Hiressam said, his fork clattering to the plate. "You do know him. We all do," and here he looked to Vara, to Alaric and Curatio, and Vaste. "Of course you know him. He is one of ours, one of our very own, and his honor is unquestioned."

"I think Cyrus just questioned it," Vaste said, far too happy for Cyrus's taste.

"That's because I don't know who he is," Cyrus said, shooting a vicious look at the troll. "But I would like to know his name before I decide that I'm not going to criticize him." He looked squarely at Hiressam. "Who is this Lord Protector?"

Hiressam stared at him, and all sound seemed to cease save for Birissa working her way through a piece of fat ham. For a long moment, he simply blinked, his lips barely parted, until he spoke. "Why, it's Lord Longwell, of course," he said, and the silence seemed to rise as his words echoed through the hall.

34.

"Longwell!" Cyrus said, coming to his feet so swiftly he nearly knocked the table over. Everyone recoiled from the fearsome clatter, save for Birissa, who snatched up the rest of the ham that threatened to topple off and then proceeded to devour it, surprisingly quietly. "We should go to him immediately. If he's in charge, he'll help us put things to the right with this Machine."

"I don't know that that's true," Hiressam said carefully, his hands folded neatly in his lap. "He hasn't been seen in public for nearing a year."

"And," Shirri said from her place at the end of the table, dripping sarcasm as the shadows played heavily under her eyes, "I'm sure he'll take the news of your joyous return with the same seriousness as he treats all such reports—none at all."

Cyrus frowned. "You're telling me if I go to his gates—"

"Well, he lives in the Citadel," Hiressam said, "so—"

"The guards will laugh you off without so much as a hearing," Shirri said bluntly. "They get Cyrus Davidon impersonators like you every day. More convincing ones, even."

"I move with the speed of a god," Cyrus said, voice rising as he stared her down, "and can use magic where few can. How are there better impersonators than I?"

"There are some … very good ones out there," Hiressam said apologetically. "Some of them … I even thought might have been truly you."

"You've met me!" Cyrus erupted. "And you didn't think *I* was real when you crossed my path earlier today!"

"Once burned, always shy of the dragon's mouth thereafter," Hiressam said, shifting his gaze downward.

"Well, my crowd of admirers seemed to realize who I was," Cyrus said.

"And dispersed quite smartly after we blew up that coal yard," Vara said. "Some before they entirely lost their hearing, I hope."

"That was just as well," Cyrus waved her off. "We didn't need company following us to the mill."

"Yes, what if they'd seen you get your arse handed to you by that human?" Vaste asked. "Truly, your following would have been over, possibly for good. Or else transferred to that Gaull fellow, which would be bad news for us indeed."

Cyrus tensed at the mere mention of Gaull's name. "We have business to attend to out there. Why are we huddling in here?"

"Because there are answers we seek before we strike out blindly once more," Alaric said, breaking the quiet that had settled over his end of the table. "I am not above a good mystery or two—"

"Or fifty," Vaste said. "A hundred. Ten thousand, maybe—"

"—But we are currently in the service of you, Shirri," he said. The young lady at the end of the table looked up at him. "And while I am content that we are doing right in helping you—it sits ill with me that your secrets seem to be the sort that are blowing back upon us like—"

"Troll farts in a tight space," Vaste said.

"Good one," Birissa said. "Spot on."

"—like ... anything but that," Alaric said, seeming to have lost the thread of his thought. "We need to know more than what you have told us if you wish our continued assistance," he said, directing his words firmly toward Shirri. "These secrets carry a peril that seems to be visiting itself upon us—"

"A secret that someone is keeping that is bringing us to peril?" Vaste clutched at his chest. "Why, I've never heard of such a thing happening in Sanctuary!"

Alaric's eye twitched slightly. "All jests aside—"

"I will never put my jests aside. You'll have to pry them from my cold, dead hands."

"That could be arranged," Curatio said, looking to Alaric. "Perhaps if we kill him, it will serve as an example to the other younglings to stop harping at us about our secrets—which are no longer secret, I might add."

"I have a godly weapon and a troll woman with a sword," Vaste said. "Come at me with everything you have, healer."

Birissa looked sideways at him, frowning. "Don't include me in your mad plans. I barely know you."

"I have a godly weapon and a hole in my heart," Vaste said, still staring at Curatio. "Come at me and I'll strike your aged groin from your body."

"I believe Curatio was making a jest of his own," Alaric said.

"I *probably* was," Curatio said dryly. "It's so difficult to tell anymore, my aged mind being not what it once was. However, my aged gr—"

"Let me stop this before it gets ugly … er," Cyrus said, holding up a hand. "I agree with Alaric. Long have we of Sanctuary embraced difficult causes and charged headlong into—"

"Death," Vaste said.

"—difficult circumstances," Cyrus said, avoiding Vaste's choice of words. "Even while our own kept secrets that might have been useful to know. But that trust does not extend to an utter stranger." And here he looked down the table at Shirri. "If you wish our aid … we need to know more than you are presently telling us."

She blinked at him, looking dully down the table. Then she stood. "No."

"Shirri—" Alaric began.

She waved a hand at him as she turned her back, striding across the Great Hall and through the doors to the foyer. Cyrus watched her, even as Alaric and Curatio called her name. She made it to the doors and opened them, disappearing out of Sanctuary without speaking a word or turning back.

"See, I can admire the lengths she just went to in keeping her secret," Vaste said. "She just walked out on the only people who have tried to protect her from this Machine. Indeed, the only ones that probably stand any chance of defending her or retrieving her magical mother from their clutches." He drummed his nails against the table, causing Vara to give him an ireful look. "That's real commitment to your secrets right there. I feel like even the people at this table could learn something from that."

"His death would be such a wonderful example to the rest," Curatio said to Alaric.

"Hush," Alaric said. "If a few japes from Vaste is the only price we pay for keeping so much from them, it is a small punishment indeed."

"I could make more japes," Vaste said, and received a withering glare from Alaric that indicated to Cyrus his patience had run out. "Or just … keep it at the current level, then. Perhaps even be a bit more sparing."

"Are we just going to let her walk out, then?" Hiressam asked.

"We can hardly compel her to stay by force," Alaric said. "Nor can we continue to throw ourselves into the fight on her behalf without any of the guidance she might provide us."

"The hell we can't," Vara said, drawing every eye to her. "We've fought for money at various points, Alaric. Death and danger for gold—"

"That's not quite right," Cyrus said. "We were sympathetic to the aims of the Human Confederation when we took their gold to defend Livlosdald and Leaugarden, or to eject the dark elves from Prehorta—"

"But we took gold nonetheless," Vara said, "for something we felt needed to be done. Here, I think, we face a similar circumstance." Her face darkened. "This Machine seems to me to be the worst possible outcome of city living. All the vile dregs of humanity clustered together to prey upon the weak. They possess all the decorum of a pack of wolves and none of the grace. I would happily strike the head of every one of them from their shoulders for nothing more than the satisfaction of doing so."

"It's quite fun, killing them," Birissa said, now holding a roll in her hand. "They make the most delightful squeals when you crush them into an airship engine. I should like to hear that sound again."

"And she seemed so civilized, too," Cyrus said.

"There's hardly anything civilized about what their lot does, little man," Birissa said, giving Cyrus barely a glance before attacking the roll. She practically swallowed it whole before continuing. "As your lady protector there said—they work in packs. It's law of nature for them, not the law of man. Reason won't work. Talking won't work— I'm happy to negotiate with someone if they show a spark of decency. But if they don't—" And her hand fell to her cloak, tearing it open, whereupon it emerged a second later with a blade nearly the size of Vara. Birissa whipped it up and around expertly, bringing the tip down to the floor with the barest clink, perfect control keeping her from chipping the stone floor. "I have ways of dealing with that, too. Same as yours, I expect." And she shoved another roll in her mouth.

"I may have to be excused for a short interval," Vaste said, his voice high. "I'm feeling a bit … flushed … everywhere."

"It's not hard to see why, either," Vara said. "You've finally found a woman who lines up perfectly with everything you've ever loved— good food, good conversation, excessively violent—why, she's practically the female troll equivalent of Cyrus." Vara's eyebrows moved subtly.

"I—I—what?" Cyrus asked, taken aback.

"She is nothing like—" Vaste looked sideways as Birissa stared at Vara, then Cyrus, with suspicion. Vaste's mouth was frozen open, his finger extended, and he took a long breath before turning back to Vara, and saying, with just a hint of surrender, "Please don't ruin this for me."

"I'm going to take this as a compliment," Birissa said, her own eyes narrowed and her hands empty of food, "seeing how as you seem to be quite fond of the black-armored little morsel. But if I catch a whiff of insult, know that the punishment for enraging me is to have your limbs plucked off one by one."

"And ... do you eat them, then?" Vara asked with mild curiosity.

Birissa just stared back at her. "No. Because I'm civilized." And she lifted a tankard and drained it in one long pull. Setting it down, she looked at Vaste, reached down, and plucked up his hand as she rose. "Come on, then, you."

Vaste stared at her paw upon his. "What?"

She took hold of him and dragged him from his seat. "Give me a tour of this place." And she moved toward the doors to the foyer with Vaste in tow.

Cyrus watched them go with some relief. "She's really quite ... forceful, isn't she?"

"As good a match for Vaste as I could've imagined," Alaric said.

"He could use someone to keep him in bounds," Vara said.

Hiressam swallowed visibly. "You think she's going to ... bind him?"

"Not quite what I meant," Vara said, lips curling in distaste. "Thank you for that."

Cyrus looked toward Alaric. "What do we do now?"

Alaric let the thought brew for a moment, and then spoke. "We find ourselves in a curious position. I agree with Vara—destroying this Machine is something we would do anyway, regardless of Shirri, for the harm they inflict upon the people of Reikonos."

"How is that a 'curious position'?" Vara asked. "It seems eminently reasonable to me."

"So does a vegetarian diet," Cyrus said, looking at the thin arrangement of lettuce and other greenery on her plate. "But I try not to hold it against you."

"Wise on your part," Vara shot back at him. "Considering the hold I seem to have over you in so many ways."

"I think we should take a short interval to reconsider our strategy," Alaric said. "To rest, to recover from your wounds—and then redouble our efforts against the Machine." He clenched his gauntlet tight and put it down on the table. "There are mysteries here, and if Shirri does not wish to enlighten us about them, it does not absolve us of the fact that she summoned us for our help. Our obligation remains, if not to her, then to the people of Reikonos, who live in fear of the Machine." He lowered his head, staring straight forward. "So we will rest. And we will plan. And we will reassess … and then we will come forth and crush this Machine with everything we have."

35.

Shirri

"They're all mad," Shirri muttered to herself as she emerged from the alley onto the main thoroughfare. "Mad and fools and ..." She let her voice trail off as the soft, hazy light of day shone down upon her from above.

Shirri blended into the crowd milling along the street. It was hardly the busiest she'd seen it; the morning traffic had died off, replaced by the market traffic of midday. People going to pick up food and wares, not bustling to the nearest factory to arrive before the starting whistle blew. She moved among the crowd with her head down, watching carefully for signs of the Machine's lackeys, the tendrils that seemed to be ever reaching for her.

The smell of thick smoke as Reikonos's factories belched heavily upon the city in the throes of midday production intruded upon Shirri's thoughts. It was always worse at this time of day; some factories did run all night, but not nearly so many as during the daylight hours. The sun, as ever, remained stubbornly clouded by smog.

"They're crazy," Shirri muttered under her breath. The conclusion was inescapable; no matter how reasonable Alaric seemed, he carried a sword and wore armor and talked of honor even as he somehow swirled into a vortex of mist, as though he'd been born from one of the innumerable smokestacks around the city. And Curatio, that timeless elf? He might have been even worse, throwing his mace out of hand and leaving himself defenseless so that Shirri would have to reveal her ability. Why, he'd probably done it on purpose, and she'd played right into his hands. Her cheeks burned at that thought of being had by them in such a way.

But ... really, hadn't they done more to hold up their end of the bargain? She'd offered them nothing and they'd pledged help. While she had little to show for it, it wasn't for their lack of trying. They'd plowed through three Machine strongholds, which was three more than she'd ever heard of anyone else doing.

"They're crazy," she whispered to herself, passing a man in a silken vest who looked at her strangely for talking to herself. "But ... they could perhaps help."

She immediately dismissed the thought. They'd offered to help blindly, before they'd realized how unstoppable the Machine was. But they'd run across its true power—or hints of it—at the mill, and look at them now. Why, they were sitting around a table trying to decide what to do next, as surely as if it were Shirri, any of the times she sat at her own table back at home, thinking through what options she had available. It was simply a matter of truth that when someone was struck, good and hard, they had to take a moment to re-evaluate, and that was what this lot was doing now, around their table in that ... hideout of theirs.

And Shirri knew the conclusion they had to come to, for it must be as obvious to them as it was to her.

The Machine was unstoppable. To continue to throw themselves against it would mean death, and Shirri wanted no part of death.

"But they have secrets of their own," she whispered to herself, then stopped short of saying the thing that would have followed after: *And I have secrets of my own.*

No, she didn't dare say that aloud, not in the streets of Reikonos. That little detail had already sparked the Machine's interest in her to begin with. She didn't need to set a fire in front of her and fan the smoke so that they would come running. Best to leave it alone.

"Mother's ... probably already dead," she said, with a cresting burn of shame. And even if she weren't ...

Well, even with those strangers' help, it didn't seem likely Shirri would be seeing her again ... ever.

All that could happen now, Shirri thought as she passed a knot of strangers who could almost be Machine thugs—if they were dressed a little worse—was that eventually the Machine would get her. This was Reikonos, after all. There was nowhere to hide here.

"I'm sorry, Mother," she said, damning herself for her cowardice. But there just wasn't anything she could do. Even if she told those weirdos her secrets ...

It wouldn't make a bit of difference.

The Machine was too big. Too strong. Too ...

Unstoppable.

So when Shirri hit the next cross street, she turned north. It'd take her a little over an hour to make it to the airship docks if she didn't take a train. And she'd need every piece of gold she could spare in order to pay for a one-way flight to Firoba. She wouldn't make it that deep into the continent; Binngard, maybe Vanreis if she was lucky, or sunny Suijnara if they had some sort of discount, or she caught the right cargo transport looking for passengers.

She didn't even care at this point. Desperation choked her. There truly was no hope left in Reikonos, and so she let her feet guide her, heart in her stomach, as she walked to where she could make her final escape—with but a quick stop along the way to pick up something she didn't dare leave behind.

36.

Cyrus

With Vaste, Birissa and Shirri gone, the table had fallen silent—not that Shirri made any noise, Cyrus reflected as they sat there in silence, the light streaming down from the stained-glass window. No one spoke; they simply stared at the table, or each other.

"Someone should show Hiressam to quarters," Curatio said at last, breaking the silence as he stretched. "I assume he'll be staying with us?"

Hiressam perked up at that. Cyrus was surprised that a several-thousand-year-old elf could manage such a youthful look. "I had assumed so, yes," Cyrus said. "If he'd like to …?"

"I would be honored," Hiressam said, bowing his head toward Cyrus, then each of the others in succession. "I have very few things and am staying at a local inn—"

"Why don't I show you to your quarters, then," Curatio said, rising, "and if you wish, you may retrieve your things from your inn and rejoin us." He glanced at Alaric. "It seems we are fated to do nothing for a short interval … is that right?"

Alaric stirred at his place at the table's head. "So it would seem," he allowed. "We could marshal our forces and march through the streets, but I suspect our general would suggest that is counterproductive."

"Better to have a target," Cyrus said. "We already probably risk ambush just walking down the street, but now that we have no idea where we're going and we know that Gaull is out there … if he's got half a brain and any sway in that organization, the Machine is going to pull back for a moment, too, while they start planning on how to remove us as their new chief problem."

"We will need a strategy soon," Alaric said. "We have hit them, but only close at hand. This city is massive and sprawling; surely they have not felt it at the other ends."

"You're probably right," Cyrus said, letting his helm thump against the back of his chair. "But I need a target first. The most powerful sword in the world is useless with nowhere to swing it."

"I will see what I can do about that," Alaric said, dissolving into soft mist. A moment more for him to filter into particulates so small as to be nearly invisible, and he was gone.

Cyrus looked over at Hiressam, and he was smiling. "I have missed seeing magic in the world," the elf said, when he caught the glance.

"Come, Hiressam," Curatio said, waving him forward, "I will show you to quarters. And then," the elder elf said, with a wry smile, "I intend to enjoy the most luxuriant of mortal pleasures."

Cyrus froze in place, eyes closed. "Don't ask—" he accidentally said aloud.

"A nap," Curatio said, already on his way out the door. "You two are young, and have so much to learn."

Cyrus looked to Vara, who was already looking at him, one of her eyes tightly shut. "I was thinking the same thing," she said, and opened her eye.

"You looked a little like Alaric there for a second," Cyrus said, looking once more at his plate. The thought of food brought little satisfaction.

"Tall and handsome, stately in my way?" she asked, teasingly.

"Heh," Cyrus let out a low guffaw. "I had a thought."

"Gods," Vara said, "tell me it's not about—" And she pointed up.

It took Cyrus a moment to realize it was their quarters she was pointing to. "Huh? No, not that." He paused a beat. "I mean, that's not what I was thinking, but if you wanted to, I could definitely get there—"

"Perhaps later," she said softly. "I am not recovered from a fresh wound as yet."

"Given the dearth of healing magic and our propensity for fighting everyone, everywhere, all the time," Cyrus said, "we might never be recovered enough for—"

"Your original thought, please?" She looked mildly impatient.

"Oh." He put a hand on the table. "I was thinking we should at least try to talk to Longwell. If he runs the city—"

"Weren't you the one who just mentioned we now risk ambush anytime we go out?" Vara asked.

"I did, but—"

"Do the Machine not own this city from one side to another?" Vara asked. "Do you not think they have spies upon every corner, aware always of everything happening within the city walls?"

"Probably, but—"

"Pfeh," Vara said, balling up her napkin from her lap and tossing it upon the plate. "I agree we should talk to Longwell. But I don't think we should rush out ourselves. Come on, General," and here she reached up and brushed his cheek with a bare hand. "We must not run these sorts of risks now that have always gotten you in trouble before. Recall the time that Malpravus, Orion and a few of our other choice foes laid a trap for you using your ex-wife as bait. If Gaull knows you are Cyrus Davidon, then surely he knows of your association with Samwen Longwell. I imagine the one thing Gaull would wish to prevent than any other—"

"Would be Longwell becoming apprised of the situation on the streets," Cyrus said, letting out a deep sigh. "Tell me, Vara ... how could Reikonos get to this state? And under Longwell's rule, no less?"

"How did Sanctuary become infected with spies during yours?" she asked, prompting him to blush. "Or thick with assassins during Alaric's?" She laid her hand upon his. "Even the greatest leader cannot watch every corner of their city every hour of the day. If it truly is Longwell that is Lord Protector, he has been alive for over a thousand years and been ruler of this city for nearly all that time. Surely his every thought is not focused upon it after that long."

"Fair enough," Cyrus said.

"We'll find a way to get word to him," Vara said, "though I suspect it will not bring immediate relief. We should go after Alaric returns, or once Curatio has woken from his nap. We could take a walk to the Citadel and return quickly, should we not find easy entry."

"It seems unlikely they'll make entry easy," Cyrus said. "We could always take the tunnels up, the way Curatio always brought us."

"Provided they still exist, yes," Vara said.

Cyrus leaned back in his seat and blew air between his lips. A wave of fatigue had passed over him, settled upon him, down to his bones. "So much has changed. I feel as though I barely got a look at the city before ... well, before we started knocking down doors and breaking skulls and fighting with swords again." He looked up at her, and gave her a wan smile. "I would wonder at why we seem to get no peace, but ... we just came from a thousand years of it."

"It seems all the more fleeting once removed from it, doesn't it?" she asked, pensive. "As though we were never quietly in the ether at all, but rather skipped straight from fighting guilds and nations and gods and went directly to fighting street gangs and thugs and some arsehole with a purloined godly weapon." Her expression darkened. "It feels like a bit of a come-down, doesn't it? From gods to this?"

"Well, I did kill all those gods," Cyrus said. "I don't suppose we can resurrect them in order to give you and I the battle we truly deserve—"

"Arse," she said lightly, slapping his pauldron. "The God of War killed me, you know."

His face darkened. "It would be impossible to forget."

She sat in silence with him for a long moment. "As tempting as it would be to dismiss this Tirner Gaull as a lesser threat than Bellarum … he may be more dangerous in his way."

"What …?"

"We are hobbled here," Vara said quietly. "Without magic at its full effect, should any of us die, it may become a permanent state— provided we're not at Sanctuary at the time. We are not full ghosts, as Alaric is, not fully part of this place. If we were to die beyond its bounds—"

"It wouldn't be able to … rechannel—reform us—whatever it did to you," Cyrus said.

"Correct," she said. "This is a truth I simply know in my bones, like a warning Sanctuary has written into my mind."

"Aye," Cyrus said slowly. "I feel it, too. The limits of our immortality."

"And that makes Gaull even more dangerous," Vara said, "for it's not as though we can simply challenge him here, inside Sanctuary—"

"Why not?" Cyrus asked with the trace of a smile. "Why not let them know where we are, and have them come for us like the sieges of old?"

Vara rolled her eyes. "I thought you were a master strategist. They have the numbers, my husband. We have a secret stronghold. Should we lose the 'secret' part of that, then we have a stronghold—and a siege. I have done a siege before, and I don't wish to again, especially now that teleportation magics are likely ineffectual."

"Oh, that's a fair point," Cyrus said, casting his eyes down. "But we should make ready for a siege nonetheless. It will likely come at some point."

"'At some point,' I can live with," Vara said. "Provided we make the siege our fallback position, the one we go to when all other plans have failed. Putting us into a defensive position now—"

"Means we lose the initiative and the ability to dictate where and how this war is fought," Cyrus said with a sigh. "Sorry. Perhaps my brain lost all sense for a moment."

"A frequent occurrence," she said, leaning in to press her forehead against his. "And why I am here. Honestly, I don't know how you survived conducting a war against the gods themselves without me."

"Well, I did have other help," Cyrus said. "Help which is sorely missed these days." His eyes lit up. "If Longwell is alive ... do you suppose some of the others could be as well? Gaull is hundreds of years old, after all—"

"I am certain some of our old friends are out there, yes," Vara said. "Still clinging tightly to their prizes of war and the immortality they bring. How long did your grandfather live again?"

"Alaric said he fought with him in the war of the—well, whatever you want to call the fall of the Protanian Empire," Cyrus said. "So ... probably some ten thousand years, or near enough? Since my mother met him and knew him on the other end of that timeframe."

"Yes," Vara said quietly, "I think it very likely that more of our friends are out there, somewhere." And here she smiled, an aura of mischief falling over her. "Somewhere out there, like Hiressam, just waiting, living their lives ... and when word reaches their ears of our return ..."

"Our sundered company may come together in union once more?" Cyrus asked.

"Indeed it may," Vara said with a faint smile. "But until then ..." And the resolve ran over her once more. "We have battles to fight."

"A war to win," Cyrus agreed.

"And that bastard Gaull's head to remove," Vara said.

Cyrus stared at her, with her flushed cheeks and dancing eyes. "Gods, I love you." And he swept in for a kiss, which she did not deny, pulling him in closer. When they broke, he added, "Minus that 'gods' business. Need to break that habit, since I broke them."

"Just remember, it was nearly the opposite," she said, and now caution fell over her fair features. "Let us not carry their hubris into our next battle with Gaull—lest we see the same or a worse outcome."

"Agreed," Cyrus said with a sharp nod. "We'll need to be smarter. More determined. Seek other help, like Longwell." He let out a heavy breath. "We need to find the hiding places of this Machine, root it out ..." Cyrus clenched his fist, "... and crush it, once and for—" He paused, cocking his head to the side. There was a sound in the distance, a deep grunt, followed by another, then another, echoing through the halls. "What the hell is that?"

"I don't kn—" Vara started to say, then her eyes widened, and she went red from her hair down to where her neck disappeared into her armor. "I don't believe it."

Cyrus stared at her. "What do you think it—oh." It went on, a steady cadence, the sound of a troll—or two—being not at all quiet in their exertion. "Oh." He blinked. "You don't think ... that's ...?"

Vara's eyes found the floor, and she nodded. "Yes."

Cyrus just blinked, the noise rising, as his lips curled in distaste. It came from somewhere above, and there was no door between it and them. He cringed. "Seriously?"

37.

Vaste

"I didn't expect that," Vaste said when it was all done, his clothes strewn all over the floor and his eyes fixed upon the ceiling. Birissa lay beside him at a small distance, breathing in and out in a slow rasp. "I mean—not that I'm complaining. It's just ... I barely know you."

"And now," Birissa said, shifting the sheets, "in this way, at least, you know me better than you've known anyone before." She turned to prop herself up on her elbow, cool amusement turning up the corner of her lip. "Let's not kid ourselves, Vaste. I haven't seen one of my own kind in a long time, and neither have you. I know why you knocked on my door. I might have done the same if I'd seen you first."

"Yes," Vaste said, "but—"

"No 'but.'" Birissa rolled onto her back, eyes pointed toward the ceiling. "Don't make more of this in your head than it is."

"And ..." Vaste said, head still reeling, "... what is *it*? Exactly?"

"What I needed," she said, throwing off the covers and rising up. She was so unlike the other troll women he'd seen before. There was not an ounce of fat upon her, her sculpted muscles rippled beneath her skin. She stooped to retrieve her clothing with a graceful motion and rose just as athletically. If he were to bend like that, he might need help getting back up again. "What you needed," she went on. "What is there?" she asked, looking right at him.

"Some ... other stuff," Vaste said. "Love. Marriage. Babies."

"I've only known you for a few hours," she said, "let's not get ahead of ourselves. Just because we might be the last two of our kind here—"

"I didn't think you were from Arkaria," Vaste said.

"I'm not," Birissa said, not looking up as she shimmied back into her underclothes. They fit ... well.

"Then how do you know, in this wider world I'm hearing about—places like this Firoba—that there are no more trolls?"

"I don't know it for sure," Birissa said, now slipping her armor back on. It was thin, well-made, mostly chain linking together larger plates, very different from what Cyrus or Vara wore. "I just know that I haven't seen any of our sort."

"Do you know where you came from?"

She shot him a quicksilver smile. "Deep question, that. Not sure I'd go probing that one if I were you."

"I meant literally, not philosophically," Vaste said. "I mean, you could answer that, too—"

"I don't have the answers to all your questions," she said, tightening a clasp and finishing the job of putting her armor back on.

"So you don't an answer for me about the meaning of life?" Vaste asked, with a sheepish smile, keeping the covers close to his chest.

"The meaning of life is that you live it," Birissa said. "That's all."

"I don't know that I believe that," Vaste said, rising up, still keeping the covers wrapped around himself. "I once heard that only a fool focused on his own navel would fail to ask examining questions of his life."

"Clearly not said by a person concerned with their immediate survival."

"It does seem the sort of thing someone wouldn't ask unless they had most of their basic needs met," Vaste agreed. "But nonetheless—what we just did here—"

Birissa strode over to him, seized him by both cheeks, and gave him a passionate—if somewhat biting—kiss. When she was done, she pulled her lips from his and said, "You are a thinker, and that is a laudable quality. But at some point, you should stop, just a bit, and act." She rose, casting a look over her shoulder. "Because if I'd left it up to you to do this ... it wouldn't have happened, would it?"

Vaste's jaw dropped. "Well, I mean ... it's true, I let you seduce me—"

"You didn't even try," she said, standing at the door. "You wanted this. You don't know me, but you wanted this. And when it came your way ... you didn't even act. Get your head on straight, Vaste. Your larger questions are just that—questions. Seems to me you keep looking around at everyone else—your friends, me, maybe—seeking something outside of you that's going to make you happy." She took a hand and put it on her chest. "Did this make you happy?"

"Well, it certainly made parts of me happy—"

"Do you feel fulfilled?" she asked, staring at him. "Was this everything you dreamed of?"

"Obviously, I ..." his voice trailed off. "No. I mean, you were wonderful but ..." He looked away. "I don't really know you."

"I had fun, too," she said, "but it lacked much feeling, all said and done, didn't it?" She was looking at him, almost biting her lower lip. "That's not to say we couldn't get there, given time, but ..." She shook her head. "Ask your larger questions. But you might want to act on getting the answers. You might want to figure out what you really want ... because some woman who looks like you and acts like you wish you were—like your friend out there in the black armor—she's not going to solve your problems for you." Her face settled into a neutral expression. "I can't. I don't even know what they are."

"I think you might have just hit upon a few of them," Vaste said, not daring to meet her eyes.

"Only the obvious ones, dearie," she said, and shut the door gently behind her as she left. "Only the obvious ones."

38.

Cyrus

"Do you think they're done yet?" Cyrus asked, staring at the dark stone corners of the dungeon ceiling.

"One would hope," Vara said, sitting beside him in the tiny cell, the door firmly closed but not locked. She moved her shoulder experimentally. "Thank goodness I cast that last healing spell. I think I managed to seal up the worst of it. Now the wound only stings a little."

"It's as though the whole world drank black lace while we were in the ether," Cyrus said, massaging a couple of his own hurts. He, too, had sealed the worst of the wounds before the time had run out on them, but angry red welts remained where they'd been, nice little reminders of what Tirner Gaull had done to him. "Say, you don't think—"

"I don't think the world can collectively drink black lace," Vara said. "I think it would have to have been us that drank it for this to happen."

"Right. True enough," Cyrus said, staring into the darkness of the cell again. "Well, I don't remember saying bottoms up while chugging any, so unless Sanctuary slipped it to us in our waking feast ..."

"Our magic wasn't working before the feast," Vara said. "We tried it in the alley fight, when we first came out, remember? It was already nonfunctional."

"Right. So it's not that."

"Well, I wasn't being serious to begin with," she said with a trace of amusement, "but no ... safe to say it's not that."

"Another theory ruined," Cyrus said. "This lack of magic may end up being the worst thing that has happened since we got here." He

215

cringed, and pointed at the ceiling. "Other than this, I mean."

"Obviously."

A seeping mist crept into the room just then, and Cyrus turned his attention to the corner, where Alaric emerged a moment later. Cyrus leapt to his feet, armor rattling, and said, "We weren't doing anything."

Alaric froze, staring at him, eyebrow raised beneath his helm, and then the corner of his mouth quirked up. "I knew that."

"He can see through walls, fool," Vara said, looking at Cyrus as though he were an idiot.

"I cannot, actually," Alaric said. "I can only see where I am present. But I did not hear any bloodcurdling wails coming from here, and thus I knew it was safe for me to appear." His mouth quirked, just slightly. "Unlike other spots … in the guildhall."

"Oh, gods," Cyrus said. "You saw …?" And here he pointed at the ceiling once more.

"I was told by Sanctuary," Alaric said. "Warned, I suppose you might say. It informs me of your presences, in much the same way it tracks danger. I have become more attuned to it in the last thousand years, specifically focusing my mind to be able to better hear what it says, at least while here in these halls."

"Sanctuary is spying on us?" Cyrus asked, frowning. "I shudder to think what it must say."

"Very little," Alaric said wryly, "though when you leave your door open, no spying is truly necessary."

Cyrus looked down, and felt Vara do the same beside him. "So …" Cyrus asked, after an appropriate moment of shame had passed, "is it safe to come out now?"

Alaric closed his eye for but a second. "Birissa is looking around, and Vaste is putting his clothes back on. It is probably safe to move about the guildhall now, but I sense you had reason to retreat down here."

"If you'd heard them, you would have retreated too," Cyrus said. "It was like the roof was coming down—"

Alaric cleared his throat. "I meant that you have a strategy in mind, something you came down here to plan, away from the rumblings of … whatever you want to call that."

"I call it the worst noise I've ever heard," Cyrus said. "And I'm including my own screams from a variety of battle wounds in that."

Vara smacked his arm, causing his armor to rattle. "The plan."

"We wanted to try and visit Longwell," Cyrus said. "We owe him at least the courtesy of a visit to explain what's going on and—who's kidding who here—we sure could use his help, especially given the circumstances. Can you ... ghost us up into the top of the Citadel?"

Alaric shook his head. "The Citadel, probably because of its advanced construction, is somehow impervious to Sanctuary's magics. My guess is that Chavoron, being both the master of that place as well as Sanctuary, managed to find some way to counteract and conceal himself from these powers while within those walls. It has remained, and I have never been able to appear within its bounds via the ether. In days of old, I had to resort to spies within the Council of Twelve in order to find out anything going on in there."

"So we can't just pop in on Longwell, then," Vara said. "That leaves us two roads—go in through the basement like Curatio showed us—"

"An idea not without its own perils," Cyrus said. "The exit comes out on the first floor. Longwell's chambers as Lord Protector are probably up top. That leaves us—I don't even know how many floors to fight our way through to get to him. Unless you're proposing disguises?"

"I wasn't much of an enchanter," Vara said, "even before this bleeding out of our magics."

"I would not trust an illusion now," Alaric said, shaking his head. "It would most certainly fail in the climb, even if J'anda himself were to cast it."

Cyrus felt a small pang at the mention of the enchanter's name. "That Shirri seems to have found a way around this problem. Shame she wouldn't tell us."

"Indeed," Alaric said. "I don't believe that door—although closed to us now—is to be closed forever. She will cross paths with us again, before this is over."

"What makes you say that, Alaric?" Vara asked. "She seemed firmly determined to get the hell away from us, secrets intact, when last we saw her striding out the door."

"Just a feeling," Alaric said with a faint smile. "Something I've learned to trust in the nature of humanity, I expect."

"That's a wonderful sentiment," Vara said, "but Shirri isn't fully human."

Cyrus blinked. "What?"

Alaric frowned. "Beg pardon?"

"She's part elf," Vara said with a smile, looking between them. "Surely you saw it."

"... Beg pardon?" Cyrus asked.

"What?" Alaric stood still.

"She is a quarter elf, at least," Vara said, running fingers over the points of her ears. "How did you miss it?"

"Because her ears were under her hair?" Cyrus asked, trying to think back to Shirri. He hadn't paid her much mind.

"I don't even recall seeing them," Alaric said in concentration, finger on his chin and staring into space.

Vara shook her head. "Pay closer attention, boys."

"I married you so I wouldn't have to pay closer attention to any woman but you," Cyrus said.

She opened her mouth in what looked like preparation to issue a rebuke, but she stopped herself before a word came out. "That ... was surprisingly wise, my husband."

"Clearly a little elvish wisdom has rubbed off on me," Cyrus said. "I wouldn't mind if a little more d—"

"And there it went," Vara said.

"Interesting, her being part elf," Alaric said, "but it hardly changes things. You are an elf. Curatio is even more elf than you. Neither of you can use magic, so I do not see how this has any bearing on the current situation, other than as a chance to point out that neither Cyrus nor I seem to pay much attention to the ears of waifs that we're helping."

"As a married man, I'm really not supposed to notice those sorts of things," Cyrus said.

"Okay, now you're just sucking up," Vara said. "I don't know that it's important—I was merely mentioning it. She may be older than you think, and thus more versed in using magic under these ... conditions. In much the same way as Curatio's spells, or that of the elder spellcasters of my race, she might have wrung power out that would seem impossible to those of us newly under this magical affliction."

"A fascinating theory," Alaric said, "And worthy of talking to Curatio about. But for now, I think, we should take action on the other thing."

"You mean the Longwell mission?" Cyrus asked.

"Indeed," Alaric said. "I see only one course of action—to go to the gates of the Citadel and announce ourselves."

"That'll go over well," Cyrus muttered.

"We don't have much in the way of other choices," Vara said. "As we've already established."

"I know," Cyrus said, "but I have to admit, I think we're going to encounter about as much success doing it this way as ..." He searched for an appropriate analogy.

"As Terian would giving up whoring and being a dark soul?" Vara asked.

"Maybe worse odds even than I would have given that, back in the old days," Cyrus said. "Though I suppose it was pretty touch and go there for a while when he was trying to kill me."

"Come, my friends," Alaric said, and he began to mist, taking hold of Cyrus's upper arm and Vara's as he stepped between them. "Let us go and make our attempts, and after we have exhausted these possibilities, we will exhaust more still—until either the problem has been thoroughly destroyed ..." And the trace of a wry smile crept upon his lips, "... or we have."

And before Cyrus could make reply to that, the endless white light of the ether took them into its embrace, and they were away.

39.

The area around the Citadel had changed the most of any Cyrus could recall seeing since arriving in Reikonos. Gone were the wooden buildings that had been so prevalent; replacing them were glorious marble and stone edifices that lined the streets around the towering capital like glory spilling out from a central cup. The largesse of the Lord Protector's government had either draped the streets nearest the Citadel in spilled-over glory, or else this area had become something of a lodestone for wealth.

The nearest building, for instance, was a glorious marbled masterwork of the sort that Cyrus had frequently seen in Termina and Pharesia. Colonnades spanned the entire front of it, and a great rooftop held up by those columns rose hundreds of feet above them, looking down from its awning above as though it were a mighty mountaintop.

"I sense the work of elven craftsmen here," Vara said.

"Really? Because I just see it," Cyrus said. "How do you 'sense' it?"

"Why, I can smell the dust of wisdom and experience in the air, of course," she said with a little more sarcasm. "It has the look of people who know well what they are doing. Competence, you see, is mostly lost among humans, and thus when you find it in a place such as this, it is all the more obvious."

Alaric let out a low chuckle. "I could not have predicted before you two ran across one another that the Shelas'akur and the son of the Sorceress would find such connection. But it is a pleasant discovery, one of the more enjoyable in my life. And certainly among the most entertaining. Probably the second most, I would say."

"What was the first most?" Cyrus asked with a frown.

"Your mother could juggle," Alaric said, "and she would occasionally put on performances for Curatio and I that would last for hours. When she would pull out the knives, our breaths would catch in our throat, and I could see Curatio lean forward, ready to leap in should she miss and wound herself. It was quite impressive."

"Well ... that is not something I would have ever known otherwise," Cyrus said. "That's fascinating."

"It does make a certain amount of sense, though, when you think about it," Vara said. "She learned nearly every trade, didn't she? Seems reasonable she might have also picked up a few other skills."

"Come," Alaric said, and led them forward.

Along the cobbled streets they trod, toward the mighty doors to the Citadel. Here stood a small wall; it was nothing like the one that ringed Reikonos, but it was new—or at least new to Cyrus. It was a good twenty feet high and stood between them and the base of the tower.

"This looks more like the sort of thing the Council of Twelve would have erected to keep the riffraff out," Alaric murmured as they approached. A set of wary guards had already picked them out of the small crowd and were watching their approach.

Only a very few people were in line for the gate entry; the rest of the crowd seemed to be simply passing by. Cyrus watched as some followed the road toward Reikonos Square, and craned his neck to try and see it. Alas, he could not; it was just a little too far, and there were a few too many people in the way. On a clear day, perhaps, he might have been able to pick out the fountain, to see what buildings had been built around its empty space.

Shaking his head, he turned back around to focus on where he was walking—

And nearly ran into a stranger, shorter version of himself.

"Hullo," said a man in black armor. The fellow wore a beard, had bright eyes, and a smile that hinted at cleverness.

"Hello," Cyrus said, momentarily dumbstruck as he stared down at this fellow. He had two swords upon his belt, neither of which looked worth a damn. Everything else was black-painted plating and chainmail that looked as though the links were already peeling.

After a brief, apprising look, the man shook his head at Cyrus. "You've got it all wrong."

Cyrus blinked, trying to figure out what he meant by that. "Beg pardon?"

"Your costuming is entirely amateur," the man said. He pointed at the cloak that was strapped around Cyrus's neck. "Look at this. It's like you're trying to hide yourself, but doing a poor job of it. As though the great Lord Davidon would ever have cause to hide himself."

Cyrus's mouth fell open, and words began to come out almost of their own accord. "Actually—"

"Indeed," Alaric said, stepping in with a look of wry amusement, and taking Cyrus's heated look in stride, "why would he ever find need to hide his bold face and endless courage?"

"Exactly," the man said, pointing at Alaric. "We're talking about the mightiest of men, the most fearless. Hiding your armor under a cloak?" He scoffed. "You should be proud to be one of the brotherhood who has chosen this path. You shame us all by trying to hide your light."

"My ... light?" Cyrus asked.

"Aye, it's all we have in these dark times," the man said. "You wear that armor, you're a beacon of hope to all these people."

"Or a nutter in black armor," Vara murmured under her breath.

"You have a responsibility to get the details right," the man said, poking a finger into the center of Cyrus's breastplate. "Look at these marks. Sloppy."

Cyrus looked down and noted there were indeed very faint scuff marks in the middle of his armor, ones he'd noticed countless times. "That was where Mortus and Yartraak and Bellarum all struck—"

"Oh, very good, you've got a canonical explanation for it," the man said. "But still, it's a flaw. It doesn't take much extra effort to get it right, lad." He shook his head sadly at Cyrus. "You're a disgrace to us all. And where's your second sword?"

Cyrus chucked a thumb over his shoulder at Vara. "She stole it."

"Blame it on her because you couldn't be arsed to procure three for yourselves." He shook his head sadly. "You're supposed to bring hope, and that takes work, real commitment—dedication." He stared at Cyrus, eyes full of a heady seriousness. "Fix it up. You're shaming us all." And with that, he turned his back and walked off.

Alaric and Vara both let out a cascade of snickers as soon as the man was out of earshot, and Cyrus was left there, mouth gaping, as the authority on all things Cyrus disappeared into the crowd.

"Well, he certainly told you," Vara said, reaching his side, shoulders still heaving with laughter.

"Yes," Alaric said, beset by a wicked case of guffaws, "how dare you leave your armor in such damaged conditions? Why, it's almost as if it bears the marks of the gods themselves trying to strike you down."

"You laugh now," Cyrus said, "but when everybody in this town realizes I've come back, that guy is going to feel like an idiot."

"Perhaps," Alaric said, moving back toward the gates of the Citadel, "but that presupposes that you make your triumphant return and are seen by everyone rather than just a few isolated souls, comparatively speaking."

"And also finding more courageous followers," Vara said. "The speed at which that crowd dispersed after the explosion at the coal yard suggested that some might not have been as faithful as you'd hope, oh mighty Lord Davidon."

"What have we here?" one of the guards asked as they approached, his hail quelling their further banter. The guard looked to his fellows. "Another Cyrus Davidon. What can we do for you today, Lord Davidon?" And he looked to Cyrus.

"I'm here to see the Lord Protector," Cyrus said.

"Of course you are," the guard said. "Who shall I tell him is calling?" At this, the guard looked most amused.

"Tell him it's your father," Cyrus shot back. "And by the by, I bring greetings from your mother. She's naked and missing me, so do be quick about letting me pass so I can get back to her before the bed gets too cold."

The guard's expression hardened immediately. "Get out."

"Make m—" Cyrus started to say, but Vara seized him by the arm and began to drag him away bodily.

"Your friends are wiser than you are!" the guard shouted after him, face a deep crimson.

"And you're dumber than your mother and I ever suspected!" Cyrus called back. "You'll regret this moment when the Lord Protector finds out I've returned."

Whatever reply the guard might have made, Cyrus missed it, because Vara was grunting as she wrestled him away. He wasn't fighting back, as such, but neither did he simply go lifeless and let her drag him.

"That was not particularly wise," Alaric said once they were far enough away that Cyrus could barely see the guard's glare.

"We weren't getting through there no matter what we said," Cyrus said, feeling the pressure of Vara's hand upon his arm. "You heard him. They must get a dozen impersonators a day trying to announce themselves to the Lord Protector. Hell, the guy who lectured me on my armor probably just did the same thing."

"Still, starting a fight with guards? Reckless," Vara said, finally letting go of him.

"I didn't start a fight," Cyrus said, "I just didn't let his insults go unanswered."

"Indeed," Alaric said, "you threw them back most adroitly, escalating the situation far beyond what it needed in order to—" He paused, turning his head. "Did you see that?"

"What?" Cyrus turned to look where his gaze had indicated. He had missed whatever it was, but—

Alaric had looked in the direction of the square, and as soon as Cyrus did the same, he did note something strange. There was a faint glow in the distance, almost like an afterimage of lightning, as though he'd turned his head a moment after it had struck and he'd only caught it for a fraction of a second.

There was a commotion coming from that way, now, shouting and scuffling, people running and trying to move away in panicked haste.

"It would appear that something is amiss," Vara said, her head cocked to point her right ear toward the source of the disturbance. "Definitely a skirmish of some sort."

"Oh, good," Cyrus said, reaching for his blade, "I could use a—"

She slapped his hand away, beating Alaric to doing the same by milliseconds. "No."

"Oh, come on," Cyrus said, plaintive.

"Perhaps we should find out what it is first," Alaric said, starting to push against the crowd, "before we rush in with violence."

"I know you've been insulted twice in the last few minutes," Vara said, lingering with him for a second more, "but do try to keep that pride of yours in check." She kissed him, then followed Alaric.

It was the mildest of rebukes, but it burned his cheeks nonetheless. "Fine," he grunted, keeping his hand on Praelior's hilt but not pulling it as he started to push through the crowd toward the square, "but mark my words—I'm going to need it, and you're probably going to wish I had it drawn, if this day continues the way it has." And he followed after them, hurrying to see what new madness awaited them ahead.

40.

Shirri

Shirri had nearly made it through Reikonos Square when it happened. She was on her long walk to the airship docks, taking a very slight detour, but still the most direct route she could without traipsing by a Machine stronghold. The docks were less than ten minutes from the square, and all she needed to make was a five-minute detour. Freedom was so close she could almost taste the dirty, oily air that hung around the docks like a cloud of grease and particulates. She'd been there before, and it was almost as though it clung to your skin, to your body after you'd been there, like the steam diffusing through the air carried that smell with it and sprayed it upon all who passed.

There was no hint of that here in the square, though. Here it was the stink of unwashed bodies that made her want to hold her nose, the scent of horse droppings all peppered throughout like tiny mountains piled all over that one needed to avoid with every step.

There was also the intoxicating aroma of bakers, of spirit sellers, of others plying their wares in some vast, sprawling enterprise that spilled over out of the widely renowned markets. Once, Shirri had heard, Reikonos had boasted the largest markets.

That was no longer true, of course. Since the days when they'd made contact with Coricuanthi, with Imperial Amatgarosa, with Chaarland, and even nearby Firoba, it had been well known that all of those lands boasted cities with markets that put Reikonos's to shame. It was a strange thing, to hear such far-off stories and think that—yes, soon, perhaps, she'd see these long-awaited mysteries for herself.

The lingering regret, though, was far more powerful than any hope she felt from the idea of escaping this place. It would take every last piece of gold, she expected, every last note she carried on her person.

She'd be starting in Binngart or Vanreis or wherever with nothing.

Still … that was better than being in the not-so-tender hands of the Machine.

Initially, the ruckus upon the square wasn't any worse than it usually was. It was always busy and noisy, the crowds surging, and Shirri did her best to avoid the largest cluster. It was moving like a sea, backwards and forwards, and she glanced over as she tried to skirt the edge. Something was happening at its center, something which had raised an outrage that she could almost hear … if she concentrated …

"He's back, I tell you!" came a man's voice, shouted high. "Cyrus Davidon has returned!"

That shouldn't have given her pause, and yet Shirri came to a stop so that she could listen, strain to lift herself up to see. She couldn't, of course, the crowd was too tall. She tried to peer through the gaps between shoulders and heads, but had little more luck. All she could tell through the forest of people was that there was a man, he was perhaps on a box of some sort to give him height, and he was shouting over a crowd that was doing plenty of shouting back.

"Liar!"

"Blasphemer!"

"I tell you, he's back!" the man shouted, even louder. "I have seen him with my own eyes, and I watched as he struck at the Machine— first he hit a slaver house, then a coal yard—and finally, went for one of the mills! He has jammed his sword in the eye of the Machine and then spit after it! The mighty Lord Davidon has seen our need and comes to answer—"

The crowd roared as something happened that Shirri could not see. The shouting man's voice stopped, and somewhere in the crowd another shout rose: "Leave him alone!" and "Let him speak, you bastards!"

Now people turned and shoved, trying to disperse, and soon enough she had a clear view of what had happened.

And it was enough to make her wish she hadn't.

A good twenty Machine thugs were arrayed around the box where the man had been speaking. They'd clubbed him down, and he was on the cobbles, blood running out from his head. Shirri's heart leapt into her throat as though it were prepared to flee her very body if she didn't start moving to get away from this—this spectacle—

And yet her feet were rooted to the spot. The surge had been there when first she'd seen them. Immediate, urgent, it told her to run, as it always had. It was that small voice in the back of her head, the one that whispered, *There is no hope in Reikonos,* and it was a compelling one. Compelling enough that she'd followed it all her life, and was even following it now—to the airship docks and then, if she were fortunate, to Firoba.

But in that moment, that small voice—that very commanding voice—seemed to get ... quieter. Something else surged to the front of her mind, something long forgotten. It was an entirely different voice, one that she recalled—vaguely—from the days before Jaimes Johnstone shoved her down in the street as a child, and she spent all the rest of her childhood avoiding him. It was a quiet voice, drowned out by the fear, drowned out by the desire to run, far, far away.

The Machine was everywhere in Reikonos. Here it stood before her, clubbing a man down for nothing more than speaking about some ludicrous man in black armor showing up to mimic an icon. Was it not news, even though this Cyrus was an imposter? Shouldn't you at least be able to speak about it without fear of being clubbed insensate, possibly even to death?

All Shirri's breath went out of her as the crowd continued to run away. She'd been afraid for so long; it had been a part of her, that voice. It wrapped itself around her very soul, constricted her heart, so much a part of her and she had not noticed its tumorous presence in every facet of her life until this moment.

Now, it was as though her eyes were opened, and a clarity swept over the world, painting in new, vivid colors. Her heart beat faster, and Shirri stared at these men—these—these—well, they were like Jaimes Johnstone, weren't they?

Thugs. Toughs. Bullies.

They were laughing and crowing over the fallen man, in their long black coats with white armbands, and she stared at them most peculiarly. It was like snapping awake after a nightmare, like the freezing cold water in a winter bath. She plunged in, though, the clear-headedness splashing upon her, and that almost-forgotten voice—it sounded, just a bit, like Alaric's—

"Enough." Shirri stepped forward where all others fled. The word left her lips before she'd fully formed the thought. The Machine visited their injustice on this city, over and over, without fail, without rest, every single day. They found you in your home, they accosted you on the street, and Davidon help you if you had a secret, because they'd try and find that, too, and never leave you alone once they knew it—

"I said *enough.*" Shirri took another step forward and raised her hand at the nearest cluster of them. She said the words in her head, as her mother had taught her, and lightning bloomed from her fingers. It sparked and danced and caught the nearest of the Machine's thugs, running from him to his nearest five comrades, and soon they all joined his dance of nerves, jerking and spasming as her spell ran through them.

"*Enough!*" Shirri said and shot another bolt to the left. It caught another group of them, and they, too, joined the dance, six of them flailing violently, the sparking, flashing light of the lightning coursing through them until it finally dispersed with a great crack and sent the thugs flying. "Enough of you!" And she shot another, catching three of them off to the side. "Enough of the Machine!" Another that sparked into two of them pulling their pistols. "ENOUGH," she raised her voice. "I ... have ... had ... *ENOUGH—*"

With the last she brought down a bolt out of the clear sky and it touched her hands for but a second before launching at the last of them. Some were fleeing, some were standing, awestruck before they got actually struck, and this blast found almost the last of them. It was more powerful and less merciless, and it left some seven of them smoking after it sent them flying.

"Gy—ahhh!" shouted the ringleader, for he was the only one left standing. He quivered, stepping back from the man who'd been speaking, the bloody man he'd struck down. His hands were up, his weapons discarded. All the fear that Shirri felt she might have just left behind had somehow found another host; it was all upon this man's face, flooding out of him as he hit his knees with his fingers laced together as though he were about to pray to her. "I'm sorry," he said, hoarse, bowing his head and looking up at her through frightened eyes. "Please—please don't kill me—"

That hit Shirri strangely, and now it felt as though she experienced a second awakening, as though she'd been in some sort of dream state. Now she found herself looking around, seeing what she'd wrought, and it sent a chill down the flesh of her back and ripped the breath from her.

The men she'd attacked ... the men she'd struck ...

They were dead. Some of them were even on fire.

She raised her hands before her, staring at them. They shook, now that the deed was done. That fearlessness, the courage that had hit her like hard whiskey, fled, and she came crashing back down to the square from the heavens where it felt like she'd been striding a moment before. She blinked, and looked at the man who'd been struck down, the speaker, and something flared to life in her, some panic, some guilt, fear of being caught doing something she wasn't supposed to—

Her hands glowed, softly, just for the space of a second, and the speaker stirred, raising his head. The blood had stopped flowing, but his eyes were glossy, and they found hers. He moaned and started to speak, but nothing coherent came forth.

"I—I don't understand," Shirri said, blinking at him. He was moaning, lifting a hand, pointing at her. She cocked her head, trying to decipher, and his finger moved, just a little to her left—

No, he wasn't pointing at her.

He was pointing past her.

She realized it just as the first heavy footstep broke its way through the crowd noise, and she spun in time to receive the club fully upon her forehead. It might have crashed upon the base of her skull had she not wheeled, but now she caught it full on, and the pain stunned her, driving her to her knees.

"Look what we have here," came a strangely familiar voice. She brought her eyes up even as blood ran into them, and found herself staring at a desperately familiar face.

McLarren.

"If it isn't our wayward mage," McLarren said, spite dripping from between his split lips. He had a cruel smile on his pale face, and his flat accent and the scar that dressed his right brow from forehead to chin, with nothing but a white and dead eye between was enough to bring back that fear that Shirri had thought she left behind only a moment before.

McLarren lifted high his club once more, and before Shirri could so much as raise a hand against him, he brought it down. The square flashed before her as though another bolt had been summoned down. Shirri fell to the ground, but barely felt it after the thud of the club against her skull, and soon enough she was simply out, in the dark, without any respite from the thing she feared … the thing that had found her at last.

41.

Cyrus

"It's like a riot going on here," Cyrus said, pushing his way into the square. It had changed, though not nearly as much as the buildings around it.

"A fleeing crowd hardly constitutes a riot," Vara said, shoving aside some poor soul who had made the mistake of occupying with their body the space she was transiting. "In a riot, there would be rage, more anger, more—"

"I feel rage," Alaric said as they burst through a clot of crowd forcing its way into the street. Now that they were in the square proper, they found that it was nearly empty save for a thickset bunch at the far end huddled around a horse-drawn cart. Cyrus's eyes followed the trajectory of the Ghost, who was moving swiftly toward the trouble, and there—

Cyrus saw it. A figure being loaded into the back of the carriage cart, small, waifish—

"Shirri," Vara said and broke into a run to follow Alaric's. Cyrus took off after them both, clutching Praelior.

A man with a deep facial scar running down his right side and a blind right eye leapt up into the back of the cart with her and slapped the side. "Go!" he urged, and the cart stirred to action as the innumerable thugs of the Machine turned to follow this man's pointed finger as he raised it toward Cyrus and his companions. "Stop them!"

"That'll work out swimmingly for these idiots, I'm sure," Vara said as she sprinted for them. Cyrus, two steps behind, held similar feelings, but was preparing himself for the fight and did not bother to express them.

Another cart was rattling into the square and clattered to a stop, replacing the one that contained Shirri. It burst open, more Machine thugs pushing their way out. These were carrying things—long, almost the length of a sword but with piping that made them look like—

"Pistols!" Cyrus shouted, throwing out a hand to point them out. These were no pistols, though; they were like the larger, meaner, older brother of pistols—

"They're called rifles, you primitive bloody fartwat!" a thug shouted at him with glee, his own pistol already raised and pointed at Cyrus. The blast and puff of smoke heralded the coming of the bullet, and Cyrus put his head down and felt the THUNK! against his helm.

More followed. A veritable rain of them, in fact, forcing Cyrus to raise his shoulders and clench his neck, darting in front of Vara as a hail of bullets pinged and spanged off his armor.

"Into them!" Alaric shouted, and they slammed into the rank of thugs who had lined up to prevent the charge after the wagon.

Cyrus didn't waste much time worrying about niceties. He cleaved arms from bodies, heads from shoulders—it was a good battle, if brief, until another thundering of bullets from the rifle company to their side cut it short.

"They're shooting their own!" Vara shouted, ducking behind Cyrus as he carefully shielded his face from fire.

"Life is cheap to the Machine," Alaric said, standing upright in the midst of all the shooting, bullets passing through him as easily as if he were not there.

"Shocker," Cyrus said as something stung him in the shoulder. He jerked, and a little pellet of metal clinked out from between his chainmail and his pauldron. It didn't have any blood on it, it had apparently just lodged between the layers of armor. "Why, my dealings with the Machine had led me to believe they had nothing but the utmost respect for life."

Another wagon came rumbling and rattling in from the direction they'd been heading, no horses to pull it. Cyrus stared at it; truly it was one of the most bizarre things he could ever recall seeing. "It's driven by invisible horses."

"I very much doubt that," Vara said, stepping behind him once more as the rifle company behind them started to reload and more piled out of the horseless carriage. "It's making a godsawful racket; it must be one of those devices like those that move airships, or that we saw cranking gears in the mill."

"Oh, yeah, that makes sense," Cyrus said and pointed to the line in front of them. "How do we handle this?"

"With grace and aplomb," Alaric said, disappearing into smoke and reappearing behind the line of men piling out of the horseless carriage. He cut through them in a whirlwind, the slashes of Aterum tearing life from flesh everywhere it landed.

Cyrus watched for only a moment before turning to Vara, pointing out the line behind them, reloading their rifles. "Come on," he said, and charged for them.

They had long rods out, pushing them into the barrels of their guns, all in a fancy line as Cyrus ran into them. Some dropped their long guns, trying to draw daggers. Cyrus made it obvious how foolish that was; they fell in ones and twos, and Vara ran in at the other end of the line, cutting her way through to him. They met in the middle, all their enemies driven to death, and Cyrus looked over to where Alaric had been and found the Ghost staring at him, beckoning him onward.

"Come," Alaric shouted. "We have little time. We must pursue—"

Another vehicle rattled into the square, horseless as the last, while the first carriage started to move again, turning around.

"Go without us!" Cyrus shouted. "You have to catch her before she gets too far away!"

Alaric looked frozen for just a moment, but then nodded and was gone a second later. His trust in them was evident; he knew they would see their way through this next trial just fine.

"Stay close to me," Cyrus said as he started toward the new carriage, Vara following a step after. He paused, stooping to seize one of these longer rifles, tossing the rod away. He would only have one shot, but that would be of some aid, surely.

"I believe I did vow that when I married you," Vara said, breaking into a run beside him. They stormed across the square, Cyrus breathing in the little details of change—the fountain was the same but everything else was different. The dilapidated buildings of wood were gone, and though these were not the grand marble edifices of just down the road, they were still grander than most of old Reikonos had to offer.

The new horseless carriage rattled and shuddered into place, its doors facing Cyrus and Vara. He readied himself even as he charged, prepared for whatever came out—

The doors flew open. Cyrus halted his charge, skidding to a stop and holding out his arm to keep Vara from colliding with him. The violence with which the doors had swung open had been too sudden, too swift. "What madness is this?" Cyrus asked, and then had his answer a moment later.

The back doors of this new carriage rattled under the force of being thrown open so hard, and before they had even settled, out stepped a new combatant. Who it was was obvious by his bearing, and made more so by the fresh wound on his face as he stepped from the carriage and into the daylight, determination turning to fury when he laid eyes on Cyrus and Vara.

Tirner Gaull.

42.

"Well, well," Tirner Gaull said with a grimace that might have been a smile if his cheek hadn't born a bandage across it, stained red with dried blood. "If it isn't my new friends, the legends." He said this with peculiar vehemence and a twist of his lips.

Cyrus could feel the blood pounding through his temples. It was as though someone had seized him by them, squeezing them between an unusually strong thumb and forefinger. "You must be lonely indeed, Gaull, to think your foes friends. Maybe it's your personality. You should, perhaps, strive to be less of a violent arse. I know—you could take up a hobby that would reinforce the threatening nature of your true being. Perhaps kitten petting. You could carry one around with you at all times instead of a sword. It would suit you, I believe—"

"You have a quick wit," Gaull said, bringing up his sword and pointing at Cyrus. "Quicker than your sword, in point of fact."

"'*Point* of fact'?" Cyrus let out a low guffaw. "Terrible pun, Gaull."

Gaull blinked. "I didn't intend that ... but ..." His face twisted again. "It wasn't terrible, was it?"

"Puns are the lowest form of wit," Vara said. "Truly, it was terrible."

"Everywhere sits a critic," Gaull said. His words were less clear than before. Cyrus realized he probably had a hole in his cheek that was causing him immense pain. Or at least one could hope.

"Mostly she sits on me," Cyrus said, trying to figure out how best to approach this fight. His initial gambit had been to see if he could stir Gaull with insults, get him to attack hastily. "And scarcely does she get too critical, thankfully—"

That wasn't it. A flicker of impatience did run over Gaull's face, but it was offset by Vara's searing look, which he could sense out of the corner of his eye.

"Oh, to hell with it," Cyrus said, and raised the long gun. Placing the wooden stock against his armor as a brace, he tried to line up the ridges at the front of the barrel with their corresponding matches at the rear. He put Gaull's face right in the middle of them and then clicked the hammer back, giving the trigger gentle pressure.

The rifle roared, but Gaull dodged aside at the last second. Cyrus let it fall, already pulling his last remaining pistol from his belt and raising it. He clicked the hammer back and found Gaull still in his spin but coming out of it—

Fire now, and he'd just dodge or throw up his sword. Cyrus needed a moment of distraction for Gaull, to get him to somehow look away for just a brief second—

A cloud of mist rolled into the square, passing through Gaull's feet and then swirling off to his side. Cyrus blinked; with Praelior in hand, Alaric's motions seemed much slower. He swirled into a man-sized object as Gaull finished his spin. Surely, Gaull had not seen—

With stunning alacrity, Gaull struck in the direction of Alaric, formless but taking shape. His blade reached out and, unerringly, picked out the spot where chain met gorget, and he thrust it home as the Ghost resolved into perfect form—

Cyrus blinked; surely—

"No," Vara whispered.

The blade struck home, and blood spurted from Alaric's neck as the Ghost staggered back, the thrust of Aterum he'd been preparing thwarted by his wounding. Alaric brought his hand up to his neck and pressed it there even as he fell back a step, then another.

Cyrus stood there in awful stasis, unable to move, unable to shout, unable to do … anything.

With a look of absolute disbelief—something Cyrus had never seen before on the steady mien of the man they called the Ghost of Sanctuary—Alaric fell backward and dissolved once more into smoke and mist, disappearing as if he were a thin cloud on a windy day.

Gaull smacked his lips together, loudly, and drew his blade back, and with a wide smile, favored Cyrus and Vara with a look of great satisfaction. "So … shall we finish this?

43.

Shirri

The waking was the hard part, the painful part, her forehead screaming agony at her as she opened her eyes. She had no control of her limbs; they had been seized by some unknown force, and she was swaying, the world moving around her.

No—the world wasn't moving. She was, she realized, just as the hands that had grasped her tightly let loose of her after a good swing. Shirri flew through the air and landed on her hands, which folded beneath her, and her knees, which stung with the impact against a hard floor. All the wind went out of her as well with the landing, her failure to catch herself resulting in her belly slapping the ground. Palms, knees, and stomach all screamed in pain, vying for her attention, with the throbbing in her skull where McLarren had clubbed her doing its level best to shout the rest of them down.

"Ungh ..." she said, lifting herself up to her elbows, her moan echoing in a confined space. She blinked in the darkness; it was not total, the glow of lamps coming from somewhere behind her, but it was thick and inky in here, and she turned her head to look back at the men who'd thrown her.

They were framed in a doorway, both retreating, another figure standing just outside, looking in, small smile of satisfaction on his scarred face. He lingered behind them as they cleared the doorway, leaving him standing there alone, looking in at her with his lone seeing eye.

McLarren.

"And now we have you at last," McLarren said, hands behind him. "Should you not have known it, Shirri? The Machine always gets what it wants."

Shirri slumped, giving up on fighting against the pull of the ground. She let her cheek rest against the cold, grainy floor, and said nothing. For what was there to say? She could spit some defiant twaddle at him, but that would be all it was—twaddle. Her head was so filled with cotton that she couldn't have constructed a spell now even if she'd possessed the strength to.

Which she didn't. The fracas in the square had drained her. Foolish, it had been, sticking her neck out like that. What had she been thinking?

It was almost as though being around Alaric and those other fools had clouded her mind. Well, this was what she got for failing to look after herself. Now, again, she was hopeless, and worse off than before.

"What are you thinking?" McLarren asked with a sly smile. "I can see the wheels spinning beneath that spiteful gaze."

"I was thinking ... I hate you," Shirri said.

McLarren was quiet for a moment. "Good," he said at last, smile not diminished in the least. "You will hate me more before we are done." And he slammed the door behind him.

"That was not the wisest retort I've ever heard," came a voice from the corner, somewhere in the darkness. Shirri raised her head to look and caught movement as a figure crawled over to her with the shuffling of hand against straw and stone. She felt both on the ground, a long piece of straw against her cheek, clinging there as she raised it up.

A man came out of the dark—but no, not a man, tall and looming. This one was short, only half the size of most she'd met, and much smaller compared to that Cyrus Davidon impersonator. He was also squatter, and limped as he came over to her and knelt. His face was covered in a black beard, and when he got close enough for her to distinguish his features, she blinked in surprise—his eyes were different, shaped very nearly like an almond.

"You're of Amatgarosa," she said in a hushed whisper. "And—"

"And a dwarf, yes, which makes me doubly strange in this place without the shorter folk," he said, examining her forehead. He had only the faintest trace of an accent. "My mother was from Vanreis and my father was an ambassador from Imperial Amatgarosa." There was a sly guile in his smile. "My name is Dugras."

"Shirri," she offered in return as he inspected the place where they'd clubbed her. His expression evinced distaste, and she wondered how bad it could be. She raised a hand, trying to draw upon the well of magic within her, but no, nothing came. It seemed all spent; not even enough to cast a small healing spell to mitigate the damage.

"It would seem you have provoked the ire of this McLarren," Dugras said, seating himself beside her. "May I ask what prompted it?"

"Ask all you want," Shirri said, feeling some of the places where she'd been most impacted. All of them hurt, none of them felt remotely comfortable. "Just don't expect me to answer."

"Ah, the mysterious sort," Dugras said, plopping down next to her. "This is going to be a boring stay in a cell with you, then. I suppose I shall have to do all the conversational heavy lifting."

Shirri groaned as a swell of pain lanced down her forehead when she touched it. "Sounds fine. Get to it, then."

"Oh?" Dugras asked. "You want me to talk?"

"Anything to get my head off this pain, yes," Shirri said. "Talk. Laugh—bloody sing, for all I care."

Dugras let a soft chuckle in the darkness. "Good enough. Hmm. Conversation, conversation—isn't it funny that you'll have a mind full of ideas and the moment someone puts you on the spot—poof, they all vanish. Oh, I know—I'll tell you about myself. You already know my name and where I am from."

"How did you get here?" Shirri asked, dragging herself on her haunches to the nearest wall and leaning against it. It was a small cell and thus a short drag.

"I was the chief engineer on an airship. The *Yuutshee*, a cargo vessel out of Amatgarosa." He dragged himself next to her. "I was enjoying some shore leave with my shipmates and went to use the privy. Someone put a bag over my head, hit me with a club, and I woke up here." He moved his hands to shrug in the darkness. "No one's asked me a question yet, they just keep me in here."

"Why?" Shirri asked, feeling another throbbing wave of pain radiate out from her forehead. The smell in here wasn't making it any better; the straw was sodden, either with Dugras's waste or that of someone else, someone who had been in here before he had.

"I don't even know who's captured me," Dugras said. "I just know I'm unlikely to see the sun again."

"Why's that?" Shirri asked.

Dugras made a snort. "Do you know what happens to someone who kidnaps a citizen of Imperial Amatgarosa?"

Shirri blinked. "Oh. I've heard the stories, of course—"

"Yes," Dugras said. "Their lives would be worthless. Their family's lives would be worthless. Their homes would be burned. Silently, without sound or word or scream. Amatgarosa does not suffer its citizens to come to harm without answer. Someone will pay for this." He shifted, back scratching against the stone. "My captain would see to it, were she to find out where I am. I can only hope she finds the correct target before loosing the—" And here he said a word she did not recognize.

"What's that?" Shirri asked.

Dugras answered, and she could hear his smile—and then a little shudder—in the dark. "Best we talk of happier things."

She let out a little laugh. "We're in a cell. In the dark. You just admitted you have no hope of surviving this. I have no better, if we're being honest—"

"Why would we not be honest, given that neither of us has any hope left?" Dugras asked.

That brought Shirri up short, and a thought presented itself—what if Dugras was McLarren's man? Oh, sure, he was a dwarf and from Amatgarosa, two things which would seem to make it unlikely, but—

If there was one thing Shirri had learned, it was that the Machine's reach was seemingly limitless. And that what they could not take by force they would take by other means. More cunning ones.

"I don't know you," Shirri said, and her guard was now up once more.

"Well, let me tell you about me, then," Dugras said. "I spend my days working on airship engines and my nights in a hammock in the engine space of the *Yuutshee*. On the best and least interesting days, nothing goes wrong and everything goes right. On the worst and most interesting days, things go terribly wrong, and I spend much time fixing the engines rather than maintaining them, and dodging our captain's considerable ire."

"He sounds fearsome," Shirri said, her mind not really on the story.

"*She* is very fearsome," Dugras said. "I would not wish to be the person who kidnapped me if she finds him."

"She sounds like a true joy," Shirri said, gently placing her head against the solid rest that was the wall. It seemed to give her strength, cool stone almost soothing her warm, aching head, as though taking the fierce resonating pain running through it and dissolving it by mere touch, catching those radiating waves of pain and taking them upon its stony self. It was soothing, strangely, and she almost felt better.

"She's not bad. I've dealt with worse," Dugras said. "So—are you ready to talk at all yet or do I need to choose another topic of conversation?"

"Best you choose," Shirri said, closing her eyes. "I reckon I've been conversed with enough for the day." She thought again of the weirdos—those strange people.

And, oddly enough, she rather wished that they were here now … or that she was back there with them.

A slow breath crept out of her lungs, regret filling the air in the cell. "I shouldn't have left," she whispered.

"A common refrain here, in this place," Dugras said. "I often find myself saying the same thing about my unfortunately timed trip to the privy. What if I'd waited five minutes? What if I'd held it until I got back to the ship? I never thought I'd spend my last days pondering the timing of a piss."

Shirri chuckled, the sound just escaping. "You sound rather amused for a hopeless man."

"I suppose I'm not entirely hopeless," Dugras said with a chuckle of his own. "Every time I think this is the end, that I'll never get out, I think about my captain turning over every stone in this city to try and find me."

"I wish someone was looking for me," Shirri said softly.

But no one would be, of course. She'd left the last people who might have behind just hours earlier.

A metallic clang followed, short, sharp footsteps at the door. Dugras barely had time to say, "Someone's coming," before the lock was unbolted and the door thrust open.

Shirri tried to stagger to her feet using the wall as support but stumbled. Dugras caught her, and she made it upright as a shadow filled the room, cast by figures in the door and light from beyond. Shirri was blinded, temporarily, and another figure was shoved into the room with a gasp. It landed at Shirri's feet and her eyes ran over the dark hair, the dirty robes, and recognition flared—

"Mother!" she fell to her knees and touched her mother's face, prompting a groan as the woman lifted her head, eyes alighting on Shirri's in the dark. Her mother could see in the darkness, always could—her elven blood at work. Shirri's was a more muddled heritage, her human father having gifted her with eyesight almost as poor as his own had likely been.

"Shirri," her mother said, reaching up to touch her face.

"Such a touching reunion." McLarren's voice dripped with mock sincerity. "And now, that you're both here, together …" the hateful tone evaporated, replaced by something far more sinister.

Glee.

"Now," McLarren said, his pause for dramatic amusement done, "we can begin."

44.

Vaste

"Pretty sure I'm not supposed to feel this bad after ... well, after," Vaste said, looking out his open door into the hallway of the much-reduced officer quarters. As near as he could tell, now there were but two rooms here, his and Curatio's. The room still bore the smell of Birissa, an earthy aroma mingled with a hint of perfume.

Vaste looked around the empty room. There was at least one floor of quarters beneath him; perhaps that was where Alaric was staying, unless he'd decided to move in with Cyrus and Vara. Or just not have quarters at all. All Vaste's things were here, of course, roughly as he'd left them before Bellarum had "destroyed" Sanctuary—actually just driven it back into the ether. A thousand years, and it had reconstituted itself perfectly.

"If only I were so easily reconstituted," he murmured, draping his robes back over himself. He'd opened the door again after Birissa left; it was mostly a sop to his pride and maybe a little bit of a spite, leaving it open in the first place during—well, during.

"If only you would shut the hell up so I could sleep," Curatio said, throwing his door open across the hall. The healer stepped out, dark and shadowed beneath the eyes. He cast a baleful gaze upon Vaste. "What is your problem now? I heard the great moaning; I assumed now that your primal crisis of virginity had been solved, perhaps some rest might be had by all—or at least me."

"I'm sorry, Curatio," Vaste said, and he truly meant it. "That was ... inconsiderate of me."

Curatio blew air soundlessly between his lips and rolled his eyes. "Of course it was. Because right now you are fully up your own arse, and thus incapable of considering others."

241

"Oh ... oh gods, I am up my own arse," Vaste said, taking a step back. "Why ... I've seen it so often in Cyrus, yet I didn't recognize it in myself—I'm up my own arse." He blinked. "I'm—I'm becoming mopey!"

"Yes," Curatio said, "very much so. Please stop."

"I'm so sorry," Vaste said. "I'm—I just—I'm having all these thoughts about—"

"Vaste," Curatio said, impatience causing him to hiss, "take it from someone who has watched the world change many times, and pondered his place within it more than you could ever imagine—you have a place in this world, in spite of your people's disappearance. You are valued. Wanted, even—though if you persist in being up your own arse for much longer, you may be less so."

"Thank you, I think?"

"The only way you will solve this problem for yourself is to see that there is a place in this world for you," Curatio said. "And the only way to do that is to go out and live in it. It's not as though you can find your place in this new world by just lying in your bed with a beautiful woman, satisfying as I know that must be in the short term."

"You have a point, I suppose," Vaste said. "But how will I know where I'm need—"

"ALARUM!" The voice rang up the stairs and was followed by the fierce ringing of a bell.

"There's a start," Curatio said. Darting out of his room without closing the door, he rushed toward the stairs.

Vaste followed only a few steps behind, tempted to cut in front of the healer but then trapped in the narrow staircase as they descended. Looking ahead, Vaste could see Hiressam a flight below, and Birissa a few below that, everyone descending at a run to the foyer.

When Vaste burst out into the open space, he realized he was in fact last to arrive. Birissa had already made it to the bell, which was mounted by the hearth, and Hiressam was only a step behind her. Both were trying to aid a figure who was struggling to stand upright, blood coursing down the front of his armor—

"Alaric, what has happened?" Curatio asked with alarm, hand already glowing.

"Unfortunately, Vaste's theorem about my weakness to godly weapons was most unfortunately demonstrated," Alaric said, wincing even as the healing spell causing his chain mail to glow around his gorget. "And by this Tirner Gaull, no less, as he battled Cyrus and Vara."

"Oh, infinite hells," Hiressam said, taking up some of the Ghost's weight as he slackened and began to fall, Birissa aiding him on the other side.

"I was forced to leave them behind," Alaric said, "lest I be decapitated in front of them."

"Hardly the sort of the thing that would aid their morale in an already difficult battle," Curatio said, hand aglow again—but red, this time.

"This Gaull is a beyond able swordsman," Hiressam said in earnest alarm as he helped Alaric to the ground and slid him against the side of the hearth. "He reminds me of elven sword-dancers, the warriors who spend a thousand years learning their craft."

"Yes," Curatio said. "Famed for their ability to duel and cut a human swordsman of great renown to ribbons in mere minutes."

"That sounds humbling," Vaste said. "But surely Cyrus the great—"

"Is a human swordsman of great renown," Curatio said tightly. "But he is practiced with his blade for a mere twenty-five years or so."

"What are you talking about?" Vaste asked with a frown. "He's a thousand years old."

"But he's spent most of that time in the ether," Alaric said with a gasp, through gritted teeth. "And he has not practiced with a sword in there. I assure you—an elven sword dancer could tear me apart on even footing."

"But he's not on even footing," Vaste said. "He's got a godly—oh. Right. Gaull has one, too."

"A godly weapon and fifty times the combined experience of his foes," Curatio said, taking another step forward. "Alaric—I know you're in pain, but we must get them out of there."

"I know," Alaric said, struggling now to get to his feet. Hiressam, looking mildly stunned, aided him while Birissa, regarding him with indifference, took a step back. "If I could but stand, I think you have healed me enough to go forth and at least take them back—"

"You should take us with you," Curatio said. "We must aid them, and if you should fail—"

"We'll need all the help we can get, right on hand," Vaste said, stepping forward. All that doubt clouding him a moment earlier was gone, now that he had something urgent to do. "Take the two of us."

"Then come back for me," Hiressam said, holding to Alaric's arm.

"And me," Birissa said with a grunt. "You can't have swordplay without me."

"I will do what I can," Alaric said, grunting. He seized hold of Curatio's arm as the healer came to him, then Vaste's, as the two of them took up the Ghost's weight from Hiressam, who moved back.

"But we must hurry, for I fear ..." He took a breath. "... I fear. Let us leave it at that."

And with a cloud of misty fog, Vaste felt the pull of the ether, and the tug into white nothingness that heralded his disappearance from this world.

45.

Cyrus

The fight was brutal and sharp and hard and horrifying. Sweat dripped down Cyrus's face and stung his eyes as he stepped sideways, back, forward, minding his footwork even as his strength began to fail.

He and Vara had Gaull surrounded, their blades raining down on him from both directions, their attacks sure and swift, the sort of onslaught the gods would have found beleaguering, the sort of offense that Cyrus had employed against Bellarum himself.

And Tirner Gaull ... was beating them.

"I haven't had a fight this good in ages," Gaull said, turning aside Vara's attack with his sword while dodging Cyrus's with ease. "It's energizing, you know? Cleansing, really." His blade moved in perfect parry as Vara's slipped across his belly but missed him by millimeters. Gaull struck true and pirouetted away, and there was nothing Cyrus could do about it as Vara took a staggering step back, blood coursing from beneath the chain mail at her hip.

Cyrus moved to aid her, but Gaull came back at him. Two perfectly aimed attacks that forced Cyrus to either commit and be struck or to move aside and stay separated. Cyrus gave way, seething all the while but recognizing the man's actions for what they were—a means to keep the two of them from presenting a united front while he danced around them endlessly, striking his little stinging blows that would gradually deprive them of their strength.

And eventually, Cyrus reflected, looking down at a wound on his wrist that was still oozing red, deprive them of their lives.

Gaull, for his part, had suffered not a single wound save for the bullet that had destroyed his cheek when last they'd clashed. It

245

affected his smile and made his speech thicker, but didn't seem to slow the man at all. Cyrus was looking for an opportunity to use his last pistol, but Gaull seemed ever on his guard, sparkling eyes turning back at Cyrus any time he tore them away for more than a second. That was cursable, and Cyrus did curse, loudly, enough to draw a smile from Gaull.

"You don't like a challenge, do you?" Gaull asked playfully. "Does it affront your ego? Sting your pride?"

"Yes," Cyrus said. "Also, the people who do it inevitably end up dead."

"Your threats carry little weight now that we're seeing the truth of your abilities," Gaull said, coming at him with a flawless offense that forced Cyrus back on bad footing. He stumbled and Gaull struck again, a small blow that nicked his elbow through the links of the mail. "Legends can die, it would seem. I think we'll be proving that shortly."

Vara came at Gaull clumsily from behind, wounded hip slowing her advance, and Gaull turned only slightly to deal with her, striking her between the plates of shoulder and breast. She stiffened, then pulled back, more red spurting out across the once-shining silver. She let a little gasp and barely kept on her feet.

A loud voice suddenly interrupted. "I don't know that you will be proving anything—other than that you're a silly little prick with a hole in his face." Vaste struck, his staff slamming into Gaull's sword, which rose to block him just in time. Gaull had moved with preternatural speed.

"Here comes another challenger," Gaull said, whirling as Cyrus attacked him just then. "The more, the merrier—and the more that will die."

"Just one will die, I think," Vaste said, coming at Gaull furiously, Letum slamming down upon his blade, rattling Gaull's grip. "And it'll be—"

Gaull stabbed at Vaste, and the troll took the hit right in the side. "You," Gaull said, smirk spreading over his face. "Time to—"

Something slammed into Gaull from behind, knocking him off his feet before he could deliver the killing blow. Curatio slipped into position next to Vaste, hand already aglow—and red. "You fool," he muttered. "I told you not to rush in."

"Oh, come on," Vaste said, grunting in pain. "Cyrus needed help."

"And this helped him, did it?" Curatio asked, mace in hand. He'd knocked Gaull asunder with a blow the bastard hadn't even seen coming, and Cyrus wasn't too proud to admit the healer had pulled it off over anything he'd managed.

"Well, he's not hurting from it," Vaste said, cringing. "Though I obviously am."

A burst of dark fog appeared next to Vaste and took up his weight; Alaric had returned. "Come," the Ghost said, and then disappeared again. Vaste was gone, but Curatio remained.

"Your numbers are fading," Gaull said, back on his feet, though a little unsteady. "Someone has called your retreat?"

That burned Cyrus, and his cheeks went scarlet. He looked around for Vara, but she was already gone. "Well," Cyrus said tightly, trying to hide his fury and embarrassment, "No legends will be dying today."

Gaull stared back at him evenly. "It's going to happen."

"But not today," Alaric's voice said, and he was there, beside Cyrus and Curatio both, then they were gone, again, into the ether.

But before they went, Cyrus saw Gaull's face one last time.

Saw the fury.

Saw the determination.

And recognized them for what they were.

He came out of the ether into a beam of light that was shining down on him, in an alleyway some distance from their fight. Vara was there, against a wall, pale and bleeding. Vaste was next to her, green blood darkening his black robes and staining the cobbles beneath him. Alaric was still cringing from the wound inflicted by Gaull, and Cyrus ...

The pains were myriad, and Cyrus thought back to Gaull's face as Alaric marshaled himself, doubtless to bring them from this area of immediate retreat back to the safety of Sanctuary ...

Gaull would not stop in his quest to kill them. And here was the proof of his power—Vaste, Vara, Cyrus, and Alaric, all wounded. Some beyond the capacity even to fight.

No, Gaull would not stop. He would be coming again, coming for them.

And he would not rest until he found them—found them and killed them.

46.

Shirri

"Tell me what I want to know and the hurting can stop," McLarren said, shrouded in shadows. He was here in the cell with them, overpowering Shirri, as her mother slumped, barely conscious, in the corner, Dugras attending her and watching with a tightly clamped jaw as McLarren asked Shirri questions, each punctuated with an attack when it went unanswered.

Shirri twitched. She lifted a hand, tried to conjure a healing spell—just a small one, to knit the wounds slightly, ease the pain—

But nothing came of it, and McLarren stomped on her hand. She could sense his grin in the stinking darkness, the fetid smell of wet straw, urine, and emptied bowels suffocating her. The pain surged in her hand and she looked at him, biting back a scream so as not to give him the satisfaction.

McLarren held something in his hand. "Have you ever seen one of these?" He threw it up in the air, like a ball, and caught it again. "It quells magic in its presence. You'll find no soothing with me—or this—around."

"I never did find you ... soothing," Shirri choked out, the taste of blood thick in her mouth.

He grabbed her by the collar and shook her furiously, eyes squinted. "Tell me what I want to know."

"I don't ... know ..." Shirri said, eyes lolling. He'd steered clear of hitting her in the head for the most part. A few slaps, sure, but mostly he'd kept from knocking the sense out of her. Part of a well-structured plan to get her to talk where her mother hadn't, no doubt.

"Oh, Shirri, I know you're lying," McLarren said, and drove a hard slap across her face. "You've been striking out at the Machine all day.

248

Carting around some Cyrus Davidon imposter, letting him do your dirty work for you—some mercenary in black armor—you think he can save you from us?" He slapped her again. "From *us*? You're going to tell me what I want to know—and now—or else—" And here he brought a knee down into her belly, which seemed to be a favorite target of his.

Shirri nearly vomited—again, for he'd already done this once—but managed to hold whatever she had left down. She sprawled across the floor, her body just screaming at her that she'd had enough, by gods, how could she not have had enough? And yet he kept going. Soon enough, perhaps, she'd even have to tell him what he wanted to know.

Perhaps. If he didn't kill her first.

"Your mother is already in our clutches," McLarren said, driving home another slap that Shirri barely felt. "You're here. You're not getting out. No one is coming for you. Your mercenaries are surely dead on the square at the hands of Gaull even now. Why would you think there's any hope for you here?" And he slapped her again, but she only felt the impact, her head rocking back, the pain …

"What hope do you have left?" McLarren hit her again, and again she barely felt it. "None. None at all. Because there's no hope for you—you street rat. You and your purloined power, this remnant, this artifact of a bygone age. Hope is for those with a future, Shirri—and you don't have one. None of your kind does. Tell me what I want to know, and I'll answer the great calling of your kind—I'll kill you. Mercifully. The suffering will end—and that's all you've lived, isn't it? Suffering? How could it be anything but, living where you live? Scraping out your life like a chamber maid scrapes out a pot? Yours is the leavings, Shirri—but you discovered something, and I'm going to give you a graceful exit for that—just tell me. Where is it?"

"It's …" Shirri sputtered, blood dripping down her cheeks, seeping out of her lips. "It's … it's …"

"Yes?" McLarren breathed in her face, and it smelled sour, like rotten leaves. "Tell me. Free yourself, Shirri. Where is it?"

"Have you … have you checked …?" She gasped, trying to string the words together as he looked into her eyes, his excitement at a fever pitch, and she managed to get out her thought. "Have you checked … up your arse?"

And she spat blood in his face.

She had a vision of Alaric smiling somewhere in the distance as McLarren rained blows down upon her. They found their mark, but again she barely felt them, and somewhere in the middle of it all there was a shriek and something hit McLarren in his middle.

Shirri blinked. Dugras was there, wrestling with the bigger man, unloading on him with a flurry of blows, the sound of them echoing in the confined cell like distant thunder, punctuated by pained squeals from his mark.

"Guards!" McLarren shrieked, and the door sprang open. Shadowy figures moved in and swooped down upon them; Dugras was sent flying a moment later and McLarren was whisked away, the door slamming behind him.

"That ... was foolish," Shirri managed to get out, trying to roll to her side. Blood was streaming out of her mouth, and she spat it again where it was accumulating under her tongue.

"I agree," Dugras said with a grunt, unmoving on the floor, "but ... I bet McLarren regrets it a lot more than I do."

"Are you all right?" Shirri asked, struggling to sit up; her head was light when she tried, so she stopped and just lay there.

"I'm better than all right," Dugras said. "But I might need a minute." And his head lolled to the side. He seemed to have passed out.

"Mother?" Shirri moaned, and gathered her strength. "Mother, can you hear me?"

"Faintly," her mother said, dark hair in shadows, her voice weak. "Forgive me for not getting up ... I'm afraid that McLarren did much the same to me ... shortly before he started on you ..."

"I'm sorry, Mother," Shirri said, and this time she was able to sit up, though still woozy.

"Don't be sorry," her mother said, and she crawled over, a few sliding feet a time. "You were right not to tell them. They ... must never know. They can never ... find it."

"We never found it," Shirri said as her mother slid into her embrace, and leaned against her, the two of them coming together like trees leaning against one another. "Don't know how we could help them."

"But we found the medallion," her mother said with a pained gasp. "That ... is more than anyone else had managed." Her hand brushed against Shirri's chest. "You don't have it on you?"

Shirri shook her head; she'd hidden it immediately after finding her apartment ransacked. "Didn't want to chance them finding it, but ... I think we might have to give it up."

"No," her mother said.

"But—"

"No," her mother said again, twice as firm. "If you've hidden it, let it remain hidden." Her eyes flared. "I refuse to give them the satisfaction. That medallion is supposed to bring hope." She touched Shirri's cheek. "Give it to the Machine ... and the little that's left in Reikonos at this point will be as dead as we will be."

Shirri nodded, though she wasn't entirely sure why. "They're going to kill us."

"Yes," her mother said. "But they're going to make sure we suffer first."

"In case you get out, Mother," Shirri said, "I hid it at—"

"Don't—tell me," her mother said, urgently, putting a finger across her lips. "Better I not know. Then I could not reveal the truth even if I wanted to." She bowed her head. "And I may want to by the end. You will, too. But you can't—you hear me? You must stay strong—for Reikonos."

"Why?" Shirri let it out as plaintive moan. "Why, Mother? It's—it's just a myth, this idea of some—some great ark filled with hope for the masses. There is no hope left in Reikonos, everyone knows it—"

"Shhhh," her mother said, and pulled Shirri's head down onto her shoulder. "There's always hope. You need only ... know where to look for it."

"But it never worked, Mother," Shirri said. "We tried it, remember?"

"It will work," her mother said. "We didn't do it right. That's all we lack—a little knowledge. A way. We were seeking for it, just as everyone here is."

"Our way is closed," Shirri said, pulling her head off her mother's shoulder. "I said the words—in desperation, even—and no ark appeared to me." She laughed, mirthless. "Just some—some Cyrus Davidon impersonator with a Vara for good measure. And a troll, an elf and—some ghostly fellow named Alaric—"

Her mother's hands gripped tightly to her shoulders. "What did you say?"

Shirri blinked in the darkness. "I said ... nothing happened. Or near enough to nothing as—"

"How did you know the name Alaric?" her mother asked, shaking her roughly. "Few would know that name, at least here in Reikonos. Where did you hear it?"

"He introduced himself as such," Shirri said, feeling the pinch of her mother's fingers. "Honestly, Mother, I—"

"What were the names of the others?" her mother asked. "The troll? The elf?"

"Curatio," Shirri said, uncertain why her mother would be so harsh, so serious. Her eyes were alight. "And the troll was Vas—"

"—te," her mother finished. "And they appeared ... after you said the words?"

"Yes," Shirri said.

Her mother's mouth fell open, agape. "They came back," she whispered in the dark.

"'They'? No, it was an impersonator—"

"One thing I can tell you about human impersonators of Cyrus Davidon," her mother said, sagging with some strange relief, "is that all are, nearly to a man, historically illiterate, for the details of history are forgotten among humans. Few know the names of the companions of Davidon, and none in these days could muster up an actual troll to stand by their side." Her mother leaned back and let out a quiet laugh, some strange blend of regret and joy escaping her. "They're back."

Shirri blinked. "Then—then the big green man—he was—"

"Vaste," her mother breathed, "the real Vaste. And Curatio ... Vara ... Alaric ... And Cyrus ... he was ... they were with the ark all this time ... but how ...?"

"Because they're not real," Shirri said. "Because they were never with the ark. Because we haven't found the ark—"

"Your answers are simplistic and lack belief, daughter," her mother said.

"And yours are blindly faithful and lack any reason," Shirri snapped back. "Faith is for children. We live in an age of reason."

"Tell me what is 'reasonable' about being governed by this Machine?" her mother replied, calm as if she were delivering a simple lecture on a sunlit afternoon in the kitchen rather than here in the darkness of a dungeon. "What is reasonable about the dark workings of this city? Of being preyed upon by these brutes? Of being beaten by this pathetic weakling, McLarren?"

"There is reason in everything," Shirri said. "McLarren wants what we have; effect follows cause. He wants, therefore he takes, and we find ourselves taken. Simple enough that any can follow it."

That drew silence. "I didn't raise you to be so ..." Her mother couldn't seem to find the right descriptor.

"You didn't raise me to be a sacrifice to the gluttonous human waste that the Machine produces, either," Shirri said, "yet here I am, about to become it, nonetheless. Effect follows cause."

"It is not over yet," her mother said softly.

"It is over," Shirri said. "Entirely."

"Sorry you feel that way," Dugras said, sitting up, cradling his head.

"It's not a feeling," Shirri said. "It's a conclusion based on the facts in evidence."

"Let me add one to your reasoning, then," Dugras said, and there was a glimmer in his eyes as he held something up. "I managed to pilfer a key to the door from one of the guards when I was fighting them."

Shirri blinked, staring at the very slight shine on the metal in the dark.

"Hope," her mother said, just a whisper in the black, as Shirri stared at the key, "is kindled."

47.

Cyrus stood in the once-mighty garden of Sanctuary and stared at all that remained.

It was so … little.

"There was a bridge here," Cyrus muttered, staring at the small pond that remained, sitting overshadowed by a willow tree that had once rested on the far bank. Now the pond was little more than a puddle, something he could wade across if he were of a mind to. The water probably wouldn't get much past his knees, either.

"Vara is going to be okay," came a voice from behind him. He turned his head out of reflex; it was Vaste, of course. He'd recognized the voice.

"Naturally," Cyrus said, looking back to the pond, to the reflection. The surface bore a strange, rainbow hue. Ash was already collecting upon it.

"Not so naturally, anymore," Vaste said, stepping up next to him. "It took all the healing magic I had, all that Vara had—Alaric was already spent—and a little life from Curatio—to put things even as right as they are at this point." He shuffled his feet. "I don't know what the hell the point of me is here, honestly. It's as though my magic was once mighty, like this pond. And now it's … much less mighty, like this pond … but perhaps smaller even than this."

"Humbling, isn't it?" Cyrus asked, keeping his eyes fixed on the wall just past the pond. The garden ended abruptly at the wall, and forbidding brick of a different shade rose above it, a factory close enough Cyrus could nearly have spat and hit it. "Seeing everything you were good at destroyed, and realizing that everything you'd poured your life into was all for naught?"

"Yes, that's exactly how I feel," Vaste said, "except I don't have statues built in my honor, and the woman I've recently slept with doesn't really care for me the way Vara does for you."

"Give it time, maybe she'll come around," Cyrus said. "It's not as though she's blessed with an overabundance of troll options."

"What if she hates me?" Vaste asked.

"She doesn't even know you."

"I'm not so sure about that," Vaste said. "We had a little tête-à-tête—"

"Yeah, I heard. You left your door open."

"Heh. I meant after that."

"Oh?"

"She hit me with some ... uh ... truths about myself," Vaste said, staring at his feet. "Ones that I didn't think would be so ... glaringly obvious ..."

"What were they?" Cyrus asked.

"She said I think too much and act too little," Vaste said.

"Well, everyone knows that about you," Cyrus said.

"Bullshit, no one knows that about me because it's not tr—oh, who am I kidding—"

"No one."

"—of course it's true. I'd rather think than act," Vaste said with a heavy sigh. "I'm not you, Cyrus—"

"Another thing that everyone knows, even aside from the obvious differences in arse—"

"I can't do the things you do," Vaste said, bowing his head. "Charging into battle the way you always have? That's not me. I'm a thinker, a planner—"

"Yeah, those battles I fought with entire armies? Totally off the cuff. No planning whatsoever. 'What do we do now, General?' 'Just sort of charge them, I guess? I don't know, throw yourselves into the maw of death, it'll all work out.'"

"That's not what I meant," Vaste said.

"It's what you said. I can't read your mind, so I have to go on what stupidity comes out of your mouth, not that which might still be brewing in your head."

"I mean I'm a ponderer," Vaste said. "You learn, you read, you think—but you act. You seize the moment." He lowered his voice. "You seized the hearts of all Arkaria. I mean, look at this ridiculous tableau—you have statues all over this city. You took action, things happened—and now you're a religious icon."

"Action ... is not all it's cracked up to be," Cyrus said.

"I don't know, it felt pretty good when I was—"

"Leaping into action means sometimes you make mistakes," Cyrus said. "Sometimes ... you get consequences you don't care for. Like the scourge overrunning the land you were supposed to save. Or gangsters taking over your home city and no one gives a damn." He shook his head, clenched a fist, felt the tightness in his gauntlet. "At least your conscience is clear, Vaste—people didn't die because you sat around thinking."

"That's not so," Vaste said. "Vara would have died in the Realm of Death because I wasn't prepared to act. You did, and she's still here with us."

That stung Cyrus for some reason. "It makes me feel guilty, you know." And when the troll cocked his head toward Cyrus, he went on. "That I don't regret that decision. I would never give her back, never, not if forced to relive that moment a thousand times. That's almost certainly the reason I feel so truly terrible every time the scourge comes up in the context of my actions—because I hate that I let those beasts loose ..." He swallowed heavily, "... but I would loose them again a thousand times, a million ... because I could never let her go."

"You killed gods for her," Vaste said. "That's the sort of epic love story that doesn't just ... fall into your hands while you're sitting around thinking about things, Cyrus. You had to act to make it happen."

"Well, pal," Cyrus said, shooting him a wan smile, "you've still got a lot of life left ahead of you, especially with that staff in your hand. You might want to learn how to act some, lest you let this life pass you by while you're thinking."

"I guess I'm going to have to learn to start doing more acting and less thinking," Vaste said, throwing up a hand to encompass the smaller garden. "I mean look at this—my favorite thinking spots have turned to absolute shit. I think we're going to have to kill all the damned scourge just so I can get back to the Plains of Perdamun and have some room to spread out."

Cyrus let out a small chuckle, then stopped, a sober thought coming over him. "I'll be honest with you, Vaste—"

"Thanks for that. It's the robes, isn't it? They make me look fat?"

"I think that's all the eating and lack of action, to be honest—but that's not what I meant," Cyrus said. "I look at this new world ... and all I see are the problems. The Machine running Reikonos. The scourge outside the gates. Who knows, even, what lies beyond all that? There are already two nearly insurmountable problems, and we've only just gotten here. A day we've spent, and look at all the difficulty before us." He bowed his head. "Against all this—and who knows what else out there beyond ... even a man of action such as myself can feel the bite of discouragement." He rubbed at the most recent wound he'd acquired from Tirner Gaull. "I don't know how we're going to fix these problems."

"Well, we've only been here a day," Vaste said, adopting a strangely cheery tone. "Give it time. I'm sure you'll find a way to fix these problems ... and cock everything up with consequences that turn into so much worse problems."

"Thanks," Cyrus said, "that really turned my frown around. I'm feeling great now, like I could take on—well, at least that squirrel—"

Vaste jerked, looking around. "Oh, haha," he said, turning back. "That was cruel. And I'd just gotten some good use of the parts they attacked." He slumped. "Does it get easier, do you think?"

"Having your genitals attacked by squirrels?"

Vaste sighed. "I meant life."

"I know I may be a thousand years old," Cyrus said, "but I've really only lived ... what ... thirty-five or so? I couldn't tell you." He sighed. "Probably not for us, no, doing what we do."

"That's what I was afraid you were going to say," Vaste said, kicking a little rock into the pond. "So ... where does that leave us?"

"Feeling helpless," Cyrus said, "in the face of the changing world. And maybe just a dash hopeless, too?"

"Yes, yes, that's how I feel," Vaste said. "So, man of action, what do we do about it?"

Cyrus just stared at the pond, the ashy residue resting on the surface creating a strange prismatic effect in the faded sunlight, obscured by the buildings standing tall around them. "I'm thinking ... wallow for a little while?" Cyrus asked, letting the air flow out of him. "Until someone comes looking for us. Then, maybe try and find a solution to our most immediate problems."

"Wallow, eh?" Vaste shuffled, his robes making a rustling noise. "I could go for some wallow. It smacks of lack of action, which, until recently, was my forte. Let us wallow together."

"Sounds ... not good," Cyrus said, "but right, at least for now." And he stared at the pond as they lapsed into silence, and the sun began to sink far below the horizon as the night crept upon them.

48.

Shirri

Discovering there were no guards at the door had been a finding of great joy, like getting bread from the baker that wasn't two days old and already filled with maggots. A rare occasion, and under different circumstances, it might have been cause for celebration.

But with the three of them as battered as they were, the celebration was muted in favor of looking around carefully and trying to determine the best route to proceed.

"They pulled me in this way," Dugras said, in that funny accent of his, something between Firoban and Amatgarosan.

"I was too out of it to have paid attention when they dragged me in here," Shirri said. It was hard not to be suspicious, but the stink of this place—fetid, rank, of blood and urine and excrement—compelled her to want to be anywhere but here. She looked at Dugras, who was turning his head swiftly in either direction, playing sentinel to their fears, "I will have to trust you to take us from this place."

"No pressure, though, right?" he grinned and limped his way forward, picking his chosen direction with care.

"Are you able to walk?" Shirri asked her mother, who limped along beside her. Blood crusted her forehead where it met her dark hair.

"Yes," her mother said, "more easily with every step, though I expect I will feel this tomorrow." A sharp cringe creased her brow. "And for some time after that, I think."

"The next hallway is clear," Dugras said from just ahead of them, peering around a corner. "This is ... very different than when I came in. They had any number of those idiots watching doors then." He looked around suspiciously. "I don't know whether they're having a meeting or they've suffered some great loss of manpower, but—I suppose we shouldn't look a gift steam engine in the boiler, eh?"

"I ... don't know what that means," Shirri said, lagging behind with her mother. She kept casting doubtful looks over her shoulder, even as her mother pushed harder to walk more quickly. The strain was showing on her mother's face, pain radiating out in her expression.

"Never mind," Dugras said. "I think there's an exit just ahead. This looks like the door where they dragged me in out of a wagon." He beckoned them forward, and then hurried ahead, still nursing that limp.

Shirri tried to aid her mother, but was waved off. "I'm fine," she said, "or as near as I'm going to be until all this heals on its own." She grimaced. "Curse that McLarren and his orb." Her hand glowed with light, and her speed improved. "Ah. We must be far enough away from him and his accursed sphere now."

With a wave of her hand and a carefully thought incantation, Shirri felt a rush of relief run through her. Her pace improved, and her mother was moving a little faster, though she was hardly swift.

"Come on," Dugras whispered from ahead. He was holding a door, and beyond it, she could see dusky sky and some sort of loading dock. He beckoned them and Shirri picked up her pace, her mother doing the same behind her.

They exited into the cool air of sundown, the whispers of the city around them. Shirri stared; there were pallets and crates, barrels and other cargo just standing everywhere. Some were filled, some seemed to be emptied, but none was apparently watched. It was as though the operation had been completely abandoned.

"There's a wagon here," Dugras said, waving them forward as he leapt onto the back of a cart. The horses, already hitched up, simply stood there, a pile of straw at their feet that they were eating.

Shirri looked ahead; an alley stretched before them, and there, beyond, entry into the streets of Reikonos, where throngs were filing past in the distance. She did not consider a mere crowd safety, but ...

She gave a quick look back at the yawning door to the dungeon building ... The busy streets offered far more safety than what was behind her.

"Come along," she said, taking her mother's arm with only a grunt of protest from her mother. She helped her into the back of the wagon, where her mother collapsed against the side, breathing a deep sigh of relief.

Dugras was already seated up front, reins in hand. "Where should we go?"

Shirri narrowed her eyes. "Don't you want to get back to your ship?"

Dugras shook his head. "I do, but—the airship docks are the most closely watched location in all of Reikonos. If I go there immediately, I might as well just walk back into that dungeon and close the door."

"Shirri," her mother said from behind her, "we have to go to them." Shirri's eyes fluttered closed. Of course she would say that.

"This city is not safe for us," Dugras said. "The Machine is everywhere. They will send messages to all their outposts to be on the lookout for us. We need to find somewhere to lay low."

Shirri let out a low breath and looked at Dugras. He showed none of the guile she would associate with a dangerous man, and yet the multiple conveniences that had allowed them to escape roused her suspicions. He could easily be playing them false, in which case ...

He wanted to go somewhere. Somewhere that Shirri chose.

The medallion. If he was a spy for McLarren, then doubtless that would be what he was after. And if that were the case ...

Better not to lead him to it. Better to lead him somewhere that he could be dealt with by people who seemed amenable to helping those in need.

And if it made her mother happy ... all the better.

"All right," Shirri said in a low whisper, "I know a place where we can go." She nodded as Dugras spurred the horses into motion, the wagon moving with a slow roll forward toward the mouth of the alley. When they reached it, she recognized the street instantly. "Take a right," she said, following the map in her memory—back to Sanctuary, where she could only hope Alaric and the others would take kindly to the trouble she suspected she was bringing their way.

49.

Cyrus

The commotion at the front gate led Cyrus and Vaste away from contemplation of the pond. With a sigh, Cyrus started around the small yard that surrounded Sanctuary. The walls on either side were like tall sentinels staring down at him ominously, and it gave rise to a sense of claustrophobia, that everything was closing in around him.

"If you were any more tense," Vaste said from a few paces behind him, "I think your long, perfectly molded buttocks armor might begin to strain from the puckering."

"It's quartal, so if it does, my arse has become strong indeed," Cyrus said, hand on Praelior and in motion toward the gate with all the alacrity that provided. Vaste was clearly drawing on Letum's power behind him, for he was keeping pace easily.

He rounded the building to find Vara already there with Curatio, Ferocis drawn and eyeing the barred gate with suspicion. Curatio, on the other hand, looked rather amused. Vara jerked at the sight of him and Vaste thundering around the corner. She spun, her sword pointed at him for a bare moment before she relaxed.

"Just us," Cyrus said, joining her. He nodded toward the gate as another heavy thud issued from it. "Who's this?"

"I don't know," Vara said, "but I don't care for the timing. It stinks of an attack."

"Oh, goodness, people," Curatio said, sighing as though long-suffering, then raised his voice to call out. "Who goes there?"

"It's me," Shirri Gadden's distinctly high voice called back, "and some others. We need aid."

"Well, that's the magic word," Curatio muttered, moving to unbar the gate, his mace still in hand. He laid a hand on the bar, then looked

261

back at Cyrus and the others. "Well, don't just gawk—make ready your weapons, in case she comes with trouble at her heels, or brings it to us in ambush."

Cyrus drew Praelior, and Vara took a ready stance beside him as Curatio removed the bar and then opened the gate slowly. Cyrus watched the gap, waiting—

Shirri came limping in a moment later, an older woman with dark hair beside her, arm draped around her shoulder and leaning on Shirri for support. The woman's dark hair partially obscured her face, but she looked up at Cyrus with brown eyes that gleamed when she saw him. Her gaze moved its way over to Vara, who met it suspiciously, and then to Vaste and Curatio in turn.

"And where ... is Alaric?" the older woman asked as she and Shirri cleared the gate and another man—a dwarf—came waddling in. Cyrus gave him a glance, then a double take. His skin tone was quite different than what Cyrus had seen before, and there was something very different about his eyes.

The dwarf caught him looking, and spoke in a strange accent. "I'm from Imperial Amatgarosa. This is the look of my people."

"I—wasn't going to ask," Cyrus said, taken aback by the dwarf's directness.

"But you were wondering," the dwarf said. "I can always tell when I walk through these streets. It's all right; I'm sure if you were in Amatgarosa, you would get looks, too. Very few of your people have been allowed there."

"What is your name, sir?" Vara asked, a little stiffly. She still had her sword at the ready.

The dwarf executed a bow, and cringed as he lowered himself. He was standing awkwardly, as if one leg were injured. "My name is Dugras, of the ship *Yuutshee*, and recently a prisoner of the Machine, now escaped, thankfully."

"You traveled here on one of those airships?" Cyrus asked, his curiosity piqued. He hadn't had a chance to ask someone about them yet.

"I'm the engineer that services the engines on the *Yuutshee*," Dugras said with obvious pride. "And as soon as I think I can make a break for it without getting caught at the docks, I'll be heading back. It might be best if I can get a message to my captain first, though, let her know what happened."

"What's going on out here?" Alaric's voice rang over the courtyard.

"We have guests," Curatio called back. "Again."

"They look famished," Vaste said. "We should feed them."

"You're hungry and looking for an excuse to eat, aren't you?" Vara asked.

"You know me entirely too well," Vaste said. "But still, let's not be rude just to spite Vaste. Come, friends—dinner awaits." And he turned, beckoning them forward as he moved up the steps.

Shirri went to follow him, the woman beside her dragging along. "That ... is Alaric," Shirri whispered to her.

"As though I couldn't tell that for myself," the woman said, a strange lightness in her voice.

Cyrus frowned and caught a glance from the woman. Her look at him was a bit more pointed and lacked the awe with which she watched Alaric. He tried to put it aside and turn his attention back in the direction of his natural curiosity, and found Dugras moving ahead without him.

"Go on, I'll just get this gate, then, won't I?" Curatio called at him, small trace of irritation bleeding through.

"That's good thinking," Cyrus called back with a grin. "You'll need to work twice as hard or healers will get a reputation for being lazy, now that you and Vaste are about the only two left. You're going to have work very hard indeed carrying his arse."

"I heard that," Vaste said. "And I'm thinking about it ... pondering action ... I think I just want to shovel food in my mouth. That counts as action."

"It does at the speed with which you do it," Vara said.

Cyrus hurried and caught up with Dugras as the dwarf was climbing up the stairs. They seemed suddenly flatter, and he did not struggle with them as he might have just moments earlier when they'd been higher. Cyrus blinked at them, then turned his attention to the engineer. "You said you work on airships?"

"On the engines, yes," Dugras said. "Though I have been known to work on other parts, if need be. On an airship, sometimes you get called to work on wherever the work needs to be done."

"Fascinating," Cyrus said, genuinely enraptured. "And ... how do you make them fly?"

Dugras stared up at him. "With the engines, of course."

"And ... what is an engine?" Cyrus asked.

Dugras let out a soft chuckle as he entered the guildhall. "It's a steam machine. Spins the propellers that produce lift—the central masts that go around and around," he made a motion with his hand suggesting up and down movement. "And we also have engines that spin the rear propellers, which allows the ship to move forward or back."

"Huh," Cyrus said, blinking. "That's amazing."

"You sound like you've never seen an airship before," Dugras said with a soft chuckle. "I mean, I know Reikonos and Arkaria are provincial compared to the rest of the world ... but come on. They fly overhead all the time."

"I just got here recently," Cyrus said as they moved through the foyer, the procession's footsteps echoing in the great space. Dugras was casting an appraising eye over everything. "From somewhere ... more provincial, I guess you could say."

"Hm," Dugras said. "Well, if you get me back to my ship, I'll gladly take you on a tour. You can ask whatever questions you want, see one up close."

"Oh, I'm taking you up on that," Cyrus said as they entered the Great Hall.

Dugras's eyes widened as he saw the feast before them. "I think it seems a pretty fair repayment considering I'm about to eat all of this."

"Give it your best shot, old boy," Vaste said, "you won't be alone in trying."

"Now, now," Vara said, "there's no need to squabble. After all, as many corpses as we made in that alley earlier, surely Sanctuary has plenty of material with which to continue making more feasts if need be—"

"... What?" Dugras asked, staring at her.

"Nothing, she's being obnoxious and trying to ruin my dinner," Vaste said as he took his seat.

Cyrus glanced around; the table had elongated further before they'd arrived, adding more seats. He sat down next to Vara, and Shirri and her mother made their way across from him, the mother eyeing him with a guarded curiosity.

"I'm Cyrus Davidon," he said, giving her a curt nod.

"I figured that out," she said, just a touch standoffish. She did not touch the food in front of her, but continued to stare at him.

"It is good to see you returned to us, Shirri," Alaric said, taking his place at the head of the table. Cyrus tore his gaze from Shirri's mother to look at the Ghost. "And even better that you brought others."

"I'm pretty grateful for that right now, too," Dugras said, already scooping up a turkey leg, barely getting to it before Birissa, who had just reached the table. She glared at him. He ignored her and began to eat swiftly and a bit messily.

"Perhaps you might introduce us to your mother," Alaric said, nodding in their direction.

Shirri seemed a bit dumbstruck, but she took a breath and said,

"This is Pamyra, my mother."

"Pamyra," Vara said gently, "you are most welcome in our halls. How long have you been in Reikonos?"

"Fifty years or so," Pamyra said, more gently to her than she'd spoken to Cyrus thus far. It elicited a frown from him.

"And from whence did you come before that?" Vara asked, as gentle a prod as he'd ever heard from her. "Pharesia, I would guess."

"Good guess," Pamyra said with a nod.

"How'd you know that?" Cyrus asked.

"Because she's an elf, obviously," Vara said. "And from what we know of the elves—"

"How'd you know she was an elf?" Vaste asked, mouth full of mashed potatoes. "You can't even see her ears."

"I saw them as she moved," Vara said. "Her hair parted out of the way on several occasions."

"I did not see that," Alaric said.

"Nor did I," Cyrus said.

Vara blew air impatiently from between her lips. "Of course not. You're not elves, and thus you pay little attention to such things."

"I didn't notice that, either," Curatio said, focusing on a bowl of black beans.

"Nor I," Hiressam said, slipping in. He reddened and looked away from Vara's gaze as he tucked in to a bowl of porridge with fresh strawberries.

"I noticed," Birissa said, around a chicken bone. "Pointed ears, right there," and she stuck out a finger right at Pamyra down the table from her. Indeed, one of the points of Pamyra's ears was protruding from beneath her dark, frizzed hair on the left side.

Pamyra wore a frown that, to Cyrus's eyes, seemed familiar in both its intensity and shape. He let out a frown of his own. "Do I know you?" he asked, and she brought her gaze around to him, rather pointedly.

"We've never met," she said, and looked away again.

"That's hardly a complete answer," Cyrus muttered.

"How," Alaric said, directing his attention to Shirri, "did you escape the Machine—if I may ask?"

"Dugras stole a key from one of the Machine's ... interrogators," Shirri said, and Cyrus got the distinct feeling she was leaving something out.

"I don't think that man's just an interrogator," Dugras said, pausing mid-bite. "He seemed like he had the run of that dungeon while I was in there. I suspect he's higher up than that."

Shirri let out a low breath. "Fine. Dugras attacked a guard while we were being interrogated by a ... higher up member of the Machine ... and we managed to escape afterward."

"How?" Alaric asked.

Shirri let her impatience flare in a flash of irritation. "I don't know. The halls of the place were near abandoned, as though they'd lost many of their number."

"That was our doing, I expect," Cyrus said. "How many of them do you reckon we killed in the square before Gaull started cutting us down?"

"Many," Alaric said. "Enough to put a dent in their numbers at their nearest base, if that was, indeed, where they took Shirri."

"And why would they not?" Vaste asked, cradling a whole chicken in his hamlike fist. "It's probably how Gaull got there so fast. He was nearby."

"If Gaull came from there," Cyrus said, "that's probably their headquarters." He turned to Shirri. "Do you know where this place is?"

She shook her head. "I've never been there before, but it's on a main road. We could probably get back if we had to, but—"

"I think I know the way," Dugras said, dumping a round of steaming asparagus onto his plate. "With her help, anyway," and he nodded at Shirri. "We could probably reconstruct a map there."

"There's no need," Pamyra said quietly, staring at Cyrus. "You'd know where it is; the building stood in your day. It's in the old guildhall quarter—though it hasn't been called that for many years."

Cyrus blinked. "I ... do know where that is, yes. Where in—"

Pamyra shook her head. "I can't recall which guild made their home there. It's one of the four biggest. You know—that all stand at the crossroads staring at each other across the main avenue."

Cyrus felt a smirk grow on his face and he turned to Vara, who was daintily picking at her salad while listening intently. "Wouldn't it be hilarious if we find Isabelle at the top of this den of iniquity? Presiding from Endeavor's old guildhall?"

Vara made a hard snort of impatience, practically wilting her lettuce as she dropped her salad fork with a clang and turned to face him with glaring eyes. "My sister is not so stupid as to choose 'running a criminal syndicate' as her career path." She paused, retrieved her fork, and said, more quietly, "Also, I would kill her out of shame if that were true."

"And now we know the wellspring of all our troubles," Alaric said, still standing unsteadily at the head of the table. "But I cannot imagine they will leave that place unguarded for long, should we mean to attack it—"

Hiressam cleared his throat. "I don't ... mean to insert myself here where I am ... perhaps unwelcome ..."

"You are very welcome here, Hiressam," Alaric said, "as are your thoughts."

"Unless you're going to be the new Ryin, in which case they're not only unwelcome, but I may stab you with this salad fork," Vaste said, brandishing his own. "It's not as though I'm going to use it to actually eat salad, after all."

"You should try it," Cyrus said. "In the absence of physical exertion, it could help you curb your arse growth."

"Your growth as an arse is quite unchecked at the moment," Vara said, looking a little scandalized that he would say such a thing among strangers.

"I find Vaste's arse quite delicious," Birissa said, attacking yet another ham. "It's plump. Moist. Like this." And she took another bite.

Vaste's eyes gleamed with triumph even as he picked at this plate. "Told you," he singsonged under his breath.

"So these are the legends of Sanctuary," Pamyra said, a little muted. She stared across the table at him. "I suppose I so long imagined this moment ... that being here, among you ... it couldn't be anything but a disappointment."

"I'm often disappointed in the presence of Cyrus," Vaste said. "Especially when he's nude from the waist down."

Vara just rolled her eyes. "That would be never, then?"

"We had lives before you thawed your cold heart for him, okay?" Vaste looked pointedly at her. "There were adventures. Countless adventures. Some did not include pants. You would know this if you hadn't been so busy spurning him for the first decade of your acquaintance in favor of a book that essentially laid out your entire romance."

"I don't think *The Crusader and the Champion* quite captured the complicated nature of our romance," Cyrus said, then flushed red. "Also ... some of things in that book sound a little uncomfortable."

Birissa leaned toward Vaste. "Have you read this book?"

Vaste glanced at her. "Yes, why?"

"We should try those things later," she murmured.

He started to open his mouth, and seemed caught between pleasure at being asked and partial revulsion in thought of what that might entail. "So ... you're saying later ... we'll—"

"This is the strangest dinner I've ever had," Dugras said.

"Sorry," Cyrus said. "We're like this all the time."

"No, you're all fine," Dugras said, "I mean, a little odd, but—" And he lifted up two dishes, one with a strange mixture in it that seemed to include small ears of corn no bigger than Cyrus's littlest finger, and another that was composed of some sort of white grain. "I've never seen rice or baby corn in Arkaria. Ever. They don't make it here from Amatgarosa, even by airship. Yet you have them both."

"Sanctuary is a unique place," Alaric said with a faint smile.

"Certainly a wondrous one," Dugras said, putting the dishes down after scooping out considerable helpings for himself. "If I'm invited again, I must bring my captain."

"Please do," Alaric said. "The more the merrier." And he turned his gaze to Pamyra. "At least … most of the time, I would say that. But there seems to be something troubling you, m'lady."

Pamyra looked at Alaric, and the intensity of her glare, apparently reserved solely for Cyrus, faded. "I have … nothing against you." She looked around. "Most of you, obviously. You seem good people, and … truthfully, I have been waiting for this day much of my life."

"You've been waiting to meet dead people for most of your life?" Vaste asked. "I thought I was the only one that did that—or at least I did, back when there were dead people around. Now I seem to spend most of my time eating and hoping that Birissa would see the virtues of my tight arse—and now that the second thing is accomplished, what's left but to eat?"

"Why were you seeking us, if I might ask?" Alaric directed his attention to Pamyra again, and shuffled uncomfortably. He seemed to be favoring the neck wound that Gaull had given him. It caused Cyrus a prickle of concern to think of Gaull and how he'd managed to bring low even the Ghost.

Pamyra drew in a deep breath, looking as if she were composing her thoughts before speaking. When she did open her mouth, the words came slow and steady. "I have long thought of you. All of you. For most of my life, now, in fact, I would say. The search for what happened to Cyrus Davidon after he rode off into legend—" And here she glared at him once more, "has filled my every day for the last nine hundred and more years."

"That's a long time to devote to this lunkhead," Vaste said. "But his bride still has you beat, I think, as holder of that record."

Vara shot him a sour look.

Pamyra stared at Cyrus, and her eyes burned and her lips curled at the side. "I have sought you for so long … questions desiring answers aching in my breast—"

"She's awfully teed off at you," Vaste said, leaning forward and stage whispering across the table at Cyrus. He then nodded at Vara. "Did you two accidentally have a baby before you left? Maybe that one has a particular axe to grind?"

"No," Cyrus said, and Vara echoed him, both of them pointed enough that even Vaste scooted back an inch in his seat.

"I am no child of theirs," Pamyra said, sounding vaguely affronted at the thought. "Nor of his alone, nor hers—"

"Whew," Vaste said. "I was afraid there was going to be some absent-father drama there for a second."

"There is," Pamyra said, leaning forward, not taking her eyes off of Cyrus. "For you … you killed my father."

The table fell into a shocked silence, to which Vaste, so helpfully, added, "You're going to have to be *much* more specific. I mean, just by killing King Danay alone he probably orphaned several hundred—"

"They were all grown," Cyrus said, turning a savage gaze on Vaste, then back to Pamyra.

"But you did kind of wreck their inheritance, didn't you?" Vaste asked. "You know, ruining the kingdom, turning it into a place where they didn't really matter as much. There are probably a ton of pissed-off former royals hanging onto a grudge for you—"

"I was never a royal," Pamyra said. "I am the daughter of a lowborn man, not a king." She stared at him with fiery intensity. "But I have a grudge, for you did kill my father."

"Again … need specificity," Vaste said, and holding up his hands, miming a long parchment. "This list would go on and on. I mean, do you know how many people's he killed …?"

"I'm sorry," Cyrus said, feeling quite struck by Pamyra's anger and keeping a close watch on her hands. They hadn't produced a weapon yet, but if she could hurl magic like her daughter, she wouldn't need one. "I don't know who your father was—"

"Oh, but you do," Pamyra said, leaning forward. "And my mother as well. She spoke of you often, told me all about how you steered my father to this place—where he met his end."

Cyrus stared at her, and a vague stirring at the back of his mind began to piece the clues together. Her familiar expression—her dark, tousled hair—he'd chalked up her somewhat haggard appearance to being a prisoner of the Machine, as Dugras and Shirri had been, but now that he looked at her, the hair especially—it seemed a natural state and reminded him of—

"My gods," Cyrus said, awe rushing over him.

"He was your best friend," Pamyra said, as a single tear streaked down her cheek, "and you led him to death against the dragons."

"Still a long list," Vaste muttered. "Getting shorter, but still—"

"No, it's not," Vara said, eyes fixed on Pamyra. "It's a very short one, indeed."

"My father was Andren," Pamyra said, looking at Cyrus with a mixture of contempt and fury, "and you ... you killed him."

"Wow," Vaste said, into the silence that fell afterward, so thick that even the clattering of silverware might have seemed like a pistol shot, "your consequences really do suck."

50.

"You're Andren's daughter …?" Cyrus asked into the congealing silence. After Vaste's wisecrack, no one had spoken. Even Birissa had stopped eating to study the impending scene. Hiressam sat uncomfortably, eyes pointed at his boots and nowhere upon the table.

"With Arydni," Pamyra said. "Perhaps you recall my mother."

"She would be difficult to forget," Cyrus said quietly. "Is she …?"

"Shortly after you left, she died," Pamyra said, her face slightly red. "But not before she told me what happened to my father."

Cyrus let out a short breath. "I'd known Andren for years. I knew he had a daughter … but I never met you in all that time."

"It is the way of elves," Vara said quietly, "to sometimes go years without seeing family. We are so long-lived, the interval seems perhaps shorter to us than it would to humans."

"My father and I had a falling out," Pamyra said, hard-eyed. "Over his drinking. But he'd written to me. Said it was … finally over. He wanted to meet, and I'd consented." She stared Cyrus down. "He wanted me to meet his new wife-to-be."

Cyrus felt the cold knife of regret slide into him. "Martaina." And now she was dead, too. Chills ran over him, tickling his skin, and he lowered his head to stare at his empty plate. "I'm sorry, Pamyra. I failed Andren. As I failed … so many people." He swallowed, the feeling of a thick knot buried in his throat threatening to choke him. "Not just the dead of Sanctuary, who I have led pointlessly into battle all these years … but the dead of Luukessia, of Arkaria, that fell because of the consequences of my actions that have consistently come back upon me like ghosts of the past, like sins I cannot cleanse myself of." He stared at his black gauntlets, palms up in his lap. He felt as though they were coated in crimson guilt. "There is no forgiveness for the things I have done. There is no hope for—"

"No." The voice was strong, definite. It rang through the Great Hall like a sounded bell, the clarity pure, and every head in the room swiveled to hear and see the speaker.

Alaric Garaunt stood, helm off, at the head of the table, his eyes upon Cyrus. "Enough of this."

"Enough, indeed." Cyrus replied. "Alaric … what is the point of what I've done? I've unleashed so much harm in this world—why would I keep doing these same things—intervening, fighting, going to war and expecting something different to happen when—"

"Because," Alaric said, "of hope."

Cyrus let out a ragged laugh. "*Hope* implies that things will get better. How do I even fix this? What's the point of fighting the Machine when—"

"Stop," Alaric said, firm. "Despair bleeds out of you like life's blood. The consequences that have come to this world are hardly the product of your choices alone, but you want to take responsibility for all of them. Responsibility is a fine thing—if you mean to do something about the problem. But if you do not—if you mean to accumulate sorrows like some strange trophies to sit in a case while you wallow paralyzed—"

"Well, I was enjoying wallowing until now," Vaste muttered.

"—then what is the point of taking responsibility? Yes, we killed Mortus. Yes, you set it off," Alaric said, heated. "But Mortus could have died by any means. You were pushed into it by Bellarum, and do you believe for one moment that if you hadn't killed him, he would not have eventually equipped and sent his servants, the titans, to do the thing instead? Or some other unfortunate soul bent into his service?" Alaric slammed a fist against the table. "Yes, you bear a part of blame, of the guilt, as do many of us at this table—"

"Not me," Birissa said, looking mildly offended.

"—but if you can't see past that guilt to a future in which you correct the problem, in which you actively work—for as many years and decades as necessary to reclaim the lands taken by the scourge— then yes, you will have failed. And what was the point of taking all that responsibility upon yourself? To simply feel terrible? Why? Surely there are reasons closer to home for you to feel terrible."

"Impotence," Vaste said.

"I don't think that's his problem," Curatio said.

"Well, he sure is acting impotent," Vaste said.

"But Alaric," Cyrus said, raising his head. "Let's just use the example before us—the Machine. Let's say we go marching over to their headquarters right now and do what we do. Kill them all, burn it down."

"I love it when we do that," Vaste said.

"Sounds like fun to me," Birissa said, ears perking up. "When do we start?"

"What happens after that?" Cyrus asked, staring at the Ghost, who stood silently watching him at the head of the table, darkness broken only by the burning hearth and the torches that surrounded them on sconces from the walls. "What steps into the place voided by this Machine when we've—"

"We do," Alaric said.

Cyrus smiled, but it lasted only a second. "Alaric—"

"Cyrus," Alaric said, cutting over him, "in case it has not become apparent to you, I don't care for the shape of this world, either. I see our fingerprints upon it all the wrong ways. The void we left behind, the empty places where we failed to act—they work upon my soul, too. The guilt, while not perhaps as raw as yours, is ever present for me as well. I hoped that the world would do well—that the land of Arkaria would thrive—in our absence. It has not." His eye glistened. "You ask me what will happen when this task is complete? And you began, I believe, to ask me what happens to this world ... when we move on again?"

A hard silence fell. Cyrus looked at him and nodded once.

"We will not be moving on again," Alaric said, and his voice rang out over the room. "For me ... this is the last stop. I will remain out of the ark this time—"

"What? Where's the ark?" Shirri asked.

"Sanctuary is the ark," Vaste said. "Keep up, will you?"

"... What?" Shirri blinked.

"—from now until the end of my days," Alaric said. "Which will hopefully be considerable." He smiled faintly. "I don't mean to leave again, the way we did last time; I would not have then save for Vara being as badly injured as she was. But our absence is keenly felt, and the day is here where we must reckon for our mistakes and for the disaster that has befallen these lands that I love." He looked down for a moment. "I speak now not only of Arkaria ... but of my home, Luukessia, as well. These places cry out for aid—and starting here, and starting right now—I mean to give it."

"This is ... really inspiring," Dugras said. He'd stopped eating, too. "I'm feeling kind of ... swept up in this right now."

"Alaric casts a mean speech spell," Vaste said.

"Spell ... what?" Dugras asked.

"We will be the guardians," Alaric said, and now his face was set, eye fixed, the determination like stone cementing his features. "The sentinels on watch for this world. And where we begin is right here. Reikonos must be freed. Arkaria and Luukessia will be saved. But this is where we start. Our duty remains clear as ever. Our ideals—those of Sanctuary—have carried us a thousand years to this place, where we are desperately needed. I have heard Shirri say it, over and over again—

'There is no hope in Reikonos.'

"Well," and here Alaric's eye glinted with determination, "I mean to change that. I will bring hope to this city, even if I am alone. I will fix that which lies broken in this place, and then I will turn my eye to the next challenge, and the one after, until there are none remaining upon these shores. I will fight these battles until I either fall or there are no more before me. I will fight for the people—for my brethren—and I will do so all the remaining days of my life."

Hiressam rose to his feet, chair clattering as he did so. He drew his sword and took it by the blade, thrusting the hilt toward Alaric. "If you will have me, I will fight with you. For all my days as well—truly, this time." He looked at Alaric, eyes burning. "I failed Sanctuary once before, and since the day I realized the gravity of my mistake, I have done nothing but try and make amends. I carried the ideals I learned here into every day I have walked since, trying to bring them to life like a faint flame in the dark—and I have failed on my own. If I may add my light to yours, if my life may serve this quest ... I will give it gladly. You need but ask."

Vaste slid his chair back and stood, wavering only a little. "I have been thinking only of myself these last days." His cheeks looked a deeper green than usual. "Worrying about *my* people. About *my* legacy. About *my* place in the world. Gods, what a selfish prick I've been—"

"Hear, hear," Cyrus said.

"Don't be an arse in my moment of confessional regret," Vaste said, "you can't pull it off nearly as adroitly as I can. Anyway ... I have been a selfish prick. A self-centered one, worried only about myself when everything around us in this city has clearly gone to shit. My life was never better than when I was surrounded by my brethren here in Sanctuary. Not when I was in Gren. Not when I was here in Reikonos, or any of the other places I've lived and felt like an outcast. When I was in Sanctuary, everything made sense because I worked toward the purpose Alaric just laid out." He looked at Alaric, and raised Letum, leaning the length of the staff down the table toward the Ghost in a gesture of offering. "I don't want to think about myself anymore, Alaric. If you're refounding Sanctuary, I want to be part of it so that I can drown my selfishness in service—and become the kind of person who is eminently worthy. Who is defined by their actions, not their stupid, self-serving thoughts."

Curatio stood and flipped his mace so that he had hold of the round end and offered the haft to Alaric. "You have long had my aid if ever you needed it, and I have pledged myself to your cause before. Now, all these long years later, I find my ardor for your ideals even more inspired, if possible. To be part of this group is to make even an old man like me feel young again. To do the good we have tried to do— and to make good all that we have failed upon—that is a noble quest which I would gladly expend all my years upon. You have my aid, too, old friend, should you want it."

Vara started to stand. "I—"

Birissa knocked her chair over getting out of her seat, and drew her immense blade, holding it delicately with one hand as she extended the hilt to Alaric. "Can I live here if I serve with this ... crew?"

Alaric blinked at her. "... Yes."

"I'm in," Birissa said, and when she saw others staring at her, she said, "Reikonos rents are ridiculously expensive. And if I can use my sword to fight people ... this sounds perfect for me." She glanced sidelong at Vaste. "There might be other benefits as well."

"Oh my," Vaste said, breaking into a smile when he saw her leering at him pleasantly.

"Well, all right then," Vara said, pulling Ferocis from its scabbard and pointing the hilt toward Alaric. "You pulled me from the jaws of death long ago and saved from a fate worse than it, I think. I had long used avarice as my guide, seeking challenges and riches—and it nearly killed me. But you saved me, you and Curatio and ..." she looked at Cyrus. "... another. You brought me here, where I found fellowship and eventually someone who could love me for the ... somewhat prickly person I am."

"We were all surprised on that day, I assure you," Vaste said. "It gave me hope there'd be someone out there for me." And here he smiled at Birissa, receiving a smile in return.

"Sanctuary has made me better," Vara said, "it made me whole, these ideals. Filled that gap in my soul—"

"Did anyone else's mind just go somewhere dirty?" Vaste asked.

"Stop it," Curatio said. "And ... yes."

"... that no riches nor conquest at the head of an army could sate," Vara said, ignoring them both. "Finding the simple joy in putting my sword toward righting the wrongs of this world was something that I had never realized I had always wanted. A curious ignorance for a paladin, but then … there I was. If that is to be our mission in this new world, I can think of no greater thing for us to do. I am most definitely in."

"Hey," Dugras said, rising to his feet, head just a little above the table. "I kinda wandered here not knowing what's going on, looking for somewhere I could hide and not get taken back the dungeon. But now you people are actively planning to go back to the dungeons … and beat the people who dragged me from my ship." The dwarf's eyes fluttered. "Okay. That's laudable. I come to Reikonos quite a bit. I've never met anyone who had the balls to throw a punch at the Machine before, let alone somebody who actually took them down a peg. That's really impressive." He shook his head slightly. "I'm not from here, and I don't know if I'll be staying long—I owe my service to my captain, you see—but … if you don't mind me serving two masters … what you've said is noble, and it inspires me." His eyes looked moist, his face sincere. "I would join you for this. And … I don't know if I can aid you completely … I'm really more of an engineer than a fighter, though I might have a couple tricks up my sleeve if you give me a bit … but I guess what I'm saying is," and he pulled one of the plain pistols that so many in the Machine seemed to carry, and turned it so that the barrel pointed toward him and the grip toward Alaric. "I'm in for knocking over the Machine and … maybe more. We'll see."

Finally came a silence at the table. Cyrus, still seated, noted he was one of only three that remained so. Pamyra still sat across from him, though she was no longer glaring. Now her eyes rested on her lap, though she flicked her gaze to Shirri at her left when there came motion from the girl.

"I'm with you," Shirri said, standing and looking down the table at Alaric. "I've lived in this city in fear … for so many days of my life." A glistening tear ran down her pale cheek, and now Cyrus could see the resemblance to her mother … and to Andren. "I don't want to be afraid anymore. I don't want to live without hope anymore. I want to believe that there could be a better tomorrow—for me, for everyone here—and that will never happen with the Machine. They have dogged my steps for … so long now. They will keep coming until there is nothing left of me but tatters. They do this to anyone they set their eye on, anyone they think they can use." She brushed her cheek with her sleeve. "I don't want to be afraid anymore. I don't want to live without hope any longer. If you want to break the Machine … I will help you however I can."

Pamyra stared up at her, mouth slightly open, blinking. "Oh ... Shirri ..."

"I'm sorry, Mother," Shirri said, keeping her eyes fixed, determinedly, on Alaric. "I can't live like this anymore. Life under the Machine is no life at all. I would rather die trying to knock them over than endure a life being crushed under the weight of fear."

Pamyra stared at her for a moment before she bowed her head once more. "Is this ..." and she looked up at Cyrus, "... why *he* fought with you?"

Cyrus met her gaze, and beneath the loathing he'd seen was pain; pain that Cyrus hadn't even dared to look in the eye. "Yes," Cyrus said quietly. "We started ... looking for riches. Andren, I, and one more. But when we came to Sanctuary ..." Cyrus swallowed hard. "Everything changed. Somewhere along the way, we stopped fighting for wealth. We stopped fighting to be the best ... and somehow we became the best anyway. And we fought for each other. For others. Andren died trying to save the elven kingdom, to save the entirety of northern Arkaria from certain doom at the hands of the titans." Cyrus's mouth felt dry. "And in this ... he succeeded ... and yet still ... we didn't entirely succeed."

"We have not failed until we have failed to try again," Alaric said, still standing tall at the head of the table, so many weapons offered him. "You mourn the loss of a battle, Cyrus—and a heavy defeat, no doubt. The casualties are high, and the field looks grim indeed. But the war we have long fought is hardly over. The enemies before us are great—but together—we can build an army again, one mighty enough to challenge them, to beat them—to win this day and all the days going forward." His eye glinted. "Join me, General ... and we will see the glorious days of Arkaria—and Luukessia—renewed once more."

"I ... would be with you for that, I suppose," Pamyra said, and now she stood, putting out her hand like her daughter had. "I learned spellcraft in the days of old, and learned to use it through the suffocating wane of magic. I taught my daughter," and she nodded at Shirri. "I fought for other guilds, for governments, in the days before the breaking of the Leagues. I fought for anyone I chose after that— and then I searched ... for something ... ever since." She still looked at the table. "For my father, I suppose. For the reason this man—this ... achingly flawed man ... would give up his life. For ... a cause, I suppose." She took a deep breath, and her shoulders moved with it. "Now ... I see it at last. The company he kept in life must have led him willingly into death. Your ideals ..." And she swallowed, "... are worthy in a way no guild I ever worked for were. Now I see it," she said, "and now ... I am with you. I only wish ... that I listened to my father ... and had seen it a thousand years ago."

"A thousand years ago ... you would have been one of many," Alaric said, "Now, you are here at a new beginning, with new skill, when we need you most."

Pamyra nodded. "Aye. I suppose I am at that."

Another silence fell, and Vaste cleared his throat and looked pointedly at Cyrus. "I'm not saying this staff is getting heavy, because it gives me godly strength, but if you don't get on your feet and declare loyalty soon, I'm going to lose patience, and the bopping of that helm of yours? It's going to be particularly epic and fueled by annoyance this day."

Cyrus let out a long breath. "You speak true, Alaric. Your words cut me to the quick."

"On your feet, asshole," Vaste said. "Join us in our foolishly grand gesture."

Cyrus skidded his chair's legs as he slowly pushed out from the table. He looked down at Praelior, hilt peeking out where it rested on his belt. "I have served Sanctuary for many years. As a member. As a warrior. As an officer and then general ... and finally ..." He lifted his eyes to Alaric, who watched him patiently. "As Guildmaster."

"And in that last role," Cyrus said, reaching up and preparing to take the chain from around his neck, "I have failed most grandly." He lifted the medallion from beneath his armor, prompting a cry of surprise from Shirri. "What?" he asked.

"Nothing," Shirri said, shaking her head swiftly. "Later."

Cyrus shook off the distraction, and started to remove the medallion.

"Hold," Alaric said.

"Why?" Cyrus asked, medallion clutched in his gauntlet. "You are the leader, Alaric. You have rallied these people—some of whom never met you until the last day—to risk their lives in pursuit of a cause that is hardly the stuff of normal life in Reikonos at this point."

"That's true," Dugras said. "I mean, normal life in Reikonos at this point? It's a little like hell, honestly. Terrible place. I never liked to visit, and that was before I got attacked taking a piss. I mean, really— who attacks a man relieving himself ...?"

"Yet you inspired them to act against a wrong that has laid in place for years," Cyrus said. "You moved Vaste to withdraw his head from his arse—"

"I was just looking at it," Vaste said, "I wasn't actually up the arse. It's so pretty, how could I not look?" Birissa made a great show of leaning back to do just that, and a chuckle ran through everyone at the table.

"You have provided a place where fellowship has stood," Cyrus said, "you provided a home where we could do ... works ... that no one else would dare. You are the leader. And I return this to you now—"

"I don't want the damned medallion, Cyrus," Alaric said, eye fixed on him. "It's just a medallion. Metal. Ether. Who cares? It does nothing we have need of right now. I will take the mantle of leadership, but I tell you now—the medal matters not at all to me. What concerns me ... and always has ... is the man wearing it."

Cyrus froze, the medal in his gauntlet. He let it slip, and it clinked against the front of his breastplate. "I suppose that's true, isn't it? Since the days you saw to my safety at the Society of Arms."

"I have an obligation to you," Alaric said, holding his gaze. There was a warmth within it. "But ... there is more, at this point, than mere obligation between us." He leaned in. "I have need of your aid ... General. I could certainly spearhead this attack—or Vara could, or Curatio—"

"Or me," Vaste said, and when he caught the amused glances, he sighed. "Well, fine. I could spearhead an attack on the Sanctuary kitchens or this table, though. The damage would be massive."

"I would join you in that fight," Birissa said, slipping a hand into his.

"I'd fight that one, too," Dugras said. "And I will ... once the standing and declarations are over." He looked around. "Are they almost over? Will we have time before the next fight?"

"—I need a general if we're to build an army again," Alaric said. "You see, here—we have the building blocks. We have enough to strike at the Machine, to take the head off the serpent, perhaps. And I will provide the guidance and the inspiration you look to me for, but if we're to conduct a war, I need—"

"A warrior," Cyrus said calmly, and pulled Praelior, reversing his grip upon it.

"A leader," Alaric said.

"A general," Vara said.

"A total arse, and a long one at that," Vaste said, and when he drew the attention of everyone in the room, "What? I thought we were talking about what Cyrus was to us. Oh, fine—a very special friend, whose best interests I almost always look after. Provided it's not mealtime, because that takes precedence."

"A godsdamned, gods-killing legend," Curatio said, amusement curling his lip as he looked at Cyrus.

Cyrus stared at the faint glow let off by Praelior. "I got this blade in service to Sanctuary," he said, looking at the curve where it met the tip. He looked up, to Vara. "Everything I have of note, of worth, save for perhaps this armor, I got in the service of Sanctuary. And even this, I would not have but by the grace of Sanctuary keeping it safe until I could take possession of it." Cyrus slid the blade, clenching tight to it, and pushed the hilt toward Alaric. "You need a general? A leader?" He shot a pointed glance at Vaste. "A godsdamned, gods-killing, legendary arsehole?"

"That's right," Vaste said, "embrace it, you prick."

"You have my sword," Cyrus said, and saw Alaric stiffen slightly, a smile slowly spread across the ghost's face. "You have my service. And, as ever ..." He looked at Vara, whose smiled glowed in the dim light of the hall, "... you have inspired me, Alaric." Cyrus smiled back. "Now ... let's go kick the ever-loving hell out of this Machine ... and get onto the next task in the long road to saving Arkaria ... and Luukessia."

51.

Cyrus was the first out the door once they were done with the proclamation of loyalties. They assembled beyond the gate without directive, Birissa and Dugras still carrying food, and all of them walking with purpose.

The ash came slowly down into the steadily deepening twilight as Curatio stared around the alley. Alaric reached the gate to Sanctuary and unbarred it, becoming ethereal in the process. "This seems likely to be a dangerous thing," Curatio said. "Any misgivings anyone has should now be aired—or else hold your peace and let us do this thing right."

"Agreed," Alaric said. "No one should be held a coward for speaking in the heat of the moment. If you have misgivings, there is no shame in vanishing quietly into the night now. No one will think the less of you for it."

"I will," Vaste said, and when he caught an ireful glare from Alaric and Curatio, he shrugged. "What? I will absolutely think less of you. Don't talk big if you're not willing to back it up. Gather the remaining threads of your dignity and press on after terrible decisions, like all the rest of us have learned to do."

"That is easier said with a godly weapon in hand," Alaric pointed out.

"I thought it even when I didn't have a godly weapon," Vaste said. "Now—let's go obliterate these thuggish idiots." And he started down the alley, Birissa a step behind him.

"Yes," Cyrus said, with a sharp nod, and following the troll now, "Let's."

"Cyrus," Alaric said, coming along beside him.

Cyrus looked at his guildmaster. "What?"

"We don't know what we're going into here," Alaric said.

"Sure we do," Cyrus said, "the headquarters of the Machine. It's in one of four guildhalls, all are massive, and surely labyrinthine inside. By now, I think we can expect the Machine will have pulled men from their other locations throughout the city in order to beef up their guard—"

"That seems foolish, does it not?" Vara asked. "Now that Dugras, Pamyra, and Shirri have escaped, would it not make more sense for them to spread their forces out on the streets of Reikonos, looking to recapture them?"

"Surely they will be doing at least some of that," Alaric said. "But it seems likely that they will also be attempting to—"

"Let me inform you about a small piece of human nature that you have perhaps overlooked in your youth," Curatio said with a knowing smile. "Never does one guard something so fiercely as after one has lost it. It is very much like closing the barn door after the horse has escaped, and it is one of the more peculiar certainties I've learned in my long dealings with humanity. We can expect stiff resistance at this headquarters now that they've been embarrassed by Shirri's escape with the others—"

"Aye," Cyrus nodded, "and I think you're right as well. The Machine will be out in the streets in great numbers." He caught a wry smile from Curatio. "They will have called up everything they have; the natural tendency once wounded in the pride is to draw yourself up, strike harder, to blind anyone who might have seen your weakness with a show of your strength. The Machine will be out in force this eve—and forceful, I think, to make up for the incident on the square and the subsequent escapes."

The moment they reached the mouth of the alley, a scream reached their ears from down the way. Cyrus's eyes were immediately drawn to a wagon, and several Machine thugs in their long coats, wrestling with a woman over the reins while a man was already downed in the street, blood spreading from a wound on his head and four thugs cackling and shouting in the night.

"This will not be allowed to stand," Alaric said, breaking into a run, boots ringing out on the cobblestones as his steps clanged on the sidewalk. "Not in our city. Not now—not ever."

"Aye," Cyrus said, bursting into a run beside him, hearing the others follow, picking up their pace. "We should see it finished this night."

"Cutting apart a hydra is no easy or quick feat," Curatio replied, only a few steps behind them, the speed of those with godly weapons carrying them out in front of the others behind. "You should know this."

"Let us at least find one head to cut off," Alaric said, "and then, perhaps, we can deal with the others as they come. Chop off enough ... no more will answer." And he sprang at the nearest of the Machine thugs.

The thug had started to turn as Alaric swept in, burying Aterum in his chest as the man swung around. The thug gasped, taking it right in sternum, the cracking of bone as the blade passed through a sickening sound in the night.

"What is th—" the one atop the wagon, wrestling for the reins, began to say. Vara leapt high through the air as she always did, striking his head from his body and coming down on the other side of her leap to slash at the next of them, a man who threw up his hands and received a blow to both, shearing them at the forearms and prompting a fierce scream.

"My turn!" Vaste shouted, and with his elongated range, swung Letum with all his force. He slammed the staff into the last of the thugs, who let out a cry of pain as it walloped his side. The crunch of bones sounded like husks underfoot as he flew sideways, swept back past a surprised Cyrus and toward the rank behind him—

The man was thrown directly into a waiting blade—Birissa, her mammoth sword jutting out, caught the man on the tip and ran him through clear to the guard of her sword. She shook him off a moment later, and he limply fell into the street and simply died.

"I did that for you," Vaste said, winking at Birissa.

"So sweet a gift I have seldom received," Birissa said, winking back.

"We were never this bad, were we?" Vara asked, sidling up to Cyrus.

"No," Curatio said with amusement, "you were ever so much worse." And without a laugh, he was on, casting a healing spell that stirred the unconscious victim back to wakefulness.

"Get off the street," Alaric commanded the woman in the wagon. "Nothing good will come from being out this night."

The woman stared at him, mouth agape, and then her eyes found Cyrus, standing in their midst, no blood drawn for him yet. She stared at him nonetheless. "Is it ..." She raised a hand to him. "Is it really you ... m'Lord Davidon?"

"It is I," Cyrus said, his voice scratching some. "Get home. Lock your doors. The Machine is angry at me, and in their ire they are reaching out with grasping hands, seeking to hurt any who cross their path. Be safe this eve—and in the morning ... you will hear from others of my return." And he strode on past her, not daring to look back.

"She's never going to forget this," Vaste said, catching up with

Cyrus to walk beside him. "First she gets attacked, then she gets saved by her own god. Not many people here have had that experience."

Cyrus gritted his teeth, determination surging through him. "Well, more are about to."

They walked on through the night, the strangeness of the buildings around them fading as Cyrus felt, rather than saw, his way through the city. It was starting to feel familiar—that bank on the corner, the shop that offered cutlets, even the candlemaker's store where they'd dealt the Machine its first shattering blow.

"You seem … more comfortable," Vara said, now beside him.

"This is not the Reikonos I knew," Cyrus said, "but it's becoming familiar. I recognize this street now. I know the direction I'm heading. I feel as though I'm becoming reacquainted with an old friend."

"I feel the same about you," Vaste said.

Cyrus merely rolled his eyes. "It's as though I've come back after a long absence to find an old ally in the thrall of a new enemy. My purpose is fixed now. All gives way to one goal—breaking the Machine."

"A suitable pursuit for a man of war," Vara said, and when he looked at her in surprise, she smiled. "Don't be shocked. Killing Bellarum might have killed the purported god of war, but it hardly did away with war itself, nor your skill at it. It may not have been what you were born to, but it is what you excel at."

"Hear, hear," Vaste said. "Now you can turn that evil you were pushed toward into something noble."

"That was almost profound, Vaste," Alaric said, falling into step beside the troll. "The sort of thing I'm supposed to say in response to your comic statements. Now what am I to do?" The Ghost wore a faint smile. "Let me try this—'A cause worth fighting for'? You mean, such as pie?'"

A round of snickers made their way from Vara, Cyrus and Curatio, as the Ghost smiled. "Very good," Vaste said. "You know me too well, Alaric."

"That is what happens after you spend a thousand years in someone's ethereal company," Alaric said.

"Yes," Vaste said. "Now I shall have to do all in my power to come up with new jests. Once more, you challenge me to rise to greatness, not only in the fight for the soul of this land, but also in the realms of repartee. Thank you for that."

There were more Machine thugs ahead, though; a cry in the night drew them forward, Dugras, Birissa, Shirri, Hiressam and Pamyra only steps behind the five at the fore. Once more, Cyrus struck no blows. The three toughs of the Machine were downed easily by Vara and Vaste, with only a little aid from Hiressam, who came surging in with a fierce battle cry at the end, and an even fiercer swing that left one of the thugs without his head.

"This will be a long night for the Machine," Hiressam said, a glimmer of pride in his eye as he sheathed his sword.

"But a short one for some of its members," Vaste said, trying to scrape a layer of blood from the tip of Letum. "Like these fellows for instance."

They moved on through the streets, dealing with the black cloaked and armbanded thugs of the Machine as they came upon them. Screams from streets away would prompt them to alter course in a dizzying, twisting path. They saved all that they found and left them, most staring gape-mouthed at Cyrus as he exhorted them, "Get inside. Tomorrow things will be different."

Cyrus recognized the awe in their faces and tried as best he could to ignore it while knowing in his gut that he was shamelessly exploiting it to his own purposes—to get them out of harm's way. When he was walking, he kept his head down for the most part, scanning the streets around them, gradually becoming more familiar with the city. Still, when he reached the cross street into the guildhall quarter, he barely recognized it. The buildings here had almost all been torn down and replaced with newer ones, built in the style of this Reikonos, and not his.

"There," Vara said, pointing at the intersection ahead, where four sprawling buildings that had been of immense height in days of old and were now modest in comparison to the buildings around them dominated the street corners. Although they had been built upon and renovated over the years, they still reflected their original architectural styles. The old Burnt Offerings guildhall was on their left coming into the intersection; its human design looked dated and the dwarven decorations upon the facade were aged and covered in ash. To his right lay the old hall of Amarath's Raiders, built in the sweeping, old style of the Pharesian Elves. Vara's eyes slid across it, her jaw tight as they passed. Across the street from it ahead was the Termina elven design of old Endeavor's hall, stained with age. And then ... across the main avenue on the left, farthest from them ...

"That's it right there," Pamyra said, pointing at the last building as they came up to the intersection. Machine thugs, their armbands and cloaks missing, but their bearing as guards obvious, stood just outside, watching these strangers approach in the dark with little concern. And why should they worry? Cyrus thought. They were at a distance, probably couldn't see the armor and swords just yet ... and who would dare attack the Machine? That told him something about the information they were getting—which was to say probably none at all.

Still ... that guildhall ...

"Naturally," Alaric stared at the edifice before them in its old Reikonosian style. "It would be this one."

"Naturally," Curatio agreed, tension in his voice.

"Oh, wow," Vaste said, providing the counterpoint to them all. "Who could have guessed the seat of all evil in modern day Reikonos would be the Goliath guildhall?"

52.

"The more things change," Alaric said into the darkness of the gas-lit street, "the more they stay the same, apparently."

"I'm putting money on Malpravus having escaped that damned seal and being behind all this bullshit," Vaste said, rustling around at his belt for change. "Who wants that bet?"

"I'll take that action," Curatio said. "Admittedly, I was ethereal when it happened, but I distinctly remember Malpravus attempting to step up to godhood. I seriously doubt he would then be content to step down to running a mere street gang when he could, instead, sacrifice this entire city on the pyre of his ambitions and become—well, you know."

"Yes, I do know," Vaste said pointedly, "because I was there to fight him when he became that skeleton thing—but do *you* know?"

"I know in general," Curatio said airily. "I heard enough discussions by your members from within the ether before we were pulled away by Bellarum's attack."

"If you didn't see," Vara said tightly, "you don't know what a horror he became. But I agree with Curatio—this would considerable step down for Malpravus. I doubt he would condescend to this level. More likely, this is either coincidence, or else we're dealing with some other member of Goliath whose evil either remains or has spawned a long legacy."

"I heard a lot of talk just now, but I'm not seeing gold to back it up," Vaste said. "Put your money where your mouth is, paladin." He blinked. "Uh, on second thought, maybe don't put money on Cyrus's lips—and, uh—never mind. Gold. Bets, people."

"What?" Cyrus asked, feeling like he'd missed something.

"So … anyone other than Curatio want to put money against Malpravus?" Vaste asked. "I've got perfectly good gold."

"Not for long," Curatio said with a smile as they crossed the street.

"Whatever," Vaste said. "You're all betting. Tacitly, because you're too scared to admit you know I'm right."

"You are not right," Alaric said tautly.

"Bet me."

"No one cares about this at present," Vara said and surged into the street. Cyrus shrugged and followed, as did the others a few steps behind.

"Tacit bet," Vaste said. "You're all going to owe me money. So much money. I'll be wealthy."

"Halt!" one of the guards on the front steps of the Goliath guildhall called out as Vara and Cyrus strode up the steps. Alarm was now evident on their faces in the lamplight. The lead started to reach for a pistol.

"Stop that," Cyrus said and charged the last of the distance between them, burying Praelior in the center of his chest, leaving him staring at the blade jutting from his breastbone. Cyrus ripped it free and claimed the head of the other with a sure swipe as he tried to pull his own pistol. Pausing, Cyrus scooped up both weapons and placed them in the empty scabbards of his belt.

"Share and share alike," Vara said, and immediately seized one from his belt and placed it in her own.

"You're worse than a tax collector," Cyrus complained.

She raised an eyebrow at him. "Do they sleep with you before relieving you of your property?"

He stared back at her evenly. "Okay, you're better than a tax collector. But this 'what's mine is yours and what's yours is yours' bullshit is getting to be a bit much."

"I would gladly share my salad with you later," she said with an impish smile, taking up position on the right hand main door of the guildhall as he moved opposite her to open the left. They were massive double doors, and Cyrus noted the lack of hinge outside suggesting they would swing in.

"Thanks for that meaningless gesture," Cyrus said, "given Sanctuary produces all the meat I can consume—"

"So long as you keep killing people on its doorstep anyway," Vaste chimed in.

"—and thus it rings a little hollow and lacking in generosity," Cyrus said.

"I give you so much more than salads," she said. "Why, you get the pleasure of my company."

"This is hardly a fair trade," Vaste said. "There are thousands of members of Sanctuary who actively avoided that for years."

"Well, that's because they didn't know me, did they?" She arched her eyebrows at him. "And certainly not as Cyrus does—which is why he puts up with my little quirks." She held the pistol beside her face in one hand, hammer thumbed back, Ferocis in the other. "Shall we?"

"We shall," Alaric said and kicked both doors off their hinges with a mighty blow that sent them spiraling in as if they'd been wrecked with a battering ram. Cyrus stared at him, eyes wide, and the Ghost caught the look and replied with a thin smile. "You assumed because I am generally quiet and mild that my strength was all in my speed?"

"I ... never thought about it," Cyrus said.

"No, you didn't," Alaric said, from behind his grey beard, "you only saw my apparent age, my reserve, and made your assumptions. And that is all fine," and he smiled, "for that is exactly what my foes do." And he plunged forward, striking down two guards that came running toward them.

Cyrus stepped inside the old Goliath guildhall and was struck by the scale of the foyer. It was comparable to the Sanctuary of old, a sprawling two-story space with high ceilings that were decorated with wood paneling and impressive art. Lamps burned in every sconce and candles hung flickering in the chandelier above. A beautiful oak staircase that was almost as wide as a city street lay before them, leading up to a landing and then to the balcony above, which spanned two sides of the room, and from atop which countless Machine guards now stared down at them, open-mouthed at their audacity.

"Knock knock," Vaste said, stepping inside, brandishing Letum. "Sorry about your doors. They looked expensive. I'd offer to replace them, but I don't like any of you, and I rather want to bash your skulls in instead." A guard stood just inside the doors, stunned, staring at Vaste. The troll reached out and struck with the end of his staff, caving the man's head in. "Like that, you see. Now—everybody form one line, I'll get to you all eventually. No shoving, no cuts—especially no cutting me. Or shooting me." He made a noise of impatience. "Come on, then. I haven't got all ni—"

"GET THEM!" someone shouted, and the room burst into motion. A bell began ringing loudly somewhere upstairs, the alarm sounding. From a hallway along the back wall to their right came a rush of guards in black coats, their armbands on display. Others began to flood down from the upstairs, and Cyrus was impressed to see them gather their courage so quickly.

Someone shot out of a side hallway and leapt from the top balcony, coming to a landing swiftly, so quickly that even with Praelior in hand, his eye had some difficulty following them. The figure came for him at a sprint, and Cyrus blinked as he realized—

It was Gaull.

Gaull kicked him full in the chest as Cyrus raised his weapon to respond. He saw him coming, but somehow Gaull moved strangely, just as swift as him but more practiced, perhaps, and when the kick landed it rammed Cyrus's breastplate into his chest and sent him flying through the wall and out onto the street, where he rolled until he reached the cobblestones in the middle of the road.

Suddenly Gaull was there, just feet from him, sweeping in, and his sword clashed with another as Cyrus got up, struggling from the hits he'd just taken. The man was no quicker than he—or shouldn't be— but he certainly knew how to use his blade to maximum effect. Compared to nearly anyone else Cyrus had fought, save gods perhaps, he moved with such ruthless efficiency and skill as to make any other foe look as though they were standing still.

"I see you've come to deliver yourself to die at my hand," Gaull said with his smile, fending off Vara with one hand, who was attacking him from behind. "Saves me the trouble of coming to look for you."

"Yeah, well," Cyrus said, springing to his feet and attacking Gaull, who now moved out of the way and let Vara overextend herself, putting her between the two of them, "don't go writing my epitaph just yet."

"I should like a try at that," Vara said, blade clanging against Gaull's in a frenzied storm, flashes of lamplight glinting off its edge as Ferocis struck Rodanthar, neither coming away with decisive advantage. "Here Lies the Great Cyrus Davidon, mostly mediocre before he met his wife and she drove him to new heights of glory.'"

"Hey," Cyrus said, bringing his blade in and forcing Gaull to alter his stance again to counter, "I graduated the Society of Arms without a blood family before I met you. That's not mediocre. No one had ever done it before."

"There are many things that many people have not done before," Vara said, "for instance, this jackass in front of us has yet to die. But when he does, it will be not grand or glorious, but very mediocre, and no one will remember him shortly after he passes." Her eyes glittered as she struck at Gaull again.

"You cut me to the quick, madam," Gaull said, amusement flickering in his own eyes as he rebuffed her advance perfectly. "But—" and he struck, catching Vara in the right arm and drawing blood as the tip of his blade made perfect contact through the links of her chainmail, "—it's all right. After all, it's not as though either of you could do any real cutting on me." And he swept toward Cyrus as Vara staggered back, exploiting Cyrus's distraction and catching him in the joint where his greaves met his boots, drawing a sharp pain and causing Cyrus to stagger.

Cyrus fended him off, and Gaull stepped back as Vara and Cyrus both recovered, blades waiting in case Gaull tried to exploit the moment of weakness. He did not, though, standing back and grinning, instead. This was not his best chance, and surely he knew it, which was why he stood back, waiting for the two of them to overextend themselves again.

"Now then," Gaull said, first blood drawn on both of them—again—his sword dancing as he waited for their next attack, "shall we finish this?"

Cyrus took a sidelong look at his wife; Alaric's encouragement had emboldened them in the face of their two defeats against Gaull thus far. But bold words only carried one so far, and here again they were confronted with the truth of the matter:

Gaull was simply a better swordsman than either of them.

"Oh, to hell with your finish," Vara said, raising a palm and blasting a spell at him, fire and force, which Gaull managed to deflect with Rodanthar. "I'll be damned if I surrender and dance to your tune." And she came at him again. Gaull responded to her attack with a great grin, and Cyrus stepped forth with an attack of his own. The battle was joined once more as Gaull continued to fend them both off with greatest ease and the occasional hearty laugh of gusty glee, but the question was—in the face of this obviously superior foe—

How long could the two of them last?

53.

Vaste

"This is all so very new for me," Vaste said, bashing in another skull. Machine thugs were everywhere, their black coats whirling like some kind of synchronized dance as they crashed in upon the line of Birissa, Hiressam, Curatio and Alaric, more daggers flashing in the foyer of the old Goliath Guildhall than any cutlery showroom Vaste could imagine.

"Less banter, more smash," Birissa called as she sheared five Machine thugs in half with one swing. Her blade was so immense and the enemy so plentiful that she was not starved for targets. And she seldom missed; it was much like a scythe going through an endless field of grain, but with blood and guts sailing in all directions. This was what Cyrus gloried in?

"I think I like the back of the battle lines better," Vaste said, smashing another Machine thug's head so that gore splattered his robes—yet again. They were soaked through now, and he sighed. "These were so nice once, too. Elven tailoring, I tell you. I paid a fortune for them. Now look at them. They're like a butcher's apron, but with more brains."

"The butcher has more brains?" Alaric asked, slashing and moving, disappearing into a blast of dark fog and reappearing behind a cluster of thugs, tearing into them. Screams filled the open foyer, loud and seemingly as endless as the waves of enemies falling upon them. "Or your clothing now does? I'm unclear. Either way, I think we can safely assume whoever or whatever you're talking about has more brains than you do, my friend." The Ghost wore a playful smile.

"Stop stealing my role, Alaric," Vaste said. "You wouldn't like it if I starting being cryptic and disappearing and reappearing everywhere.

Acting all fatherly toward everyone."

"You acting fatherly presupposes you showing maturity," Alaric said, "and I think I would welcome it."

"Well, you'll see it, then," Vaste said, whipping Letum forward and dashing another thug's brains across his robes. "In the fullness of time."

"Speaking of fatherly," Alaric said, reappearing next to Vaste and catching a Machine thug just as he slid in to stick a dagger in Vaste's side. Alaric cleaved him in two, and both halves hit a nearby wall, making a considerable mess. "How do you suppose our wayward warrior and paladin are faring outside—you know, against their great challenge?"

"I don't know," Vaste said, his voice evincing a little strain as Hiressam darted in front of him. Thugs were swarming at him now, apparently picking the largest target in the room and trying to overwhelm him. It was almost working; the length of Letum made it more difficult to work up a good swing, and by crowding him they threatened to eliminate the space in which he built up the momentum he was using to kill them. "I'm hoping your words inspired them, and they'll come back in, covered in his blood, with Cyrus wielding two blades again, triumphant, a little happy—not too happy, you know, because if he gets too happy he gets insufferable—"

"I have a better question," Alaric said, looking to his side. Birissa was near at hand, letting out a bellowing roar as she ripped apart another press of Machine thugs, "where did our guests go?" He whipped his head around. "And where is Curatio?"

But there was little time to answer, for it seemed as though the Machine was pouring everything it had at them. Vaste tensed as they continued to rush in, and he began to feel the stings of the occasional blade landing upon him even as he swung his weapon even more wildly and swiftly, trying to batter them all away and keep them from surging past into the street to attack Cyrus and Vara—who probably had enough to contend with.

54.

They'd gotten separated and forced down a hallway, not because they wanted to, but because when a clutch of Machine thugs came at you with blades and guns, and you lacked a weapon to strike them down, that was what you did. Shirri was desperate; she hadn't even had time to call out to Alaric to let him know what was wrong—no magic at all, thanks to McLarren and his accursed globe, probably—and off they'd gone, her, her mother and Dugras, separated from the body of the Sanctuary assault and now running through winding, twisting corridors in the Machine's base.

"Do you have any spellcraft yet?" Shirri asked her mother as they ran past endless doors. This section of the building did not look anything like the dungeons; a definite plus in her mind.

Pamyra raised her hand, stared at it for but a second, then shook her head. Lamps glowed, hanging from the walls, but it was still dim in here indeed. "No. Wherever McLarren is, his defense against us still works, it would appear."

"They're coming," Dugras said, strain showing on his face as he urged them around another corner. He'd led them thus far, and the two of them had tried to keep up with him. He could move surprisingly fast given his shorter legs. Shirri had actually had to hurry a few times to keep pace.

"We're in the middle of their base," Shirri said dryly. "I should be surprised if they stopped coming anytime soon. Unless Alaric and the others simply bleed them completely dry of soldiers."

"These are not soldiers," Dugras said, opening a door off the hallway and swiftly closing it again. "Though it would appear they live in something approaching a barracks style."

"Well, they're as good as," Shirri said, "for purposes of hunting us." And she followed them around another corner.

"They're here! Over here!" someone shouted from just behind them.

"Not really," Dugras said, but he was hesitating. "They're more like dogs. But without the decency, loyalty, or adorableness." He stopped at a corner and cocked his head. "Say, things are starting to look different here. Maybe this is—"

Dugras's face flickered with pain as something struck him from behind and drove him forward. The dwarf struck a wall, then slumped, bleeding from the head as another figure came out from the corner.

The scarred face surprised her, leering as it did from beyond the corner, the blank eye staring back at her. And clutched in the man's hand ...

Was the orb that deprived her of all magic.

"Hello, Shirri, Pamyra," McLarren said with cool precision, showing just the smallest hint of pleasure that he'd found them.

Shirri just stared at him, gape-mouthed, and the last flicker of hope within her was like a candle when the hard winds swept in; it took only a moment for it to gutter ... and then go out.

55.

Cyrus

"You fight with such passion," Gaull said, landing another pointed blow on Cyrus's shoulder, and Cyrus staggered back. The pain seemed to throw the world around him into astonishing clarity. The smell of Reikonos was everywhere, the black ash falling from the sky like a gentle rain. Cyrus took two faltering steps as Gaull moved away. Raising his hand to try and conjure a healing spell, he saw the glow turn red, and cringed as the dull sense of pain that accompanied draining his life to turn it to magic worked its way through him.

And still the blood seeped out.

Cyrus pulled one of his pistols and furiously fired it at Gaull, who merely raised Rodanthar at the last second as a shield, stepping out of the way of Vara's attack. The bullet spanged off the blade and then he was back at it again, coming at Vara with precision, not fury.

Vara met his attack cannily and carefully, but it seemed little headway could be made. As Cyrus watched, tossing aside the pistol, Gaull drove in at her side, and a spearing attack moved Vara back, leaving a little trace of red bleeding down her side where his blade had pushed through the chain once more.

"But passion is hardly a guarantor of victory," Gaull said, smugness seeping out, the tip of his sword dripping crimson. "Skill, my friends. Skill will carry you through where passion fades. Skill is the bridge, and you ..." He let out a small chuckle. "You are clearly in deep water already."

Vara's eyes met Cyrus's, and they flashed for a second. He knew what she would do before she did it, and tried to join her in time. Vara came at Gaull in an attack, and Cyrus lurched forward to do the same. A pincer—another one—coordinated, careful, trying to land an attack where none had been successful thus far.

Gaull saw them coming, of course; the charge was too grand, his eyes too quick and his mind too canny. He met Cyrus with a kick that came out of nowhere and knocked him over backward, and then clashed with Vara as Cyrus landed, hard, end over end.

The impact left Cyrus with the taste of blood in his mouth, and an ache in his side. He lifted his hand, trying to decide if it was even worth it to try and cast a meaningless heal. Staring up into the night sky, things seemed ... dark indeed.

No help ... is coming, he thought, the dark staring down, clouds of black hung above him like draperies.

And as he lay there, trying to catch his breath, Cyrus wondered if the dawn would see him dead—this time, for good.

56.

Vaste

"This ... is going downhill rather quickly," Vaste said as the room seemed to flood with Machine thugs and the bullets started to whizz around as more and more of them began to jerk their pistols and go to work. Certainly, they were hitting themselves more than they were succeeding in hitting him—or Alaric, or Hiressam or Birissa, for that matter—but they were still damned sure trying, and it was getting loud, and he was having to constantly duck out of the way of pistol shots, while simultaneously take advantage of them by pushing Machine thugs into their path. Hilarious, yes. Exhausting, also yes. They were heavier than they looked, those thugs, and his energy of movement was hardly boundless.

"It's because you're too busy thinking and not acting," Birissa said as she cut another swath through the enemy. They were still roughly in the center of the room, almost at the foot of the stairs, and down came the flow of endless thugs in black coats. Vaste was swinging Letum for all he was worth, and bodies were flying across the room, heads were erupting with his strikes like tiny volcanos of gore.

And still ... they came.

"Has anyone actually seen Curatio?" Vaste called. Hiressam shook his head as he plunged his blade into the center of a thug's chest and back kicked another. "So ... we're missing more than half our allies in the middle of a battle that's not going our way."

"Have faith, brother," Alaric said, appearing and disappearing once again with a blast of fog. It was nowhere near as impressive now with a godly weapon in hand, but Vaste had to admit it still looked damnably cool when he did that, and Alaric was certainly generating his share of carnage.

"I'd rather have a plan," Vaste shouted back as the Ghost disappeared again.

"Why can't you have both?" Birissa asked, and she met his eyes across the battle. "Faith in yourself and your comrades," and she dealt a blow that sent five more thugs flying in pieces, two of them discharging their pistols into the air in surprise as they flew, "*and* a plan?"

Vaste froze. Cyrus always tended to have a plan for these things, didn't he? But it often went awry. When they went to Enterra, he had plans—and then the goblins swept in and shit went wrong. The same thing happened in the Realm of Death with Mortus.

"Okay," he said, feeling a little grim, "maybe a plan is not all it's cracked up to be. But still—"

He stopped when his eyes caught motion at the top of the balcony above and across the room. There was a line of black there, thugs with the long weapons, leaned against the end of the balcony, ten or twelve of them, all taking aim to fire. He looked up and saw more on the opposite balcony; elevated and looming over them, they had Vaste, Birissa and Hiressam in a crossfire.

Vaste blinked. Their hammers were back, and their weapons raised. The shots would come, and soon, and there would be no avoiding them this time—not all of those. He could see death coming now, a hailstorm of metal bullets tearing him to shreds, with no healing spell to save him, no resurrection to bring him back.

The death of magic would, apparently, be the death of him.

57.

Cyrus

Pain lanced through him, and Cyrus ached as he tried to sit up. Vara was giving Gaull hell—or as near as she could without actually striking an effective blow. She was stalling him, nothing more, and the sound of their swords clashing in the night was the only thing other than the taste of his own blood and the smell of ash that Cyrus was truly aware of outside of the pain.

He braced himself, trying to rise, and suddenly someone was there, standing over him; white robes turned grey with ash and face set in a serious expression. "So …" Curatio said, "… how goes it?"

"Have you been watching?" Cyrus asked, trying to push to his feet. "He's cutting us into tiny cubes of meat which I presume he's going to use to feed—I don't know, probably himself, since I doubt he gives a fig for the poor or has any pets."

"He strikes me as the sort to favor cats," Curatio said, calmly watching Gaull battle Vara, as though the subject before him were of no more interest than a landscape painting. The healer raised a hand and Cyrus felt a little better.

"Curatio … he's going to beat us both," Cyrus said, winded, breaths coming out with urgency.

"Yes," Curatio said, matter-of-factly. "He has nearly a thousand years more experience than you; and he's quite right about passion. It will carry you only so far against someone who has studied footwork so long that any move you make comes as no surprise to him. Every muscle movement betrays you, for he has lived more lives than you and trained harder."

"How the hell do I beat a guy like that?" Cyrus asked. "And why wasn't Bellarum like that? He'd lived lifetimes."

Curatio wore a hint of a smile. "Bellarum was effectively immortal, never worried about actually battling his way through life." He nodded at Gaull. "This one, though ... even with Rodanthar in hand, he feels the bite of mortality. Look at what you did to his cheek; surely he has other scars as well. It spurred him to keep working, to always be wary, to put his arrogance aside and earn his life every day. No god you ever met felt need to do that. Cosseted by their magic and insulated by ten thousand years without challenge ... what need would Bellarum, or indeed, any of them, have of learning what Gaull has learned by hard experience?"

Cyrus sagged, watching Vara manage her stance carefully as Gaull swept in on her nonetheless, striking another blow. "I can't beat him. And neither can she."

"Do you need to?" Curatio asked, still calm.

"What the hell does that mean, Curatio?" Cyrus nearly exploded. "In order to win this, yes, we have to beat him."

Curatio smiled. "Do *you* need to beat him? Does your ego require it, General?"

Cyrus stared at the healer. "Hell no. Let's kick his ass together, I'm fine with that."

The healer rolled his eyes and thrust out his hand. "Give me your sword." Cyrus stared at his open palm and hesitated only a moment before pressing Praelior into it.

"Ahhh," Curatio said with a long sigh, then deploying the spikes on his mace from his other hand. "Now ..." And he turned to Gaull, "let us see what over twenty thousand years of fighting experience can make of this foe." And he whistled, shockingly loudly, causing Gaull to glance at him briefly. "You there—time to leave the children alone and face a real challenge."

Gaull evinced a flicker of surprise. "So ... the legend in black throws in the towel of defeat." He smiled, a little cruelly. "I don't think I ever really believed in you, Lord Davidon," he said the title mockingly, "but this ... handing over your sword and giving up? Truly, this is lower than a legend would stoop."

"Before I was a legend, I was general, dumbass," Cyrus said. "I command troops to win the battle. I don't siege the entire enemy line my own damned self." And he watched as Curatio stepped up and Vara moved to match him—

"No," Curatio said, indicating with his head that she should move away. "I appreciate the thought, my dear, but ... you'll only cramp my style."

"Your style—" Gaull started to say mockingly, but was forced to go on the defense a second later and never managed to finish his goad.

Curatio came at him with lightning quickness; Cyrus had seldom seen a godly weapon turned loose when he didn't have one in his own hand, and it was dizzying to watch the battle unfold at such unbelievable speed. The healer whirled and struck a blow with one weapon against Gaull, then another, and Gaull was forced to react and counter—but poorly. Every time Curatio struck with Praelior, the mace followed to a different spot a second later, and within three parries, Gaull took his first hit.

A long slice of scarlet over the Machine leader's arm gleamed red under the gaslight. Gaull staggered back and Curatio waited, patient, the hint of a smile on his lips.

"I must thank you for this," Curatio said as Gaull came at him and was rebuffed, taking another strike, this time to the leg, for his troubles. "My friends here have long labored under the perception that simply because I was unable to fight by the laws of our time, that I was, perhaps, unable to fight at all."

"No, I saw you wield that mace in the halls of Enterra," Cyrus called back as Vara limped up to him, hand glowing red and weariness on her face. "We knew you could fight. We just didn't know ..." he waved his hand vaguely, "... that you could kick our asses so handily."

"I could kick all of your asses handily," Curatio said, never taking his eyes off Gaull as the Machine leader came at him again. Praelior met the edge of Rodanthar, and Gaull received a spike from the mace to the face. He staggered back again, bleeding from the forehead. "Do you know how long I spent in war in my youth? It was endless; those were the days of battling elven tribes, the days before we discovered and turned magic to our own purposes. It was me with a sword in my hand and an effort to survive by being better than any other."

Furiously, Curatio moved in on Gaull. "Then came the days of my ambassadorship to the Protanians. Do you know why I became an arena fighter?" He struck, and Gaull took a long, bloody gash to his flank and spun as Curatio stood above him, sword raised. "Because I enjoyed it."

Curatio brought down Praelior, a thin smile perched on his lips. Gaull took the blow across the wrist and his hand was cleaved from his body with delicate strength and speed. With a backward swish, Curatio sent it in Cyrus's direction. Rodanthar, still gripped by the severed limb, came to rest at Cyrus's feet.

Cyrus blinked, then stooped, picking up his father's sword and discarding the hand still wrapped around the hilt like fetid garbage.

"Well ... look at that," he said, brandishing it for Vara.

"Very nice," she said through a pained grimace, "to see it back where it belongs."

"No," Gaull moaned, holding the stump where his hand had been. His knees hit the cobblestones, then he slumped to the ground.

"Yes," Curatio said, turning around and leaving Gaull in the middle of the street. "You see, this is the problem with relying only on skill and not having any passion, nor—indeed—wiser friends to fight alongside you." His eyes glimmered with amusement as he made his way back to Cyrus and offered Praelior, hilt first, to the warrior. "Eventually, you will run into someone better, and then who do you fall back on?"

"You should probably keep that for now," Cyrus said, waving Rodanthar. "Just for the battle, you know."

"And maybe a while longer," Vara said. "Until we're out of peril."

"Well, that'd be forever," Cyrus said in complaint. "And I really like that sword. I can use two, you know. I was, in fact, until somebody stole one off my belt—"

"We can take up this discussion afterward," Curatio said, smiling. "For now, though, perhaps you can take care of this one," and he nodded at Gaull, "from here?"

"Oh, yes," Cyrus said with a smile of relish. "I think I can handle this modest challenge." And he drew a pistol with his other hand.

"Then I shall rejoin the battle inside," Curatio said, walking toward the doors as Cyrus moved toward Gaull, who was gasping in the street.

"Come," Vara said, "let us be done with this," and she led him out to Gaull.

Gaull looked up at their approach, and stretched his remaining hand before him in austere defense. There was no escape, no hope. His teeth were clenched, and defeat was draped across his features with the pain.

"I'd say 'well met,'" Cyrus said, "or something similar, but really ... poorly met. I wish Zarnn had gutted you a thousand years ago and hung your entrails all over the swamp." He swung Rodanthar before Gaull's eyes, and the Machine thug watched the sword as though it were his fondest hope come back to visit him. "You truly are among the most vicious scum I have ever met, Tirner Gaull, and I can only say that if I grant you a merciful death here, it's because I wish you to be out of my presence, not because I think you deserve any measure of lessening in your suffering."

"I ... could tell you things ..." Gaull said, shaking, pain bleeding out along with the crimson life coming from his many wounds. "About the Machine. About who runs it."

"And I could listen," Cyrus said, uncaring, "if I could tolerate you for a moment longer and had but a damn left to give."

He raised the pistol and leveled the sights on Gaull's face. The flash of it firing was like summer lightning, illuminating the street more effectively than any gaslamp, but only for a moment. When it was done, Gaull was left twitching, a crushed hole in the top of his head the diameter of a good sword hilt at its widest point.

Cyrus turned his back on the man as the guttering gasps replaced the dying sound of the shot, and he walked way, Vara at his side, toward the open doors of the old Goliath Guildhall, still a seat of evil after all this time—

But not for much longer, he thought.

58.

Shirri

"Tell me where it is."

McLarren had her by the throat; her mother and Dugras were already down, McLarren having taken particular pleasure in lashing out and striking down her mother as the older woman came at him in a futile physical attack.

Shirri felt the hard pressure at her throat, the air failing to enter her lungs, the blackness clawing at the edges of her vision, spots of light dancing before her as consciousness waned.

McLarren had her at his mercy, and his interrogation was merciless. His eyes stared into hers with the full expectation of answer. He raised the orb in his other hand and then pocketed it, bringing his now-free hand around to slap her. "Tell me where it is, and this can all be over."

"I don't ... want anything to be over," Shirri said, clawing at his hand, surprising him so much that he dropped her. He stood back defensively, as Shirri fell to her knees and stayed there, looking up at him with the fury of a lifetime. "I want ... to live my life without you ... you people ... always at my back. I want to live without your Machine constantly trying to keep me down ... your men accosting us in the streets ... your decisions in councils across this city ... the thousands of them that you make that tangle in every aspect of our lives ... I want to be free to be me ... to live my life!" It was all coming out in a burst of raw anger. It was a lifetime they'd been here, on her back and the backs of every citizen of Reikonos that hadn't participated in their little gang and thus reaped the rewards of corruption. "I just want to be left alone by you people ... and you couldn't let me have even that."

McLarren let out a low chuckle. "Because, you fool, you're not a person, though you think you are. None of the citizens of Reikonos are people unto themselves. You're part of a greater whole, you see … part of a great chain, and we could no more leave you alone than you could leave babes unsupervised. You belong to us—all of you." McLarren's eyes grew narrow. "There's no hope in Reikonos—because who needs hope when we have the Machine? Hope is elusive, foolish—the Machine is a guarantee. As certain as the sunrise, we remain. You will render everything unto us … and then you will be allowed to die. There are no other options."

"I choose death, and will render nothing," Shirri said, staggering to her feet. "I care not what you have planned for your Machine's future—I don't want you in mine. I would rather die than serve this fiendish thing you've built by giving you one iota of aid—and I'd rather choke to death on my own blood than ever give you that medallion."

McLarren stared at her, cold and smoky, but it seemed a decision had been made. He shrugged. "Fair enough," he said and came at her—

A blade sliced through his chest at heart level, and McLarren gasped. It was perfectly curved, like a half-moon of death, and it stuck out below McLarren's breastbone. All the air went out of him, and he stared, open-mouthed, at it sticking out of him.

"I found your office," Dugras said, peeking out from McLarren's side. "I wondered where my things had gone. I guess you were going to keep my tanto as a trophy?" The blade slipped out of McLarren's chest, and the Machine man dropped to his knees, red drizzling down his front. Dugras stepped around and reached into McLarren's pocket, emerging with the orb in hand. He nodded to Shirri and tossed it to her gently.

She caught it, staring, and wondered at it for a moment. Wasn't there a spell to activate objects such as this? Oh, right. She remembered the words now.

With a whisper, the orb glowed for a moment, then went dark, its steely surface cold in her palm. Raising her hand at her mother, Shirri cast a healing spell, and the familiar glow was produced once more. It fell over her mother's fallen figure, and Pamyra stirred.

"You … can't win …" McLarren said as Dugras came around, a small pistol drawn and in his hand. It was no single barrel, either; it had many independent barrels that rotated. Multiple hammers stuck out from the center of it like spokes from a wheel, and Dugras held his finger upon the trigger and thumbed back three of them in a row, keeping it pointed at McLarren. "Against us ... against the Machine ..." Blood trickled down the corner of McLarren's mouth. "We're too much for you. We ... are always moving forward ... and you can't stop ... the Machine ... for we are ... progress. We were here before you came ... and the Machine will be here long after both of us have turned to dust ..." He chortled, and a wet, hacking cough sprayed blood from his lips.

"I'm half-elf," Shirri said, and raised her hand to brush back the hair around her ears. "But I'd outlive your Machine even if I weren't. The people out there," and she waved her hand all around, to encompass the city outside these walls, "will see their freedom restored. They will walk these streets without fear of your kind. Because I'm not here to fight you alone, McLarren—though I would, now," she said fiercely, "if it came to it. But I have help." And the words stirred the heat in her soul, and some strange feeling of conviction came from within, burning its way out of her like her soul was on fire. "I have seen people rise against you, to knock back your Machine's twisted 'progress.' You squeeze the life out of us and call it 'progress.' I know what you are, though," she whispered, and stared him in the eye. "And I will not fear you—or your Machine—anymore." Magic swirled around her fingers. "I will help break the gears of your Machine however I have to."

As the spell swirled around her hand, building, McLarren eyed it, dazedly, seemingly unable to move. "You won't win ... he won't let y—"

A burning blaze flew forth from Shirri's fingers, some power she'd long feared to loose. She thought back to the alley, only days before, and the fear that had choked her as the toughs had closed in. Everything had seemed impossible then—and facing McLarren had seemed the most impossible thing of all.

But as her spell magic faded, McLarren was dead. His legs toppled with a thump, dusting the floor with black ash like the smokestack refuse had found its way in here.

"Not bad," Dugras pronounced with a nod and turned. A dozen Machine thugs were standing there. "Oh. I didn't realize you were here." He raised his pistol and rattled off six shots in rapid succession, dropping several of them and then flicking a lever that broke the pistol down the middle. Pulling a small, metal pre-packed cartridge from his belt, he reloaded it quickly and flipped it closed with a satisfying click.

It seemed unnecessary; the remaining toughs had broken and run, fleeing back the way they'd come. McLarren's death by immolation must have made an impression, Shirri thought distantly, as her mother stirred and rose to her knees, clutching her head.

"Did I miss anything good?" Pamyra asked, one eye still closed in pain.

"Your daughter threw off the yolk of the Machine," Dugras said with a half-smile.

"That must have been something to see," Pamyra said, rising to her feet with a helping hand from Shirri. She looked into Shirri's eyes, and there was a faint smile there, as well. "Did you find something you lost, my daughter?"

Shirri didn't have to think long about it before answering. "Hope." And she looked back down the hallway they'd come from. "We should probably get back to the others ..." The shrieks and clangs of battle could still be heard in the distance, and that told her that Alaric and the others were still fighting the good fight. "You know ... give that help we swore them, now that we have our magic again."

"And now that I'm not toothless anymore," Dugras said, clicking his pistol closed cleanly. "I swear, you Arkarians and your primitive one-shot weapons ..." He made a scoffing sound. "Shall we?" And his eyes glinted with mischief, dagger in one hand and his gun in the other.

"We shall," Shirri said, and with a nod at her mother she took the lead, surging in front of the dwarf, a spell ready on her lips for any unfortunate Machine thug who happened to cross her path between here and the members of Sanctuary who labored somewhere ahead.

59.

Vaste

The sight of two rows of riflemen taking aim at them from the elevated balconies above was a worrisome sight for Vaste. These weapons were beyond dangerous, and though he did not subscribe to Alaric's belief that they were necessarily dishonorable, he did want to curse them right now for being incredibly inconvenient to his continued drawing of breath.

"Shits," he said, and swiped out with his staff, cracking one of the wooden balcony pillars nearest him with all his strength.

A fierce splintering ran through the pillar and echoed in the foyer; stone from floor to ceiling, bearing an ancient look, it broke cleanly as the wooden beam snapped cleanly in the middle.

The whole balcony above on that side lurched, and all the riflemen lurched with it. A distraction, perhaps, but only that, Vaste knew. And it had worked on only half their number—

He turned his head to look at the others, preparing himself to dodge the incoming hail of fire, but something was moving up there. Black fog was wafting off the upstairs balcony on the other side of the room. A sword was flashing, and there were cries he could not have picked out of the chaos. Something was happening, that much was sure, and it was—

Alaric. Of course.

The Ghost razored through the gunmen with godlike speed, striking through them as impressively as Birissa cut through a dinner. Vaste grunted and leapt forward, aiming for the next balcony support. It seemed Alaric had the other side of the room under control, which left him to deal with this one.

He smashed the next support, causing the balcony to lurch further.

Gun barrels hung over the edge, their wielders unable to get their balance to steady their aim. "Heh," Vaste said, neatly spared from their wrath by being in the shadow of their weapons.

"STOP HIM!" someone shouted—a Machine thug in a hat was pointing right at him. Vaste felt a bit singled out; there was so many of them in here, though their numbers were perhaps fading off a little now. Still, at least ten men swiveled on him as Vaste hurried toward the last pillar. They were in hot pursuit but lacked the speed granted by a godly weapon—

Birissa swung her blade and cleaved five of them as they surged for him. Pieces of the men were flung through the air, Vaste paused, admiring what she'd done there. Her face was twisted in rage, lips snarled with anger—

Gods, that was sexy.

"Hihi," he said to her, waving, as he swung his weapon like a hammer at the last pillar. It rang true as it found its target, and the beam burst, a grinding crack issuing from above him as Vaste threw himself past the five men sweeping toward him—

The balcony he'd been standing in the shadow of a moment earlier broke loose and collapsed, swallowing up his pursuers in the resulting wreckage as he hot-footed it back to where Birissa and Hiressam were being joined by Curatio—with Praelior in hand, no less!—finishing the clean sweep of the dwindling Machine thugs making their way into the entry hall.

"Seems you've about got things wrapped up in here," Cyrus announced a moment later as he and Vara re-entered the hall. They both looked a little worse for the wear, but were standing and not bleeding torrentially, which—combined with Cyrus holding Rodanthar once more—suggested they'd been triumphant.

"Looks like you avenged the honor of the last of the trolls," Vaste said, nodding at the sword in Cyrus's hand.

Cyrus looked at him coolly. "Zarnn was hardly the last of the trolls, Vaste." And his gaze flicked, subtly, to Birissa.

"Perhaps not," Vaste said, catching a lone Machine thug on his back swing and causing a geyser of skull matter to hit the ceiling. "Perhaps not, indeed."

"You killed them," Shirri's voice echoed over the room as the last of the thugs met their end with Alaric's sword through his chest. The Ghost looked up and smiled as Pamyra, Dugras, and Shirri re-entered, looking a little bruised and bloody but still walking under their own power. Vaste considered that a win. Especially given how hard it was to heal non-ambulatory persons in these damnable days.

"All that we could find," Curatio said, "though I expect more are lurking within the depths of this place."

"We should root them out," Vaste said. "You know, make sure Malpravus isn't lurking somewhere in the dark, ready to spring upon us all."

Curatio gave him a quirk of a smile. "You're just hoping to collect on that ill-advised bet of yours."

Vaste pursed his lips. "I'd also like to make sure they're not keeping any other prisoners we should free before we burn this place to the ground, once and for all." He let his gaze flick around a little. "But ... yeah. I don't really want to pay you any gold, so ... best to be sure the necromancer isn't hiding out in a dungeon room."

"He's not here," Cyrus said with great conviction. "This is below him. This is the petty scheming of a tyrant, not a god-in-waiting." He shook his head. "Whoever rules here ... they want to keep Reikonos their personal fiefdom, and milk it for all its power. To keep the people under a boot, not to rip the lives from them cleanly in the course of their own apotheosis." He clenched Rodanthar tight in hand. "I want to find the person behind this Machine. I want to carve their heart out of them, to drain their blood the way they've done to this city." His eyes narrowed. "I want to turn the very people they prey on against them, and make them fear us the way they've made everyone else fear them."

"Hear, hear," Shirri said, sounding a little choked, but her voice became stronger. "I am fully on board with that plan."

Alaric smiled. "As am I. But first ... I agree with Vaste." He favored the wreckage of the Goliath hall with a disgusted eye. "Let us search this den of snakes for secrets and prisoners ... and that done, let us burn it so that no evil may rise here again." He stood, imposing, in the middle of them all, though he was fully several feet shorter than Vaste and at least a head shorter than Cyrus. "Let us burn it down, here—and then we will stake the other heads of this hydra, until we reach the very last."

60.

Cyrus

The searching of the Goliath guildhall was surprisingly quick; the setting of fires all throughout, a slightly slower one. They'd run from room to room setting bedsheets aflame, putting correspondence to the torch, not lingering to watch it spread. By the time Cyrus had reached the main hall again, he found the others waiting for him, lingering, and when the last of them—Dugras and Hiressam—came out of one of the lower hallways, smoke was already curling around the ceiling of the might entry foyer.

Cyrus led the way out into the street, the others just behind him, and as his eyes adjusted to the darkness of the street, he was hardly surprised to find a waiting crowd. They let out gasps as he emerged, a black-armored figure striding out of the guildhall, the black smoke rising in columns from behind him.

"Oh, look, it's your admirers," Vaste deadpanned as they reached the center of the street. Smoke was pouring out of side windows of the guildhall's upper levels further down the street. "Seems they've found you again."

"I think these are new ones," Cyrus muttered, looking over the crowd for familiar faces. He didn't see any, but neither did he see Machine thugs in their familiar leather coats or with their white armbands and strange symbology.

"Whatever, your believers are endless in number," Vaste said, drifting away from him toward Birissa, who surveyed the scene with definite skepticism. "You should probably encourage them or something. You're good at that."

"I would," Cyrus said, "but I'd be too afraid you'd mock me under your breath."

"You've gotten pretty good at ignoring my jibes during your speeches," Vaste said. "But I think I have better things to do right now than pillory you with words while you try and inspire people to whatever hairbrained cause you intend to have them take up." His eyes flashed. "Have at it … General." And he moved to stand next to Birissa, who watched Vaste coming with …

Delight? It was faint … but Cyrus saw it.

"Vaste is right," Vara said, slipping up next to him.

"Don't let him hear you say that," Cyrus murmured.

"You should say a few words," Vara said. "And don't worry—we'll keep the secret of Vaste being right between us." She smiled and faded back, joining Curatio a few steps behind Cyrus. "That's a very nice sword for a healer," she said to him.

"Do you like it?" Curatio asked, raising Praelior up. "I got it secondhand."

Cyrus tried to tune them out, focusing on the crowd ahead. They were spread out over the street, eyes flicking from the fire burning behind him in the guildhall to him, standing there before it, at the head of his new—and burgeoning—army.

He turned, looking them over. Vaste and Birissa stood a few feet away, Vaste awkwardly looking at her. Finally Birissa rolled her eyes and put an arm around his shoulder, dragging him close to her as Vaste's eyes widened, and he broke into a smile under her touch. Cyrus almost laughed, but instead turned; Shirri and her mother were talking quietly, Shirri nodding at something Pamyra was saying. When Pamyra caught him looking, a cloud fell over her expression, and she met his gaze evenly. Cyrus moved his gaze onward.

Hiressam stood behind him, watching him. When he found Cyrus looking, he nodded once and saluted. Cyrus gave him a nod in return, and then caught Alaric doing the same; staring at him, waiting for him to speak. The Ghost inclined his head in Cyrus's direction, and Cyrus knew his mind. Curatio and Vara were speaking to each other in quiet tones, a smile on his wife's face. She looked at him and turned that smile his way, giving him a nod of encouragement.

They were all behind him. They were all doing the things that normal people did when the tension of battle dissolved. It was a small army—much smaller than the last he'd led, into the Realm of War … but …

They'd just done something no one else had done.

"People of Reikonos," Cyrus said, raising his voice as in the days of old, when he'd addressed armies. This was no different, in spite of the changed world. These were people—scared people, looking for a leader to do that which they could not do alone:

Crush the damned Machine.

"My name is Cyrus Davidon," he said, booming voice ringing out over the crowd. "And I have been gone for too long. But I am returned to you now—when you need the help most." He threw his thumb back. "This building was the headquarters of the Machine, the seat of its wicked power. For too long these thugs have reigned over you, harried you, robbed from you, exhausted you and stolen all your hope.

"That day is over."

A ripple ran through the crowd. He knew skepticism when he saw it, and this was more than a little of it. But beneath it all . . .

These people wanted to believe. He could taste their desire for hope.

"The long night of the Machine's reign is over," Cyrus said. "Dawn is coming."

"It's metaphor," Vaste said, and Birissa chortled. "But also literal, see?" And in the distance, Cyrus could see the faint hints of light on the far horizon to the east.

"I caught that, yes," Birissa said. "Very serendipitous."

"Five syllables," Vaste breathed. "Glorious."

"Tomorrow, seek me in Reikonos Square," Cyrus said. "At midmorning. Tell your friends. Tell your families. Tell all who will listen: I have returned," he said, trying to put Rodanthar into his scabbard and finding the blade far too wide to fit. "Tell—dammit." He sighed and gave up on that. "Tell everyone. And I will see you on the morrow."

The crowd stirred, silent, for just a second. Then a ring of cheers, applause, cries, some mixture of relief, of worry that had broken came ringing out at him, loud in the quiet city night. Cyrus waved, once, and then turned to Vara. "How did I do?"

"It was beautiful," Vaste said. "I think that thing with the sword might have undermined your serious moment. And I didn't even have to be involved!"

"You're such a jackass," Cyrus said. "Curatio—" And he looked and found the healer had already stripped Rodanthar's scabbard from Gaull's belt and was holding it out to him. "Thank you."

"I didn't want people to see you robbing a corpse after that speech; it would do more to undermine your credibility than anything Vaste could," the healer said, a trace of amusement curling his lips.

"What do we do now?" Hiressam asked, looking at the crowd, which was now roaring, chanting Cyrus's name.

"I don't know about you guys," Vaste said, "but I might need some sort of stomach remedy to stop the churning now that I'm hearing them chant his name. I mean, really," and he sent an amused look at Cyrus. "Who do they think you are? Some sort of god?"

"He did just do something that no one else has ever done," Shirri said, easing up to them, looking a little less meek than when they'd first encountered her. She cast her eyes toward Cyrus, and he saw some small measure of difference in the way she looked at him now. "I think they believe ... that he's Cyrus Davidon, returned."

"And what do you believe?" Alaric asked.

Shirri glanced away for a second, then looked back up, eyes shining. "I believe he's Cyrus Davidon, returned." And she looked at him, almost apologetically. "But ... not quite as impressive as the legends."

"Oof, that's gotta hit the old ego," Vaste said.

"I was never as impressive as my legend," Cyrus said, looking right at Shirri. "Your mother could tell you that. If I ever had any secret to my successes ..." And here he looked at Pamyra, trying to put as much warmth and compassion into his voice as he could, "... it's that I always had great people standing with me in whatever endeavor I took on ... and it's to my eternal regret that not all of them made it out of those battles alive."

Pamyra's gaze did not soften at first, but after a few seconds, she seemed to relent, at least a fraction, though she said nothing.

"Come along, my friends," Alaric said, waving them forward. "This night approaches its end, and morning will be here before you know it, along with a new day for Reikonos. We have much to do before then."

"Such as ...?" Vaste asked, sounding mildly perturbed. "We just fought an epic battle against a man with a godly weapon, people who could shoot seemingly endless amounts of metal killing balls at us, and—" He looked at Shirri. "I don't know who you faced, but I'm sure they were very difficult."

Shirri stirred, looking over at Dugras, who nodded once. "Yes," she said, "it was one of the key leaders of the Machine, and he had the ability to completely nullify magic in his presence—with this." And she brandished a metallic orb from her pocket.

"Interesting," Curatio said, and held out his hand. "Do you mind if I take a look at that ...?"

She shrugged and handed it to him, and the healer pocketed it.

"See, everyone faced down their troubles with great courage," Vaste said. "Hope was restored. The Machine was beaten, their headquarters lost. Cyrus managed to avenge the honor of the last of the trolls. And I was able to conquer this trifling issue I had with a lack of romance." He nodded at Birissa, who cleared her throat, looking a little nonplussed. "Birissa was able to conquer this trifling issue I had with lack of romance," Vaste amended. "So tell me, Alaric—what could we possibly have left to do before Cyrus's speechifying on the morrow?" He looked at the lightening sky to the east. "Or in several hours, at least."

Alaric cleared his throat, and smiled, faintly. "I rather assumed we would return to the guildhall, feast, sleep ... do ... whatever—or whoever—tickled our fancy, in some of our cases. With doors closed, this time, I do hope." He cleared his throat. "A just reward for a job well done, you know."

"Oh well, if it's feasting and—well, you know—I'm all for it," Vaste said, and raised his hand. "Let us depart—and do much of what Alaric calls work but is actually much fun stuff!" And off he went, Birissa's arm around him.

"You're feasting again?" Dugras scratched his beard, and inclined his head. "The captain can wait until tomorrow, I suppose. Though if you keep feeding me like that last meal, I may just have to stick around."

"I am surprised," Hiressam said, nodding as he fell in beside Dugras, "we had a cook that handled all this before. I had assumed with her departure that perhaps the quality of the meals would fall, but they've been stellar thus far ..." And off he went, beside the dwarf.

"I could use a night of sleep," Shirri said, her mother beside her, "and our apartment is ... wrecked."

"We have an abundance of beds at Sanctuary," Alaric said. "I'm certain we can find you accommodations, temporary ... or otherwise," he said slyly.

"Perhaps we'll go with 'or otherwise' for now," Pamyra said warmly to Alaric, but when she looked back at Cyrus, that same coldness persisted, if a degree or two less cold than it had been.

"You know what has to happen here, right?" Alaric asked, sidling up to Cyrus once Shirri and her mother had moved on, down the street, with the others.

Cyrus looked over his shoulder. The crowd was easing toward him. Calling his name. Asking him for things. Imploring him for aid for their various maladies. Soon they would be upon him; fear, perhaps, kept them at a distance, but it was dissolving, emboldening them the longer he was here. "I can't just walk down the street back to Sanctuary," he answered.

"No," Alaric said, with a shake of his head. "It's not befitting a legend such as yourself ... and they would follow."

"And the Machine might not be fully defeated yet," Cyrus said as Vara slid up to him. Curatio had gone on, with the others, leaving only the three of them to stand before the crowd, which was growing restless, getting closer to him. The first of them were only feet away—shouting and begging him for aid, some of which he could not have given even had he wanted to. "It would be unwise to lead them back to our gates."

"Aye," Alaric said, and slipped in close behind Vara and Cyrus, who now stood side by side. "Say your farewells—and make it dramatic."

"As though you even need to tell him that," Vara muttered.

"Come to Reikonos Square on the morrow!" Cyrus shouted, voice booming so loudly that half of those that had nearly reached him took a step back at the sound. "I will be there. I will speak to you. And we will make tomorrow a better day."

"That will do it," Alaric said and touched Cyrus on the shoulder. Light infused the air around him, brightening, as he slipped into the ether and the gasps of the crowd faded into the night.

61.

Vaste

"So ... you were right," Vaste said, light of day streaming in through his window, which seemed wider somehow than it had been before he'd left. He frowned at it; really, he should have a balcony, like Cyrus and Vara, he thought. But for now, maybe he'd settle for a wider window. "I'm sure you like the sound of that, don't you?"

Birissa sat on the edge of the bed, which was unbowed despite the weight of both of them on it. She studied him with a furrowed brow. "I don't particularly care—though I find I am often right, often enough that it is no particular occasion to be amazed when I am. What about, in this case, may I ask?"

"You may, and that was a very polite way to say it," Vaste said. "I mean, I'm used to trolls who don't so much have manners—it's more, 'Answer or I clubs you. Urgh urgh.' That sort of thing."

Her frown grew more pronounced, her lower fangs jutting higher out of her lips. "That ... is appalling."

"I agree, which is why I left my people," Vaste said. "But that's a bit off topic. What I was trying to say was that you were right—about me." He bowed his head slightly. "I do think too much and act too little. I've long been content to be a follower, to move with the herd, to make my funny jokes rather than stick my neck out and command action. And ... that has extended to every area of my life. Obviously." And here he gestured at the bed, as though that would make everything clear.

"It's hardly a sin to think," Birissa said, more quiet than usual. "It's only a problem when it keeps you paralyzed. Holds you back from doing what you know is right ... or going after what you truly want."

"I know." Vaste tapped his fingers against Letum's ebony surface.

318

"But my desire to sit back, to suggest action rather than take it, to bury myself in Council and not drive things forward—well, it is a kind of paralysis, at least the way I do it. It has to change. I'm going to lead more as we head into this—I don't know—revolution, maybe? I'm going to be better. Not just make funny jokes. I mean, I'll still do that, too, because—hell, it's me. How could I not?" He clenched his staff hard in his grip. "But I will become a man of action, worthy of remembrance in my own right—and worthy of the legacy of the trolls now lost." He felt a strange gravitas creep through him. "I think all my life ... I've wanted to meet a certain kind of alpha troll ... someone who possessed the definitive qualities that I thought our race should have. And I never have. Because I had magic, was too bookish, too pensive. I have a godly weapon now, though, and little magic, and no excuse not to act." He gave a sharp nod. "It's a new world. Time to be a new me."

Birissa just looked at him, a little mischief playing in her eyes. "And this new you ... is he going to truly take more action? Become stronger?" She flexed her arm.

"I suppose I'll have to," Vaste said, pulling his chin up. "Why?"

Her eyes danced. "It's nothing, really ... just noticed your arse could use ... a little tightening."

Vaste sagged. "Truly?"

"Just a little." She held her thumb and forefinger a small length apart.

"Well ..." he said, letting out a little sigh, "at least I don't have to try and figure out how to shorten it." He patted his backside. "It's okay, my perfect plum. There's room for improvement everywhere, I suppose. Besides," and he brightened just a little, "you don't have to have a perfect arse in order to be remembered for a thousand years ... clearly."

62.

Shirri

When Shirri woke to the sound of someone at the door, it was from the deepest, most satisfying sleep she'd had in months. The bed was heavy down; she'd sunk into it when it was still dark outside her windows and now the light was streaming in. She opened her eyes and lifted her head from the comfortable pillow, mumbling, "What?"

Whoever was at the door took that as an opportunity to enter, and she jumped slightly, worried about propriety.

It was Alaric, and he was in before she'd even had a chance to sit upright. Shirri felt an edge of panic, and started to clap her hands about her person. "Wait—I'm not decent—" She said, before looking down and realizing she'd gone to bed in her clothes. She was perfectly decent.

Alaric paused, hand on the door. His helm was under one arm, clutched there, and a puzzled expression came over his face. "I think I would find it curious to know what your definition of 'decent' entails, if it does not include being fully clothed."

"Sorry ..." She blinked back the drowse, pushing away the urge to dive back into the pillow. "I was sleeping. Didn't realize what I was saying until—never mind. What are you doing here, Alaric?"

"We were about to leave," Alaric said, "Cyrus, Vara—all of us—to head to the square. I came to offer you the chance to stand with us. If you don't wish to—"

Shirri tried to suppress her yawn and failed. "I—I wish to, but—"

Alaric let a coy smile slip across his lips. "But you wish to sleep as well?"

Shirri felt a little dumbstruck by that, but matched his smile with a slightly guilty one of her own. "Yes, please."

"That is perfectly fine," Alaric said, starting to close the door. "I haven't seen your mother yet this morning, either. Perhaps I'll let her sleep rather than wake her to ask."

"Please," Shirri said. "She went through a lot in the Machine's dungeon, I think. She could use some rest."

"Very well," Alaric said, and he started to withdraw, closing the door behind him.

"Alaric, wait," Shirri said, and he paused, cocking his head. "Thank you."

"For what?"

"No one else in Reikonos would have helped me the way you lot did," Shirri said. "And I have a feeling … you're going to help a lot more people before this is over."

"*We* … are going to help a lot more people," Alaric amended with that same smile. So reassuring.

"We, then," Shirri said, and a powerful yawn came over her.

"We'll see you when we get back," Alaric said. "There's food on the table in the Great Hall if you wake hungry."

"I expect I will," Shirri said, already on her way back down to the pillow by the time he shut the door. Sleep claimed her moments later, a content one, filled with hope and rest, free from worry; a sleep such as she could not recall since childhood.

63.

Cyrus

Reikonos Square was abuzz, wild and full of people. There was an aura of excitement in the air, reminding him of a war rally of old and the madness those entailed. The difference was the hint of uncertainty; people were waiting for something they weren't sure was coming.

"Well," Cyrus muttered, "it's here now."

"What's here now?" Curatio asked. "Madness?"

Cyrus felt a very slight smile creep onto his face. "Hope."

Curatio looked at him sideways. A few of the others were listening in.

"Shirri kept saying there was no hope left in Reikonos," Cyrus said, and nodded at the crowd before them. They hadn't caught sight of Cyrus yet; he was at the edge, about to plunge through toward the fountain, leap up on the edge and use it as a dais to speak. "What is this, if not hope?"

"There is always hope," Alaric said, coming up beside him. Hiressam was just a little past him, Vara lingering at the edge of their small group. Vaste and Birissa were under cloaks, but towering over the crowd even here at the edges. And Dugras was somewhere in Vaste's shadow, using him as cover and following the troll closely. "Even Shirri had it all along, though I doubt she realized it." The Ghost's eyes danced. "Hope is the most resilient of human qualities, and its loss, though felt acutely, is almost always an overreaction. Smother it—kill it, even—it rises again. Truly, I have met none whose hope could not be returned through a most modest set of circumstances. It may lie dormant for years, but it beats, always, in the breast, ready to return with but a little breath to revive it."

"I don't know about a little breath," Vaste said. "Seems to me this city needed a resurrection spell of hope."

"A shame that magic is lacking, then," Curatio said.

"I don't think so, Vaste," Cyrus said. "Look at this. Look at these people." And he threw a hand up. "Their faces are pinched with worry, sure—but they're waiting with anticipation for something to happen. Something that will change their lives forever."

"And you think seeing your long arse is it, then?" Vaste cracked, deadpan. "Well, best get on out there and show your arse."

"I can always count on you for exactly the support I need," Cyrus said, shooting him a smile. And then he began to make his way through the crowd.

"Hope is not so fragile a thing as most believe," Alaric said, at his side, as Cyrus started to brush past people. He was getting looks; no one as tall as he could possibly make their way through a thick-packed crowd without doing so. He heard a gasp. Someone tried to grab his cloak, but he brushed them aside, then took it off and tossed it to Vaste.

"What the hell ...?" The troll said, catching it easily. "Am I now to be your clothier?"

"Yes," Cyrus said, without looking back, "now that you've got little in the way of magic, I find I have need of you as more than a skull crusher. Hold my cloak."

"I'm going to give it away to one of these poor unfortunates in the crowd," Vaste called back at him. "Look at them, these beleaguered. They could use a good cloak. Or at least a slightly above-average one such as this." A pause. "You know, this is actually pretty good. Is this elven tailoring?"

"Hell if I know," Cyrus said, "I took it off a particularly tall corpse after I left the Society of Arms, and it's been with me ever since." He looked back to find Vaste now holding it at arm's length. "Kidding. I bought it from a tailor here in Reikonos after Sanctuary started making good gold."

He made his way through the crowd, which was now starting to surge around him, his movement catching eyes. "Move back," Vara said, coming along beside him and shoving a man away when he started to make a movement toward Cyrus. "Give him some room." Then, to Cyrus, she said. "I would swear I've seen the cloak you came to Sanctuary in still hanging in our closet."

"I do still have that corpse-robbed cloak," Cyrus agreed. "It's not half bad. I keep it to remind me of how far I've come."

Vara smiled impishly as she gently turned aside a screaming woman about to heave herself at Cyrus. "I assumed my presence would be enough for you. From bottom of the barrel warrior to ..." She looked around them. "Well ... this." The crowd was going mad, shouts being issued in all directions, some crazed relief as people started to realize ...

Cyrus Davidon might actually be back.

They reached the edge of the fountain, and Cyrus stepped up without further delay, rising up to stand on the edge and looking over the crowd from an even more towering height than he normally commanded. Vara slipped away a step below him, giving him a last, reassuring smile before turning to deal with the crowd, which was beginning to grow truly wild. Alaric and the others formed a perimeter around him and stood there, blocking people from getting too close as Cyrus cleared his throat, and a silence fell.

The crowd spread to the edges of the square and beyond. He had seen them crowding the avenues and thoroughfares on his approach, and tried not to think about how many people were crowding around here, waiting to hear him speak, instead focusing on what he needed to say.

Hope.

"Hello, Reikonos," he let his voice boom out. "It's been a long time."

A rush of uncertainty ran through the crowd, and he tried to think—what would they want to hear?

What did he need to tell them?

"For a thousand years I've been gone," Cyrus said. "I left this world thinking that I'd cured its ills. The gods of old were dead. Men were in charge of their own destiny. Little did I know that after I left, other forces would sweep in. In my days ..." He coughed as Vaste shot him a look of glee; Cyrus sighed, thinking the same thing the troll probably was, that his last words made him sound like a curmudgeonly old man, "... humanity had a Confederation that allowed us to spread from the River Perda in the west to the Sea of Carmas in the east; from the shores of the Torrid Sea here in Reikonos to the Bay of Lost Souls in the South and beyond. It was an imperfect government, and we were imperfect people—but we were free. You could walk out the gates of Reikonos, if you were so possessed, and go anywhere else. Even the poor here were free. Now, though ..."

A grumble of agreement ran through the crowd. Cyrus felt it; he was getting through, harmonizing with them.

"Now, I see people in chains," Cyrus said, "prisoners to fear. A Machine that crushes the people under its weight," he added, running his eyes along the edge of the crowd, where black coats were creeping in, their white armbands like beacons that shone in the midday sun. There were dozens of them, a hundred of them, more maybe, pushing their way through the masses, their eyes fixed on him. He knew predators when he saw them, and these were animals on the hunt, stalking through the crowd. "I walk these streets and I see freedom give way to fear. I see a laughing, victorious army of bandits that know that they are unchallenged," Cyrus said, locking eyes on the Machine thug nearest him. Vara was watching, too, and elbowed Alaric, murmuring something to him, then pointing out the trouble coming. Vaste was already fixed on two more that were threading their way through the crowd toward him. Their goal was clear—get to Cyrus.

"Hope," Cyrus said, and the crowd grew quiet, "is fleeting. You walk these streets ... you live in these places ... you raise your families here ... and there is nothing to look forward to. All belief that your children will see a better tomorrow has fled. You are captives in this city, with only the smallest chance to escape it.

"I will say this to you—words that have echoed in my life, over and over—do not be afraid," Cyrus said, looking over them all. "Fear will make you its prisoner—"

"Fear will make you its bitch," Vaste said.

"—and you will always be subservient to it, if you let it rule you," Cyrus said, ignoring the troll. "And you will not live. Not truly. This place, this city—there are things to fear here." And he looked at the Machine thug easing up on him. "But one thing you will not fear much longer ... is the godsdamned Machine." He stared at the man easing through the crowd at him, and the thug froze, finally realizing that Cyrus was looking at him. "Last night, my comrades and I destroyed the Machine's headquarters. Yesterday, we ransacked one of their mills ... and a coal yard ... and a candlemaker's shop. All Machine outposts, and every last one of their people within ... we dealt with in the manner that the Machine can expect from me." He stared at the man in the crowd. "I have no mercy in my heart for those who would terrorize and oppress the people of Reikonos simply to enrich themselves, and I will show how I feel about you ... scum ... you villains ..." Cyrus glared down at the nearest Machine thug, pale and poxy, sores on his face, and the man seemed taken aback, his forward motion halted by the attention he was getting, "... every chance I get. So ..." And here he looked up again, at the next nearest Machine thug, and the next after that, "... give me a chance, Machine ... if you'd like to be broken."

"Terrible," Vaste pronounced. "I see what you were going for there—'breaking,' 'machine,' because machines break, but—no. It's a very overused metaphor in these days, I would think."

"I suspect it will connect well with the audience, though," Hiressam said. "It's very easy to understand as an analogy."

"Works for me," Dugras tossed in.

"Could we perhaps save the critique for some other time?" Vara asked. "When we're not being closed in on by Machine thugs in an already unruly crowd?"

"Wait, there are Machine thugs closing in on us? Damn my height, damn this crowd," Dugras said.

"If I waited until I was out of danger to offer critiques, I would never offer critiques," Vaste said. "I mean, what do you expect me to do? Remember them all and spew them in the five seconds per year we're not in peril? I'd be forever writing them down, lest I forget. And they'd lose at least ninety percent of their humor, what with the context having long passed. They'd land with a thud, all amusement stripped from them."

"That would be a merry occasion," Curatio muttered. "Vaste, with all his humor removed."

"It'd be the opposite of merry, actually," Vaste said. "It'd be joyless. Like you, old man."

Cyrus stared down at the poxy Machine goon who was closest, and the goon stared back, suddenly looking rather like a hare frozen in place by the sight of a falcon flying above him. Cyrus did not relent, and the man began to melt back into the crowd. Unable to move very fast, he kept his eyes locked on Cyrus, and reached up for his white armband with the strange symbol on it. Sliding it off, he raised it up between himself and Cyrus, then let it drop. It fluttered, disappearing into the crowd. He swallowed visibly, almost comically, waiting.

Cyrus nodded, once, and the man seemed to breathe for the first time in ages. He shoved through the throngs of people, making his escape. Others of the Machine's servants seemed to take their hint from him, pushing their way back where once they were shoving forward. It was a retreat, and an obvious one. The crowd shouted at them, shoving them as they tried to push through.

"The day of the Machine is over," Cyrus said, "and whatever is left of them … will topple soon." He drew breath, watching the remainder snaking their way through the crowd, their courage broken. "These are the last of their days, and soon enough, you will no longer fear to walk these streets."

A ragged cheer came from the crowd, and Cyrus could feel the relief, the hope, surging through them. They were more than unruly; so long had they been pushed down that he suspected a backlash brewing. There was an anger that ran like lightning in this square. Point it in the wrong direction and something would surely be destroyed.

Cyrus drew a long breath and began to say something else, but a martial shout in the distance caused a hush to fall over the assemblage. At the edge of the square there was movement, wild shoving as something happened, and he turned his attention to look.

A double line of guards marched their way into the square, wearing the white livery of the city watch. They carried rifles in hand, more dressed for battle than the formal guards Cyrus had seen very occasionally thus far in Reikonos. They marched, and the people gave way for them as they headed straight for him upon the fountain, in formation and very serious. There were a hundred or so, and tension filled the crowd. This sort of raw show of force did, after all, suggest a very specific goal, and Cyrus could feel it in the air as they marched up and the crowd continued to give way until the front of the line had nearly reached Vaste and Hiressam, and someone within their rank shouted, "Company! Halt!" and they stopped.

Cyrus looked down at them with a wary eye, hand resting on Rodanthar's hilt. There came a moment of silence as the captain of their number moved up from the back of their rank, sliding in between the armored forms like a mouse bulging within a snake as he passed through their double-file line.

When he reached the head, he found himself staring up at Vaste, and past him, to Cyrus. The man looked warily at the troll, and Vaste grinned back down at him.

"Hihi," Vaste said. "You have a message?"

The guard captain cleared his throat uncertainly, and the tension hung thick in the air. Cyrus wanted no trouble with Longwell's guards, but he had a bad feeling about what was to come. If it was an order to dissolve the crowd, Cyrus had a plan for dealing with that but suspected it would come to no good end.

Another wild murmur ran through the crowd. Someone shouted, "Hang them!" and a roar commenced as Cyrus threw up his hands to stay their madness. There was that quicksilver sentiment he'd detected; the rush of anger that would turn this crowd into a mob and then into a mad riot that would burn the city with its rage.

"No," Cyrus said, as emphatically as he could. The guards were eyeing the crowd nervously; they could feel the tension in the air. Cyrus watched the guard captain; what came next would hinge upon his words. If it was an order to disperse ...

Well, there would be only so much Cyrus could do to quell a crowd gone mad.

The guard captain unfurled a long scroll of parchment, and cleared his throat. His ruddy face nearly buried beneath his helm, he glanced up at Cyrus and began reading his missive.

"General Davidon," the guard captain said, and Cyrus felt a strange prickle of relief at the mere effort—the olive branch, really—offered by addressing him by his own title, "the Lord Protector has heard of your return and sends his compliments. He wishes to speak with you immediately, if possible." The guard captain paused. "If you are amenable, I am to escort you to him presently. If, on the other hand, you need some time to, uh ..." The guard captain looked at the crowd, briefly, and returned to his scroll. "... In any event, the Lord Protector calls upon your long friendship and seeks your aid. He would like to discuss with you ... a, uh ... a peaceful resolution to the problems plaguing the city."

Cyrus frowned. "Would he?"

The guard captain swallowed heavily. "He would. My lord." And he bowed at the waist.

"It seems the Lord Protector would like a word about solving the problems of Reikonos," Cyrus announced, and there was a lusty cheer from the crowd.

"You don't suppose this is some sort of trap, do you?" Vara asked, moving to his side as Cyrus stepped down. The guard captain, at least a foot shorter than Cyrus, twitched as he moved forward.

"I have a hard time believing Longwell capable of treachery against his friends," Cyrus said, "but I suppose it's been a long time. Best we be on our guard." And he looked around at his little band and nodded once.

Alaric nodded back, and so did the others, one by one. "Caution is always a wise mantle to cloak yourself in," the Ghost said, and Cyrus noted that every hand that could hold a godly weapon was touching it, even if lightly.

"If you'll follow me," the guard captain said, and beckoned Cyrus forward, "my lord."

"I will follow you," Cyrus said, waving to the crowd as he began to pass, moving in the wake of the city watch formation as they threaded their way back through the crowd toward the Citadel rising in the distance.

64.

They were marched to the Citadel gates, which were open wide, guards standing on either side to allow them to stroll right through. Cyrus glanced at the guard standing to the side; a familiar face. It was the guard who'd sneered at him only the day before. He stared, mouth agape, at Cyrus, who maintained his amused smile and proffered a little wave as the line of guards dissolved and he was ushered in by the captain. The gates were closed behind them, the clanking of metal as they shut giving Cyrus an uneasy feeling, a strange punctuation to a day barely begun.

"Be at ease," Alaric said. "On your guard, but unworried. The gates were closed when we visited, after all. I expect they are not open much of the time."

"Speak for yourself with that 'relax' crap," Vaste said. "I plan to panic fully, because now we're totally trapped in here ... with people who don't have godly weapons and can't use magic." He blinked. "What do we have to fear again?"

"You taking inappropriate action," Birissa said, giving him a slap on the bottom that stirred him into motion again as Cyrus moved to follow the guard captain into the Citadel.

The sprawling entry was the same as ever. Timeless, even, Cyrus thought, looking at the slightly glowing walls, still as flawless as if he'd passed through here only yesterday rather a thousand years ago.

"This place has not aged a day," Curatio muttered to Alaric.

"No," the Ghost said, and there was a trace of sadness in his voice as they made their way to the metal cage in the center of the entry, with sturdy chains rising up through the center of the building. It was secured along the back wall of the room, and Cyrus frowned. He'd ridden the contraption when first he'd come here, but it had been removed shortly thereafter. He'd not even noticed, given that it simply stood along the back wall, rising up a shaft through the floors above. "Save for perhaps that," Alaric said.

They were ushered into the box, Cyrus looking around warily as the guard captain got in with them. Once they were in, the operator pulled shut two cage doors, both metal. The old one had been wood, but this one seemed to creak just as much, the black iron straining under their combined weight.

"Sorry," Dugras said as it let a particularly loud squeal, "shouldn't have had that second cruller this morning."

"I doubt you're the problem," Hiressam said, looking around with an awed expression.

Vaste must have caught it. "Why, my good man. You look as though Cyrus Davidon himself might come jumping out at you at any moment."

Hiressam let out a small chuckle, and the tension went out of his shoulders. "Very good. You are correct—what has yet to come can hardly top what has gone before." A hint of the tension came back in his bearing. "Still … I find myself worried, nonetheless."

"A smart quality in a warrior," Cyrus said, looking up through the iron bars above them. "Especially when we're suspended many levels above the ground in a confined space with no easy escape." His own voice betrayed tension. Taking this contraption was perhaps not the best of ideas, given all the uncertainty inherent in their current position.

"Indeed, for all we know this is brand new," Vaste said, "and the method by which the Lord Protector assassinates his enemies. They're lulled into a false sense of security by the relief at not having to climb thirty floors straight up, and then—whoops! Someone drops the rope holding this thing up and it's SPLAT! down at the bottom. What a tragic end for my beautiful arse. And the rest of me."

"I have worked here for many years," the guard captain said, looking somewhat insulted, "and in that time, we have never had an accident with this device."

"So what you're saying," Vaste leaned toward him, "is that you're due?"

The guard captain seemed to realize that arguing was a futile pursuit, and he shut his mouth as the box clanked upward. The sound was eerie, chain upon metal, and the air seemed to grow cooler the higher they climbed. Cyrus could see floors passing by now, nearly empty or completely so. The days of this tower being an administrative capital for the Confederation seemed to have passed. About a third of the way up, suddenly the floors ceased being occupied entirely and fell to near darkness, only the glow of the walls shedding any light.

Their rise slowed close to the top, and soon enough it stopped completely. The guard captain opened the gated doors on a small room that opened onto a balcony. Cyrus felt a pang of recognition as he looked at it; once upon a time he'd come along right after the Empress of Enterra had been pushed off it by a particularly cruel guard.

"Memories, eh?" Alaric asked, at his side.

"That's the problem with a place that hasn't changed," Cyrus said as they moved forward toward grand doors that were manned by two guards in much more opulent dress than those of the city watch, their livery gold and their armor shining, as though it had never seen the wear of battle. "It does tend to bring them back."

The doors were thrown open then, and inside lay a sweeping room with a throne against the back wall, grander than the wooden dressings of the place back when the Council of Twelve had made it their court. It was draped in finery, silks and curtains, and a glorious purple carpet lay across the entirety of the floor. Torches burned on small sconces within, and the air held the aroma of incense.

A man sat on the throne, draped in finery of his own, of a sort that reminded Cyrus, just slightly, of the King of the Elves and his brilliant rainbow garb.

"Nothing about this is familiar," Vaste said, blinking as they all paused with Cyrus just outside the room's entry.

"Your voice is," came the call from the figure on the throne. At this distance, Cyrus was hard-pressed to tell that it was Longwell. The skin tone was right, but his features were indistinct. Cyrus took a couple careful steps into the room, slowly making his way forward. The figure rose upon the dais, pushing off the opulent arms of his seat. He stared down at Cyrus, an intensity to his expression. Cyrus stared back.

Where once there had been benches for people to sit in a gallery before the Council of Twelve, now there were wide open spaces, appropriate for a throne room where audiences were given, rather than a gallery where petitions could be heard and Councilors addressed with both grievances and requests. Everything about this room was different, and the finery made Cyrus feel cold, the very atmosphere chilling his skin.

"The décor is definitely an improvement," Vaste pronounced.

"A compliment from my old friend Vaste," the Lord Protector said, sounding amused. "A rare reward."

"He remembers me," Vaste said, clearly pleased. "Thank the dead gods someone does. Finally!"

"You are a hard one to forget," the Lord Protector said, reaching the end of the dais. Something in his voice, his cadence—it was all wrong. Cyrus stared at him; the features were indistinct, lacked almost any weathering. Which would be expected—he probably hadn't aged, not with Amnis, the Spear of Water, in his possession, but still ...

Cyrus edged closer to the dais, but carefully, easing through the wide space of this throne room.

"Come closer, my old friends," the Lord Protector said, almost a quiet awe seeping into his voice. "I see Alaric—not gone after all, eh? And Curatio! And ..." He took a step down. "Vara herself ... returned from death at the hands of the God of War ... Truly wondrous ..."

There was a sort of naked hope in the Lord Protector's voice that seemed earnest in his delight at seeing them all, and yet still ... some small rankling suspicion ran through Cyrus's body, tickling the back of his neck.

"It is us," Cyrus agreed, now only twenty or so paces from the Lord Protector. He stared into the face, seeking signs of familiarity; clearly Longwell recognized them. Why, then was Cyrus having such difficulty recognizing this visage—albeit not entirely clear at this distance and somewhat hidden by the strange headdress framing his face.

Was this the King of Luukessia that he'd ridden with for years?

"Truly, it is ..." The Lord Protector agreed. "Has Sanctuary preserved you all this time? You have not aged a day—any of you ..."

Cyrus blinked. Longwell knew about Sanctuary?

"It has," Cyrus said cautiously. The Lord Protector beamed down upon them, hands clear of any sort of weaponry. He looked into the face and ...

It was not right.

"Who are you?" Cyrus asked, impatience causing him to ask it flat out. Vara thumped his vambrace at the bicep, albeit gently, but he barely noticed. He only glanced at her out of the corner of his eye, and, by way of answering her reproach, said, "The features are wrong. The voice is wrong. And ... where is Amnis?" Cyrus took another step forward. "Where is the Spear of Water, Lord Protector?" He glared at the man before him. "Who are you? And where is Samwen Longwell?"

The man stared down at him, and a cool expression fell over his face like a curtain dropping on a performance. "I haven't the faintest of idea about Lord Longwell's whereabouts ... Cyrus."

"You do know me," Cyrus said, staring back at him. "You know *us*.

Who are you?"

"Who I am is unimportant," The Lord Protector replied. "What is important ... is how we can help one another."

"Let us end this charade," Curatio said, and stepped forward, thunderheads boiling over his face, clouding it with anger. "I cannot perhaps do what I once could with magic, but what I have left should be sufficient to this task—"

He spun his hand and made a circle, throwing his palm out at the Lord Protector, who started to recoil as a blast of light hit him squarely. Gone in an instant were the glorious robes, gone then was the headdress that gleamed like a sun. The light in the room dimmed a little, but what was left showed the Lord Protector plain, and what remained ...

Was a skeletal figure in dark robes, with navy skin, staring out at them from sunken eyes.

"Malpravus," Cyrus said, and he drew Rodanthar instinctively. The only sound behind him was every other weapon being unsheathed, and the shouts of guards behind them echoing and ringing down the tower, though for good or ill, in surprise at Malpravus's sudden unmasking or alarm at these intruders pulling their weapons at their master, he neither knew nor cared.

The old necromancer drew himself upon the steps to the dais, templing his bony hands back together, and looking at Cyrus with a glint in his eye. "Truly ... it is good to see you again ... dear boy. All of you, really."

And into the moment of silence that followed, rang one voice, as Vaste shouted loud enough to be heard down on the street. "*I WIN!*" He pumped his free hand furiously, Letum clutched in the other, and looked at each of them in turn. "You all owe me SO. MUCH. GOLD. And also ..." His face fell, and he slapped Letum into both palms, gripping the weapon tightly, ready for battle. "... Shit."

Cyrus Davidon Will Return in

CALL OF
THE HERO
The Sanctuary Series
Volume Ten

Coming Late 2018!

Author's Note

Thanks for reading! Obviously after eight main books (now nine) and three side volumes, Cyrus and company are well known to most of you, as is the land of Arkaria. And what do you even do for a follow-up after having them face gods and something that feels like death itself?

Well, if you're me, you fast-forward them a thousand years, destroy their homeland, and leave them a hell of a lot of problems to solve. Because putting them back in a pastoral, peaceful, slightly different version of Arkaria where everything is beautiful and it's all glorious, firm troll arses and honey mead would be BORING. Though I'm sure our friends would enjoy themselves in such environs, you, the reader, would be bored out of your skull. I mean, I like to think I'm a decent writer, but creating dramatic tension out of a peaceful world would be like me spinning straw into gold, and last I checked, my name wasn't Rumple-anything.

So here we go – into a new world, with new challenges. Maybe it's a little dark or off-putting to you. I understand. Trust me when I tell you I'm setting up another epic story, one that will hopefully top the end of the story arc you saw in LEGEND (Volume 8). But it's going to take some time to set up, and honestly – I can't write books as large as CRUSADER and LEGEND anymore. They just kill me, for more reasons than one, and they also take forever to get out (some of you probably remember CRUSADER taking a year or LEGEND arriving months late – and thanks to those of you who didn't write me angry emails about that, cuz those books were GINORMOUS). So expect to see more reasonable sized works in the realm of AVENGER, CHAMPION and WARLORD in the future, which will keep you happy because they show up regularly and me happy because banging my head against the wall constructing doorstopper-sized tomes does not make me enjoy life at all. It makes me angry. And you won't like me when I'm angry, because the author gets angry – you probably guessed it – PEOPLE DIE. Including your favorite characters.

So let's keep the author happy, shall we? In an effort to keep the body count down to manageable levels and stave off anymore unfortunate incidents like that one time in the Dragonshrine with all the deaths and crying and yarghhhh – yeah, you remember that. Let's not do that again.

As has become somewhat standard for this series, I'm not going to be setting release dates, so if you want to know immediately when future books become available, take sixty seconds and sign up for my NEW RELEASE EMAIL ALERTS by visiting my website. I don't sell your information and I only send out emails when I have a new book out. The reason you should sign up for this is because I don't always set release dates, and even if you're following me on Facebook (robertJcrane (Author)) or Twitter (@robertJcrane), it's easy to miss my book announcements because...well, because social media is an imprecise thing.

Come join the discussion on my website:
http://www.robertjcrane.com!

Cheers,
Robert J. Crane

ACKNOWLEDGMENTS

Editorial/Literary Janitorial duties performed by Sarah Barbour and Jeff Bryan. Final proofing was once more handled by the illustrious Jo Evans. Any errors you see in the text, however, are the result of me rejecting changes.

The cover was once more designed with exceeding skill by Karri Klawiter of Artbykarri.com.

Thanks to Jennifer Ellison and David Leach for being my first readers on this one.

The formatting was provided by nickbowman-editing.com.

Once more, thanks to my parents, my in-laws, my kids and my wife, for helping me keep things together.

Other Works by Robert J. Crane

The Girl in the Box
and
Out of the Box
Contemporary Urban Fantasy

World of Sanctuary
Epic Fantasy

Defender: The Sanctuary Series, Volume One
Avenger: The Sanctuary Series, Volume Two
Champion: The Sanctuary Series, Volume Three
Crusader: The Sanctuary Series, Volume Four
Sanctuary Tales, Volume One - A Short Story Collection
Thy Father's Shadow: The Sanctuary Series, Volume 4.5
Master: The Sanctuary Series, Volume Five
Fated in Darkness: The Sanctuary Series, Volume 5.5
Warlord: The Sanctuary Series, Volume Six
Heretic: The Sanctuary Series, Volume Seven
Legend: The Sanctuary Series, Volume Eight
Ghosts of Sanctuary: The Sanctuary Series, Volume Nine
Call of the Hero: The Sanctuary Series, Volume Ten* *(Coming Late 2018!)*

A Haven in Ash: Ashes of Luukessia, Volume One *(with Michael Winstone)*
A Respite From Storms: Ashes of Luukessia, Volume Two* *(with Michael Winstone—Coming Early 2018!)*

Southern Watch
Contemporary Urban Fantasy

Called: Southern Watch, Book 1
Depths: Southern Watch, Book 2
Corrupted: Southern Watch, Book 3
Unearthed: Southern Watch, Book 4
Legion: Southern Watch, Book 5
Starling: Southern Watch, Book 6
Forsaken: Southern Watch, Book 7* *(Coming in 2018!)*
Hallowed: Southern Watch, Book 8* *(Coming Late 2018/Early 2019!)*

The Shattered Dome Series
(with Nicholas J. Ambrose)
Sci-Fi

Voiceless: The Shattered Dome, Book 1
Unspeakable: The Shattered Dome, Book 2* *(Coming in 2018!)*

The Mira Brand Adventures
Contemporary Urban Fantasy

The World Beneath: The Mira Brand Adventures, Book 1
The Tide of Ages: The Mira Brand Adventures, Book 2
The City of Lies: The Mira Brand Adventures, Book 3
The King of the Skies: The Mira Brand Adventures, Book 4
The Best of Us: The Mira Brand Adventures, Book 5* *(Coming in 2018!)*

Liars and Vampires
(with Lauren Harper)
Contemporary Urban Fantasy

No One Will Believe You: Liars and Vampires, Book 1* *(Coming Early 2018!)*
Someone Should Save Her: Liars and Vampires, Book 2* *(Coming Early 2018!)*
You Can't Go Home Again: Liars and Vampires, Book 3* *(Coming Early 2018!)*

* Forthcoming, Subject to Change

14646283R00185

Printed in Great Britain
by Amazon